# THE SEVERED THREAD

## ALSO BY LESLIE VEDDER

*The Bone Spindle*

# THE SEVERED THREAD

## LESLIE VEDDER

RAZORBILL

# RAZORBILL

An imprint of Penguin Random House LLC, New York

First published in the United States of America by Razorbill,
an imprint of Penguin Random House LLC, 2023

Visit us online at penguinrandomhouse.com.

Library of Congress Cataloging-in-Publication Data is available.

ISBN 9780593325858

Printed in the United States of America

1   3   5   7   9   10   8   6   4   2

BVG

Design by Suki Boynton
Text set in News Plantin MT Std

*For my partner, Michelle,*
*everything is more fun with you*

# THE SEVERED THREAD

# PROLOGUE

—»»»— —«««—

## Red

RED STOOD AT the boundary between the Forest of Thorns and the black waste. Her scarlet cape swirled around her as the night wind shrieked in her ears, the desolate landscape streaked with shadows and whipping sands. Still, it all felt familiar—like home.

The monster wolves prowled through the forest behind her, their yellow eyes gleaming in the perpetual dark. Brittle thorns snapped beneath their massive jaws, and their claws dug deep gouges into the sand. The giant white wolf sat back on its haunches, staring up at the sliver of moon, and howled. Usually, the rest of the pack would have raised their voices to join him, but not this time. Tonight, Shadow cried alone.

There was a rustle in the forest. Slowly, another wolf crept out. In place of Shadow's rotted body and hulking twisted bones, this one was very much alive, with shaggy brown-and-white fur covering its small, gaunt frame. It crawled on its belly past the monstrous wolves three times its size. Red bent down, and the wolf pushed its nose into her hand, whining at the sight of the traveling pack by her feet. He knew what the canvas bag meant.

"I know, Cinzel," Red soothed, digging her hands into his ruff. "But we can't stay. Our prey is out there, and it's getting away."

A shiver ran down Red's spine like a phantom hand. Prince Briar Rose had woken from his hundred-year sleep and escaped with Filore Nenroa, and Red hadn't been able to stop them. Fear gripped her like a vise at the thought. So many things had gone wrong that weren't Red's fault, but that wouldn't matter to the Spindle Witch.

Red was no fighter. She was a spy, a relic hunter, sometimes an agent of death from the shadows, but she was going to have to find a way to capture Briar and take care of Fi. Her only other choice was to tell the Spindle Witch she had failed and beg for mercy. Red shuddered, burying her tan fingers into the soft undercoat of Cinzel's shaggy fur.

Not that. Anything but that.

Briar Rose was restored, and all his magic with him. The Witch with the paper scraps was powerful enough for his magic to breach the Forest of Thorns. Even Fi had proven to be more than just an annoyance. And Shane . . .

An image of the huntsman flashed through Red's mind— her hair wild, her eyes burning as she'd faced off against the transformed Briar Rose in the Forest of Thorns. Red's hand lifted to her throat almost unconsciously, resting against the small scratch from the prince's claws. Shane had saved her, even knowing who Red was—even after Red betrayed her and nearly killed them all.

An unfamiliar feeling crept over Red, a flutter in her stomach like anticipation . . . or dread. Red had gotten close to people before, but she'd always had a reason, and she'd never forgotten it. That made it easy to walk away.

Shane was the first person who made her want to forget. Red closed her eyes and held one fragment of a moment in her mind: spinning with Shane on the balcony in Bellicia, dizzy from the wine and the candlelight and the heat of Shane's body only a breath away. Out here, among the beasts and thorns, it seemed more like a dream than a memory. She'd forgotten herself that night, let Shane get too close. That couldn't happen again.

Dreams were nothing but fantasies, and this one was over. Red had a job to do.

Her thoughts were broken by a sudden screech as a giant black crow flapped through the tangle of thorns. Shadow leapt up, snapping at the bird. Its taunting caws sounded like laughter as it settled on a branch over Red's head. Milky-white eyes fixed on her, glowing like the moon.

Red fell immediately to her knees.

"I'll catch them," she promised. "I have a plan. They won't escape me again. Please . . ."

She didn't get to finish. The crow's wings beat angrily against the dark thorns. Its beak clicked like a disapproving tut. Shadow growled, his ears laid back against his ragged fur, and Cinzel slunk to his stomach with a helpless whine. Red shushed them both, focusing on the crow.

3

When it took flight again, she followed it, motioning the wolves back as she navigated through the twisting thorns. The crow landed every few feet, looking back at her with those sinister eyes. As though Red would dare defy it.

At last it perched in the branches of a calcified white tree, one of the corpses of the long-dead forest. It had been carved into something of a pedestal. Red swallowed hard. She hadn't been called to this altar in many years. She'd hoped the thorns had swallowed it whole by now.

Nestled in the white branches outstretched like bone arms lay a polished black rod, wound round and round with rust-stained bandages. Red's hand ached just looking at it. She could only make out the barest details under the bandages: the sharp thorns that snagged in the old gray cloth, the golden thread that trailed from the base like dangling spiderwebs.

The rod was a piece of the Forest of Thorns, and a piece of the Spindle Witch, and the blood that crusted it like a second skin belonged to Red. It was a magic relic of sorts. But unlike the ancient relics Red usually sought out, this one was crude, crafted by the Spindle Witch herself. One that Red hadn't been forced to use in a long time.

The crow stared expectantly at Red. She shivered again, numb all the way through as she inched forward. If the Spindle Witch wanted her to take this, Red couldn't refuse.

As soon as she had the rod, the crow took off, its wings silhouetted against the sky as it disappeared. Red tucked the rod into her belt and made her way back to the wolves. Shadow was pacing restlessly, and Red held his massive head to her chest, whispering in his ragged ear.

"Don't worry, I won't be gone long. I've just got a little something to take care of."

She pressed her fingers to her lips and whistled, calling Cinzel to her side. Red shouldered her pack, feeling the weight of the rod at her hip. The black waste almost seemed to part before her.

She would catch up to her prey in no time.

# 1

## Fi

**FI SLIPPED THROUGH** a narrow gap in the rock, sucking in a breath to squeeze between the towering russet slabs. High sandstone walls rose around her on both sides of the thin gully, which cut a tight, zigzagging path between sheer canyon walls.

She cursed as her sleeve snagged in a spiny cactus. It wasn't even really *her* sleeve—the creamy silk blouse had originally been Briar's. A hundred-year-old blouse wasn't Fi's idea of good traveling gear, but her own shirt was in shreds after the fight in the Forest of Thorns, so borrowing Briar's had been her only option. He'd kept his velvet coat and his short-sleeved undershirt, while she took the impractical antique. It fit her more like a tunic, belted at the waist.

Her companions weren't looking much better. Shane's dusky-red coat was infested with burs, and there was a long black smudge up the center of Briar's shirt like he'd been dragged on his stomach. Even the Paper Witch looked a little worse for wear after a week of hard traveling through the wilds of Andar.

Fi glanced at the quickly rising sun, already too warm on her tan skin. Her short brown ponytail clung to her neck. If it wasn't so hot, she could have at least kept her coat on instead of tying it awkwardly around her hips. Without it, the bell-shaped sleeves were a menace.

Fi eyed the cactus. It didn't look like it was going to budge. With a horrible ripping sound, she tore the sleeve free.

A few rocks slid out from beneath her, skittering and popping down the sloping path and almost clobbering Shane in the head.

Shane shot her a glare. "That time, it was definitely on purpose." The huntsman's ash-brown hair was looking more than a little unkempt in its braided bun, and her fair cheeks were definitely sunburned.

Fi winced. "Still just an accident." Just like the last time, and the time before that.

"Well, why don't we switch places, and we'll see how many rocks I *accidentally* kick down on you," Shane grumbled. She lost interest in Fi as her wedge heel stuck in a fissure between the stones, almost bowling her over when she yanked it free.

Fi rolled her eyes. "Even you would not be able to squeeze past me right now."

Three days ago, when they had finally left the wastes behind for the high bluffs rising out of the desert, Fi had felt nothing but relief. The Paper Witch had called this place the Sunset Narrows. She thought she could see why. Battered sandstone slabs rose around them like a labyrinth, some of them spear-point sharp, others smeared with black dust like scorch marks. By day, they were a dull rust color, but the sinking sun set them on fire, the scarlet light blazing in every craggy rock face until they glowed.

She had underestimated the *narrows* part, though. The maze of stone passages didn't make for easy traveling—even Shane could barely wriggle through the tightest gaps, and Fi's knees and elbows were purple with bruises. It was a good thing the Witches of Aurora's line were tall and willowy, or she had a feeling they would have lost Briar and the Paper Witch a few forks back.

"Need a hand?"

Fi looked up. Briar was just beyond the next bulging rock, reaching down to help her up. His pale skin had a slight rosy color, and his golden hair was messy from the climb.

"It's better to go over, trust me." He jerked his chin at the gap along the wall, which barely looked wide enough to stick a leg through.

Fi hesitated, then kicked herself for hesitating. "Thanks."

His hand was warm around hers, the once-smooth skin rough with new blisters already turning into calluses. Briar shot her one of his dazzling smiles, holding on tight as she scrambled up the rock.

"I'm just glad you didn't see the part where I tried to squeeze through and almost got stuck for good. Luckily, we've been eating light."

"Don't let Shane hear you say that," Fi warned. Her partner had spent all morning ranting after she nearly broke a tooth on the thin rye loaves from the Paper Witch's pack.

It was called traveler's bread because it kept forever, but it was also hard as a rock and tasted about the same. Unfortunately, they didn't have much choice. The Paper Witch was a vegetarian, and even if he wasn't, the only signs of life in the canyon were a few cockeyed lizards and the nesting swallows darting in and out of holes in the bluff. Neither looked very appetizing to Fi.

She slid down the far side of the rock, and Briar reached up to steady her, catching her by the arms. Fi's stomach lurched. She had landed too close to him, almost toe-to-toe, with nowhere to look except up into those twinkling blue eyes. She could feel her face heating up, and not from the sun.

Briar brushed something off her cheek—red dust, she realized, as his fingers came away stained with it. Then he stepped back, letting go abruptly and leaving Fi off-balance. She pretended to retie her bootlace just to keep her head down until the blush faded.

Things with Briar had been different. Fi wasn't sure where they stood now, barely a week since she'd rejected him in the tower. When she'd woken him with a kiss from his hundred-year sleep, she'd meant it to be goodbye. A clean break so that they could both walk away.

In the end, nothing in the castle had gone the way it was supposed to.

Now they were just partners, with a promise to save Andar together. But *together* was harder than she'd expected. There was a distance between them—a certain look Briar got staring into the fire at night, like he was a thousand miles away, where Fi couldn't hope to reach him. She wasn't sure she should even try. She was the one who'd rejected him, after all. And none of her reasons had changed.

Her gloved hand curled over the Butterfly Curse seared into her palm. She was no closer to removing the mark and ending the devastation it could bring. As long as they kept moving like this, she was safe, but if they ever stopped for longer than three days . . .

*Misfortune. Destruction. Calamity.* Fi felt cold grip her heart, like a cage of icy fingers. Briar had enough on his shoulders without bearing her burdens as well.

Fi finished fiddling with her boot and straightened, squashing those pesky feelings down. *For good this time*, she promised herself. They had much bigger problems, starting with the Spindle Witch who still held Andar's castle in a stranglehold and extending to the Witch Hunters who were after their heads. The lawless wilds of Andar were Witch Hunter territory, and they roamed freely in the red hills and canyonlands. One of the many reasons they were squeezing through this impossible path.

Besides, from the way Briar acted, Fi doubted he was even thinking about what had happened between them anymore. She was probably flattering herself, assuming his feelings for her were even a drop in the ocean compared to how badly he wanted to save his kingdom.

"Haste, Filore." The Paper Witch stood in the mouth of the gully ahead. He pushed a strand of blond hair from his pale face, motioning them forward. "The longer it takes to reach the Ironworks, the more danger we are in."

So far they'd avoided any run-ins with Witch Hunter

patrols, but they'd had more than a few close calls. It felt like Witch Hunters lay in wait down every passageway, treacherous as the dust-colored vipers that lurked in the dry sagebrush, invisible until they struck. The night before, they'd almost stumbled right into a Witch Hunter camp, and only Shane's quick application of her fist to the sentry's nose had stopped him from raising the alarm. After that, the Paper Witch had turned them toward a different path—an ancient forge, made by the Witches of Aurora's time, which he said ran right through the heart of the hills. But his face had been tight with worry ever since, and Fi had serious doubts about a shortcut the Paper Witch was reluctant to take.

With a great cursing and clatter of rocks, Shane burst through the narrow gap, looking positively livid. "I put my hand in a hole crawling with centipedes!" she growled, flicking one of the wriggling insects at the Paper Witch before it could crawl up her sleeve. It fell miserably short. "There's no way this is the best route to your legendary Witch city!"

The Paper Witch looked annoyed, though it was hard to tell under all the dust. "It is not the *best* route to the hidden city of Everlynd," he said, emphasizing every word. "But with the Witch Hunters out in force, it is the only route that remains open to us."

*Everlynd.* Even just the name sent a thrill down Fi's spine.

When the Paper Witch had met them at the edge of the Forest of Thorns, he hadn't just come to light their path. He'd come to fulfill one final duty passed down from his great-grandmother, the Rose Witch: to lead Briar to the hidden city of Everlynd, the last bastion of old Andar. Concealed in the fallen kingdom, powerful Witches had kept the magic of Andar alive in secret for a hundred years, waiting for their prince to rejoin them and lead them to victory over the Spindle Witch. Ideally, it wouldn't have just been Briar, but King Sage and all the Witches from the castle, too, but . . .

Fi shook herself. Just a place like Everlynd existing was more than she'd ever dreamed possible. A place of magic and learning, where the most precious of spell books and relics had been secreted away after the kingdom's fall. A tiny piece of the old Andar preserved like a ship in a bottle all these years. Fi couldn't wait to see it.

Shane was less impressed. "If these Witches are so powerful, I don't see why they can't at least come out and meet us halfway."

The Paper Witch shook his head, either in fondness or defeat. "The city is almost impossible to enter, and only a select few ever leave. It's how the Witches have remained hidden all this time. I am one of a handful of people who knows the way, and even then, the path is—"

"Full of danger, and traps, and killer tests. I remember," Shane groused, waving him off. "Fine. But I want it known that when we get to Everlynd, I expect a royal welcome. You have to be good for something." The last part she aimed at Briar, who laughed.

"I keep telling myself the same thing," he said as they set off again, catching Fi's eye and throwing her a wink. Fi tried very hard not to smile.

It took another hour of climbing and sliding before the Paper Witch led them down a crooked gully that dead-ended at a towering slab of rugged stone. Fi craned her head, shading her eyes and staring up and up and up. A glittering vein of smoky quartz wound through the granite, the uncut crystals glittering like dark stars against the rock. It was beautiful, in a way, but . . .

"I don't see anything that looks like a door," Fi said, wiping her sleeve across her sweaty brow.

"The entrance to the forge is hidden in the rock, and it will remain sealed until we find the keyhole and unlock it." The Paper Witch pressed his lips into a thin line. "Unfortunately, I don't know how to do that."

Shane gaped at him from where she'd leaned back against the rock. "Wait—you dragged us all the way up here to a door you can't even open?"

The Paper Witch chuckled. "Contrary to your frequent accusations, Shane, I don't actually know everything. Certainly not everything about ancient Andar. I've never traversed the Ironworks myself. But Witches who have passed through the forge describe the silver vein of quartz near the entrance, so it must be close." He offered them a smile. "Fortunately, I travel with two enterprising young treasure hunters whom I'm sure can figure out the rest."

"Treasure hunters usually get some *treasure* for their trouble," Shane muttered, but she pushed to her feet, banging her knuckles against Briar's shoulder. "Come on. We'll start by looking for the basics—pressure panels, trick rocks. There ought to be some of those magic squiggles Fi likes so much. Just don't stick your hand down a hole without checking it first or something will probably bite it off."

Briar looked a little pale. Fi rolled her eyes. "She's exaggerating. Between the vipers and the centipedes, you're much more likely to end up poisoned."

"That's not as reassuring as you think," Briar told her. Still, he followed Shane over to the rock wall, scouring the crags and fissures.

Fi hung back, staring at the glittering quartz and trying to remember everything the Paper Witch had told her about this place. As much as Shane liked to complain about it, context and history were everything when it came to ruins.

The Ironworks had been built in Andar's earliest age by fire Witches and earth Witches—Witches who could manipulate metal and rock and feel the veins of crystal deep beneath the ground. Together, they carved out a great forge and bellows under the hills that burned all through the night. Early storytellers of Darfell had imagined the mountain to be the lair of a Witch who could transform into a great fire-beast, so massive that when it raged the entire northern sky turned red with the smoke of its fetid breath.

But those were just old stories. Fi tugged on her earlobe, thinking. Real people had worked here—Witches who would have been coming and going all the time to gather raw materials for their creations, everything from the iron gates of Andar's fortresses to the spears of its soldiers. So what had they done?

Her eyes followed Shane, picking her way along the slope while Briar cautiously peered into the rainwater divots. A spark of light magic glowed in his palm.

*Could it be a magic lock?* Fi wondered. For Witches powerful enough to build the forge, using earth magic to reveal a keyhole would be effortless. But immediately she dismissed the idea. Fire Witches had worked here, too, and iron Witches. A door that required a specific magic affinity would be too inconvenient.

The Paper Witch had moved away from her, crouching beside a boulder slick with lichen and filling their precious waterskins from a small stream dribbling through the rocks. Wildflowers bloomed out of the crevices around his feet, bright purple scorpionweed and white snowberries following the dark stream of water until it vanished at the base of the wall. Fi bent and pressed her ear against the rock. She could hear the water trickling inside, loud like it was moving through a vast hollow space—*like a hidden passage.*

Anticipation tingled in Fi's stomach. The door was right in front of her. She just had to figure out how it worked.

"Filore?"

The Paper Witch was watching her, curious.

"There's something here." Fi flattened her hand against the sun-warm stone. She could almost imagine that heat was bleeding out of the rock, the ancient fires still burning in the heart of the mountain. The smoky crystals winked between her fingers.

*Smoke. And fire.*

Fi's eyes widened.

"Shane, Briar!" she called excitedly. "Come back. I think I've got it." Her eyes roved over the sandy basin until she spotted a spiny clump of sagebrush. She fastened her gloved hand around it and tugged hard. The shrub came out of the dry soil surprisingly fast, sending her stumbling back into Shane.

Shane caught her shoulder. "Please tell me that bush isn't the key to an ancient Witch ruin."

"Not by itself." Fi kicked the last clumps of dirt out of the brittle roots. Then she dug out her old flint and tinder. The shrub was half-dead already, and it caught the first spark, the dry branches withering so fast she worried she wouldn't have enough of it. Before she lost the flame, she lifted the burning sage and thrust it against the quartz.

The change was immediate. The smoke inside the crystals began to billow, as if it was being blown away by a soft wind. Fi moved the flame along the rock. A swirl of smoke rushed away from her, all the stormy colors bleeding out of a crystal the size of her fist and leaving something in their place: a long, narrow slit in the rock, half as long as her thumb.

"The keyhole," the Paper Witch murmured in approval. Hidden among the dark crystals, it had been completely invisible. "So the stone itself is the lock. Well done, Filore."

"We're not in yet," Fi warned, coughing as the sage's pungent smoke got in her lungs. She studied the sharp, narrow keyhole, so tight it was hard to imagine wedging any key in there. But it was the perfect size for a thin steel blade . . . "Shane, your dagger. Quick, before we lose the fire."

"If this snaps off in there, I'm going to be pissed," Shane grumbled. But Fi could tell her partner was smiling as she leaned around Fi and drove the dagger into the rock, all the way to the hilt.

Fi held her breath as Shane twisted—but to her surprise, the lock turned easily, the clump of pale crystals rotating like tumblers in any other door. The earth rumbled beneath her feet. Briar pulled her back as a fissure creaked open in the rock face, the seam of quartz and granite separating to reveal a long black tunnel. Rivulets of water snaked down the rough sloping passage and disappeared into the dark.

Shane yanked her dagger out, looking satisfied. "That's more like it."

Fi dropped the sage and stomped out the last tendrils of fire, mesmerized. The lock had been relatively simple, but the power to build a doorway right into the stone . . . that was incredible. Fi felt like it was finally hitting her. These weren't just ruins like the ones on the edge of Darfell; they were in the heart of the kingdom of magic now.

A tarnished iron archway engraved with runes was set into the rock just inside the passage. The marks were old, some melted so deeply into the stone they were barely visible. Fi laid a hand over a series of interlocking triangles. The giant script was twice the size of her palm.

"These look familiar, but I can't place them." She craned her head back. "Is this Riven Earth script?"

"In its infancy," the Paper Witch said. "The Order of the Riven Earth grew from the magic practiced here."

Fi traced a finger along the curve of the metal. When she thought of magic, she always thought of the spells recorded in her parents' library, ancient tomes filled with rituals and recipes and sketches of lost relics—the secret knowledge of generations of Witches. But this magic was even older, from the Witches who came before them, the ones who had tested the limits of their raw power and built something brand new. Before spell books. Before the Orders of Magic.

The Paper Witch's hand settled on her shoulder.

"We should hurry," he said. "The door won't stand open long."

"I guess I'm leading," Briar said, stepping around her into the mouth of the passage. Crackles of light magic leapt to his palm. He shot Fi a teasing smile. "Hopefully, there aren't any giant spiders this time."

Fi shuddered. Now that she was thinking about it, an old forge seemed like perfect cave spider habitat.

"Just for saying that, I hope they eat you first," Shane told him. Then she set off down the passage, the rest of them following her into the dark.

# 2

---»»»—«««---

## Shane

**SHANE WALKED SIDE** by side with Fi, listening to the watery echoes of their footsteps bouncing down the smooth cavern walls as they moved deeper in. The musty air of the tunnels was cold and stale. Fi slipped her jacket back on with a shiver.

The forge was a warren of passages, with dozens of openings cutting away into the dark. The Paper Witch said most of them let out somewhere in the Narrows, and as long as they kept traveling in a straight line, they should come out in the right spot. That was one more *should* than Shane was comfortable with, wandering through a creaky ruin held together by thousand-year-old magic. Trickles of dust rained down on their heads, and she could hear the distant rumble of rocks shifting deeper in. She had a feeling this ruin was just itching to bury somebody alive.

Briar walked at the head of the line, his light magic

blazing in his hand like white fire. Grudgingly, Shane had to admit her partner was right—the prince could be *useful* from time to time. Of course, he'd be a lot more useful if they were walking right behind him, but Fi kept stopping to inspect the iron archways that carved a path through the mountain like a massive metal spine. As far as Shane could tell, every arch was identical to the one ten feet in front of it. But try telling a historian that.

"Be careful," the Paper Witch called back. "The floor drops out quite suddenly here."

Shane nudged Fi forward with her elbow, not as gently as she had the first three times. Where Briar and the Paper Witch had stopped, the stone walls suddenly peeled back and the tunnel opened out into a vast hollow cavern.

Now Shane could see the Ironworks. Smelting furnaces and crumbling chimneys black with scorch marks towered over them in the gloom, the long trenches for carrying water and molten metal cut right into the stone. At her feet, a deep pit plunged into the floor, revealing a spiderweb of underground tunnels glinting with carts and pulleys on rusted chains.

It reminded Shane of the great smelting mine in Rockrimmon. The mine was somewhere her father had forbidden her to go as a child—so naturally she'd gone there all the time, dragging Shayden with her down one of the old coal chutes and coming back soot-streaked from head to toe. Grandmother always threatened to grab her by her ankles and dunk her in the pond headfirst. But Shane liked the way it felt to stand deep inside the earth, surrounded by the noise and the heat. The forge felt alive: the bellows like lungs, the bubbling liquid iron running like thick blood in molded

21

veins, the clang of the metalsmith's hammer pounding like a heartbeat.

This place was long dead. A burned-out smell lingered in Shane's throat, and the pits had been picked clean, nothing left but a boneyard of creaky gears and rusted mechanisms. The crystals bristling along the walls glowed with other-worldly light—just one of those little reminders that she was standing in a Witch ruin. Huge iron archways stretched across the ceiling like a cage of massive ribs.

"It's magnificent," Fi breathed, taking a careless step forward. Shane grabbed the back of her jacket before she could step right into the mine shaft. *Magnificent* was definitely going to be her partner's last word one day.

"Only you would say that." Shane felt more like she was standing in a hollowed-out corpse. She touched the battered handle of an old crank, and the whole thing crumpled into a rusty pile at her feet, the springs squealing. Fi shot her a look like she'd done it on purpose. "You sure this is a shortcut, not a death trap?" Shane asked.

The Paper Witch gestured to the ceiling. "The magic engraved into the iron archways is very strong. As long as the runes are intact, the cavern will hold."

"You hope." Shane was starting to think they should have taken their chances with the Witch Hunters. She'd known a lot of Witches, and they all put too much stock in magic—especially crusty old magic nobody had been upkeeping.

"I think my sister told me about this place once." Briar craned his head back in awe. "It's where the ruby in Aurora's crown came from, right?"

The Paper Witch nodded. "According to legend, it was

discovered by a great scholar of magic who lived in Aurora's time. He came here looking for secret veins of magic deep within the earth itself. In the core of the mountain, he found a ruby of matchless quality. Before it was carved into a rose and set into the queen's crown, it was known as the Hollow Heart of the Hills."

That was downright creepy—to Shane, anyway. Fi just looked more fascinated.

"I don't think I've ever heard of this scholar," she said excitedly. Shane could practically see her flipping pages in her mental library. "What was his name?"

The Paper Witch shook his head. "Unfortunately, that information is lost to time. The scholar disappeared, along with all of his research."

Fi looked disappointed. But Shane wasn't surprised. The kind of person who crawled around in the bowels of Witch mines prying out rubies with ominous names was just *asking* to go missing.

The footing got more treacherous as they traversed the forge. Shanks of rusted metal cracked like brittle bone under Shane's boots. They were only about halfway across when Fi stopped so abruptly Shane nearly crashed right into her and sent them both tumbling to their death. A chasm the length of the entire cave stretched in front of them, at least ten feet across at the narrowest point. Shane kicked a small rock into it and watched it fall, banging against the side on the way down. She never heard it hit the bottom.

"Is there another way?" Briar asked, glancing around.

"I don't think we'll need one. Look." Fi pointed at the far ledge.

Shane squinted through the dim. Her partner had spotted an old, rusted drawbridge, so narrow it was more like a long iron plank, that looked as though it was meant to be lowered over the gap. Too bad they were on the wrong side to use it.

Briar considered the chains holding up the bridge. A little curl of magic swirled in his hand. "I could try to knock it loose—"

"No!" Shane and Fi said at the same time. Shane made a face. "Don't start throwing magic in here—who knows what you'd hit." The last thing they needed was Briar bringing the ceiling down.

Fi peered up at the tangle of ancient pulleys hung from a long crossbar. "If I could get my rope around the windlass, I might be able to swing across."

"I think you mean *we* can swing across," Shane corrected. "Unless you figure you can pull that thing down yourself." The winch at the base of the bridge looked decidedly rusty. "You're the brains and I'm the muscle, remember?"

Fi rolled her eyes. "Suit yourself." She was already grabbing for the rope at her belt, sizing up the distance across the gap. The Paper Witch pulled Briar back to make room. Fi swung in a tight circle and released. The rope sailed out toward the bridge, the dull ring clanging as it bounced off the windlass. Fi yanked it back.

"Second time's the charm?" Shane suggested.

"I thought it was third time," Fi muttered as she wound up again. She spun the rope even faster, and Shane's guts clenched a little as her partner's boot slid dangerously close to the edge.

This time the metal ring wound all the way around the

iron bar, crossing over itself as the rope snagged tight in the chains. Fi tugged gently, and then harder, turning to Shane with her eyebrow raised.

"Ready?" she asked as Shane got a good grip on her waist.

"Be careful," Briar said. Shane had a feeling she wasn't the one he was worried about, but she wasn't taking it personally.

"Ready," Shane told her partner, sucking in a breath in anticipation. Then they leapt over the edge together. Shane's stomach did a backflip in the second they sailed across the drop, suspended over nothing. Then the far ledge was under her, and she let go, her boots crunching over loose gravel as she stumbled a few steps to absorb the momentum. Fi landed awkwardly, twisting to keep hold of her rope and yank it down after them. The ring nearly clocked Shane in the face.

"Are you guys okay?" Briar called.

Shane waved him off, following Fi as she bent to inspect the winch. The mechanism was smeared with dark grease, and there was a healthy supply of rust crawling up the chains.

Fi gestured with a thumb. "All yours."

"Yeah, yeah," Shane muttered, grabbing the grimy handle. Her back muscles protested as the winch screeched, the old gears turning painfully slowly. "So far, those Witches really aren't pulling their weight."

Fi chuckled. The chains rattled and the bridge shuddered, creaking down inch by tortured inch.

Shane glanced across the chasm to find the prince still staring at them. Well, at Fi. There had been a lot of that— the staring—since they came down from the tower, and not all of it from Briar. She shot her partner a look, coaxing the winch another handspan. Fi's account of how she broke Briar's sleeping curse had been suspiciously light on details, but Shane had noticed the new distance between them. Then again, considering the monstrous thing Briar Rose had become in the Forest of Thorns, maybe a little distance wasn't such a bad thing.

Not that Fi knew about that, as far as she could tell. It wasn't really her place to blab, but she hated keeping secrets from her partner. It made her itchy all over.

Shane cleared her throat. "So, uh . . . has Briar talked to you about, you know . . . anything?"

She cringed at how awful that came out. Luckily, Fi was too busy being defensive to notice.

"What would we have to talk about?" she asked, her voice clipped.

Well, that was ridiculous. Even from Fi *keep-your-nose-out-of-my-business* Nenroa. "Gee, I don't know. Dark curses, evil Witches . . . whatever happened between you in that tower. I assume you kissed him, since he's awake."

"Is any of this helping you pull the bridge down faster?" Fi bit out, her arms crossed and her cheeks a little pink.

That wasn't a no. Shane cranked the handle, gritting her teeth against the strain as the bridge dropped another few feet. "So you kissed him. And then . . ."

"And then we mutually agreed to work together, for the good of Andar," Fi finished blandly.

Shane snorted. "Yeah, that's pretty much how I remember that fairy tale."

Fi sighed so heavily, Shane was surprised she didn't bring

the cave down. "It's complicated," she muttered, pinching the bridge of her nose.

Shane shook her head. "It always is with you." With a final heave, the bridge dropped into place, smashing the crust of crystals clinging to the opposite ledge. The chains shuddered. As Briar and the Paper Witch started across, Shane wiped the ancient grease off on her pants, fixing her partner with a serious look. "Just . . . be careful around him, okay?"

Fi shot an incredulous look toward Briar. Shane admitted he didn't really look much like the monster from the Forest of Thorns, all scraggly and sunburned in his ragged coat. He didn't even look much like a prince anymore. "I think I can handle it," Fi said drily. "Besides—like I told you, there's nothing between us."

"Right. Obviously." That's why Fi was blushing red enough to light up the whole cavern. But Shane let it go. She wasn't really the person to be spouting off romantic advice anyway, since she was in love with a girl who'd probably kill her the next time they crossed paths.

They walked on for hours, traversing the twisting maze of passages in the eerie half-light. Shane was thoroughly sick of the place by the time the tunnel began to slope upward and then opened out into another cavern.

It reminded her of the forge, but in worse shape. Hulking boulders had fallen out of the ceiling, and heaps of discarded coal and scrap iron littered the floor, disguising long trenches cut into the rock. In some places, the floor cut away completely, exposing steep chutes that plunged into the dark levels below. Maybe they'd once been channels for water runoff, but now they just looked like a really good way to lose somebody in the lowest levels of the mine, probably forever.

A passageway in the wall to Shane's left was completely blocked, a broken iron archway just visible through the rockfall and rubble. "What do you think happened here?" she asked.

Fi had already crouched down, examining the splintered metal. "The runes on the archway are broken. I guess that's all that was holding it up." She gave the iron ribs on the ceiling a wary glance. "It won't be long until this whole place comes down."

"And by *not long*, you mean . . ." Shane had been burned before.

Fi shook her head. "I'd be surprised if it lasts another ten years."

Shane rolled her eyes at Fi's back. *Not long at all*—if you were a rock, or some kind of ancient relic like Briar Rose. Still, she felt uneasy. She was starting to see why the Paper Witch had been squirrelly about coming this way. There was nothing natural about this place, the crushing weight of the earth held back by just a handful of old spells. The mountain was going to win that fight eventually. Shane didn't want to be here when it did.

"We should be close to the exit." The Paper Witch shook the dirt from his robes. "Look for a passageway with stone steps leading up to the surface."

Shane's boots crackled on layers of forgotten metal shavings as she moved between the boulders. She lost sight of her companions in seconds, all of them but Briar, the globe of white magic burning in his hand. The bitter smell of sulfur and coal tar burned in her nose. Some of the trenches in the floor were still greasy with pitch. She passed a few tunnels cut into the ash-streaked wall, but none that had stairs.

"Anything?" she called, mostly to break the suffocating silence.

"There's another archway over here," Briar called back. "But I can't tell where it goes. I'll get a closer look."

When had Briar gotten so far from the rest of them? Shane's guts clenched, some nasty prickle crawling up the back of her neck. The air in the room felt tense, like the cave was holding its breath, taut as a bowstring. Waiting. On instinct, Shane reached for her ax.

Something clanged off her boot. Shane bent down. Just a lump of scrap iron, but there was something else here, pressed into the ashes and dust. A faint set of footprints.

Shane's mouth went dry. The footprints were small, not even as big as hers. But it was the mark next to them that twisted in her stomach like a knife, a different print smeared into the pitch and grease.

A wolf print.

Suddenly, she knew exactly what was waiting for them here.

Shane took off at a dead run. "Briar! Look out!"

Briar turned. But it was too late. Already, Shane could see a figure framed against the dark tunnel behind him. The dim underground light burned in her scarlet-lined cloak.

"Red," Shane choked. The name ripped out of her like a vital organ.

Red smiled. Then she pulled something from beneath her cloak—a burning lantern, the glass shattering as she threw it down into the trench at her feet.

Flames roared to life in the ancient stone trench. Shane reeled back just in time, shielding her face as the wave of heat rushed over her. Her arms felt seared even under her coat. The red-orange flames raced up one trench and down the next, cutting the room into pieces—Red and Briar on one side, and the rest of them stuck uselessly on the other.

Through the haze, she watched Briar whirl around, light magic crackling in his raised fist.

"You!"

"None of that, now, Your Highness." Red whipped something through the air—a twisted black rod studded with thorns. Briar gasped in pain as the thorns bit deep into his arm, his light magic snuffed out as he sagged against the wall.

"Briar!"

Fi's scream echoed in Shane's ears. She could hear her partner skidding through the rocks, trying to find a way around the flames.

Shane swore under her breath. She'd let her guard down. Nowhere else in the forge still smelled like tar and grease—just here, where Red had laid her trap. And they had walked right into it. She'd been so preoccupied with the Witch Hunters, she'd forgotten what they were really running from.

Her fingers clenched around her ax handle. "What did you do to him?"

"I just drained a little bit of his magic. Very temporary, I'm afraid," Red lamented, seizing Briar's coat. "But enough to take him with me. Sorry our reunion has to be cut so short." Briar's head lolled back against the wall, his eyes unfocused.

Shane gritted her teeth. This was not happening—not on

her watch. She was the one who'd let Red go, and that made Red her problem. And Shane handled her own problems.

"Get the fire out somehow," she shouted, not knowing or caring whether Fi and the Paper Witch could make that happen. Then she tucked her ax under her arm and pulled her jacket over her face, and threw herself into the flames.

Everything was smoke and searing heat. The flames stung her skin, licking greedily at her red coat. She hit the ground hard on the other side and rolled, just working from the assumption that some part of her was on fire. The ax handle jabbed into her ribs, and her lungs squeezed like they were clenched in a fist. But she came up where she meant to—right at Red's feet, staring up into those astonished, unbearably beautiful brown eyes.

Shane kicked Red's legs out from under her. The girl crumpled with a shriek, and then Shane was on her, the two of them rolling end over end through the rocks. Shane came up on top, pinning that deadly rod to the stone with her ax blade. From the corner of her eye, she could see Briar crawling away. Red struggled viciously, kicking at her shins.

"Red! Stop it!" Shane shouted, smashing her to the floor. "Stop it, I don't want to hurt you!"

Red stared back at her, speechless.

She had forgotten the wolf. The beast burst out of the shadows and slammed into Shane like a battering ram. She felt the nauseating crack of her knees hitting the stone as the wolf wrestled her down, dragging her dangerously close to the plunging chute. Her boots licked the empty air. Those razor-sharp claws dug into her shoulders, its stinking breath hot on her neck.

Red was whistling frantically, and the wolf responded, sinking its teeth into the sleeve of Shane's coat and shaking so hard, Shane thought her arm would pop out of the socket. The ax flew from her hands, spinning wildly across the floor.

"Shane!"

Shane forced her eyes open. Through the haze of teeth and fur, she could see the Paper Witch had stomped out a tiny gap in the trench. Fi had Briar's arm looped over her shoulder, her frantic eyes locked on Shane as she hauled him up. But Red was already getting to her feet again, the thorn rod clenched in her white-knuckled grip.

They weren't losing Briar Rose now. Not after everything they'd gone through to save him in the first place.

"Fi, get him out of here!" Shane shouted. Desperate, she threw all of her weight into rolling over, forcing the wolf off and jamming her boot into its ribs.

Nothing she'd done to the wolves in the Forest of Thorns had even left a mark. But this one yelped in pain, its grip on her sleeve loosening for just a second. It was all she needed. Shane scrambled to her feet and tackled Red, their bodies slamming hard into the wall.

A horrible shriek of splintering metal filled her ears. Shane jerked her head up. The wicked thorn rod in Red's hand had screeched across one of the iron archways that held up the ceiling, cutting through the ancient runes like they were nothing but water. The arch glowed an angry, molten red. Shane watched in horror as the runes sank into the hot metal, the spell unraveling right in front of her. Suddenly, the whole cave was shaking.

"It's collapsing!" Fi gasped. "Shane—"

Shane couldn't hear her anymore over the groan of ancient rocks and the teeth rattling in her head. The arches were splintering one after another. The fiery glow ran up one arch and down the next one, the tarnished metal suddenly bowing under the weight of the mountain. This whole cave was coming down on them. But she had nowhere to go—nowhere except down the shaft of the dried-up waterway.

A crack split the ceiling, a shower of dust and crystal shards pelting her face. Red was right under the fissure. Shane knew she was going to kick herself for this later. But she was already moving, sliding madcap across the floor.

"Meet you on the other side, partner!" she shouted, hoping Fi could hear her over the cacophony. Then she hooked her arm around Red's waist and jerked her back, straight into the chute. The wolf skidded after them with a whine.

Her last dizzy glimpse was of Fi, holding tight to Briar as they raced for the final archway. Then everything was vertigo and twisted limbs and pain—just her and Red sliding down the channel into the endless dark, and the total certainty that she was going to regret this when she hit the bottom.

# 3

## Fi

FI'S LUNGS BURNED with the last tendrils of smoke as she raced across the cavern. The fire was mostly out in the ancient trenches, but that was the least of her problems now. Cracks slithered across the ceiling, sending chunks of granite and crystal hurtling down over their heads. Any second, the entire cavern was going to collapse.

She kept her arm around Briar's waist, holding on tight as the floor shook and his knees almost went out. Briar was keeping up with her now, but he still looked ashen from whatever Red had done to him before she and Shane—

*No!* Fi shoved the thought away before panic could rise up in her chest and overwhelm her. Shane's last words were still ringing in her head—*See you on the other side.* Fi wasn't going to let her down. She had to concentrate on getting Briar out of here alive.

Briar stumbled. She grabbed his elbow, desperately trying

to keep them both from falling. Her eyes cut down to his feet, and her heart leapt all the way into her throat.

Shane's ax. He'd tripped on Shane's ax.

Emotions surged through Fi like a torrent. She couldn't just leave it there. She ducked under Briar's arm, stretching out her left hand. Shards of iron and broken rock scraped her knuckles as her fingers curled tight around the handle.

"Quickly!" the Paper Witch shouted. "You must make it to the archway where the runes are intact!" Her wild gaze locked on him, braced under the immovable iron arch of an open passageway with his hand outstretched toward her. The cracks had reached the wall around him, but the arch was holding above him.

They were so close!

Fi tried to run, but the floor was too unsteady. She could barely see, choking on dust and smoke and ash. Her eyes were watery, and Briar leaned heavily on her shoulder. Silt and gravel rained down from the fissure in the ceiling. Fi yelped as a sharp rock bounced off her shoulder.

"Fi, watch out!" Briar shouted.

There was a terrible groaning sound. Boulders crashed down just behind them, splintering against the floor. She caught half a glimpse of the giant slab falling directly above them. She would never make it—but Briar might. Fi surged forward and shoved Briar with all her strength, trying to get him clear.

Briar staggered. His head whipped back, his expression morphing from surprise to fear. He screamed out her name, an almost feral sound, as his hands burst to life with magic like Fi had never seen. Vicious red sparks crackled at his fingertips. The magic burned so hot it felt like a wave of fire against her skin.

Briar leapt forward, smashing his hand against the falling stone. Time seemed to stop—the slab hung frozen over their heads, the crumbling cave halted in its collapse as Briar's magic flared out of him like a wave. The red light was so blinding his hand looked like a pale shadow against it. With a crack like thunder, the giant slab split, exploding into chunks. The Paper Witch shouted, and Fi threw a hand up to cover her face. She felt Briar's arms close around her—then they both hit the ground, the ceiling thundering down on top of them.

Briar's magic disappeared. Fi's head smashed against the blunt edge of a rock, and a wall of darkness slammed over her. At first, she thought she'd lost consciousness, but if that were true, her head wouldn't be pounding. So the dark meant they'd been buried in the rubble. Briar's magic had blown the rocks back just enough to make this tiny hollow around them.

*Briar!* The thought made her shoot up from the ground, and then she almost did pass out. Her body rippled with pain, emanating from the fingers on her left hand, trapped under a fallen rock. She tried to pull it free and almost screamed as the agony spiraled up her arm, pinpricks of fire exploding inside her head. She could feel the handle of Shane's ax still clenched in her fist, the carved wood crushing her fingertips against the floor.

"Fi?" Briar's voice was close and worried. She heard him scrambling up, his breathing ragged as he knelt beside her. "Are you hurt? What happened?"

"My hand . . ." She couldn't get the rest out. When Briar moved, a single shaft of light had pierced the darkness from a small chink in the fallen stones. Her eyes were riveted to the massive rock that had crunched down onto her fingers, squeezing all those tiny bones until she thought they'd pop. The sickle edge of the ax blade gleamed under the rubble.

Briar's eyes went wide with horror. "Hang on, Fi—just hang on. I've got you."

Fi shook her head. "Your arm . . ." she croaked. She could just make out the crimson stain on the sleeve of his velvet coat.

"It's fine," Briar promised, his voice tight. "You're the one I'm worried about."

Fi couldn't answer. Every nerve was an ember, scorching her from the inside.

Briar gripped the stone and heaved it backward, struggling against the weight. Fi shoved her other hand into her mouth and bit down hard. She couldn't scream—the pieces of the broken slab leaned precariously over their heads, and it would be all too easy to bring the unsteady pile down around them.

Briar wrestled the rock away, and the sharp pain became a dull ache as all the blood in her body rushed to her throbbing hand. But she still couldn't move, her fingers pinned under the ax handle.

Briar looked at the buried ax, then at her. His eyes were dark and wary. "Fi . . . you have to let go," he said softly. "I can't get your hand free unless you let go of the ax."

Fi knew he was right. That didn't make it any easier.

Her heartbeat pounded in her head as she forced her hand to uncurl, releasing the ax. Briar pried the handle up just enough to squeeze her fingers free.

His lips were pressed into a tight line. "You shouldn't have pushed me out of the way like that."

"I had to. I couldn't stand to lose . . ." *You.* The word stuck in her throat. "Someone I care about."

"Neither could I," he said, the words so soft she felt them like a gentle hand on her face. Like Briar's hand, hesitating just short of cupping her cheek before he pulled away. He wiped streaks of dirt from his forehead. "Sorry for this in advance." Briar turned her hand over as gently as he could, but it still made her gasp.

"How bad is it?" Fi hissed.

Briar looked ghostly pale, and she didn't think that was just the bad light. "I wouldn't look at it," he advised.

Fi knew he was right. But she couldn't stop herself. She glanced down quickly and then away, instantly wishing she could erase that image from her brain. Her whole hand was swollen under the fingerless glove, her two littlest fingers crunched and bloated like sausages. She felt like she was going to be sick.

Something swooped into the hollow through the gap in the stones. It flashed in the shaft of sunlight like a tiny white bird—then Fi realized it was a scrap of paper, torn to give it wavering wings. It circled the hollow twice and fluttered to the ground. Fi got the sense the spell had been performed hastily, imbued with just enough magic to find them.

"The Paper Witch," she breathed. Through the blood rushing in her head, she thought she could hear the distant sound of rocks moving, the Paper Witch digging to reach them.

"He'll get us out," Briar said.

Fi swallowed. Her mouth was dusty, and even though she was gasping, it felt like she couldn't get a full breath. It was too dark to tell if her vision was going black. She tried to hold herself steady, but her fingers were shaking, numbness crawling up her hand from the fingertips.

*Don't think about it*, she told herself. *Don't think about whether they're broken. Don't think about Shane and Red. Don't think about the fact that the rocks could come down again any second . . .*

*Don't think about it.* She must have told herself that a hundred times since the Forest of Thorns. After what happened at the castle of Andar, she'd been forcing herself to take it one problem at a time, step by practical step, refusing to dwell on the enormity of what they were facing. But now, with everything literally in pieces around her, she couldn't.

They were in the wilds of Andar, alone, with no host of powerful Witches from the castle or warriors from Everlynd at their backs. The Spindle Witch was still after them, and the Witch Hunters were all around them. Briar, the last hope of an entire kingdom, crouched next to her, bleeding, buried in a cave-in. She felt the weight of it all crushing down on her, her breathing too shallow.

"Fi," Briar whispered. "Hey. Look at me."

And then suddenly the hollow was filled with brilliant light as Briar lifted his hand, slowly uncurling his fingers. Soft pink light washed over her—not the harsh sting of daylight, but the faintest blush like the first light of a sunrise. Fi stared.

A small white tree rose from the center of Briar's palm, its bare branches twined and thronged with blossoming roses.

The pain was still there, but Fi was able to force it back until she could get a breath. She looked at Briar through the branches of the rose tree, taking in all the tiny details. The flowers shivered as though in a breeze, and the skin of his palm was dappled with shade. This was too intricate to be something Briar imagined—it had to be something he had seen. A real piece of Andar.

She knew Briar was trying to distract her, and honestly she was grateful. In the dark, with only the magic between them, she could pretend she was a thousand miles from here, sitting beside a campfire under the stars while Briar whispered to her about his kingdom.

The Paper Witch was getting closer. She could hear his labored breathing now, the thud of rocks being rolled away from the pile. The slab shifted over their heads, sprinkling them with another fine layer of dust. Fi kept her eyes on the tree. There was something about it—it was too smooth, too perfectly white to be wood. It looked like marble. There was a pattern carved into the trunk, too, but she couldn't make it out even when she stared until her eyes burned. It seemed almost like the language of the Divine Rose, but as soon as she thought she recognized a letter, the image shifted and the words were unreadable again.

Fi frowned, leaning in until her nose almost touched the tree. On the other side of the branches, Briar smiled.

"What does it say?" she asked.

"You tell me," Briar shot back, raising an eyebrow.

Fi didn't know. But as soon as she could think through

the pain, she was going to have a hundred questions. Suddenly, she was so grateful it was Briar with her—Briar who knew her well enough to create a mystery for her. Briar whose beautiful magic always lit up the darkest places. She blinked back the prickle of tears. She was supposed to let him go, for both their sakes. But after everything, Briar was still here, right beside her, not asking her for any promises or explanations. Maybe the Butterfly Curse meant that she would have to leave him one day. But not yet.

A sharp crack echoed through the rubble. Light flooded into the hollow. The little gap was wide enough now that Fi could make out the Paper Witch's anxious face on the other side, and beyond him a set of stairs that led up toward daylight. The glowing tree in Briar's hand disappeared in a rush of sparks as he shot her a weary smile.

Fi sagged against the rock in relief. They would get out of here. They would escape these caves. And Fi would unbury Shane's ax no matter how long it took—because her partner was alive and would be waiting for them on the other side.

Fi wasn't sure she understood everything that had happened between Shane and Red. But if it came down to a fight, Fi's money was always on her partner.

# 4

## Red

**RED LEANED HER** head back against the rough stone wall, staring across the cave at the unconscious form of the huntsman. Shane lay slumped on her side, her feet almost dangling into the shallow underground stream that cut through the channel, just a trickle of water meandering into the dark.

A few glowing crystals had broken off and tumbled down the chute with them, and they cast a wan light across Shane's face. Her ash-blond braid had come free from its bun and lay uncurled around her head. She looked deceptively peaceful. Red had already checked twice whether she was still breathing, laying her fingers featherlight against Shane's neck. Her own heart thudded almost too loud to feel the steady pulse under her hand.

The urge to go over and check again was strong. Red held herself back. Mostly because she wasn't sure what she was hoping to find. That the huntsman was still alive, or that she was dead.

Red closed her eyes. Cinzel whined, pressing close to her side, and she buried a hand in his shaggy ruff, scratching deep to soothe him. She huffed out a laugh as he raised his head and bunted his furry cheek against hers.

"I'm fine," she whispered. But even to her own ears, her voice sounded shaky, some part of her still trembling from the near miss.

Watching the cracks spread through the cave ceiling, the molten runes splintering over her head, Red had felt something she hadn't felt in years: fear. Not for herself—she'd always known her days were numbered. But for the girl now sprawled out on the rocks, bruised and bleeding and utterly determined to be a constant thorn in Red's side.

Red had been so close. She had gambled that Briar Rose's companions would know the old passageways, that they'd trade the exposure of the Narrows for the deceptive safety of ancient places. She'd planned her ambush so she could grab Briar Rose and disappear without a fight. Everything had gone perfectly—except she'd underestimated Shane. Again.

And Shane had saved her life. *Again.*

Red turned her face up to the light filtering down from the hole in the ceiling. She wasn't sure how far they'd fallen or how deep they were. Her body throbbed from skidding down the chute, but she wasn't hurt, not really—probably because Shane had been wrapped around her, taking the worst of it. When they finally landed, Red had been so dizzy, she'd mistaken the broken crystals for shattered glass. She'd shot up, ready to continue their fight, only to find it was over. But it didn't feel like she'd won.

Her eyes flicked back to Shane. Even from here, Red could see the dark bruises blooming over her left arm, the grooves where Cinzel's claws had sliced through Shane's coat. The cuts in her back would be shallow, barely a nuisance. So much less than he could have done. But Cinzel had understood her far too well, when Red whistled frantically to him and he'd dragged Shane away, careful not to crush her arm in his powerful jaws. He'd heard what Red hadn't even known she was saying—not just *take her down*, but *don't hurt her*.

She hated herself for that.

The black rod lay at her side, sinister and gleaming. Red reached down and laid her hand over it, feeling the ever-present prickle of the thorns.

She should kill her. Shane was the reason she'd failed the Spindle Witch again, and she'd made it perfectly clear that she would never stop getting in Red's way.

And yet . . .

Fear surged through Red, the same strange crush of panic and heat that had overwhelmed her in the cavern above. Shane scared her. Not because of her skill as a warrior, or her stubbornness, but because Shane pierced through her walls to something locked away deep inside Red, a part of herself she thought had withered and decayed a long time ago.

Anger rose like bile up her throat. She didn't need this. Red had a job, one she was good at. She had her freedom—at least to a point. She had Cinzel. She had worked so hard to build a life out of the waste and ashes she'd been given. And Shane could take all of that away so easily.

Red tightened her hold on the rod until a trickle of blood slid down her finger. One more spot of crimson soaked into the rust-stained threads. One more coil in the bindings that held her.

The golden threads on the relic had been strung by the Spindle Witch herself, back when Red was young. A shiver ran through her at the memory of phantom hands carding through her hair between knotting each string.

*This rod is a little bit of me, a little bit of the Forest of Thorns, and a little bit of you, Red. The part that is the forest is unbreakable, sharp enough to slice through anything you encounter.* Long fingers brushed the curls from her face, but Red kept her eyes on the floor. *The part that is me will eat at the magic of any Witch you wield it against, but only for a moment. It's just a piece of me, after all. A fragment of unimaginable power. And the part that is you, Red . . .*

The fingers suddenly dug into her head, forcing her face upward. The Spindle Witch's eyes glittered behind the dark veil.

*That part is your blood. You will feed the rod with your life, for as long as you fail to master your own power and must rely on such a trinket.*

Red had feared the Spindle Witch. She'd hated the Spindle Witch. But she'd never defied the Spindle Witch. Her hands shook as she lifted the rod to slash the huntsman's throat.

But she already knew she couldn't do it. Just like Shane couldn't leave her to die.

Her breath caught remembering the Forest of Thorns: Shane framed against the black vines, her gray eyes blazing into Red's. *If I could do it all again—even if I'd known every-thing from the beginning—I'd still try to save you.*

When had Shane's voice become a ghost in her head, haunting her with all those bittersweet moments she desperately wanted to forget?

Red stumbled back. She let go of the rod and reached for something else—the coil of thick cord tucked into her pocket. Crawling forward, she bound Shane's hands, cinching the knot tight.

No more mistakes. She could still turn this around. She wouldn't let Shane get the best of her one more time.

Shane groaned, her fingers twitching. Red's heart jumped. Then she scooted away and arranged her face into a charming smile, the one that belonged to the girl Shane would recognize. The girl the huntsman had fallen for.

# 5

❧

# Shane

SHANE AWOKE WITH a jerk, lurching up and blinking into the dim. She was in some kind of underground cave. The darkness echoed with the sounds of flowing water. Her mouth was dry like she'd swallowed a fistful of sand on the way down the chute, but that was nothing compared to her head, which throbbed like she'd nailed herself in the skull with her own ax.

Shane let out something halfway between an expletive and a groan, trying to reach up and feel her head. She couldn't move her hands.

"Careful," a soft voice murmured, closer than Shane expected. "You have a nasty goose egg back there. Though I guess you'll just have to take my word for it."

Shane's sluggish brain caught up all at once. *The fight. The cave-in. Red.* She whipped around to find Red leaning back on her hands beside a tiny underground river, the very picture of uncaring. Like it didn't bother her at all to be stuck down here together after everything that had happened between them. Apparently, Shane was the only one suffering from a bad case of emotional whiplash, feeling torn in a hundred different directions at once.

Anger won out.

"Red," she growled. The wolf at the girl's side bared his fangs in warning, but Red just smiled.

"I like the way you say my name—always so full of feeling." Red soothed the wolf with a single touch. Shane could only see a slice of her face, but her eyes were dark and depthless in the crystal glow, her lips twisted in a mocking smile. "Has anyone ever told you, you wear your heart on your sleeve?"

Shane ground her teeth together. She had gotten that particular warning a few times, mostly from her grandmother, and mostly about not letting her emotions get the better of her. Which they were definitely in danger of doing at this moment.

It should be so easy to hate Red. She'd tried to kill Fi in the Forest of Thorns. She'd tried to take Briar again. And even though Shane had saved her, she'd still woken up with her hands bound.

Her grandmother had always told Shane she was a glutton for punishment because of her reckless fighting style. She couldn't even imagine what that wizened old bat would have to say about her newly reckless heart. Probably the exact same thing.

*If you insist on rushing in and leaving yourself wide open, don't be surprised when someone takes advantage of that.*

Shane scooted away from Red, letting her back thunk against the wall and ignoring all her new aches. "You know, this is a pretty lousy way to repay me for saving your life . . . twice," she added, blowing her hair out of her face.

Red gave a little shrug. "Well, I thought about smashing your head in with a rock at least twice, so I'd say we're even. Besides, you're only alive right now because I need your help."

Shane bristled. "With what? Dragging Briar Rose back to the Spindle Witch? Because I'm not going to do that. If this is you making me the same offer you made in the Forest of Thorns, you can forget it."

Red clicked her tongue. "Sadly, no. That offer expired when you got in the Spindle Witch's way." She combed her fingers through her tousled hair, carelessly pinning up the curls that had fallen out of the high knot. "I was thinking more along the lines of working together toward a common goal . . ."

Shane snorted in disbelief. Her and Red, common goals? *Unlikely.* Aloud, she just said, "I'm listening."

Red inched closer, her shadow rippling over the glowing crystals embedded in the walls. "Well, you are an experienced treasure hunter." She tossed her chin to indicate the cavern. "I want out of these tunnels, and I think you're my best chance of making that happen."

Shane peered around. She squinted up at the dry chute they had tumbled down—now precariously blocked by rocks and debris—and then along the trickling stream to where it disappeared down a narrow tunnel.

She'd definitely escaped worse than a natural cave system.

Once, she'd made her way through an entire underground maze carved from magnetic rock that sent compasses spinning and left anyone who entered too dizzy to see straight. She'd navigated the whole ruin blindfolded, half for the bragging rights, and still come out of it with a pocketful of jingling silver-backed sapphires. Of course, her partner at the time had just been puking left and right because he couldn't keep his blindfold on, not waiting to stab her in the back in the dark. Which was probably what she could expect from Red.

"And what do I get out of this bargain?" Shane wanted to know.

"Your freedom," Red promised. She wagged a finger at Shane. "You're far too unruly to make a good hostage. Get me to the exit, and I'll let you go."

Red's voice had the familiar teasing lilt, but Shane sensed there was something else there, something lurking just underneath the surface. Shouldn't Red want to kill Shane, too? Why would the right hand of the Spindle Witch ever let her go?

Unless something was holding her back. Maybe Red wasn't as unaffected as she was pretending to be.

Red leaned suddenly close, smirking. "What? Waiting for me to sweeten the deal?" she teased, one finger pressed to her lips.

Suddenly, Shane was remembering the feel of those soft lips against hers, the heat of her body and the sound of Red's laugh—her real laugh, breathless and surprised. All the memories she had tried to extinguish burned to the surface. Shane supposed her feelings were all over her sleeve again, or at least her face, but she wasn't the only one. She didn't think she was imagining Red's breath coming a little faster as Shane mirrored her, leaning in until their lips were a whisper apart.

"You think if you flirt with me enough, I'll forget what you've done? Who you work for?"

Red was so close, Shane felt the shiver on the other girl's skin. "No," Red whispered back, the words almost a kiss before she pulled away. "But I think we've both realized we're not going to fight to the death down here. So what other choice do you have?"

Shane hated that she had let herself be taken hostage. She hated that Red's brown eyes could still look so beautiful to her, even knowing all the dark things that must be concealed behind them. But she hated most of all that Red was right. Shane wasn't sure if the magnetism between them would pull them together or fling them apart or just set her internal compass spinning until she was hopelessly lost. But one way or the other, they were at a stalemate.

Red stood up, calling the wolf with a quick whistle. "Cinzel. We're leaving." She looked expectantly over her shoulder. "Well?"

Shane swallowed. But there was really only one answer.

"I'll stop you, Red," she promised, struggling to her feet. "I'll protect Fi and Briar, over and over. As many times as it takes."

Red smiled like she'd expected nothing less. "But first you'll have to get out of here. Who knows what's happening to them while you're stuck with me?"

That was a sobering thought. Shortcut or no shortcut, this was still Witch Hunter territory. If it came to a fight,

Shane ought to be the one at Fi's back, not the peaceful, animal-loving Paper Witch, whose most dangerous weapon was a very disapproving look.

"Truce, then—just until we get out." Shane nudged her messy braid over her shoulder, waving her bound hands. "So maybe we can lose these?"

"I think I'll feel a little better if they stay on," Red said, gesturing for Shane to take the lead.

The wolf—Cinzel, Red had called it—growled at Shane as she passed. Shane glared right back before heading off down the narrow passage, following the little stream. It was as good a place to start as any.

The light was much dimmer in the underground tunnels. The great swaths of crystal that lit the caverns above were sparse this far down, most of them clustered into the ceiling and high on the walls. They gave off a watery glow, almost like moonlight.

The cave system was clearly natural, which made it hard to pick her route. Some tunnels tapered off into holes barely big enough for a gopher, while others stretched out into vast glittering halls, the crystals reflected a thousandfold in great pools as still as glass.

Shane tried to follow the waterways—no easy feat when the streams kept crisscrossing and vanishing into fissures in the rock, but at least they were all basically moving in the same direction. She remembered the Paper Witch saying there was a river on the other side of the ruin, drawing it with a stick in the dirt the night before they'd entered the forge. Part of her wished she'd been paying better attention to Fi's nine hundred follow-up questions. The other part of her knew there was only so much navigating you could do from stick drawings in the dirt. It was a good bet the underground waterways and the river flowed to the same place, though, which made it her best chance for meeting up with the others.

Something moved in the shadows. Shane jumped as the wolf lunged past her, utterly silent until he scrabbled over the rocks and snapped at the eyeless fish flickering in the stream. She kept forgetting about him, and the crackle of fish bones crunching in his jaws wasn't a real cheery way to remember.

The scraggly brown-and-white wolf didn't look like much compared to the twisted monsters Red had commanded in the Forest of Thorns, but even this one had almost taken her arm off. Shane was really wishing she had her ax right now—for a lot of reasons.

Her eyes darted over to Red. Unlike Shane, who was caked so thick with grime and dust she probably looked like she'd been buried alive and then crawled back out, Red still looked unfairly put together. She wore an outfit suited to traveling, a fitted red tunic that flared at the hips over black pants, with a wide black belt cinched at the waist. Her crimson-lined cloak flashed around her ankles. In the soft light, she was mesmerizing, her cheeks glistening with the exertion of the march.

Shane cursed under her breath. The next time she tripped, she'd make sure to break her fall with her head. She had clearly knocked something loose in her brain if she was still mooning after Red.

The tunnels stretched on and on. Red had her waterskin, which they were quickly draining, but she didn't have any food, and only Cinzel seemed to be enjoying the slimy fish.

It was impossible to tell time in the perpetual twilight, but if Shane's protesting muscles were any indication, they might have to find a spot to rest soon.

She was about to suggest they call a halt when they came on an archway carved into the rock. Where everything else was mottled and raw, this looked like it had been chiseled at, the stones scarred by deep grooves. The area beyond was pitch black, not a crystal in sight, but the trickle of water she'd been following led straight into it.

Shane wrinkled her nose. "We need to go through there, but . . ."

"But what?" Red demanded crossly. "Let's go." She stepped around Shane, pinning her with a glare. It was somewhat undercut when she immediately caught her foot on a rock, tripping and almost tumbling into the stream.

"I was going to say we need some light first," Shane said smugly. "I would have tried to catch you, but . . ." She waved her bound hands.

The look Red shot her was positively murderous. Shane's chuckle died as Cinzel butted his big shovel-shaped head into the back of her knee and she lurched forward, cracking her elbow against the rock.

Shane swore. Red hadn't even given the wolf any kind of signal!

"Very funny," Shane told the mangy creature. His tongue lolled proudly out of his mouth.

Red had a little *serves-you-right* smirk, but it faded as she stared down the tunnel. "So what do you suggest? Unfortunately, my pack and everything else useful is still above ground, while we're stuck down here." She shot Shane a look, to be sure the huntsman knew who she blamed for that.

Shane ignored her. Her eyes landed on the softly glowing crystals. "Maybe we can pry one of those out," she said, nodding toward a fist-size crystal about shoulder level in the wall.

"Cinzel, guard," Red said offhand. The wolf sat obediently on his haunches, yellow eyes fixed on Shane, while Red slid a thin hunting knife from her boot and set to work prying at the crystal. The blade kept sliding against the glassy surface. Red cursed as the knife flew off, chipping against the stone.

"I'd give you a hand—you know, if I could," Shane offered, holding up her wrists again. Red's eyebrows drew together in frustration, and Shane wasn't sure whether she wanted to drive her blade into the wall or into Shane.

"Fine," she said at last, jerking her head. "Make yourself useful."

Shane approached slowly—no sudden movements with a wolf at her back. She almost expected Red to pull the wicked rod from her belt, just to be doubly sure Shane wouldn't try anything. Instead, Red took Shane's hands between her own, lifting the small knife and gently sawing through the layers of frayed rope cord.

This close, with the crystals all around them, it was impossible not to notice the scars on Red's hand. Most of them were old, jagged white lines scratched into the center of her palm, but there were some new wounds, too. Punctures that were raw and red even though they had long stopped bleeding.

Now Shane knew where those came from. The thorn rod. The weapon Red used as the right hand of the Spindle Witch—one that clearly hurt her to wield. With Red's hair pinned up, Shane could see a flicker of the faded tattoo on the back of her neck: the two snakes, fangs extended, frozen forever in an unwinnable battle. Fi had said it was a sealing tattoo, something the Witch Hunters had done to Red when she was a child. To them it represented magic and evil devouring each other. But Shane couldn't help thinking of a different kind of battle altogether. The battle being waged in the girl right in front of her.

There was the Red who had clearly suffered horribly and been forced to do whatever it took to survive, and there was the Red who now used that suffering to justify whatever horrible thing she was asked to do. One of them could be saved. The other one . . .

The bonds fell away. Before Red could pull back, Shane reached out, catching her wrist.

"I was hoping you'd run away after the Forest of Thorns." Her voice was low, just a breath in the dark.

Red arched an eyebrow. "I did run away, if you recall."

"No. I meant away from the Spindle Witch and all of this."

Red jerked back, her hand slipping out of Shane's grasp. She laughed, but it sounded hollow. "Oh, Shane. Don't you ever get tired of being so wrong about me?"

That stung. But Shane refused to give up, because she had realized something about Red—something important. Red was at war with herself, whether she knew it or not. There had been one moment, more than any other, when she had given herself away.

"That night, outside of the Forest of Thorns, you asked me to run away with you. You meant it, didn't you?"

Red's expression didn't change, but her scarred hand fisted in her cloak. Shane had a feeling she'd struck a nerve.

She pressed on, staring deep into Red's eyes. "If I'd said yes, you would have left the Spindle Witch and disappeared with me. You were asking me to save you."

"You're wrong." Red shook her head, like she could chase the words away. "I only asked because I knew you would never agree."

"Red . . ."

"I cut you loose to get that crystal," Red bit out. "Don't make me regret it."

Shane had so much more she wanted to say. But there was a coldness in Red's gaze now, a warning that she was about to cross an invisible line that would put them back at each other's throats.

"Fine." Shane held out her hand for the knife. She wedged the tip of the blade in between the rocks and then smashed her palm into the hilt, hard enough to create a crack. Two more good hits and the crystal came free. She offered it to Red, who refused.

"You're leading, remember?" Her arms were crossed tight, every inch of her radiating *leave me alone*. She didn't retrieve the cord, though, or bind Shane's hands again before they splashed under the archway. It was a start.

The cavern beyond was cold and damp. The rocks above the archway were reinforced by thick iron beams bolted to the rock, which seemed reassuring until Shane passed under them and caught sight of a long split through the center where the crossbeam was bowing in. The smell of rot hovered around them. Shane held up the crystal, swinging it around to light the vast empty space. Where she would have expected veins of crystal, there were deep gouges carved into the walls, like everything of value had been torn out. There were even deep holes scored with hatch marks from a pick or a shovel, where someone had been digging and digging—like they were searching for something.

One strange mark held her gaze, carved into the wall between two hacked-out fissures: a great curved X with an eye on either side. The carving was simple, but something about it pricked the hairs on the back of Shane's neck. She wondered suddenly if this was where the scholar had found the massive ruby he called the Hollow Heart of the Hills. It certainly felt hollow now, and empty, and bitter cold.

"Hurry up," Red snapped.

Shane let the light drop away, but the feel of those eyes followed her long after they'd left the cavern behind.

She didn't try to talk to Red again. Whatever she had uncovered was too raw and too fragile—and too dangerous. For both of them.

# 6

---※≫—≪※---

# Briar Rose

**BRIAR LEANED INTO** the heat of the fire, looking out over the darkened world. The half-moon shone like a severed coin over the canyons, and the night was filled with the sound of insects whirring in the wild grasses along the steep slope.

They had come out of the underground passages near the top of a high bluff. The sun had already been sinking over the Sunset Narrows, bathing everything in brilliant reds and golds as they set up their small camp. It was little more than a few blankets around a pit of smoldering embers, protected by the overhang of the tunnel entrance at their backs and close enough to the edge to look down on the ravine and river below. To keep watch for Shane.

Fi was trying to act normal, going about small tasks, tending to the fire, but every few minutes her gaze flickered to the dark landscape stretched out below them. It was obvious she was worried about her partner. Guilt squeezed Briar's stomach like a wet rag. He was the reason they'd been separated.

As the night deepened, the Paper Witch had taken the first watch, and Fi had gone off to forage for something more appetizing than the hard traveler's bread. Which left Briar alone with the fire, trying to wash the blood out of the sleeve of his velvet coat.

He wrung the fabric out over the dirt, inspecting it in the low light. He'd done his best to wash the stain out, but the fabric was mottled and rough around the tear—it would never be the same again. Unbidden, the feeling of the sharp thorns sinking into his arm returned, making him shudder. In that moment, it felt like all his magic had been sucked away from him, leaving him empty and hollowed out, barely able to stand.

Briar squeezed his hand over the bandaged wound, wincing. The small cut still stung where the thorns had broken the skin. But he'd take the pain over the memory any day. His eyes slid to Shane's ax, propped against a rock on the other side of the fire.

He'd been useless down in the forge—worse than useless. Shane had rescued him, and they'd lost her. And then he'd almost lost Fi, too. He had reached for his magic, and just when he needed it most, it hadn't come. The light inside him had guttered—failing, just like Briar was failing. Staring into Fi's wide hazel-green eyes as the rock hurtled toward her, he had reached out desperately, dredging deeper and deeper until he found a different power—a darker one.

The power of the Spindle Witch.

A shiver of revulsion crawled down Briar's spine as he

stared at his hand against the glow of the fire. For just one moment, as that wild red magic crackled all around him, it had changed. Bone claws had stretched out from his nail beds, gleaming in the light. It wasn't his hand that blasted through the rocks—it was the hand of the monster he'd been fighting so hard not to become. The creature that still haunted his dreams, lurking like a shadow under his skin just waiting to get out. He dragged his fingers down his arm as though he could scratch the truth away.

He could have killed Fi. He could have killed them all. In that moment, all he'd wanted was power, and the second he felt it coursing intoxicatingly through his veins, he'd almost forgotten why. If Fi hadn't been right there, he would have lost himself to that overwhelming magic. Only this time, there would be no Great Witches to save him—to pull him back from the brink of darkness and tuck him to sleep.

The sleeping curse that had protected him for so long was broken. He'd come dangerously close to losing himself once in the Forest of Thorns already. If he succumbed to that dark power completely, he would really be gone this time—*forever*. Worse, in the hands of the Spindle Witch, he would betray all of them. His kingdom, his people . . . and Fi.

"Briar? You okay?"

Briar raised his head at the sound of soft footsteps. Fi stood on the other side of the fire, wisps of her brown hair shivering in the breeze.

He didn't know what she'd seen on his face in the moment before she stepped into the firelight. But he pushed all the dark thoughts away, offering her an easy smile.

"Fine," he promised. She had enough to worry about—he wasn't going to be one more thing. "What do you have there?"

"Dinner," Fi said, as if it were obvious. She had turned his old shirt into a makeshift pouch, the billowing hem stretched out and loaded down with globes of bright red fruit. Briar was pretty sure he'd seen the same little fruits clinging to the scrawny cactus he almost sat on the day before.

"Can you really eat those?" he asked, a little wary.

Fi poured the cactus pears out into the dirt. "As long as the spines don't get you." She stuck her thumb in her mouth, as if soothing a puncture, but he thought she was smiling at him.

The bandage the Paper Witch had fixed around her left hand was coming loose. Fi fussed with it, trying to tighten it one-handed until Briar cleared his throat.

"You know, I can fix that for you."

"Can you?" Fi asked, crooking one eyebrow. "I'm surprised a prince would have any experience with broken fingers." Still, she took a seat next to him, holding out her hand.

Briar peeled the bandage off, careful not to jostle her as he inspected her hand. Some of the swelling had receded, but the middle finger was badly bruised at the joint. Her ring and little fingers were a patchwork of puffy blue-and-purple skin, and the smallest nail was blackened and cracked. Her pinkie was definitely broken, but miraculously it seemed to be the only one. Honestly, it made him a little sick to look at. Especially knowing his magic had played a part in causing it. He dredged up a reassuring smile.

"I don't have any personal experience with broken bones,"

Briar admitted. He wiggled his fingers at her playfully. "These were considered priceless treasures. But I did get the chance to splint my brother Sage's fingers. And they are, I assure you, *mostly* straight."

"Mostly?" Fi protested.

"I kid. Sage's fingers are perfectly straight."

"Clever of you to pick something I have no way of verifying," Fi muttered.

Briar chuckled. He had to swallow around a lump in his throat at the thought of Sage still asleep in the castle, trapped by the Spindle Witch's threads.

"Seems like a king should have been treated by a proper healer," Fi pointed out, hissing just a little as he tightened the bandage splinting her little finger to the one beside it.

Briar smiled at the memory. "It was a matter of pride. Sage didn't want the whole castle knowing he'd foolishly reached up into a fireplace chute and the damper came down on his hand. Of course, that might have had to do with the important letter his *adorable* little brother shoved up the chimney to stop him from going back to work. But in my defense, I couldn't read yet, so I didn't know how important it was."

Fi snorted, probably at his use of *adorable*, and shot him the flat look he'd been hoping for. Briar liked it when Fi got that look, like something—often Briar—had measured up exactly to her expectations.

He considered her hand, reaching for her black fingerless glove. "The bandage might stay better if you took this off—"

"No." Fi's voice was suddenly sharp. She cleared her throat. "I mean, it'll be fine. Just leave it on."

"Right," Briar said awkwardly, wondering again what Fi was guarding so closely. She never took the glove off, not even at night. He had caught a glimpse of the black mark on her palm once or twice, but never clearly enough to make sense of it. It had looked like some kind of tattoo or burn. He hoped one day she'd finally trust him enough to tell him.

"So, you never told me about that tree," Fi said, as Briar wrapped the bandage. When he looked up, her eyes were curious. "What was that? The illusion you made down in the rocks?"

Briar had almost forgotten it. After the shock of Shane sacrificing herself and his magic going haywire, it had been the last thing on his mind.

"It's called the Tree of Roses. One of Andar's many secrets." He tied off the bandage, then reached for another. "It's a gravestone of sorts. Those patterns you saw carved into the marble aren't just words. They're names—the real names of all the most powerful Witches who've ever belonged to the Divine Rose."

Fi looked skeptical. "I didn't think those names were recorded anywhere."

"They aren't recorded anywhere *else*," Briar agreed. "Just the Tree of Roses in the castle gardens. Many of the Witches of the Divine Rose were ancestors of mine. When they chose to devote themselves to the order, they took a Witch title and gave up their claim to the throne, and their names along with it."

"But I couldn't read any of them," Fi insisted.

Briar shrugged. "You wouldn't be able to even if you were standing right in front of it. They're etched into the tree

64

with very particular binding magic that makes them unreadable. Supposedly, it was invented by the first queen Aurora herself, though, to be honest, she gets credited with a lot of the Divine Rose's more brilliant spells."

Fi's eyes glowed with curiosity. She was leaning toward him now, her broken finger all but forgotten. Her face was sunburned and streaked with dust, and her hair was a rat's nest at the back of her neck, but he liked her best this way: Fi the historian, eagerly soaking up every detail.

"Did every magic order do something like that?" she asked.

Briar shook his head. "I have no idea. In my time, the orders kept to themselves, remember? You'd have to tell me."

He could practically see the wheels turning in her mind. "I don't know. There isn't much written about memorials erected by the Orders of Magic, but if the writing's unreadable, maybe there wasn't much to record. Rivarrcha has an entire volume of excavation records—it would be easy for something like that to get lost in the footnotes." She fixed Briar with a penetrating stare. "You're absolutely certain it's unreadable? You've seen it in person?"

"I stood before it many times," Briar said wistfully. He could still see it so clearly in his mind: the memorial of white marble carved into a tree whose long, intricate branches twined with scarlet roses. Briar had spent hours beneath it—his mother's grave, and his sister's, even while she lived. Their names were up there somewhere, carved into the boughs, undecipherable even to him.

The Spindle Witch had taken them both from him—his mother when Briar was days old, too young to remember her face. And his sister, Camellia, sixteen years later, ripped from him when he fell under the sleeping curse, lost to time.

Fi wasn't giving up. "Did you ever try tracing the letters with your fingers? How about a charcoal rubbing?"

"I was not nearly so bold," Briar said with a laugh. He could just imagine the Great Witches stringing him up by his ankles if they caught him in the act. "But when we go back . . ." The words caught in his throat, but he forced himself to go on. "When the Spindle Witch is finally gone, you're welcome to try anything and everything you like."

"I'll hold you to that," Fi said.

Briar wondered if she heard the promise underneath the promise: that she could imagine coming back to Andar, as a friend or something more. It warmed the part of him that had been icing over ever since he awoke in the tower with her goodbye kiss cooling on his lips. Sometimes, when he couldn't sleep, Briar stared into the dark and made the same wish over and over, until his heart ached: that he could slip back in time to that moment in the tower, right before their goodbye, and this time he would say something different, something better, something that changed her mind. But when he woke up to the gray sky streaked with pink, he still didn't know what he wanted to say. He'd poured out everything he felt about her, and she'd rejected him.

Briar had tried to put it away and focus on being her partner, but in moments like this, he couldn't help wondering if maybe he still had a ghost of a chance.

*Or maybe he was just being unbearably selfish.* Briar shoved those feelings down deep in his chest, where they couldn't push their way out.

"Well, you're in luck," he said, voice light. "I can't imagine anyone denying the savior of Andar a small thing like a charcoal rubbing. But if somehow you don't have quite enough clout to get away with it, mine should do the trick." Briar knotted the last bandage around her wrist to hold it in place. "There. Ready for your next round against the cactuses."

Fi looked down at her hand, surprised. She tested the bandage with the tip of one finger. "Thanks. Maybe one day I can return the favor, if anything ever happens to your *priceless treasures*." She wiggled her fingers at him teasingly, but her smile was warm.

"Here's hoping," Briar agreed, crossing his fingers in jest.

The quiet of the night was broken by the arrival of the Paper Witch. He moved with impossible grace and stealth for someone navigating the wild hills in long robes. As he stepped into the firelight, he raised a hand, pushing his silvery-blond hair behind his ear.

Fi twisted to face him. "Any sign of Shane?" she asked hopefully.

The Paper Witch shook his head. "Not yet. But she would have a much longer path to navigate, coming from the caves beneath the Ironworks. We'll move to the riverside tomorrow. The lowest tunnels run along natural streams, so she should come out somewhere down there. Shane is the most resourceful treasure hunter I have ever known—I am sure she will find us, given time."

Fi got to her feet, retrieving her rope and throwing her cloak around her shoulders. "I'll take the next watch," she offered.

Briar rose to follow her, but the Paper Witch held him back. "A moment, Briar Rose." He waited until Fi was out of earshot, his lips set in a grim line. "I've warned you not to be reckless with that magic. What happened in that cavern *cannot* happen again."

He'd seen—the Paper Witch knew what had almost happened. Briar's throat tightened at the memory of bone claws.

The Paper Witch laid a heavy hand on Briar's shoulder. "It might be best, for the time being, if you avoided using magic as much as possible."

Briar bristled. "You expect me to hang back and let Fi and Shane fight my battles for me?"

"I expect you to remember that there are more important things at stake here than any one of us." The Paper Witch's gaze seemed to pierce right through him. "You are the key to the Spindle Witch's defeat. Whatever happens, we cannot risk losing you. For the sake of all of Andar."

It was the last thing in the world Briar wanted to hear. He knew his first duty should be to his kingdom, to the people trapped in the castle, to the Witches of Everlynd, whom he had never met but who'd been waiting a hundred years for him. But Fi and Shane were real in a way that all those distant figures weren't, and he wanted so desperately to belong with them. Not just a prince to be rescued, but a real partner, someone they relied on in return. For once in his life, Briar didn't want to be locked away like a rose under glass—too precious to risk.

He'd waited a hundred years to start living again. But even now, away from the castle and free of the sleeping curse, he was still the ill-luck prince, just as useless as the moment he'd been put to sleep.

The Paper Witch sighed, the bell in his hair tinkling as he released Briar's shoulder. "Small wishes, Briar Rose—remember? For now, try to get some sleep," he urged. Then he moved off, retiring to his blanket beside the fire.

A cold pit sank in Briar's stomach. He clenched his fist, sending a twinge of pain up his wounded arm. What was the point of having powerful magic if he could never use it to save anyone? What was the point of being a part of some great destiny if all it meant was that his life was never his own?

As long as Briar could remember, every Witch he'd ever known had urged him to tread carefully, to use just a drop from that great well of power inside him. He could still remember crouching next to his sister Camellia, her hands over Briar's as she helped him trace the Divine Rose script, teaching him the mysterious language and all the secrets it held.

He had mastered the spells so quickly. Magic came to him effortlessly and obeyed his every whim, even complex illusions manifesting with just a twist of his fingers. But no matter how much he excelled, there were certain pages in the spell books that she would never show him, pages she had stitched closed with little roses in crimson thread.

*Small wishes*, she had told him over and over—when she'd refused to teach him binding magic and oath magic, spells even the novices of the Divine Rose learned. When she'd again refused his request to learn the ancient battle magic of the first light Witch, the spells Queen Aurora had used to conquer the warring fiefdoms and unite the kingdom of Andar a thousand years before.

Finally, he'd lost patience. *Why won't you teach me anything important? How am I supposed to defend myself when the Spindle Witch comes for me?*

He could still remember her expression then—how she'd whirled away from the window of the Great Witches' tower, her blue eyes wild, staring at him like he'd brought something impossibly wicked into the sunlit room. He wondered what specter she was searching for in his face, and whether she found it before she steadied herself against the window, one hand pressed to the stained-glass roses.

*Your magic is very powerful. But you must be careful how you use it.* Her fingers tensed. *Imagine you are on one end of a string. And the Spindle Witch is on the other. It is magic that connects you, and so magic—the wrong kinds of magic—can draw her closer to you. You must never use your magic in anger or fear, never to do harm.* She offered him a thin smile then, one that didn't reach her eyes. *Your magic is meant for small wishes, Briar Rose.*

Briar had never questioned her. But now he wondered if there had been more to her hesitation—if she'd worried about making him too powerful, what might happen if he fell to the Spindle Witch's will with all the magic of the Divine Rose at his fingertips. A precaution, in case she couldn't save him.

Maybe *small wishes* hadn't just been a mantra to protect him, but to protect everyone else.

Briar looked down at his pale hand. Just a hand. The same hand that had bandaged Fi's fingers—the same hand that had called up the image of the rose tree. There hadn't been any darkness inside him at that moment; his light magic sprang to his fingertips almost before he reached for it. Maybe because in that moment he had had only one wish—*a small wish.*

But what about when small wishes weren't enough?

Briar curled his hand into a fist. He could still feel the crackle of power there, waiting.

# 7

## Shane

SHANE SWIPED HER elbow across her sweaty forehead, scraping a chunk of quartz down the blunt edge of her dagger.

"You know, I'm starting to think you lied about knowing how to open this door," Red complained, leaning over Shane's shoulder to get a better look at the incredibly stubborn chunk of smoky quartz set into the wall. It was just like the one back at the entrance—which meant they needed fire.

"You want to give this a try?" Shane grumbled, wincing as the crystal slipped and left an ugly scratch down the blade. It was the dagger her former fiancée Kara had given her, though the engravings were slowly being obliterated by her banging. This whole thing was hard enough without flint and a fire starter—and harder still without any real kindling. The clump of torn fabric under her dagger remained stubbornly unlit.

Red didn't offer to take over, just heaved a dramatic sigh,

cracking her neck. The scratching sound from farther down the tunnel meant Cinzel was digging up some rodent or nest of worms he planned to eat. Shane was getting pretty close to joining him. Her stomach felt like a tiny shrunken pebble.

They'd navigated the tunnels until late the night before, only stopping on the algae-slick banks of a small underground pool to get a few fitful hours of sleep. Every drop of sweat and speck of dirt stuck in Shane's clothes felt like a centipede crawling down her shirt, and when she finally managed to drift off, she kept dreaming of Fi buried under a ton of rubble. She shot awake over and over, reaching for an ax that wasn't there.

The emptiness at her back stung. Her grandmother would have kicked her from one end of the armory to the other for losing that battle-ax, a weapon that had been passed down through generations of Steelwight kings. Shane had carried it so long it was like an extension of her own body—not to mention her last connection to her family.

She shook that thought away hard. It wasn't just the ax that had been forged in Steelwight; it was Shane herself. Countless hours of training under her grandmother's strict eye until her muscles ached, a hundred lessons on how to survive in the forests and winter wilds. Which was how she knew it was possible—*hard but possible!*—to make a spark against a dagger as long as you hit it with a rock that was harder than the metal.

*So why wasn't it working?*

Red tapped her foot obnoxiously, and Shane almost smashed her thumb in frustration as she slid the crystal down the dagger one last time.

A spark flashed in the darkness. It landed in the cloth, and Shane dropped to her stomach, breathing gently on the fabric as it smoked and then sprang to life, crawling with fire.

"Ha! Take that," Shane crowed, shoving her dagger into the burning scrap and lifting it to the bulging quartz set into the wall. The crystal swirled with smoke and flame as the slit of the keyhole appeared. Shane didn't waste a second, flinging the burned cloth aside and turning the dagger in the rock.

"About time," Red announced.

The rock trembled and groaned. A fissure split the crystals on the wall, the passage slowly creaking open. Midmorning sunshine spilled into the gap. It was even later than Shane had expected.

Red closed her eyes, tipping her head back and breathing in the fresh air with relish. Her tan skin seemed to glow in the sunlight. Cinzel padded up to her side, the white fur on his belly shining.

"I guess my gamble on you paid off." Red tossed Shane a fond smile. "We're out—you're free to go wherever you want."

"Eager to get rid of me?" Shane asked, brushing off her pants and moving past Red into the doorway.

"Isn't that the other way around?" Red murmured, almost too soft to hear.

Shane blinked against the onslaught of light. The stone door had let them out into a narrow gully bristling with spiny cactus and dry sage. Slabs of the same old red stone towered over her, but through the gaps she could make out the low hills in the distance. They were almost through the Narrows. Clear water trickled through the rocks at their feet.

Somewhere ahead, Shane could hear the rushing of a river and a pounding waterfall.

"Looks like you're stuck with me a little longer," Shane said, waving at the high sandstone cliffs. "There's nowhere to split up."

"So our truce extends to the first fork, then?" Red suggested. Her voice was light, but her smile didn't quite reach her eyes.

More than anything, Shane wanted to say, *It could last longer than that, if you would just come with me.* But she swallowed it down. "Sounds about right."

They walked side by side down the narrow passage, picking their way through the rocks. Without thinking, Shane reached out to help Red over a patch of prickly cactus. *Traitor*, she thought, staring at her hand on Red's elbow. Cinzel growled half-heartedly, nipping at her dusty coat.

"Snap at me, and I let her take a needle bath," Shane warned. The wolf studied her for a moment before settling all the way down on his belly, watching her with rueful eyes. Shane blinked. "Did he actually understand me?"

Red threw her an amused look. "Not the way you mean. But wolves are very intelligent. Cinzel's smarter than most people—he's almost certainly smarter than you."

"Then maybe *he* can help you over the next cactus patch," Shane muttered, and wished her stomach didn't turn a somersault when Red laughed, tossing her head back. For a second, she was the girl from the market again—the mysterious, intoxicating stranger who could set a match to Shane's heart just by looking at her.

Shane wasn't imagining this. There was still a connection

between them, and Red felt it, too. Shane wasn't ready to let her go again, but she didn't know how to avoid it. If she had more time, maybe she could change Red's mind . . .

Red had sauntered ahead, but she stopped suddenly, pulling up short. Shane hurried to catch up. In front of them, the canyon split into two narrow passages—one branch running toward the river, the other toward the hills. They had reached a fork in the road.

*So much for more time.*

Red offered her a tiny smile. "End of the line, I guess."

"Red—" Shane began. She never got the chance to finish.

"Well, well, well. What do we have here?"

Shane whirled around. Four figures had appeared around the bend, half-hidden in the shadows of the narrow passage. Her blood ran cold as her gaze swept the two men and two women.

*Witch Hunters!* Their dark cloaks were thrown back in the heat, but there was no mistaking the saw-toothed blades hanging from their belts, or the massive topaz amulet swinging at the leader's neck. He was the one who had spoken.

"Looks like a couple of rats scurrying out of their holes." His gruesome smile showed off a handful of missing teeth. "Hello, little rats."

Shane sized up the Witch Hunters. The hulking man with the pike seemed three times her size. Four against two would be bad odds even if Shane had her ax. Without it . . .

"On my signal, we run," she hissed to Red. "Get back to the door, and then—"

Something hurtled down from the top of the gully. Shane caught one glimpse of a cloaked figure sliding toward her—

then a fist plowed into her cheek, throwing her back into the rock wall. Pain exploded across her face.

"Shane!" Red screamed.

Shane's eyes swam. Every nerve in her head was on fire. She braced herself against the rock, choking as the spines of a wicked saw-toothed blade dug into her neck.

"Don't do anything foolish." The pasty Witch Hunter whose fist had so rudely introduced itself to her face leered down at her, his heavy sword pressing into her shoulder. Shane groaned. Trust the Witch Hunters to have one filthy scout at the top of the gully, just waiting to get the jump on people.

"Cheap shot," she coughed, spitting a mouthful of blood. Her lip was definitely split open, and her mouth was numb, but at least she wasn't choking on any broken teeth.

Over the scout's shoulder, she could see Red frozen, her back pressed to the wall of the passage. Cinzel crouched in front of her, his ruff bristling and his jaws open in a snarl.

"What happened to running?" Shane shouted to her.

Red's face was ashen with fear, but she managed a withering look. "I didn't realize *the signal* was you getting clocked in the face."

"Wait. That wolf . . ." A blond woman threw her hood back, her eyes narrowing as she studied Red. "I know who you are. You're the Witch Ivan's been after all these years."

*Ivan?* An excited murmur rose through the Witch Hunters at the name. Shane felt the sword ease off her neck as the scout craned his head, trying to get a good look at the Witch. Red's hand clenched around the thorn rod on her belt.

"So Ivan's still alive. Shame." Red's words were careless, almost bored. But Shane could see how tense her shoulders had gotten, all the blood draining out of her face. Whoever Ivan was, just the thought of him terrified her.

*Maybe he was the monster who put that mark on her neck.*

Shane hadn't even eaten anything, but that thought made her want to hurl.

"If we bring her in, Ivan will reward us with anything we want," the man with the pike hissed, his eyes gleaming. "Our pick of the treasure, or a promotion to the Eyrie. No more scut duty out in the waste."

Cinzel was positively vibrating with rage, and so was Shane. Maybe Red was an enemy, but the Witch Hunters were worse—nothing but scum-sucking vultures, preying on people and doing ugly things for money. Shane wouldn't wish them on anyone. Not even Red.

Especially not Red.

She threw a glance at the dagger in her boot. All she needed was one second of distraction. She'd get this Witch Hunter off her, get hold of a weapon, and then . . . well, she'd figure the rest out if she got that far.

The leader of the Witch Hunters took a step toward Red. "Looks like your luck's run out, little Witch," he said, drawing the saw-toothed blade in his meaty hand. "Take her alive, if you can—Ivan hates it when someone ruins his fun."

"Over my dead body," Shane growled.

The sword twitched against her neck. "Careful," the scout warned. "You're halfway there." Then he turned to shout over his shoulder: "What about this one?"

Shane didn't wait to hear whether she was keep or kill. She seized the scout's moment of distraction. She ducked under the sword, hooking him by the back of his neck and smashing his forehead against the rock. The man's shriek roiled in her ears.

"Red, run for it!" Shane yelled.

The Witch Hunters leapt into motion, scrambling for their weapons. She could see two of them racing for Red, but she didn't have time to worry about that. The scout came up roaring, so close Shane could smell his rank breath as he swung wildly at her. She ducked just in time. The saw-toothed blade screeched against the rock, leaving an ugly white groove in the wall over her head.

For the first time ever, Shane was glad she was short. She surged up and jammed her shoulder into his chest just below the breastbone. The Witch Hunter crumpled, almost taking her down with him as his weight sagged against her—then she was out, surging through the gap beneath his arm and staggering to her feet.

"Red!" she shouted.

Red's sudden gasp made her turn, just in time to see Cinzel's teeth closing around the blond Witch Hunter's arm. The woman screamed, dropping her weapon and backing away.

Red had her back against the rock, holding the wicked thorn rod so hard a rivulet of blood ran down her wrist. The rest of the Witch Hunters were surrounding her. The leader of the squad lunged as if to grab her, and she lashed out cat-quick, dragging the rod across the Witch Hunter's leg. The man howled.

"Back off," Red warned.

"You'll pay for that," the Witch Hunter spat, clutching his bloody thigh. "Kill her! Ivan will have to settle for her corpse."

Shane didn't like the sound of that—or the look of four on one. She pushed off the wall and rocketed across the passage. The dark-haired Witch Hunter rounded on her, but Shane was faster—she dropped to her knees, kicking the woman's legs out and then driving her boot into her opponent's chin for good measure. She felt the bones creak as the woman toppled into the shallow water, clutching her face.

"Forget about me already?" Shane taunted, scooping up the woman's short sword and spinning it in her hand. The remaining three Witch Hunters watched her warily. The blond woman had retrieved her sword, and her eyes gleamed with feverish hate, her bloody hand clenched around Cinzel's bite.

"Keep her off us, Von!" the leader shouted, pushing the giant beefy man with a pike toward Shane. "We'll get the Witch."

Red's terrified eyes locked on Shane's. Shane really wanted to get in there and help her, but she'd have to take care of her own problem first. The man with the pike rushed her, bringing his weapon down hard enough to shake the ground. Shane scrambled out of the way, swearing as she barely blocked another crushing blow. Her whole arm juddered with the force.

Out of the corner of her eye, Shane saw Cinzel leaping at the Witch Hunters in a flash of white-and-tawny fur. The monster with the pike came at her again. Shane still had the short sword, but against a pike, it was basically useless. Von swung wildly, forcing her farther and farther down the narrow passage—away from Red. That had been the point, she realized with a lurch as the other Witch Hunters flooded in between them, cutting her off.

"If you want a fight, come at me, you cowards!" Shane yelled. She ducked another swing, rolling under the giant's arm and coming up behind him—then her back exploded in agony as the butt of the pike smashed in between her shoulder blades. She'd been careless, rising too fast and forgetting the pike's massive reach. Through dancing black spots, she realized the blond woman had forced Cinzel away from Red, cornering him against the rocks. That left Red facing the leader alone.

"Red!" Shane shouted, as Von wound up for a swing. "Red, get out of there!"

Red didn't seem to hear her. Panicked, she lashed out with the thorn rod, too far from the Witch Hunter to even graze him. The man whipped his heavy sword up and caught the rod between its gleaming teeth, and Red shrieked as a twist of the blade ripped the rod out of her hand. It clattered into the rocks, the golden threads dark with blood. Then the saw-toothed blade crunched down again, and Red screamed as it sliced a jagged gash deep into her arm. That sound echoed on and on in Shane's ears.

Cinzel's howl rattled her teeth. Von swung again. Shane threw herself into the shallow water, feeling the whiff of the pike staff passing overhead as she twisted onto her back and slammed her thick heel into the giant's burly ankle as hard as she could. Von crumpled to one knee. It wouldn't keep him down forever, but it gave Shane enough time to stagger to her feet, blood racing and shoulder throbbing. *She had to get to Red.*

It was the only thing that mattered in this moment. She sprinted across the rocks and plowed into the leader full tilt.

Shane smashed the hilt of her short sword into his fleshy side, right above the floating rib. From the way he bellowed, she was pretty sure she'd given him a broken bone to remember her by.

The Witch Hunter backed away, clutching his gut.

"Who else wants their ribs rearranged?" Shane shouted, putting herself in front of Red. She hoped she sounded intimidating instead of winded. In top condition, she had no qualms about kicking Witch Hunters down as many times as they wanted to get up. But after long days of hard travel on little food and less sleep, Shane could feel she was almost at her limit.

Luckily, the Witch Hunters were, too.

"Retreat!" the leader growled. His eyes burned into Shane's. Then his gaze darted to Red, a nasty smirk curving his lips. "Your days are numbered, girl," he spat, before lurching back down the gully with the rest of the pack limping after him. Shane had never been so glad to see a bunch of Witch Hunters' backsides. The giant with the pike brought up the rear, his massive hands wrapped around something black and gleaming . . .

"My rod!" Red lurched up from the wall like she was going to chase after them.

Shane caught her around the waist, yanking her back. "Are you out of your mind?" she demanded.

Red struggled frantically against Shane's grip. Her face was flushed, her eyes wild with terror. "They took the rod! I have to get it back!"

"Forget it—they're gone!" Shane spun Red to face her. "Do you have any idea how lucky you are to be alive at all?

You'd have to take on their entire camp to get it back. It's suicide."

For one moment, Red looked like she was going to argue. Then, all at once, she slumped against Shane, her legs crumpling.

"Red?" Shane dropped to her knees, holding Red against her to keep the girl's head from cracking against the rock. "Hey! Talk to me—what happened?"

"I don't . . ." Red squeezed her hand over the jagged cut on her arm. Her fingers came away wet with blood. She lifted them to her nose, her lips twisting. "Poison," she croaked out, halfway between a laugh and a moan. "The Witch Hunter's weapon must have been coated with poison."

All the blood rushed to Shane's head as Red pressed her fingers to Shane's cheek, her lips trembling.

"I guess you won't get to stop me after all," she whispered, almost wistful. Then her hand fell away, leaving a wet smear on Shane's face.

"Red! Hey! Snap out of it," Shane yelled desperately, shaking her. Red's head lolled against her arm. Cinzel nipped at her elbow, scared and confused, but Shane had no time for Red's mangy wolf.

She stared at Red's unconscious body, her mind churning. She didn't know anything about poisons. But the Paper Witch would. She lurched to her feet and hauled Red up onto her shoulder.

"Don't make me regret this," she muttered. Then she raced for the river with Cinzel at her heels, really hoping this wouldn't come back to bite her.

# 8

⤜⤜⤜ ⤛⤛⤛

# Briar Rose

**"SHANE SHOULD BE** here by now."

Briar lifted his head, looking up at Fi from where he knelt at the riverside, refilling one of their precious waterskins. The other dangled limply from Fi's fingers.

Briar followed her gaze. The Narrows were beginning to flatten out, the bluffs around the river blunted and growing thick with weeds wedged between the rocks. They'd broken camp at dawn, making their way down to a riverbank shaded by leaning ash trees. Tiny yellow flowers bright as buttons dappled the grassy bank.

Briar corked the waterskin, moving to Fi's side. "The Paper Witch seemed pretty sure Shane would pass this way no matter where she came out," he said, trying to sound reassuring. "And he's taking a look around right now, just in case. All we can do is wait."

Fi didn't seem to like that answer much. She pinched the

bridge of her nose. "I know in my head that running around in the rocks and passages just makes us more likely to miss each other, but . . ." She shrugged helplessly. "I just can't help thinking, what if something happened? Maybe Red got the better of her."

Briar's hand fisted at his side. "I don't think the Witch would hurt her." A memory of Red backed against the thorns, his own gleaming claws wrapped around her throat, flashed through his mind. "She owes Shane, after all."

Fi nodded absently, and Briar felt a sick wave of heat rising through him at her worried expression. Fi didn't know just how much Red was indebted to Shane, because Briar still hadn't told her what really happened in the Forest of Thorns—that he had almost lost control and killed Red, and that Shane had been the one who stopped him. Every time he opened his mouth to say something, he imagined Fi's face twisting into a look of fear . . . or worse, disgust. Briar didn't think he could stand that.

He pushed the thought away. Fi was worried about her partner. The least he could do was cheer her up.

"You know, Shane would probably laugh if she could see us right now," Briar said, shaking the hem of his coat and raising a cloud of dirt. "I think I'm still wearing half the dust from that cave-in."

"Me, too," Fi admitted, wrinkling her nose. She bent and dragged her fingers across the surface of the river. "It's cold," she said. "But we might as well get cleaned up while we have the chance."

Briar shifted awkwardly. "So . . ."

Fi rolled her eyes. "Come on," she said, and then nearly

killed Briar when she shucked off her shirt without a word of warning.

His stomach jumped. Fi still wore her ragged undershirt, shored up with strips of her old torn blouse, which she'd wound over her chest and tied off at the shoulder. He couldn't tear his eyes away from her. She kicked off her boots and socks and then slipped all the way down to her small clothes, splashing into the river up to her waist.

"It's rude to stare," Fi said, clearly embarrassed. She pressed her bandaged hand to her arm. "I already know I'm all scratched up and bruised—you don't have to rub it in."

Honestly, Briar hadn't even noticed. He was too busy admiring the glow of Fi's bare shoulders and the sprinkling of deep-brown freckles that dusted her collarbones. In the spill of warm sunlight, she was radiant.

Before he accidentally blurted any of that out, Briar turned away, pulling off his jacket and undershirt and throwing them aside. The muscles in his back tensed as he imagined Fi watching him strip down. Now he understood why she had been so embarrassed. He felt like all of his flaws were on full display, and he wished fervently that he wasn't so pasty. When he turned around, though, Fi was looking studiously in the other direction. Briar was almost disappointed until he realized the tomato-red blush had crept all the way to the tips of her ears. *She had looked.*

Fi ducked her head under the water, scrubbing at her hair with her right hand, and then tossed it back in a spray of droplets. Briar swallowed against his suddenly dry mouth, reminding himself how unattractive and itchy he was. It worked—too well. He hurried into the river, though he kept his pants on. Anything else was just too much for his brain to handle.

The cold water swirled around him in gentle eddies. Briar dunked his head under, scraping a week's worth of dust and grime off his skin. The scratch from the thorn rod stung a little in the water, but the redness had faded.

When he was done, he made his way back to the bank, feeling like a person again—if not quite a prince. He took a seat on a wide, flat rock that stretched into the shallows, shaking out the rest of his clothes and giving the worst patches a quick rinse. The castle tailor would have been scandalized to see what became of his velvet coat.

Briar wasn't in much better shape himself. His muscles ached from days of hard travel, and the soles of his boots felt like they were about to flap right off. Objectively, he knew he should be miserable. But he wasn't. All he'd ever wanted was to get out of the castle, and now that he had, he wanted to spend the rest of his life just like this—exhausted and hungry and blistered from head to toe, and seeing the whole world with Fi, if she'd let him.

Fi slipped out of the river and perched beside him, kicking her feet lazily in the water. Her wet undershirt clung to her skin. Briar leaned away, tossing his coat onto the shore, and then gasped in surprise when a fingertip brushed the center of his back.

"Sorry," Fi said guiltily. "You have an awful bruise here. It must be from the rocks coming down." Her cold hand slid across his spine. Briar yelped in surprise—though he'd like to think it was sort of a manly yelp.

"It's fine," he said, inching away.

Fi's brow crinkled in confusion before a knowing smile bloomed on her lips. "Ticklish?" she guessed.

"Unbearably so," Briar admitted. "My brother used to tickle me mercilessly whenever he was losing an argument." The memory made him chuckle—though he didn't remember finding it funny at the time.

"I'll keep that in mind." Fi nudged his elbow playfully. "In case I ever need to win an argument."

"Hey," Briar protested, but there was no bite to it. Secretly, he loved every little slip of Fi's tongue, when she said something about the future like Briar was going to be in it. Unconsciously, he found himself studying her again, her eyes closed and her head tipped back to enjoy the breeze. The heat of her so close was intoxicating. Briar stared at her parted lips.

If he stayed here like this, he was going to do something he regretted. Briar got quickly to his feet, scrambling for an excuse as Fi blinked up at him.

"I think there might be one more wineskin to fill in the pack," he said.

"I'll help you look for it." Fi pulled her feet out of the water, splashing after Briar toward the shore. She only made it a step before her foot slipped and she pitched forward wildly. Briar reached out instinctually to catch her, their bodies colliding as Fi locked her arms around him.

Her fingers were like icicles from the cold river, but somehow they still left a line of fire everywhere she touched him. Briar stifled a groan. He was trying to keep his distance, but she really wasn't making it easy.

"Sorry," Fi said sheepishly, braced against his shoulder.

"Anytime," Briar said, a little breathless. "Just be careful. The moss on these rocks is pretty sli—"

Briar's foot slid out from under him before he could even finish the warning. Fi grabbed for him, but it was too late, and they both went down in a tangle, sprawling onto the grassy bank.

Briar landed on top of Fi with her arms wrapped awkwardly around him. *Smooth,* Briar thought, wishing he'd bashed his head open on the sharp rocks and spared himself a lifetime of trying to live this down. He could feel Fi's knee crunched into his stomach and her breath on his bare shoulder. She was wheezing. Briar pushed up on his hands, horrified.

"Fi, are you hurt?"

Only she wasn't gasping for breath—she was laughing, so hard she was shaking with it. Their eyes met, and Fi lost it again, pressing her hand over her mouth, and in a second Briar found himself laughing, too.

They had to look ridiculous, sopping wet and splayed out on the shore, but Briar didn't care, not even when Fi's knee jerked and clocked him in the ribs, because she was laughing, really laughing, and this moment felt fun and easy—the first thing that had really felt easy between them in a long time.

"Who needs to be careful now?" Fi asked, offering him a wry smile.

"Me," Briar agreed, staring down at her. But it wasn't mossy rocks he needed to watch out for. It was his heart, galloping away with him. He felt exhilarated, watching her chest heave as she smiled up at him with some of the little button flowers mashed in her hair.

It was perfect, and the only thing that would make it more perfect was if they kissed. It would have been so easy to lean down and press their lips together. He didn't even think Fi would stop him right now. But as sure as Briar was that he wanted that, he was equally sure it would be a mistake. Fi was his partner, his friend, and it would be all too easy to push her until he ended up pushing her away.

She'd rejected him, but she'd also risked her life for him, because he was still someone she cared about—*someone she couldn't stand to lose.* That meant there was something between them, even if it wasn't quite what he wanted. Yet.

He had been quiet for too long. Fi was staring at him curiously. Briar braced himself on one hand and plucked a few mangled yellow flowers from her hair, twirling them in his fingers.

"Unless you wanted to keep these, as accessories?"

Fi brushed the flowers away. Briar flopped over in the grass so they were lying side by side, staring up at the blue sky. The light breeze was cool on his bare skin. Fi started to sit up, but Briar grabbed her elbow.

"We can't go anywhere until the Paper Witch or Shane shows up. You might as well rest."

Fi pinned him with a look. "Trying to add a sunburn to your list of problems?" she asked drily. She didn't get up, though, just scooted forward until she could hook her foot under his coat and toss it back at him. There was a loud tearing sound. Fi shot up with a wince.

"I think I ripped it," she admitted.

Briar folded his arms behind his head. "At this point, one more hole isn't going to make a difference."

Fi didn't look relieved. She lifted the coat, examining it closely. The fabric had snagged on the spines of a small barbed thistle they were probably lucky they hadn't tumbled into. There was a jagged tear in the lining between the second and third button, right under a pair of tiny embroidered roses.

"I think there's something in here," Fi said.

That got Briar's attention. He sat up fast, scooting closer and peering over her shoulder. Fi was right. Something was tucked between the layers of fabric. Fi reached in, working her fingers around until she could pull out a piece of parchment folded tightly into a square. She unfolded it carefully— it was at least a hundred years old, after all.

The page was about twice the size of her palm, creased with deep grooves from the folds, and it was filled from corner to corner with numbers, all grouped off into sets of three. Briar recognized the curves on the sixes and the soft curls at the bottoms of the ones.

"This is Camellia's handwriting," he breathed, touching the paper with his fingertips. It felt delicate as a dragonfly wing. His sister must have been the one to hide it in his coat . . . but why? And when?

Fi frowned, tracing one finger over the numbers painstakingly inked onto the page. "I've seen groupings of numbers like this before. I think it's a book code."

"A book code?" Briar repeated. "Why would she go to all the trouble to hide a code in my jacket?"

"Maybe she was worried about her message falling into the wrong hands?" Fi's voice was hushed. "Think about it, Briar. If Camellia wanted to make sure you got this, she'd have to hide it in something she knew you'd still have no matter how many years you were asleep. This was what you were wearing all that time."

Briar fingered the two roses that had been sewn right over the hidden page. "But what does it mean?"

"Well, if I'm right and it's a book code, then each of these sets of three numbers represents a word. The first is the page number, then the line number, then the word number."

"So we need a particular book to read it." Briar shrugged. "There are definitely no books sewn into this coat, and I can assure you there were none hidden in the bed with me."

"Of course not," Fi said excitedly. "If the book was right there with you, it wouldn't be a very secure code, would it? But since the code was written by *your* sister, hidden in *your* coat, it's intended for you. She would have picked a book that meant something to you."

She stared up at him expectantly. Briar swallowed. Fi's theory made sense, but he had no idea what book it could be. Camellia was an avid reader, and she'd used dozens of spell books, some of them secret tomes only shown to the highest-ranked Witches of the Divine Rose. She had shared that love of books with Briar, reading to him every night, but the only ones they read over and over were the illustrated storybooks, probably because they all had happy endings.

When he was young, he'd treasured those nights and those stories, but as he'd gotten older, angrier, lonelier, he'd pushed her away. He wasn't sure how well they'd even known each other at the end. How could he possibly know what book connected them?

FI AND BRIAR were both dressed and poring over the code when the Paper Witch returned. He hadn't found Shane. Fi's shoulders sagged in disappointment. Briar filled the Paper Witch in on what they had discovered.

The Paper Witch lifted the code and blew gently across the square of parchment. The numbers seemed to shiver, as if the edges might lift off the page. He smoothed a hand over them to press the ink back into the parchment. "There is no enchantment hidden within the ink," the Paper Witch said, handing the code back to Briar. "I believe Filore is right. It's a code."

"But what message would Camellia need to give me like this?" Briar asked.

"I don't know," the man admitted. "But the Rose Witch was not the type to leave anything to chance. If there was even the slightest possibility there was knowledge you would need, she would make sure you had it." His eyes grew distant. "There was a rumor among those who fled Andar at the very end, that the Great Witches were crafting a spell strong enough to rival even that of the Spindle Witch. Whatever the secret, it's been entrusted to you, Briar Rose. You *must* remember that book."

The Paper Witch and Fi were both staring at him again. Briar wanted to have the answer—more than that, he *should* have it. Camellia had left this message for him. She had trusted that he could figure it out, just like the Paper Witch and Fi were trusting him now. He stared down at the little piece of paper.

His concentration was broken by a great clatter of rocks. Briar jerked up in surprise to see a very familiar figure bolting toward them from the canyon.

"Shane!" Fi yelled, springing to her feet.

Briar stuffed the code hastily into his pocket. Shane's eyes were wild, and her cheek was smeared with blood. His eyes riveted to the body slung over her shoulder.

"Are you hurt?" Fi asked, running to her partner's side.

"Not me. Her." Shane lowered Red to the ground, her eyes locked on the Paper Witch. "You have to save her."

Briar fisted his hands in his coat. *Red*. The right hand of the Spindle Witch. And Shane had brought her right to them.

## Fi

FI LOOKED DOWN at the unconscious figure on the bank. Red was laid out carefully on her scarlet-lined cloak, her face pale and feverish in the shade of the stunted ash trees. Her breath came fast and ragged. Fi couldn't see the grisly wound on Red's arm anymore, thanks to the bandages scrawled with Divine Rose runes, but just thinking about it made her a little queasy.

She had managed to keep busy while the Paper Witch tended to Red by taking care of her own partner, mopping up Shane's split lip and getting her account of the fight. But now there was nothing to distract her from their very real problem.

The Paper Witch sighed. "I've done all I can for her," he said, perching on one of the weathered gray rocks. "But I'm afraid the news is not good. This poison is one I've seen before—something the Witch Hunters brew using the venom of pit vipers, along with a few other distasteful things. It's slow-acting, but without an antidote . . ."

"How long?" Shane cut in. The words were muffled by the cloth she held bunched against her lip, spotted with blood.

The Paper Witch shook his head. "A few days, at most."

Shane's jaw clenched so hard Fi could see the muscles standing out in her neck. The riverbank was suddenly deathly quiet, only the rush of the water and the quiet shushing of the tree branches in the breeze. The Paper Witch wore a pained expression, and Briar was looking pointedly away. They all knew what he was saying. Red was going to die unless they helped her. And they shouldn't.

Red was their enemy—an agent of the Spindle Witch. And the fact that Shane cared about her made her twice as dangerous. But the thought of abandoning her in a desolate place like this left Fi cold all over.

"So where can we get this antidote?" she asked, breaking the heavy silence.

"The Witches of Everlynd would have it. But . . ." The Paper Witch hesitated. "We cannot bring such a dangerous enemy into their hidden city."

Shane bristled. "So you're saying we leave her here to die."

"I would not wish that fate on anyone. But I don't have an alternative." The Paper Witch pressed a hand over his eyes. "The stakes are simply too high. We cannot take the risk."

"Forget that! This is Witch Hunter territory," Shane argued, shaking the bloody cloth at him. "If we leave her here, they'll kill her, *or worse*—"

"You're bleeding again," Fi interrupted, grabbing her

partner's hand and pushing the rag against the trickle of blood sliding down Shane's chin. Shane didn't seem to care.

"Look at her—she's helpless!" She threw out her hand toward Red's unconscious form. After the Paper Witch moved away, Red's wolf had crept out of the spiderweed along the bank and hunched at her side, pushing his nose against his master's limp hand. "She's not a threat to anyone right now." As though to agree, the wolf whined low in its throat.

"Shane . . ." the Paper Witch began.

"You can't underestimate her." Briar's voice was quiet but intense. His eyes hadn't left the Witch since Shane laid her on the bank, and Fi realized his hand was clenched over the rust-colored stain on his sleeve. His eyes flicked to Shane. "She almost killed Fi in the Forest of Thorns, don't forget that."

"Oh, trust me, I haven't forgotten *anything* that happened in the Forest of Thorns," Shane growled. "And I'm not sure Red's the one we should be worried about."

Unease crept through Fi. Looking between them, she got the feeling she was missing something very important. Before she could ask, the Paper Witch stepped forward, his hands raised.

"Even if Red herself is no longer a danger, the threat of the Spindle Witch is not to be taken lightly." He tipped his head, looking at Shane as if imploring her to understand.

Shane ground her hands into fists. "I'm not going to abandon her out here for those vultures. If you're leaving her, you're leaving me, too."

That was one thing that was definitely not happening.

"We're not leaving anybody," Fi said firmly. She stepped

forward, squeezing Shane's shoulder. "And we're not going to become murderers, either. We take Red to Everlynd." She locked eyes with the Paper Witch. "We'll manage the risk. It's the right thing to do."

That was what Fi had learned, having the ridiculously loyal huntsman for a partner: that sometimes doing the right thing was worth the risk. Fi could go back and forth a hundred times, weighing the pros and cons of helping Red. But even with her lip split open and her face roiling with ugly purple bruising, Shane always seemed dead sure of what was right. This time, Fi was going to follow her lead.

Shane threw her a grateful smile. The Paper Witch pressed his lips into a thin line, asking without words if she was sure. Fi didn't budge. His eyes flicked to Briar. "It's your kingdom at stake, Briar Rose," he said, the bell in his hair tinkling softly.

"I'm with Fi." Briar's eyes had lost that hooded look, and his expression was once again soft.

The Paper Witch sighed. "Clearly, I am overruled. But I warn you, we are still a few days from Everlynd. However quickly we travel, we will be cutting it close."

He paused, considering, then turned to Shane.

"There is an outpost just beyond the last defenses of the city. We'll leave the two of you there and send help back." He raised a hand, forestalling the protest Fi could see building on Shane's lips. "The last leg of the journey is by far the hardest. It would be quite impossible for Red in her condition. When we reach the city, we will ensure you get the antidote *and* that the Witches of Everlynd have the chance to take precautions before bringing her inside. That is the most I can agree to."

Shane nodded tightly. "I can live with that."

The wolf let out an excited whine at Red's side, drawing everyone's attention. Fi could see the girl's fingers twitching. She was coming to.

"Let me talk to her alone," Shane said, turning toward Red. "She's not going to be all that excited to see us."

"Wait, Shane. One more thing." Fi jogged over to where they'd left the pack. With a lurch, she heaved the ax up into her arms. "I figured you might want this back." The gleaming silver head felt like it would leave a crater in her shoulder, but it was worth it for the huge grin that lit Shane's face at the sight of it.

"I thought it was gone forever." Shane took the ax, lifting it as though it were nothing, and then suddenly Fi found herself grabbed in an awkward one-armed hug. The ax handle dug into her ribs, and her broken fingers twinged, mashed in between them. But it was the heat that surprised her, the surge of warmth in her chest as Shane said, "Don't know what I'd do without you, partner."

"Are you talking to me or the ax?" Fi grumbled, embarrassed by the display.

Shane laughed. "Whichever one put that funny look on your face." She thumped Fi on the back, then hurried over to Red. Fi watched as Shane helped the girl sit up, nudging the wolf back with her elbow when he tried to lick Red's face. She couldn't hear what Shane was saying, but she could guess well enough by the way Red's eyes flared in surprise, her fingers clenched in the wolf's pale fur.

Briar stood beside her, his gaze fixed on Red as well.

"We won't let anything happen," Fi promised. "I trust Shane."

Briar shook himself, his complicated expression falling away as he offered her a smile. "And I trust you."

Fi was already too warm from Shane's hug. Briar's words made the heat rise up to her cheeks. She looked away, desperately missing the old traveling hat she used to be able to pull down over her face.

THEY SET OFF in the late afternoon. With the Narrows at their backs, the Paper Witch led them through barren country, the fields of boulders changing to scrubby gullies thick with scraggly pines and dry foxtail grass. The air buzzed with insects and the chittering of small rodents poking their heads up from a warren of holes.

Red and Shane walked about ten paces behind the rest of them, Red's hands loosely bound in front of her. Fi caught glimpses of the wolf appearing and disappearing through the rocks like a specter, its ears flat against its head. Whenever they stopped, he would crouch low and inch close to Red, watching the rest of them warily. He didn't seem aggressive, but Fi was still very glad Shane was the only one getting within biting distance. The wolf and the huntsman seemed to have some sort of understanding. Fi even caught Shane pouring a little bit of her water into the depression of a rock for the wolf to lap up.

They finally stopped for the night in a copse of knotty pines near the shell of an abandoned house. Not much was left of it but the skeleton of the beams and the ancient fieldstone wall, both of them seared with scorch marks from some long-ago fire. Fi kicked a few seasons of rotted moss out of the old firepit and struck the flint with practiced ease, coaxing their little fire to life.

Looking at the wild pink hollyhock growing over the charred remains of the house, she couldn't help thinking of the seeds that only opened after the heat of a wildfire. She wondered if Andar was like that: a seed locked tight under the ashes and the waste, just waiting to erupt into blossom again.

Shane and Red had set up camp a short distance away, in the shadow of a fallen tree. Fi blew on the flames one last time, laying some larger logs over the embers, and then made her way over to her partner, the old travel pack with their provisions slung over her arm.

Shane was ripping one of their precious few blankets into strips for more bandages. Someone was going to be sleeping cold soon—and they were all going to be left wearing nothing but rags. She looked up as Fi approached.

"You'd better not be bringing me any more of those prickly pears," the huntsman said, waving her dagger in warning. "I've lost too much blood already."

Fi rolled her eyes, dropping a few dark-purple prickly pears into the moss next to the last of their traveler's bread. Their supplies were getting thin. "If you roll them in the dirt with your boot before peeling them, the spines come right off."

Shane snorted. "Tell that to my tongue, which I almost impaled this morning. No thanks."

Fi snuck a look over at Red, slumped against the fallen tree. Her eyes were closed, and her face was gray with the strain of the long march. Still, Fi was glad to see Shane had left her ax with the Paper Witch, far out of their prisoner's reach. The wolf lay at Red's side. His yellow-gold eyes stared back at Fi, unblinking.

"How's she doing?" Fi asked under her breath.

Shane made a face. "Well, she had enough spirit left to laugh at me when my foot got stuck in a gopher hole. So I'm not counting her out yet."

Fi hoped Shane was right—and that they'd be showing up on Everlynd's doorstep with a hostage, not a corpse.

She made her way back across the clearing, swallowing a smile as Shane tossed the rock-hard bread to the wolf. Briar had taken a seat near the fire, staring hard at the scrap of parchment inked with Camellia's code.

"Be careful with that," the Paper Witch warned, picking at the wild strawberries and brown-capped mushrooms they'd foraged near the river. Briar dutifully moved farther from the fire and the spitting sparks, while Fi made a mental note to memorize that code as soon as possible.

"Any luck figuring out the book?" she asked, dropping down next to Briar.

"No." Briar scrubbed a hand through his disheveled curls. "There are just too many possibilities."

Fi propped her hand on her chin, her hunger forgotten. Book codes were maddening, because unlike other riddles and ciphers, she couldn't even guess at the words without the right book. Her father had adored them for exactly that reason. When she was younger, he had always given her a code for her birthday and then watched her scour the house for her present with an unbearably smug expression, refusing to give her any hints about which book decoded the cipher—which, in the vast Nenroa library, was less a fun scavenger hunt and more an exquisite form of torture. Apparently, he'd hidden her mother's engagement ring the same way, and the ensuing three-hour treasure hunt almost convinced Lillia to change her answer.

Briar leaned suddenly close, eyebrows raised. "What's that smile for?"

"Nothing," Fi said, flustered. *Probably best not to be thinking about engagements sitting within kissing distance of a dashing prince.* She tugged at her earlobe, forcing the blush down and trying to remember the book code strategies her exasperated mother had taught her. "Maybe we can at least narrow it down," she suggested. "I mean, there are some things we can tell just from the code itself."

Briar laughed. "By all means, impress me." He wiggled the paper at her, eyes twinkling.

Fi cupped the code gingerly in her bandaged hand. "Well, for starters, we're probably not looking for a picture book. The highest page number listed is one hundred eighty-four. This next part is just a guess, but since the numbers don't go any higher than that, it's also probably not a massive reference or historical volume."

Briar leaned back on his hands, looking thoughtful. "Camellia had her own spell books. She was always marking them up with notes and observations and extra spells in the margins."

"Fascinating," Fi breathed, her mind racing at the thought of all the tiny wisps of knowledge that had to be tucked away in a book like that. "But it's probably not one of those, either. With a whole bunch of annotations, it would be hard to know which words the book code was pointing to. Plus, a lot of spells are written in magic languages and runes, which would be hard to count accurately."

"Brilliant as usual," Briar teased, and Fi cursed her heart for its traitorous little flutter. "But I'm afraid I still have no idea. The Library of Andar is so vast it has literally thousands of volumes, and it could be any one of them. Not that that helps us, since they're all back in the castle." He sighed heavily, but Fi felt a sudden thrill of excitement.

"Briar, you're right!" she said, shooting up. Her hand grabbed his sleeve. "We've been thinking about this the wrong way. This was a backup plan, right? Some information so important Camellia wanted to make sure you would have it no matter what happened." Briar nodded vacantly, like he wasn't following at all. "So she wouldn't have left the book in the castle, where it was in danger of being found. She would have taken it with her when she left—into Darfell."

Briar's face tightened. "Then we have no clue where it might have ended up."

"Actually, we do. Because we know where Camellia ended up. I've been there." Fi could feel her mind racing. "The Rose Manor—the ruin where I found the bone spindle—there was a whole shelf of books there. What better place to hide something so important? As long as they're still there . . ."

"They're not, I'm afraid." The Paper Witch's face was grave. He knelt beside Fi and reached out to brush the back of the paper. "After you and Shane departed, I traveled to the Rose Manor myself, only to find it had been looted by Witch Hunters. What they didn't take, they burned."

Fi's heart sank. "Then the books . . ."

"I believe they were taken." The Paper Witch's eyes grew distant. "The Witch Hunters had been looking for that particular ruin for a very long time. It was something of a fixation of theirs."

It was cold comfort. Even if the books were still intact, they were in Witch Hunter hands. Fi couldn't imagine how they would ever get them back.

Her feelings must have shown on her face. The Paper Witch tipped his head, giving her an encouraging smile. "Everlynd has an extensive library of its own. Perhaps there will be a copy of the book we seek there."

"If I can even remember it," Briar muttered bitterly.

"You will," Fi reassured. She held out her hand, offering him the parchment back.

He didn't take it. "You hold on to it," he said, giving her a wistful smile. "I have a feeling if anyone can solve that code, it'll be you."

Fi didn't know what to say. She tucked the code into her pocket, but it was a long time before she forgot that distant look on his face—like he was still the prince in the white tower, entombed in roses, fading like a dream.

# 10

## Shane

**SHANE WOKE TO** someone shaking her.

"Wake up," Fi hissed.

Shane groaned, every muscle in her body protesting as she dragged herself from the clutches of sleep. They'd had two hard days of travel since leaving the riverside. At this point, her blisters had blisters. Fi better have a really good reason for jabbing her awake.

Shane braced herself on her elbows, looking around the sparse camp. There hadn't been much of a fire to begin with, but it had burned down until it was no more than a soft red glow. The rest of the camp was still asleep, Briar and the Paper Witch by the fire and Red curled around her wolf. The creature's eyes were luminous in the dark as he stared at Shane.

*The dark?* Shane blinked fuzzily up at the moon still hanging in the sky. "It's the middle of the night."

Fi rolled her eyes, offering Shane a hand. "Hardly. It's

a couple hours till dawn, at most." She pulled Shane to her feet. "There's something you should see."

Shane started to grumble about inconsiderate partners, but Fi put a finger warningly over her lips, beckoning her to follow. Shane cast one last glance at Red. The girl was sweating even in her sleep, her brow crinkled into a pained frown. Shane resisted the urge to press her hand to the girl's forehead and feel for the fever she knew she would find. The Paper Witch had said they would reach the outpost by midmorning, and he'd better be right.

Fi ducked low, climbing the sloping ridge at the edge of their camp and shooting Shane dirty looks every time her foot slid in the rocks, like she was doing it on purpose. Shane bit down the retort that she'd be a lot more coordinated if she'd had more sleep. Together, they crept to the top of a hill covered in scrubby cypress trees. Fi pulled Shane down beside her in the weeds, pointing over the edge.

Shane sucked in a breath through her teeth. A long line of horses and wagons was rolling through the sparse canyons toward the mountains in the distance. Cloaked figures with burning torches rode up and down the lines, their features sinister in the red light.

*Witch Hunters*, Fi mouthed, looking grim.

Shane inched forward on her elbows to get a better look. The Witch Hunters were armed to the teeth, with saw-toothed blades slung through their belts and curved daggers strapped to the saddlebags. She could hear distant voices shouting and laughing, clearly not bothered that their caravan was visible from a mile away. The Witch Hunters were the most dangerous thing out here, and they knew it.

The wagons creaked, every one loaded high and covered in heavy canvas to protect the loot. Shane had no trouble imagining the Witch Hunters crawling all over Andar like parasites, burrowing into every old ruin and stripping them clean like the scavengers they were.

*Relics?* she mouthed back.

Fi shrugged. Shane supposed it really didn't matter. Whether it was stolen treasure or stolen magic relics, she was just relieved there was no cage down there with Red inside it. Her guts twisted at the thought of the girl chained up and presented like a prize. Her body itched for a fight, but there were too many.

Fi tugged her arm, leading her back down the slope to a broken boulder, far enough from the camp not to disturb their companions but out of sight from the ridge. Shane followed her and slumped down against the jut of rock. A night lizard with bright eyes flicked its tongue at Shane and then scurried away as she stretched her legs out.

"Where do you think they're taking all that?" she asked.

Fi grimaced, as if remembering an unpleasant taste. "When I used to . . . spend a lot of time in Bellicia—"

"With an arrogant little slug-weasel," Shane filled in helpfully.

Fi rolled her eyes, but she looked like she was fighting a smile. "I used to hear the Border Guards talking about the Witch Hunters' headquarters hidden away in Andar. I never put any effort into figuring out where that was. But now, knowing there's a good chance that's where Camellia's book ended up . . ."

"Trust me, finding the Witch Hunters isn't going to be

the problem." It was dealing with Witch Hunters that was the real pain.

They were quiet for a moment before Fi let out a long, slow breath. "You were right about what would have happened to Red if we'd left her."

"Well, we didn't leave her." Shane tipped her head back against the rock and then pinned Fi with a serious look. "Thanks for that—having my back about Red."

"You've had mine a few times," Fi admitted grudgingly.

Shane huffed out a laugh. "Still. After everything she's done, I wouldn't have blamed you if you didn't want to help her."

"Well, I don't know if you're right about being able to save her." Fi pulled up her legs, resting her chin on her knees. "But I don't think she deserves to die."

Something swept through the trees—a dark shape on soundless wings—and Shane whipped around, relieved to see an owl and not a crow gliding between the trunks. She couldn't help picturing the tattoo on Red's neck, the two snakes endlessly consuming each other. Even if there was another side to Red—the one Shane had fallen in love with—who was to say it was the stronger side?

"You think I'm fooling myself that I see something in her?"

"I think if anyone can save Red, it's you," Fi said softly. "And if you can't manage it, then no one could."

There was a lot of Fi-style hedging in that statement, but if you really dug down deep, she was saying she believed in Shane. "Thanks," Shane said, bumping their shoulders together. "I needed to hear that."

"You know, I didn't say I was *sure* you would succeed," Fi hurried to add.

"Nope," Shane said with a grin. "Too late. Can't take it back now."

Fi grumbled a little about Shane taking everything out of context, but Shane could see she was smiling. It made her feel a thousand times lighter, like some weight she hadn't known she was carrying around had just slipped off her shoulders.

Fi was a hard one to read. From the first moment they had become partners, Shane hadn't been totally sure she was welcome, and she'd continued to wonder now and then if their partnership was on equal footing. If Fi actually cared about Shane as much as Shane cared about her, or if one day she'd be able to walk away from this partnership and never look back.

But sitting side by side, Shane felt a sudden surge of warmth. Fi believed in her, even if she was too prickly to say it out loud. And she'd done her share of fighting for Shane, too. Shane wouldn't forget she'd gotten those broken fingers saving her ax from the rubble. They were partners in every way that mattered.

Fi climbed awkwardly to her feet. "I'm going to get everyone up," she declared, sliding back down the hill. "We might as well head out before dawn."

Shane shook her head fondly. That was the partner she knew best, ruthlessly rousing everyone before the sun.

On the other hand . . . Shane threw a glance over her shoulder, thinking of the caravan of Witch Hunters moving off into the dim. For once, her partner might be right about leaving in a hurry.

RED WAS GETTING worse, not hour by hour but minute by minute.

Not long after they set off, the girl had stumbled so many times Shane had passed her ax off to Fi and switched to carrying her, hoisting Red's nearly limp form high on her back. She left Red's hands bound, but only to keep her from slipping off. The cord of the rope cut into her neck as Red's body bounced around on her back, sagging bonelessly against her. Shane blinked away the drops of sweat trickling down her forehead and into her eyes.

The wolf seemed to sense that something was wrong. He was no longer keeping his distance but padded at the heels of Shane's boots, winding up underfoot more times than Shane could count. Fi kept throwing her worried looks, but Shane just put her head down, concentrating on putting one foot in front of the other.

She was surprised when Red's arms tightened around her neck.

"What happens to me in Everlynd?" she croaked into Shane's ear.

"You get treated," she said, shifting her grip on Red's legs to push the girl farther up her back. "We save your life."

"No." Red choked out a feeble laugh. "I mean, what happens after? If you're just taking me to your Witch city to be executed, you should save yourself the trouble."

"You won't be executed."

"But I'll be a prisoner." Red's voice was weak, and she pressed her flushed cheek to Shane's shoulder.

Shane felt her own voice growing hoarse. "You'll be alive, Red," she said. "And you'll be my prisoner—I won't hand you over to anyone. I promise."

The silence stretched on for so long Shane wondered if Red had passed out again. Then Red's shivering breath burned against her neck. "You and your promises."

Those words followed Shane the rest of the way to the outpost as they doubled their pace.

The sun was right overhead when the Paper Witch finally led them into a small stone building partly embedded into a rocky hillside. The door squealed on rusty hinges. The outer walls were speckled and pocked with damage, and Shane had a feeling she knew what from. For the last few hours, the wind had been growing steadily stronger, pelting them with dust. In the distance, she could see a storm raging that reminded her of the waste at its worst—a great swirl of whipping sand that howled like hungry jaws.

As she laid Red down on the pallets, Shane locked eyes with Fi over her shoulder.

"I guess the rest is up to you." She made a face at Fi's grim expression. "Here's where you say something encouraging, like *We'll be back in no time* or *She's never looked better.*"

Fi pressed her lips into a tight line. But all she said was, "We'll be as fast as we can."

Sometimes Shane wished her partner was a better liar.

# 11

## Fi

FI PUSHED HER hair out of her face, staring in disbelief at the immense sandstorm that raged in front of her. The Paper Witch had said it wouldn't be easy to reach Everlynd, but nothing had prepared her for this. The angry midday sun burned above them, all but snuffed out by the clouds. The storm was so thick it was as though they stood at the foot of a giant wall. There was no way Red would have made it through this. Fi wasn't even sure about the rest of them.

"How are we supposed to get through?" she called, holding up an arm to shield her face and squinting at the Paper Witch. His robes whipped around him, his crystal earring dancing madly. Briar stood close behind her, his chin tucked into the collar of his increasingly ragged blue coat. "Do we wait for the storm to pass?"

"This storm never passes," the Paper Witch called back. "It was created by the Witches of Andar to protect Everlynd."

"How is that possible?" Briar asked. "A spell this vast . . . only the Great Witches had that kind of power."

"Perhaps alone," the Paper Witch agreed. "But this spell was woven by many Witches working in unison. When the Spindle Witch took the castle, some Witches escaped into Darfell, but many others fled to Everlynd. They drew rocks from deep in the earth and pulverized them to make the storm. It's the reason Everlynd has remained safely hidden for a hundred years, the last great haven of magic." He tipped his head. "We're very close. Come, Filore—you can help me find the way."

Fi and Briar traded dubious looks. "I don't think I can see in this any better than you can," she called.

The Paper Witch chuckled. "Then it's fortunate it's not your eyes I need. Get out your rope."

Fi didn't know what good her rope could possibly be, but she did as she was told, winding it carefully around her left palm. The swelling in her hand had disappeared, leaving only an ugly bruise, and she had removed all of the bandages except the one keeping her broken little finger tied tightly to its neighbor. As long as she didn't bang it around, it didn't even hurt too badly anymore.

She looked up at the Paper Witch expectantly.

"We're searching for a marker." The Paper Witch waved at the haze in front of them. "The path to Everlynd is clear to those who know what they're looking for. Just swing your rope out, dear. The first marker should be very near."

Fi squinted through the dust, searching for stone cairns or flags, anything that might give her a direction. She couldn't see a thing. Still, she moved forward a few steps and then whipped the rope over her head, releasing it in a wide arc. It disappeared almost immediately into the storm. Without the heavy weight on the end, it would no doubt have been carried away by the wind. The cord slithered through Fi's fingers, unwinding as it flew. She was just about to yank it back and ask for better instructions when she heard the telltale clang of the ring striking something. The rope tugged as the end caught fast.

"Lead the way," the Paper Witch suggested.

Fi hesitated, all too aware of the dangers of traveling through a sandstorm. She unspooled the tail of the rope and handed it back to Briar and the Paper Witch.

"Stay close," she shouted over the wind.

Fi put her head down and turned into the maelstrom. Within moments, she couldn't even see her hands on the taut rope. The only sign of Briar at her back was the way he bumped into her every few steps. She'd barely whipped out fifteen feet of rope, but it took longer than she expected to follow. Her feet dragged as the thick sand sucked at her boots.

She had just taken another heavy step when something loomed out of the storm. It looked like a giant snake, coiled at the base, ready to strike.

Fi yanked on the rope in surprise. It wrenched free, and she smashed backward into Briar. The creature disappeared into the sand. It took Fi a moment to steady her racing pulse and realize that the snake hadn't been moving. It was made out of stone, and it was probably the marker she was looking for.

"Are you all right?" Briar called into her ear.

"My rope came loose," she lied, gathering it up. There

was no way she was admitting she'd just been frightened by a statue. "I think we've found it." She grabbed Briar's coat and pulled him forward until the coiled snake once again surged out of the blowing sand.

The statue was at least ten feet tall. It was carved of hard speckled granite, the snake's coils bulging and its jaw unhinged to show off the broken nubs of long fangs. The raging winds had stripped most of the details away, but when she was right beneath it, Fi realized that the few scales remaining were round like flat pebbles. She recognized that design. This statue had been created by the Order of the Rising Rain in the form of the Snake Witch.

The stone had been sculpted with a hollow at its center, just big enough that the three of them could cram inside. It would be tight, but at least they wouldn't have to shout at each other.

"This is cozy," Briar said with a chuckle, squeezing up beside Fi to make room for the Paper Witch, who was carrying the pack and the last of their supplies.

"I hope you know the way from here," Fi said, coughing through the dust.

"I don't," the Paper Witch said simply. "There are many paths through the storm, and I've never taken this one before, but there are instructions on the markers. Look around— something should be written here." He lifted one hand, brushing the caked dirt away to reveal a line of ancient runes carved into the wall. The first character curved like a long, sinuous S.

"Briar, make a light!" Fi said excitedly. A strange look

passed between Briar and the Paper Witch, one Fi couldn't guess at, and then Briar lifted his hand, pressing his fingers together to gather light at the tips. At the first spark, Fi dragged him forward, holding his hand close to the wall. The magic flared to life, white and luminous.

"I knew this would be your most useful talent," she said, shooting him a distracted smile before turning back to the runes. Each letter was long and thin, like the path traced by a winding drop of water. "It's the language of the Order of the Rising Rain." Fi pictured the ruins of the giant school they'd passed in the waste. As one of the largest orders, the Rising Rain had left behind whole stacks of spell books—enough to make a pile taller than she was when she'd first started studying the language. All of her uncertainty transformed into wonder as she deciphered the words. "These are directions. It reads *fifty steps from the snake's tail, sixteen steps right.*"

"And there we will find another marker, and another, and so on until we reach Everlynd," the Paper Witch filled in.

Briar's magic faded, and Fi let go of his wrist. She was in awe of what an undertaking the markers must have been—not just creating the giant statues, but arranging them with perfect precision to create a path through the storm. Still, something was bothering her.

"Couldn't anyone who knows the script of the Rising Rain follow this path?" she wondered aloud. That didn't seem particularly safe.

"Clever Filore." The Paper Witch reached out to pat her shoulder. "Certainly, if all the markers were written in the language of the Rising Rain. Each marker gives instructions in a different magic language—one for every order whose Witches reached Everlynd. Even between us, I doubt we can read them all."

Fi balked. "So how will we make it to the other side?"

The Paper Witch's eyes crinkled, the bell in his hair tinkling. "Have a little faith," he said. "I may not be quite the linguist you are, but I have a few tricks up my sleeve."

Fi swallowed back a retort. She wasn't entirely satisfied with that answer, but she was familiar enough with the secretive Paper Witch to know it was all she was going to get for now.

The snake's tail stuck out sharply from the stone, pointing like an arrow into the thick storm. This time the Paper Witch took the lead, with just enough rope between them that Fi wasn't trodding on his heels. Honestly, she was glad to let him set the pace and decide exactly what constituted a *step*. She kept count anyway, growing nervous as she took her fiftieth shuffling step forward and the Paper Witch came to a stop.

He dragged his boot heel through the dirt, drawing a wobbly line, and then led them carefully in the new direction. Fi squinted through the blowing sand. Just as she took her sixteenth step, she caught a glimpse of jutting stone—it was only a few feet off their path, but they'd nearly missed it. Fi snatched the Paper Witch's robes, pulling him back before they overshot their mark. Clearly, they were going to have to be very careful.

Fi sent a silent apology to Shane back in the outpost with a quickly worsening Red. They'd go as fast as they could, but hurrying was only going to get them all lost.

At first Fi couldn't make out the new shape at all. Then she realized the craggy tower of stone was actually a massive hourglass, each curved bulb higher than her waist. Someone had rubbed flecks of gold onto the dark granite to give the illusion of brilliant sand running through the neck. Fi slipped inside, taking cover.

"The Order of the Golden Hourglass," she said.

The Paper Witch nodded. "Of course. Everlynd was originally the hidden school of those who practiced dream magic and prophecy, after all."

Briar had been combing sand out of his hair, but at the words he whipped his head up in surprise. "That's what Everlynd is? The city of the dream Witches?"

Fi could only imagine all the things that secret city might mean to Briar, but she knew exactly what it meant to her. The city of the Golden Hourglass was her mother's favorite legend of Andar. For as long as Fi could remember, nothing delighted Lillia like finding tiny scraps of information about the hidden school tucked away in spell books and forgotten histories. She'd never heard the name *Everlynd* before—in the old texts, it was referred to only as *the city of waterfalls.* Its location was a closely guarded secret even at the height of the kingdom's power.

One summer, Fi and her mother had spent two whole months riding between the towns along the border of Darfell, up to their elbows in the dusty stacks of small libraries, looking for clues in the oldest maps of Andar. They never found much, but at night, lying under the stars and the black ring of tall pines, they had made a game of imagining that lost place: an entire city built behind the veil of a soaring waterfall, or a tower of shimmering gold brick where everyone was forever asleep. Fi seemed to remember having a few of those conversations right there at the Paper Witch's kitchen table while the Witch listened in, innocently slathering his scones with strawberry jam.

Though they were wedged in tight, Fi craned around until she could give the Paper Witch a flat look. "I can't believe you kept this a secret from my mother all these years."

The man laughed, a hearty laugh that warmed Fi like she was sitting in that sunlit kitchen again. "There were a number of times it nearly slipped out. I hope Lillia will forgive me if I can bring her here one day."

"She'd forgive you in a second," Fi agreed softly.

With Briar's magic for light, they read off the next set of directions: *thirty steps from the statue and then twelve left.* Almost before they'd caught their breath, the Paper Witch marched them on through the whipping winds. They found the next two markers easily, one for the Order of the Riven Earth and another belonging to a tiny sect of Herb Gatherers whose writing Fi was only able to piece together because her mother still used a few of their gardening books.

As they set out again, Fi began to think, impossibly, that this just might work. But those hopes crumbled as they hunched beneath the next statue, a tower studded with arched windows.

"I've never seen this script before. What is it?" Fi asked, scrubbing dirt off the wall and revealing not letters but a pattern of tiny stars.

"It's the language of the Celestial Stargazers," the Paper Witch said, squinting at the runes. "They use constellations in place of words, but it isn't simply a matter of recognizing the shape—the north-south orientation of the constellation matters, too. I've never found the time to learn it."

"Briar?" Fi asked hopefully.

The prince offered her a sheepish look. "There was a Celestial Stargazer in Sage's court who offered to teach me a few things," he admitted. "But he told me I'd need years of study before I could even read their spells, so I never took him up on it."

Fi felt cold, her skin tingling where the sand had rubbed it raw. Without the directions, they were stuck. She squinted at the stars through stinging eyes. Her parents had taught her how to pick apart new magic languages, looking for common runes or letter shapes from languages she did know, but this one was just too different. A knot of worry tightened her throat.

"How close are we to the end?" Briar asked.

The Paper Witch shook his head. "Too far to chance an educated guess. Most paths to Everlynd use ten markers, so we're just over halfway." His gaze moved to Fi, as if he could see her recounting their steps and trying to decide if they could backtrack through the storm. "Faith, Filore," he reminded her. "Magic created this storm, and magic will guide us through it. Here, take the pack—and Briar, hold out your arms."

The Paper Witch dug into his pack and pulled out a long cylinder wrapped in silken blue cloth: a scroll of pristine vellum. He unwound it and draped the thick blank paper across Briar's outstretched arms, and then began rolling up his left sleeve. Fi watched in fascination. She'd never seen the Paper

Witch in anything but his long robes, and now she knew why. Though the Paper Witch was pale, from wrist to shoulder his arm was covered with dark bands of tattoos in a series of thick rings, as if he'd dipped it into paint. No, not paint—*ink*, Fi realized with a gasp as the Paper Witch pinched the skin of his wrist and then slowly drew his fingers upward, and impossibly the ink came with him, dangling from his fingertips as if he had pinched a shimmering black ribbon. He pressed his fingers to the vellum, and suddenly Fi could make out letters and words—line after line of sharp black text erupting onto the scroll as the Paper Witch slid his finger along. The ink uncoiled from his arm and hung in the air as long curls of waiting words. As it unwound, the black color around his wrist grew lighter until Fi could see the gaps between overlapping letters.

"It's a book," she breathed.

The Paper Witch smiled. "Several books, actually. This one is a key—it gives the directions for each of the markers. There should be a symbol at the end of the inscription—" He nodded toward the wall, and Fi noticed for the first time a pair of diamonds carved after the last constellation. "The same symbol is in this key, along with the directions. It's how Everlynd's scouts navigate the storm. We carry the key on our bodies instead of a scroll to ensure it never falls into the hands of the Witch Hunters."

"Ink magic," Briar said. His blond hair flopped into his face as he leaned over the scroll. "The royal couriers used that. When Sage had to send an important message to the distant territories, an ink Witch would bind it to the messenger's arm so the message couldn't be altered before it was delivered."

"That's where the Witches of Everlynd got the idea," the Paper Witch replied. "Though we've taken it a bit further."

Fi had forgotten all about the storm. She had seen the Paper Witch's magic many times, but this was so far beyond writing small charms. As she'd always suspected, he was much more powerful than he let on.

Mesmerized, she leaned into Briar to get a better look. Just as the Paper Witch had said, she could see that each set of directions was preceded by a symbol, like a tiny bookmark. She saw a rose, a sickle moon, a leaf of ivy, a bird in flight, but no diamonds. The Paper Witch unrolled another line and frowned as he reached the end of the scroll.

"This marker must be farther in. I don't have enough paper. Filore, your arm, please?"

Fi stuck out her arm so fast she almost elbowed Briar in the ribs. The Paper Witch grabbed the line of ink dangling from his wrist, and Fi sucked in a sharp breath as he looped it around her forearm. The ink magic stood out like a brilliant tattoo. She could hardly feel it, a maddeningly light tingle floating just above the surface of her skin. The sensation grew stronger as the Paper Witch plucked the very first line from the scroll and wound the ink delicately around his fingers, pulling new lines of text onto the scroll using Fi's arm as a pivot. The magic slithered forward like fabric on a bolt.

Fi couldn't tear her eyes away. She had mostly grown out of wishing for magic herself, but her heart surged at the thought of carrying her own personal library on her skin. She would cram as many books as she could wrist to shoulder, and maybe wrap a few around her ankles, too, as long as that didn't interfere with the spell.

"You said Everlynd's scouts all use keys like this?" she asked hopefully. They couldn't all be ink Witches. Maybe the Paper Witch could teach her how to use this magic even without any of her own.

The Paper Witch shot her a knowing look. "I always feared the day you discovered this particular ability. When the battle for Andar is won, we can *discuss* doing something similar for you—but bear in mind that inking takes a long time, and you can't carry as much as you'd think. You'll have to choose your books carefully."

"You can use me for overflow," Briar offered, close to her ear. Fi's breath quickened. Agreeing to ink any book she wanted onto his skin—that felt awfully permanent, compared to their temporary, as-yet-undefined partnership.

"At last. Here they are."

Fi's gaze jerked back to the scroll. The Paper Witch tapped a finger against the double-diamond mark, and after it, a set of simple directions: *forty steps from the tower window, then nine left*. Fi looked at the carved constellations again, amazed that an entire language had developed out of the positions of the stars.

The wind howled beyond the doorway as the Paper Witch retracted the shimmering ink ribbon, winding it carefully back around his arm. "We should hurry on," he said. "The afternoon is slipping away from us, and the storm grows more treacherous after dusk."

Briar wrapped up the scroll, and they set off again. The air seemed thicker and the gusts wilder—or maybe Fi was just getting tired, her legs aching with the effort of plowing through the drifts. She counted down the next three markers in breaths of sand. As impossible as this had seemed, they were somehow at the second-to-last marker. She looked up as a shape rose out of the gloom.

It was a tree—or it had been once. Stone branches had been shorn off by the brutal winds, and what had once been beautifully carved roots were now worn away almost to gravel. Chunks of broken rock littered the sand. There wasn't even a hollow to protect them from the wind—which meant there was no hollow to protect the carved words, either.

Fi rushed forward, swiping a crust of sand from the wall. It was useless. As hard as she scrubbed, there was no inscription left to find, just a few deep strokes dug into the smooth stone. She recognized the squared-off letters as the language of the Order of the Wandering Roots, one of the hermitic orders who lived in the eastern forests and mostly kept to themselves. The tiny finishing mark had been completely erased.

"It's gone," Fi said. The word dropped into her stomach like a stone.

"What do we do now?" Briar asked the Paper Witch.

"We have no choice," the man replied, his voice grim. "Without the mark, I cannot use the key to guide us. We must retrace our steps. Tomorrow we will try to find a different path through the storm."

"Red doesn't have that much time, does she?" Fi asked. The Paper Witch's silence was answer enough.

Fi bit her lip. Shane was counting on them. There was no way the huntsman would give up if she were here, so neither would Fi.

Fi stared at the remaining runes, trying to piece together

anything that looked like a word, or even just half of one. There had to be something here she could use. At the base of the statue, she could still see the outline of the trailing root that pointed into the storm. If they at least had some idea what the first instruction had been, maybe they could find their way from there.

Fi pinched her earlobe, squeezing her eyes shut tightly as she pictured the first set of runes. She imagined her own hand writing the script of the Wandering Roots. Could it be fifty steps? No, the lines didn't quite match up. Most of the directions had been round numbers, though, and fifty was the highest she'd seen. Twenty, then? She traced the carved marks. Something seemed off about the spacing. Thirty would fit better. *Thirty steps.* The rest of the inscription was too worn to even take a guess.

Briar and the Paper Witch were still arguing.

"Even if we can backtrack, you're talking about spending the night on the edge of the storm," Briar argued. "What if we run into Witch Hunters?"

"You don't understand the danger of this storm, Briar Rose," the Paper Witch warned. "It is designed to turn people around and trap them. If we wander with no idea where we are going, we will die."

"What about *some* idea?" Fi interjected. Briar and the Paper Witch turned to her, and Fi ran her finger along the impression of the letters. "I think the first part here would read *thirty steps.* Would that get us close enough to find the last marker?"

The Paper Witch pursed his lips. "How sure are you?"

Fi took a breath, picturing the script in her mind. All of the strokes fit. "Sure enough to bet my life on it."

The Paper Witch nodded slowly. "Then, if you are both certain this is a risk you wish to take . . . ?"

It was for Shane. There was only one possible answer.

"Yes."

"Absolutely."

Fi and Briar responded at the same time, and Fi shot Briar a smile from the corner of her mouth. With a last glance at the remnants of the statue, she wrapped her jacket tight and followed the Paper Witch into the storm. Her heart hammered in her chest with every step—she didn't think she was wrong, but she couldn't say it was impossible. Whatever happened now, it was on her. She closed her eyes, burning the runes into her mind. She *was* sure. She had to be.

Long, agonizing minutes crawled by before the Paper Witch held up a hand. "This is thirty steps," he shouted.

Now for the hard part. Each marker had listed a second set of steps in a different direction, but usually not more than fifteen. Fi raised a hand to shield her face and peered into the gloom. There wasn't even a glimmer of a marker—not a single clue as to where they should go next.

"I'm going to use my rope," she called to her companions. That was how they'd found the first marker, after all.

Fi stepped forward to swing the rope, and immediately she found herself alone. Her stomach dropped, but before she could panic, Briar plunged out of the storm and grabbed her arm. His other hand was hooked firmly in the Paper Witch's elbow.

"We can't get separated!" he shouted, putting his lips against her ear. "Hang on." He stripped off his ragged coat, leaving him in just his thin undershirt while the wind and sand raked over his bare skin. He leaned toward Fi, winding the fine material of the sleeve around her belt. Then he backed off, fisting his hand in the cuff of the opposite sleeve so Fi had a little room to maneuver.

The wind rose into a high wail as Fi whipped the rope over her head, once, twice. Then she threw out her hand and sent it sailing into the storm. The force of the gale was even stronger here, and Fi was sure her rope had only flown half the distance she intended. Still, she whipped it sideways, dragging it through the sandstorm and hoping to feel it catch on a marker. No such luck. Fi yanked the rope, and the ring crawled toward her, dragging a heavy pile of sand as she gathered it up.

*Again*, Fi told herself. She whipped the rope faster over her head, spinning it longer and throwing all her weight into it as she released in another direction. It flew farther than before, but it hit the ground uselessly just the same.

*Again*, she told herself—and again, venturing farther from Briar until the coat was stretched out precariously between them. Her arms burned, and the pain was flaring up in her broken finger as she used it over and over, but Fi made herself keep throwing. There was a marker out there somewhere— she could imagine it, just out of reach. A flutter of panic made her throw too wild, the ring bouncing off the sand before she even lost sight of it. They'd left the marker behind; there would be no backtracking now. This had to work.

With a scream of frustration, Fi released again, throwing

the ring with everything she had. The rope sailed out in a high arc. She wrapped both hands around the rope, whipping it wide, willing it to find something. The sand shifted under her feet, and she stumbled forward, losing her balance. She had pulled free of Briar's coat.

The storm closed in around her instantly, cutting her off from her companions. Panic shot through her. She took a bad step and nearly tumbled, but just then her rope went taut, cinching tight around her arm. She could feel the impact as the ring snagged on something and held. She had found the marker, but she had lost Briar and the Paper Witch. She looked behind her desperately, searching the blowing winds, not daring to let go of the rope. How far away from them had she gotten? Five steps? More?

"Briar!" she yelled. She could barely hear her own voice, and she choked on a mouthful of sand. "Briar!" she screamed again. She stretched backward, swinging her hand desperately through the storm. All she caught was dust. Fi looked between her empty palm and the rope, its long tail whipping around her. There was a voice inside her head insisting that the practical thing to do was keep hold of the rope, even if she had to go forward alone and come back with Everlynd's scouts, because without that rope, none of them would ever survive the storm. But it was drowned out by the much louder voice shouting that surviving wouldn't mean anything if she had to leave Briar and the Paper Witch behind.

Her grip loosened, the rope slithering through her hand with the force of the wind.

At the last second, a figure surged out of the storm. Briar's arms locked around her so tight she couldn't breathe.

Fi gasped and clenched her fist, grabbing the very end of the rope before it escaped. The Paper Witch was right behind Briar, the two of them bound together by the ragged blue coat, and Fi couldn't help laughing in relief.

"I found it!" Fi shouted, pressing the rope into Briar's hands.

"I found *you*," Briar shouted back. They shared a victorious smile.

They used the rope to guide them, pulling themselves forward to the final marker. Just as they reached the base of the statue, a shaft of sunlight speared the swirling clouds, and Fi looked up to see what had caught her rope: the curl of a twisted vine beneath a trio of stone roses, the petals wide in welcome. It was the marker of the Divine Rose that had saved them, the dark granite radiant against a patch of blue sky.

Briar brushed the sand reverently from the hollow, and Fi read the final inscription. A trailing leaf at the back of the statue pointed them straight toward Everlynd. The storm receded as they fought their way up a steep slope of sand, leaving them beneath a wide blue sky with their backs to the sun, which was just starting to sink into the west.

When they crested the hill, Everlynd lay before them. Fi stared, hardly trusting the vision of towering golden cliffs rising out of the ground, their sharp faces cut by dozens of shimmering waterfalls as bright and delicate as veils. At the foot of the cliffs, a vast lake shone like a pane of flawless glass, and built all around it was a city of the same golden stone, the many-storied buildings tucked side by side like the chambers inside a pearly shell. Great curtains of vines spilled down the walls from lush rooftop gardens bursting with brilliant red and yellow flowers. After so much time in the barren landscape, the colors almost hurt Fi's eyes. Her chest hurt, too, her ribs suddenly too tight around her swelling heart.

It reminded her of Pisarre, of Idlewild. It reminded her of the kingdom of Andar, the one she'd fallen in love with so long ago in the pages of her parents' history books. The one from Briar's memories. When she'd dreamed of the magnificent kingdom of magic, this was what she'd dreamed.

"Andar," Briar breathed.

"A small piece of it," the Paper Witch agreed. "Welcome home, Briar Rose."

# 12

## Fi

THE PAPER WITCH hurried toward Everlynd, Fi and Briar right on his heels. Long before they reached the gates, they were intercepted by a pair of scouts. The two women surged up from the dunes with crossbows raised. Fi had just a second to take in their flame-red cloaks and the sharp iron bolts before the taller of the two recognized the Paper Witch. She pressed her hand to the shorter woman's shoulder, both of them lowering their weapons slowly.

"Paper Witch. Forgive me. It's been many years since you returned to Everlynd."

"Longer than I thought, if the soldiers of the Red Ember now greet visitors with crossbows," the Paper Witch replied.

Fi recognized the name. The Red Ember had been an order of Witches dedicated to combat magic, skilled soldiers loyal only to the crown. Their ancient symbol had been a tongue of flame, but she could see that the scouts' cloaks were embroidered with the image of a white tower instead. Briar's tower. These truly were Briar's people.

"Nikor's orders," the scout told them. She looked curiously at Fi and Briar. "I'll escort you to Everlynd, but it will be the steward's discretion whether your friends can enter the city."

"For some things, even Nikor must step aside," the Paper Witch said. Though his tone was even, there was a steely undercurrent to it that made Fi wonder if they weren't as welcome here as the Witch had implied.

They followed the scouts across the last hills of sand. A small crowd had gathered beneath the watchtower at the mouth of the city, watching their approach, and Fi saw the knot of men and women in red cloaks break apart to let two figures through. The first was a tall man with pale skin and a well-trimmed blond beard. He wore a silk tunic with a purple vest and carried a small gold scepter. Fi decided he had to be Nikor, the steward. On his arm hung a woman old enough to be a grandmother, with curly gray hair that fluttered down her back. Her fine blue dress looked heavy on her thin shoulders. The man raised a hand as they approached, and when the woman lifted her head, Fi was surprised to find that her eyes were cloudy and white, staring vacantly in their direction.

"So it is you, Paper Witch." The steward didn't sound particularly pleased. "We thought perhaps you had tired of us for good."

"I could never tire of Everlynd, though I do not quite recognize it," the Paper Witch replied. He gave Nikor a hard look. "Every time I return, it seems more Witches have joined the Red Ember. I didn't realize Everlynd had such a pressing need for soldiers."

"These are dangerous times," Nikor said. "But you gave up your chance to have a seat on the ruling council long ago, and with it, your right to have an opinion in these matters." His gaze traveled across Fi and Briar, not at all welcoming. "Everlynd is my responsibility. Until the curse is broken and the rulers of Andar return to us, I will protect it by any means necessary."

"Then you will be relieved to hear that burden is no longer on your shoulders." Nikor's eyes narrowed, but the Paper Witch swept away from him, speaking instead to the soldiers and the curious citizens watching from the street. "This is the day we have waited so long for," he announced. "After a hundred years, Prince Briar Rose has finally returned to his people."

There was an audible gasp from the crowd, and the old woman whipped around, her cloudy eyes fixed on them. Briar tried not to fidget, lifting his dirt-streaked face to the crowd.

"The prince . . ." Nikor's hand tightened around the gold scepter. Then he took a step forward, bowing low from the waist. "Your Highness. Everlynd welcomes you with open arms." He gestured for the soldiers to clear the way, as if they were suddenly a nuisance. "I am Nikor, your steward. My family has been looking after Everlynd in your stead."

"Thank you," Briar said. "It's . . . a relief, to find some part of Andar survived."

Nikor's face softened. "It's a relief for us as well, to know that everything we've waited for has not been in vain. This is the Seer Witch, my advisor. The other members of the council will be eager to—"

He stopped abruptly as the Seer Witch seized his arm, pulling him down to whisper harshly in his ear. Nikor frowned, and Fi found herself the focus of that ancient gaze as the old woman turned to stare right at her. Her empty eyes were cold.

Nikor cleared his throat, looking troubled. "I'm afraid your companion is not welcome inside the city."

"What?" Briar demanded.

"Nikor . . ." the Paper Witch began.

"She knows why." The Seer Witch's voice was a low rasp. Her eyes dropped to the black fingerless glove, and Fi's skin prickled under that empty gaze. The Seer Witch was looking right at the butterfly mark. She could almost feel the curse mark crawling on her palm.

She hadn't thought about the curse in weeks. They'd been traveling almost since the moment Fi had touched the bone spindle, never staying in the same place for more than a day. There was nothing the Butterfly Curse's misfortune could do to Andar's barren hills. But looking at the beautiful city of Everlynd spread out before her, Fi felt the familiar shackle of dread squeezing her heart. *Welcome home, Briar Rose*—that was what the Paper Witch had said. This was Briar's home, or the closest he had to it. And Fi cared about Briar, more than she had ever cared about anyone—which meant the Butterfly Curse had power here, enough to destroy it all.

Fi clenched her hand, as if she could hide the mark inside her fist. It would be three days before the curse caught up with her, but the Seer Witch was right. Everlynd would be safer if she never set foot inside.

Briar had stepped toward Nikor, righteous and angry. "You don't understand who this is—"

Fi caught the sleeve of his coat. "Briar, don't," she said softly.

"I understand your misgivings," the Paper Witch broke in over both of them, directing his words to Nikor. "But this girl, Filore, is the one who freed the prince from his curse. All of Andar owes her a great debt."

"And we are certainly grateful, but it sounds like she has already played her part." Nikor's face could have been carved out of marble. "I do not take the warnings of the Seer Witch lightly. And in case you have forgotten, the council ruled that I have final authority over who is allowed into Everlynd. My decision stands. She will not be a guest of this city."

Fi's stomach churned. She didn't know if it was relief or regret.

"And what if she was my personal guest?"

Fi's head shot up at the new voice. A young man with brown skin had jumped down from the steep staircase of the adjacent watchtower, making his way through the red-clad guards.

"Would anyone voice any objections to me?"

He looked a little older than Fi, maybe eighteen, with short curly black hair and a friendly smile. Though he had dropped from the tower, he wasn't wearing the telltale red cloak—just a pair of plain pants under a belted shirt embroidered with purple leaves. His rolled-up sleeves showed off a band of black ink around his forearm. Fi wondered if he also held the key to traversing the storm.

The Paper Witch met him with a quick embrace, looking

him up and down. "Perrin, you've gotten so tall," he marveled.

"That's what happens when you're gone for five years," the boy said with an easy shrug.

The Paper Witch placed a hand on the boy's back, turning to Fi and Briar. "Allow me to introduce Perrin, great-nephew of the Dream Witch."

"There are a few more greats in there," Perrin admitted. "But that's too much of a mouthful."

"The Dream Witch," Briar repeated softly, a look of wonder on his face. Fi could see the resemblance now, remembering the Dream Witch, whose lush curls shook when she laughed. She and Perrin seemed to have the same smile.

Perrin turned to Nikor, eyebrows raised. "So? What'll it be? Are you going to deny me?"

Nikor looked like he was grinding his teeth. "As a descendant of one of the oldest magic families, you are granted special privileges. But this is not wise, Perrin."

"I'll take my chances," Perrin replied. Fi thought he threw her a wink, but Briar was standing right next to her, and it could just as easily have been for him.

"She's your responsibility," Nikor hissed. Then he turned on his heel and walked away, leading the Seer Witch by the arm. The old woman leaned into Nikor, her body bent like a withered tree, still whispering into his ear as they vanished into the crowd.

Fi watched them go. She was grateful to Perrin for the rescue, but the old woman's warning squirmed around in her gut. Fi had sworn she would never let the Butterfly Curse hurt anyone again. It was the reason she hadn't seen her parents in over a year—the reason she'd said the hardest thing she'd ever had to say in the tower and turned Briar down. Maybe she could talk to the old woman, find out if she'd actually seen something or if she just sensed the curse's malevolence. And she would be sure not to overstay.

Her eyes darted up to the sun, which was high in the afternoon sky. She wasn't sure exactly when she'd entered the city. After all, they'd entered the sandstorm created by the Witches' magic at noon. Three full days would be cutting it too close. She'd leave before the final morning—even if it meant running away in the dead of the night. No matter what happened, she would leave before the curse could strike.

The crowd had largely dispersed. Fi guessed that news of Briar's arrival was spreading fast. The Paper Witch led them into the city past the last few soldiers.

"I will see the captain of the guard about dispatching help for Shane," he said. "And then I must go after Nikor. In spite of his private contempt for me, he will understand the need to convene the council. They will want to speak to you, Briar Rose."

Perrin cleared his throat loudly. "Might I suggest a detour for a change of clothes? I think the prince might be better received after a bath, when the councilors can tell who he is under all that dirt."

Fi couldn't argue with that. The sand was so caked onto her skin it felt like she'd grown scales.

"A very good point," the Paper Witch agreed. "After I've seen to Shane's aid, I will do the same. Briar Rose, be ready when I come to collect you." He set off down the same path Nikor had taken, clouds of dust flapping from his long sleeves.

Fi felt a little of the tension ease from her shoulders. As long as Shane could hold out a little longer, they would be rescued.

"Well, I guess that leaves us two choices," Perrin said, turning to them. "We can go straight to my house, though the bath won't be ready yet, or I can send word ahead and we can take the scenic route."

Fi glanced at Briar. He smiled back like she shouldn't even have to ask.

"We'll take the scenic route," Briar said.

"I was hoping you'd say that," Perrin replied with a grin of his own. He said a few words to one of the guardsmen, and then the three of them fell into step together, moving up the wide cobbled street toward the waterfalls. "We should have just enough time to see the highlight of Everlynd, in my humble opinion. It's the oldest part of the city—the school of the Golden Hourglass."

*The school of the dream Witches.* "Are you serious?" Fi asked, trying not to sound too eager. She had a feeling Perrin could tell anyway.

He smiled warmly. "Well, we haven't had a royal visitor in a hundred years. I wouldn't want to disappoint."

It couldn't last—not with the Spindle Witch still searching for them and the Witch Hunters at their backs, not to mention the Butterfly Curse like a ticking clock on her skin. But just for this moment, Fi stepped into the world of her dreams.

# 13

⟫⟫⟫ ⟪⟪⟪

## Shane

SHANE PACED IN front of the windows, staring out at the swirling storm. She could still see the wall of sand in the distance, but the wind was getting stronger here, too—she could feel it battering the outpost, banging the ragged shutters against the pockmarked walls. She had no idea how long ago Fi and the others had set out. But she knew they were running out of time.

Red lay on a pallet of moldering old sheets, tossing and groaning. Shane had wrapped her in all three of their blankets and her red-lined cloak, but even with Cinzel's great furry body curled up against hers, Red wouldn't stop shivering. The skin around her wound seethed with ugly red streaks all the way up to her shoulder. The poison was deep inside her now. Shane kept pacing from the pallet to the window and back again, counting the breaths moving in and out of Red's parted lips.

The outpost was painfully bare. Shane had already prowled through it twice, kicking the desiccated chunks of firewood around the hearth into a pile. It felt good to slam her foot down on something and feel it break. Whatever this had once been, she got the sense nobody used it much these days. There was nothing here—no water, no food, no glistening vial labeled *Witch Hunter Antidote* stuffed in the back of the barren cabinet. Just a warped table and a crumbling old hearth, and Shane and her ax and the wolf. And Red, dying too fast.

Shane ground her fist against the windowsill. She longed to unsling her ax and heave it into something. Too bad none of her current problems could be solved by putting a gaping hole in the wall.

Cinzel lifted his head, giving a long howl that echoed off the stone.

Shane gritted her teeth. "Knock it off! You're not helping." If Red could sleep through that, she was really in bad shape.

Cinzel howled again—a low, mournful sound that rattled her all the way to her bones. Shane dropped down next to the pallet and found herself face-to-face with the wolf, staring directly into his yellow-gold eyes for the first time.

"Hey, Cinzel! Stop it."

Maybe it was her imagination, but the wolf seemed to respond to its name. He broke off the howl and pushed his nose into Red's leg, looking up at Shane with sorrowful eyes. Cautiously, she reached out and dug her fingers deep into his fur, scratching his neck like she'd seen Red do. Under the coarse outer layer, he was softer than she'd imagined.

"She's not dead yet," Shane said quietly. "Don't give up on her."

Red thrashed against the blankets. Her expression was twisted and pinched, and her lips opened around a moan, the sound caught in the back of her throat. Just hearing it ripped Shane open.

"Red. Hey."

Red moaned again, softer this time—just a scared whimper. That was all Shane could take. Her hand settled on Red's arm, gently shaking her awake, and Red surged up with a gasp, struggling against the itchy blankets. For one second, her eyes were wild and empty, like she saw someone other than Shane looming over her.

"Nightmare?" Shane asked. She couldn't stop herself from reaching out, pressing the backs of her fingers against Red's flushed cheek.

"No," Red snapped, collapsing back onto the pallet. "Just dreaming."

"You were moaning," Shane said simply.

"Moaning?" Red repeated. Then a mocking smile curled her lips, and she twisted to face Shane, arching one eyebrow suggestively. "Maybe it was a really *good* dream about you."

Shane snorted. "Now, that would be a nightmare."

Red tried to laugh, but she broke off coughing, her face twisted in pain. Shane ground her teeth, feeling horrible and useless. She'd gotten Red this far, but what was that worth? She couldn't do anything except sit here, waiting.

When she could breathe again, Red wiped a hand across her mouth with a grimace. "Don't just sit there with that dour look on your face. The least you could do is entertain me."

Her eyes lifted to Shane's. "Tell me one of your silly stories from Steelwight. The ones that always have such impossibly happy endings."

Shane swallowed hard. All the words felt stuck in her throat. Right now, looking down at Red, she didn't want fairy tales and stories of fated love, the short, easy version you got to share over drinks in a crowded tavern if you lived through all the hell first. All she wanted was for Red to be okay.

Maybe there was one story she could tell. Shane slumped back against the wall, rubbing the heels of her palms into her eyes.

"Fine. I'll tell you a story. It's about a girl—the daughter of a War King. And her twin brother, born three and a half minutes after her. She was the best warrior in a generation . . ."

"So this is definitely a fable," Red scoffed.

Shane nudged Red's boot. "Shut up. You're ruining the mood." She took a deep breath—as deep as she could, like if she breathed deeply enough, maybe she'd be breathing for Red, too. "Best warrior in a generation, but she never seemed to do anything else right as heir. And one day, she met her betrothed, a princess from Icefern . . ."

As the wind howled through the chinks in the stone, Shane told Red everything—how she'd walked away from Steelwight with nothing but the ax on her back, how she'd set out to make a new life and lost a lot of herself before she found her way again. She wound up telling Red other things, too. How much she missed the salt of the sea breeze on her face when she stood on the fortress walls. How when she looked up at the night sky, she still saw the Steelwight constellations first. Things she'd never told anyone, not even

Fi, because talking about them brought the pain close again. Somehow, she thought Red would understand. She had a feeling Red had lost a lot, too, and maybe she hadn't always gotten much back.

She stuttered out when she reached the new parts of her story—meeting Fi, meeting Briar, meeting Red.

Red made a face, coughing into her elbow. "I hate unfinished stories."

"Well, I'm not sure how this one ends yet," Shane admitted. Then she leaned down, bumping her fist softly against Red's shoulder. "Your turn. Why don't you tell me a story? Tell me how a person ends up working for the Spindle Witch."

For a moment, Shane thought she wasn't going to answer. Then Red tipped her head back, resigned, her eyelashes dark and wet against her ashen cheeks.

"Once there was a Witch, born the daughter of Witch Hunters."

Shane stopped breathing. "What?"

Red threw her a baleful look. "Now who's interrupting?" Still, she pushed herself up to lean against the wall, her body sagging against the worn planks. Cinzel rested his shaggy head in her lap. "The girl's father loved her as much as he hated the magic inside her. He did everything he could to get rid of it . . ." Red's lips trembled as she cupped the tattoo at the back of her neck. ". . . but nothing worked. So in the end, he just had to get rid of her."

Something flared in Shane—outrage, quick as a match striking. "Monster," she hissed.

Red gave a hollow laugh. "Monsters find other monsters, Shane. Maybe the girl was right where she was supposed to be." She closed her eyes. "Only one person was willing to take her in—a Witch who was cruel but powerful, who only saved the girl because she could use her. And that's when the girl realized the only thing that matters in this world is power, and whether you have enough of it to be on the winning side. And she swore never to be so weak again."

Something was building in Shane's head like a roar. It was anger, she realized as she ground her fist into the dust—anger at the Witch Hunters, and the Spindle Witch. Anger at everyone who had ever failed Red and left her like this, chewed up and spit out by hurt and grief and hatred. But she was angry at Red, too—for giving up, for believing them when they told her what she was worth. Shane was so angry it felt like it was blistering her insides.

Red sagged against her, pressing her temple to Shane's shoulder. Her words were so soft Shane almost lost them in the screaming of the wind.

"And then, when that girl had finally made a place for herself, she had to go and meet someone like you. Someone who makes her question whether she was wrong about everything."

Shane's mouth went dry. "Red . . ."

Red shook her head. "It's just a story," she said, sounding tired. "Don't take it so seriously."

Shane stared down at Red. Even now, with dark circles under her eyes and her skin waxy, Red was still pushing her away. As sick as she was, Shane wanted to shake her. She'd been trying to tell Red she had choices—that she could still change her mind, change sides, change her whole life. But Red never seemed to hear her no matter how loudly she shouted.

The door banged in the wind. Red inched away from Shane, pushing her sweaty curls out of her face. "What are you still doing here? Just go. I'm as good as dead already."

"They'll get here in time," Shane insisted. "Just hang on."

"I'm not talking about the poison," Red spat. "I lost my relic. The thorn rod." Her expression faltered, her voice cracking. "I already failed the Spindle Witch by letting Briar Rose escape. She warned me this was my last chance. Now that I've lost the relic, she'll assume I've betrayed her. No one crosses her and lives, at least not for long."

Shane bent close, gripping the back of Red's neck and catching her eyes. "Your story doesn't end like this. I promise."

Red laughed. Not a nice laugh. "The Spindle Witch or the Witch Hunters . . . what does it matter? I'm a corpse."

"Why are you so set on dying all of a sudden?" Shane demanded.

Red's breath was coming too fast. "Why are you so set on keeping me alive?"

"Because . . ." Shane clenched her teeth over the answer. Because she couldn't stand the defeated look on Red's face— like she knew that if she died here, not one person would care. It made her sick, especially because Red was so wrong. Shane would care. That mangy wolf would probably guard her body until it starved. And Red ought to care, because she could be so much more than this.

Something inside Shane snapped, sharp as a bone breaking. Suddenly, her head was crystal clear. She was going to save Red from everything—from the Spindle Witch and the Witch Hunters and even from herself. Shane was tired of fighting Red, and fighting to get through to Red, and fighting to remember that Red was supposed to be her enemy. But mostly, she was just tired of fighting her heart.

Shane surged up from the wall, grabbing one of the bloody bandages and binding Red's wrists tight. "That's it. We're going."

Red's eyes fluttered open in shock. "Shane," she croaked. "What are you—"

"Shut up!" Shane growled. She hooked Red's arms around her neck and swung the girl up into her arms, banging the door open with her bruised shoulder. "You're not done. This isn't how it ends between us."

The wind hit her full in the face. Shane threw herself into it, her legs churning as she raced through the sand. The fleabag wolf loped alongside her, crooning, and even though Shane couldn't speak his language, she thought she knew what he was trying to say. For once, they were on the same side.

*There is no after—not for us.* That was what Red had told her outside the Forest of Thorns. But Red was wrong. They could still have that *after.* As enemies. As friends. Maybe even as something else, something better. She wasn't going to let Red die and leave them both with a heart full of regrets.

Red's weight sagged in her arms. Shane could barely see anything through the whipping winds. But in the distance, appearing from the wall of sand, she thought she could just make out the shape of five figures, their red cloaks flapping, each one emblazoned with a blinding white tower. She'd know that tower anywhere.

Shane fell to her knees in relief. Her partner had come through after all.

# 14

## Fi

**EVERLYND WAS EVERYTHING** Fi had ever wanted and more.

Her chest buzzed with anticipation as she walked through the city, lagging a few steps behind Perrin and Briar to try to look at everything at once. The busy streets rambled past tall stone houses under wild rooftop gardens, and the air was heady with the smell of lilacs and ripening apricots. The windows were shuttered by lattices of dark wood twined through with blue and purple wisteria. Briar stared around, just as enthralled as she was.

They were getting some stares of their own. Red-caped soldiers stopped in the street to watch them pass, and a young girl whose eyes were already cloudy like a seer's stared after them, her dark springy curls braided with a dozen tiny bells. At least no one in Everlynd knew or cared who

Fi was. Briar, on the other hand, was making quite the first impression.

They were nearly to the waterfalls when Perrin turned and led them through a trellis shrouded in vines. "Ready?" he asked, already grinning. Then he swept the curtain of leaves aside.

Fi's heart soared as she caught sight of the Order of the Golden Hourglass—a tower of glistening golden stone that shimmered like a mirage in the sunlight, each of its six levels shaped like interlocking stars. Up close, it was dazzling, but Fi guessed that from a distance the points of the stars mimicked the uneven face of the golden cliffs, hiding the tower in plain sight. Arched doorways led out into lush gardens that changed with every level: at the base a thicket of mossy linden trees, and then a level planted entirely with scarlet flowers, and one of shallow reflecting pools, and on and on. Mist rolled over the tower from the glassy waterfalls leaping out of the rock face. One of them, long and thin as a horsetail, thundered onto the top of a bronze pavilion that crowned the very highest level of the tower. From there the water flowed down the chains of tarnished bronze discs that surrounded it like a veil, finally pouring into a channel that wound lazily down the tower before rejoining the river.

"Magnificent," Fi breathed.

"More so on the outside than the inside," Perrin admitted. "The inner tower is mostly private chambers for the Witches who came to study here. There's no great hall or anything. They didn't have to get together in person, after all," he added, pressing his finger to his temple.

So they had met in dreams. *Her mother had been right!* Fi tried to engrave every image into her mind. More than anywhere else she'd been, she knew this was the story her mother would want to hear over and over.

"What's that humming sound?" Briar asked. Now that she was listening for it, Fi could hear it, too—a low hum like a sustained note floating under the rush of the waterfalls.

"It comes from the river." Perrin pointed at the shallow channel of water that looped around the tower, crossing the dirt path at every level in a row of smooth stepping-stones. The channel was lined with small bronze balls that twirled in the slow-moving flow. "The intersection of the path and the river represents the crossroads of the waking and sleeping worlds. New initiates of the Golden Hourglass are supposed to walk barefoot up the waterway to the pavilion, but the sound is sort of hypnotic—I fell asleep standing up."

"Do they . . . disqualify you for that?" Fi asked. She wasn't sure how strict the initiation rituals were.

Perrin laughed. "Maybe I would have had to repeat it, once. We've loosened up a little now that there aren't enough Witches left to bother with the orders anymore."

Fi jerked back. "The Orders of Magic are gone?" Briar looked equally stricken.

Perrin nodded. "A few of the more powerful Witches still choose an order, but it's basically just picking a favorite color. There are more spell books in Everlynd than Witches who could learn them. For now, we're just safeguarding the knowledge in the hopes that the orders can be restored one day alongside the kingdom of Andar."

They were quiet for a moment, looking out at the ancient

tower, which seemed suddenly very empty. Fi thought of the ink books wrapped around the Paper Witch's and Perrin's arms and wondered how many other ways the Witches of Everlynd had kept the old knowledge safe. And what it had cost them.

"What about the Red Ember?" Briar asked.

Perrin scrubbed a hand through his short hair. "They're not exactly an Order of Magic anymore. Many of the soldiers don't have any magical ability at all. But they're definitely recruiting every Witch that Nikor can get his hands on." A frown pulled at his lips for a moment before he shook it away. "I'm sorry we don't have time for a closer look, but any longer and I'm afraid we'll have to throw a bucket of water over you and send you off to the council still dripping, Your Highness."

Briar shifted uncomfortably at the title. "Just Briar, please," he begged.

"Briar works for me," Perrin agreed.

Perrin was serious about not delaying. He hustled them through the back roads, not stopping until they arrived at a lanky three-story building at the end of a busy lane.

As soon as they entered, Fi was reminded of the Paper Witch's tower. Perrin's house was roomy and warm, thick with the scent of rosemary. Heavy wooden tables jigsawed between a bright kitchen and the wooden circular stairs winding up to the next floor. Every surface was strewn with open books, their pages pinned under heavy mugs or held by makeshift bookmarks improvised from dried leaves and quill feathers. But what really drew her eye was the wide glass window set into the front wall.

The deep nook held three tiered shelves cut right into the stone, and every one of them was filled with glistening hourglasses. Some were large, like they could count out whole days; some were tiny with just a pinch of gold dust that would barely last seconds. As Fi watched, one of the hourglasses turned over, swinging gently in a wooden frame carved with little moons. Was Perrin safeguarding these hourglasses? Using them? He'd said he wasn't nearly as powerful as his great-aunt, but less powerful than one of the Great Witches could still be a lot more powerful than most.

"Do you live here alone?" Briar asked.

"Yep." Perrin shrugged. "My parents were members of the Red Ember. They died six years ago." His eyes flickered almost unconsciously to an alcove tucked into the corner, where Fi noticed a small square painting of a man with Perrin's curly hair. The paint was thick and uneven, like the work of an amateur—but the smile on the man's face was soft and full of love. Fi wondered immediately if Perrin's mom had painted it. A silver necklace hung from the corner next to a few other keepsakes, along with a torn piece of a red cloak. Mementos.

Fi's chest ached. The loss hit too close to home.

"I'm so sorry." Briar bent to take a closer look at the painting. "You got your father's looks."

Perrin smiled fondly. "I'm told we both take after the Dream Witch. I've always wondered if that was true. You knew her, right? What do you think?"

Perrin lifted one eyebrow, striking a pose. Briar chuckled.

"You certainly have her sense of humor."

A bittersweet smile flashed across Briar's face, and Fi

wondered how strange it must be to lose people to time. Did he see the ghost of his old mentor when he looked at Perrin? Little pieces of his life turned into flickers of familiarity in the faces of strangers?

Fi cleared her throat over a sudden lump, turning to Perrin. "So, did your parents have dream magic, too?" she asked curiously.

"Not a drop," Perrin replied. "They weren't even Witches, just soldiers devoted to the city. I'm a bit of a throwback, actually." He shook his head, as though at some private joke, before heading for the stairs. "Come on."

Fi studied Perrin's wide back as they followed him up the circular steps. The boy talked about his magic like it was nothing special, but Fi was certain Perrin was more important than he was letting on. And more powerful.

Upstairs, Perrin pushed open a door with a flourish. "Here we are."

Warm steam wafted from the room beyond. The washroom was twice as big as Fi had expected, with two porcelain baths sitting side by side, separated by a cream-colored privacy screen. The lattice over the window threw diamonds of sunlight across the floor. Heat rose in Fi's cheeks at the thought of bathing in the same room as Briar, even with a screen between them. She turned to Perrin, not even sure what she was going to ask, but he was already backing away.

"I'll go rustle up some more appropriate clothes," he said, stepping out and swinging the door closed. "Take your time."

Fi shot Briar a nervous look. Her heart just about leapt out of her chest as the door banged open and Perrin's head poked back in.

"Not you," he amended, pointing at Briar. "You hurry. You, though—Fi—enjoy." Then he was gone again.

Fi stepped behind the privacy screen, but she waited a moment to make sure Perrin wasn't going to reappear before reaching for the hem of her ragged shirt. Or rather, Briar's shirt. Her eyes cut to the screen. Briar was closer to the window, and she could see his silhouette against the cream fabric—the shadow of him laying his coat aside, and then the curve of his back as he pulled the undershirt over his head.

An image of Briar's bare chest as he stood in the river flashed through Fi's mind, and she looked pointedly away, shucking off the rest of her clothes and slipping into the bath. The water was heavenly, not just warm but downright hot, and she felt her muscles relaxing as weeks of travel melted away. She had always loved a bath. She heard the soft splash of Briar climbing into his own tub.

A handful of bottles had been left beside Fi's tub, and she grabbed the one that looked like soap, slathering it into her hair. Next to her, Briar's silhouette lounged with his head tipped back, one foot dangling over the rim of the tub. Fi couldn't help smiling even as she rolled her eyes. She was willing to bet Briar had never hurried through a bath in his life.

There was a splash as Briar sat up, leaning out of the tub. "Do you have any good soaps or oils over there?" he asked.

Fi pressed a hand over her chest, self-conscious even though she knew Briar couldn't see her. "There's a couple things."

"Excellent," Briar said. "Because they have really underestimated my needs as a prince. Pick me something that smells good?" His hand appeared around the edge of the screen, held out expectantly.

Fi was now beet red, trying not to imagine how Briar smelled. *Get ahold of yourself!* she thought sternly. She rifled around and picked something floral. She kept herself covered as she placed the bottle into Briar's wet hand, fascinated by the drop of water that traveled from his finger to hers.

Fi slid quickly back into the tub. She hadn't really thought much about her looks, especially how she looked naked, but she couldn't help wondering if there was something ideal and lovely about her skin or her freckles—or any part of her, really—or if she just looked like one of those hairless mole rats, all tan and wrinkly. It was a ridiculous thought, she could recognize that, but that didn't mean she could get rid of it. She wasn't about to ask Briar for his opinion, though. Fi scoured her skin with a washcloth and then held out her arms for inspection. At least she wasn't dirty anymore.

She watched Briar's shadow opening the bottle, a strong scent of lavender filling the room. Briar was too pale, starved for sunlight after years in the castle, but he was still beautiful. Fi knew that from the bits and pieces of him she'd seen, but more than that, because every part of him would be Briar— fun-loving, teasing, breathtaking Briar.

"Fi."

Her head jerked up. Briar's shadow had stopped moving, his face turned toward her. His voice was unusually serious.

"What was that, with the Seer?" he asked. "What were they talking about—*you know why you can't enter*?"

Of course that was what he wanted to know. The water felt suddenly colder, sending a shiver up her spine. "It's nothing you need to worry about," she told him.

"It's about the mark on your hand, isn't it?" Briar lifted his own hand, holding it out as if he would press it to the screen between them. "What is it? What does it do?"

Fi looked at her left hand. It was still ugly and discolored, and she worried the broken pinkie was healing crooked, but by far the ugliest thing was the butterfly. "It's . . ." Why was it so hard to say the words? Fi pulled her knees up to her chest. "It's an old problem, but I've got it under control. I won't let it affect you or the people of Everlynd."

"I'm not worried about these people—I don't even know these people." Briar's voice was hoarse. "I'm worried about *you*. We're partners. Let me help you."

That word *partners* panged around in her rib cage. Fi forced herself to take a deep breath. She'd probably put this off as long as she could. Briar would find out one way or the other, when she had to leave in three days. He was right— they were partners, and she owed him an explanation. She had to tell him.

Fear churned in her stomach, but there was another feeling, too—relief that she wouldn't have to hide her secret from Briar anymore. Fi closed her eyes and pressed her forehead lightly against the screen.

"Briar . . . I—"

The door banged open, and they both yelped, Briar diving back into the tub with a great splash.

"You're not ready yet?" The Paper Witch stood in the doorway, dressed in a clean white robe with a silk sash. "Haste,

Briar Rose! The scouts will be back with Shane before you have even finished your bath."

"They found her?" Fi called hopefully.

"Word just came," Perrin offered, his head appearing from behind the Paper Witch. "Though it may still be a while before they make it through the sandstorm. In the meantime, I've brought, uh . . . I'll just set these here." He carefully looked over Fi's head as he set a pile of clothes by her tub and a second one by Briar's, then retreated to the hall. The Paper Witch closed the door firmly, but Fi could still hear the impatient tapping of his foot from the other side.

Briar surged out of the tub, drying off and hurrying into his clothes. Fi decided to do the same before anyone else came banging through the door without knocking. The outfit left for her was not a dress, as she had originally thought, but a pair of loose pants and a long silk jacket that flared at the knee and had multiple large pockets. Best of all, they fit and didn't have any holes in them. The only thing she fished out of the pile of her old clothes was the fingerless glove, which she pulled over the butterfly mark. She slipped Camellia's code into the pocket of her new coat.

Satisfied, Fi picked up a small hand mirror, using her fingers to comb through her wet hair. It was long enough to feather around her neck—she'd have to cut it soon. A flash of blue appeared in the mirror, and Fi turned to see that Briar had emerged from behind the screen, fully dressed and looking every inch the prince of Andar. He wore black trousers and a cream silk shirt under a blue satin vest, which shimmered with a line of silver buttons. A knee-length cape of midnight blue was fastened to his shoulders, darker than his usual coat but still dazzling with his eyes. What surprised her most was the circlet of gold gleaming in his blond curls. Somehow, she'd never pictured Briar in a crown.

He flicked drops of water from his hair, careful not to upset the circlet. "How do I look?" he asked.

"Like you're going to be yelled at for being late," Fi teased. She reached out to straighten his cape but stopped before she touched him. "You look fine."

Briar glowed like it was high praise, catching her arm on the way down. "You look good, too—too good for me to do it justice now. I'll find you later and we can finish our talk. Don't forget what you were going to say."

How could she, when it was going to change everything between them? Her hand squeezed into a fist as she watched the Paper Witch usher Briar out, his regal cape swishing behind him. He suddenly seemed very far away. Maybe everything had already changed for them—or more accurately, maybe the time they had spent beside campfires and tumbling through the dirt together had been the lie. Fi had been dragging a prince around like he was a common traveler or treasure hunter, but he wasn't.

Fi could still remember the look on the Paper Witch's face when she'd first told him about pricking her finger on the bone spindle, and he'd said this was the moment *the descendants of Andar had been waiting for all their lives.*

Fi fisted her hand over the butterfly mark. She might have feelings for Briar, and they were probably even returned, but in the end, it didn't really matter. Briar Rose had always been a powerful Witch and a royal prince, miles above Filore Nenroa, daughter of a tiny Border House. The Butterfly Curse was just the final nail in the coffin. There were all kinds of goodbyes in life, she had learned, and as she watched Briar Rose go to meet his people, she wondered if this was one of them.

To Fi's surprise, Perrin knocked politely on the edge of the doorframe, though he didn't wait for a response before entering.

"Lovely," he said, looking her up and down.

"Flirting will get you nowhere," Fi warned.

Perrin held up his hands. "I was referring, of course, to the outfit I picked out."

"Oh. Right." Fi plucked at the red silk robes. "I guess your taste isn't so bad."

Perrin grinned. "I had a feeling you were the scholarly type. I could tell by that little crinkle between your eyes from squinting at too many books."

Fi reached up unconsciously, pressing a finger between her eyebrows, only to be met with Perrin's laugh.

"Again, kidding. You don't have any wrinkles. It was all the rapid-fire questions about the dream Witches that gave you away."

Fi felt a little color rising to her cheeks. She'd been trying to hold back, clearly not as successfully as she'd hoped. But how could she? This was a once-in-a-lifetime opportunity for a historian. One she'd almost missed out on.

"I wanted to thank you for earlier," Fi said, tugging at her sleeve, "when you stood up for me at the gates. You didn't have to do that."

This time Perrin's laugh was soft, almost rueful. "Everlynd is . . . not what it used to be. It's easy to find yourself on the wrong side of the council these days."

"Even you? The heir to one of the Great Witches?" Fi asked, surprised.

"Especially me." Perrin grimaced. "I told you I was a bit of a throwback. I didn't just mean my magic. My parents believed that Everlynd was the hope of this kingdom. That we should be doing more than waiting for someone to come along and break the curse for us—protecting Witches, driving back the Witch Hunters . . ." He sighed heavily. "My parents were Nikor's main opposition on the council, but I'm afraid my voice doesn't carry the same weight as theirs did. I'm just a thorn in his side these days."

Fi frowned. "Then aren't you just making it worse, going around him to help a stranger like me? Not that I'm not grateful—" she rushed to add.

Perrin shrugged. "Maybe. But it's the right thing to do. You risked your life to save Briar Rose, right? So you risked your life for Andar, and for all of us. My mother would haunt me from her grave if I stood by while they threw you out. Probably the Dream Witch, too."

Fi couldn't help but smile as Perrin searched around for some wood to knock on after invoking their spirits. He reminded her of the Witches from her old storybook, the ones who solved problems with wisdom and kindness, and sometimes just practical advice. If Perrin was anything like his great-aunt, she understood why Briar had loved the Dream Witch so much.

Fi slid her hands into the wide pockets of the scholar's coat. Something tickled her fingertips, and she fished it out, holding up a long purple tassel.

"Sorry, I should have checked the pockets more carefully."

Perrin reached for the string. "It's just a book ribbon from the more ancient section of the library."

Fi barely heard anything except the word *library*. She couldn't even imagine the wealth of information about the Spindle Witch and Andar that might be hidden away here, protected by the storm. Not to mention the possibility of finding the book they needed to decipher Camellia's code. "I don't suppose you're familiar with this library?"

Perrin's eyes were bright. "I am its very best patron," he said. Remembering the state of his workspace downstairs, Fi didn't doubt it. "And the library just happens to be in the Main Manor, where your dear prince is right now standing before the council of Everlynd. I'd be glad to take you." He offered an elbow.

"Lead the way," Fi said gratefully.

# 15

### Briar Rose

**BRIAR STOOD STIFFLY** before the members of the council. Nikor, the Seer Witch, and two others sat around a half-moon table in what the Paper Witch had called the Main Manor, a three-story building of white stone that stood apart in the heart of the city. The small chamber was lit by three arched windows that looked out over Everlynd's vast lake.

The Paper Witch introduced Briar to Captain Hane, who led Everlynd's guard and the Witches of the Red Ember. She was a tall woman with brown skin and a cloud of dark hair that floated around her face. Though she sat rigidly straight, she seemed to be a friend of the Paper Witch, and she offered Briar a quick smile.

The final seat at the table was filled by the Stone Witch, an old man with a tan, craggy face who looked as if his mind was made up even before the Paper Witch finished telling the story of Briar's rescue and the fate of those still locked in the castle.

It took all Briar had not to fidget with the tiny silver buttons on his vest. He looked like a prince again, but he still didn't feel like one, standing mutely beside the Paper Witch. As the sun sank behind the cliffs, attendants lit the lanterns in niches in the wall, and in the half dark, the Paper Witch paused for a breath, his hands tucked into his wide sleeves as he looked into the councilors' faces one by one.

"With the return of Briar Rose, the time is upon us. We must marshal what forces we can to retake Andar."

For a long moment, no one spoke. At last Nikor leaned back in his chair, rubbing a hand over his neat beard.

"You've been gone too long," he replied. "The situation in Everlynd has changed. The Witch Hunters are more numerous than ever. All the sects have been recalled to Andar, and they roam within a hair's breadth of this city. If not for the storm, they would have found us long ago."

"He's right," Captain Hane supplied, throwing the Paper Witch a glance like she was sorry to have to confirm Nikor's account. "The Witch Hunters are no longer a loose coalition fighting for power among themselves. About a decade ago, a new leader took power. He's named himself their High Lord, and he's been bringing all the sects to heel. They've moved their headquarters to the Eyrie, the old watchtower to the north, scant days from here."

Briar had seen the Eyrie once, in a dream. His brother Sage had traveled to the ancient watchtower to mediate a dispute between the local lords, and Briar had begged the

Dream Witch to show it to him until she finally relented. He could still picture the gray tower perched at the edge of a ragged gorge and ringed by rickety rope bridges, the battlements curled around its head like a crown of dark horns.

"The Witch Hunters are mere parasites," the Seer Witch hissed, speaking up suddenly. "Andar has only ever had one true enemy." The room seemed to darken as she said it, as if black wings had passed over the window. "As long as the kingdom is under her power, any attempt to restore it will fail."

"Is that prophecy, or merely a prediction?" the Paper Witch asked.

Nikor's voice was tense and angry. "It doesn't require a gift of foresight to know it's madness to go to war with the Spindle Witch while the Witch Hunters are at our backs."

"No more so than hiding in Everlynd forever, hoping they don't find us," Captain Hane said through gritted teeth. "As I have said many times." She shot an angry look at Nikor. "The Witch Hunters are getting more aggressive every day. It's time we dealt with them once and for all. If we take the head of their leader, their alliance will crumble. My soldiers are ready to fight for the prince."

Her gaze settled on Briar. He tried not to jump, his heart jerking with a sudden hope. Nikor snuffed it out with a wave of his hand.

"Even if you could take the Eyrie, you'd never keep it. The Witch Hunters have us badly outnumbered. This is not the time to be carried away by old loyalties."

The tiny bell in the Paper Witch's hair tinkled as he fixed his eyes on Nikor. "You and I have disagreed on many things, but we were always united in our belief that restoring Andar must be the highest goal."

Nikor scoffed. "That was when you led me to believe that breaking the sleeping curse was the key to everything. And yet here we are . . . Prince Briar Rose has been awakened, but the Spindle Witch remains undefeated, the people of the castle are trapped in sleep, and you come here with nothing but your hand out, seeking our aid. Everlynd owes you nothing."

"Nikor, you go too far." The Stone Witch turned to Briar. "Don't misunderstand, Your Highness. We all wish to restore Andar. But your people are safe for now. We sacrificed so many to build this one small haven." He passed a hand over his face, as if banishing old grief. "The sandstorm keeps the Witch Hunters at bay, and the Spindle Witch hasn't bothered us—"

"She hasn't bothered you because you insist on doing nothing," the Paper Witch cut in, losing patience. "But the prince is awake now, which means it is only a matter of time—*a very short time*—until the Spindle Witch begins to move. Seize this moment to stand against her."

"And how do you expect us to do that?" Nikor demanded. "You have brought us nothing! No king, no Great Witches, no army . . . just one ill-fated boy."

The Paper Witch said something in reply, but Briar couldn't hear him anymore. The air had begun to rush in his ears, and as Captain Hane and the others joined in, all of the raised voices bled together in a great roar. He could feel hope slipping away like grains of sand through his clenched fist.

He wasn't the prince Andar needed, and he never had been. He felt as if he were twelve years old again, crouched in the chamber of the Great Witches, listening to other voices debating what should be sacrificed for him.

**THE CHAMBER WAS** where the Three Great Witches met with the heads of the Orders of Magic. Unlike the castle's formal audience chamber—a gray stone hall with slit windows and Sage's rosewood throne—the Great Witches' chamber was radiant and bright. Set high into one of the castle's many towers, the room spilled over with tapestries and plush sitting cushions and shelves of magical reference books. The air was musty with the smells of amber and charcoal and cinnamon and a hundred other things tucked away in the tiny drawers of a tall apothecary cabinet. The round walls were studded with stained-glass windows set to face east, south, and west, so that as the sun moved it illuminated different scenes—snow-white gardenias at sunrise, mottled oak trees at midday, and at sunset a window seething with scarlet roses, so bright the lines of lead between them looked like tiny dark thorns. At night the stars poured into the room through the great skylight.

Briar had come looking for Camellia that night, but it was Sage's voice he heard through the half-open door. Briar froze with his hand over the knob. He couldn't remember Sage ever entering the Great Witches' chamber before. Nor had his brother ever sounded so angry.

"Enough! I only agreed to meet with you because you said it was urgent. This is not urgent. I have made my position on this matter clear many times."

Briar hesitated only a second, turning sideways so he could slide through the cracked door. He crouched behind the apothecary cabinet, breathing fast.

Sage stood at the center of the tower, glowing in the moonlight that spilled through the high window. Two men stood across from him, both dressed in the blue-and-ivory robes that lords of Andar wore at court. Like Briar, Sage still wore his formal clothes from the evening meal: a deep blue doublet, intricately embroidered, and his golden crown shimmering in his short blond hair. They had similar features, but that was it—Briar was all knees and knobby elbows, with pants that hovered above his ankles and a circlet he knocked off every time he ran his fingers through his too-long hair. Sage was every inch a king, strong and sharp-eyed as he stared down the two councilors.

Briar recognized the first as Nestor, a ruddy-cheeked man with a thin beard and hard eyes that made him seem perpetually sour. The second was Aldwin, an older man with brown skin and hair that was beginning to go gray. Briar didn't know what they were arguing about, but Nestor's mouth was twisted into a scowl, his voice rising as he stepped into the circle of moonlight.

"It is only a matter of time—" Nestor began.

Sage cut him off. "I'll not hear this."

"With all due respect, Your Majesty, I think you have to. Better here than in front of the entire council." Aldwin glanced toward the door, and Briar ducked low, biting his tongue as he accidentally cracked his elbow against the floor. He held his breath, waiting to be discovered, but the old man went on. "There has been deep unrest in the villages near the northern mountains. The Topaz Knights are speaking openly against you, and their numbers grow with every passing day."

Briar risked a glance around the cabinet. He knew a little about the Topaz Knights, a minor order that rejected all magic and claimed Andar's reliance on Witches would be its downfall. The Snake Witch had said they were extremists, not worth worrying about. But the serious expression on Sage's face told a different story.

Aldwin's voice was soft. "An order that decries the evils of magic is very seductive to those living in fear of the Spindle Witch's vengeance. And the part Prince Briar Rose might play in it."

Briar went cold at the sound of his own name. The darkness of the tower suddenly seemed closer and thicker, like a great black cloak that threatened to smother him. Everyone knew about the Spindle Witch's vow to destroy Andar. But what did Aldwin mean, the part he might play?

"Don't try to spare his feelings, Aldwin. He's not a child anymore." Nestor's voice was harsh, his lips curled back in disgust. "Briar Rose was meant to die, and nothing but misfortune has come of the foolish bargain your mother made to save his life."

Sage's hand seized the collar of Nestor's robe, wrenching him closer. "Watch your tongue," he snapped, but Nestor just spoke faster and louder.

"He is forever marked by the Spindle Witch's curse, and he will bring her wrath down on all of us!"

Briar couldn't breathe. His head was pounding, those words echoing inside his skull. He pressed his hands over his ears and closed his eyes, searching for that well of white-hot magic inside him, the light magic that Camellia said was too beautiful to ever be evil. But for once all he could find inside himself was darkness and doubt, and a tiny voice whispering in the back of his mind. He had killed his mother. He was poisoned by a curse. What if Nestor was right? What if the years of darkness the seer Witches predicted, the destruction of Andar and the fall of the Great Witches—what if it all started with him? Briar lowered his forehead to his knees, and his circlet slid off into his lap, the gold as dull as brass. He clenched his fists around it.

By the time he lifted his head, Aldwin had placed his hand on Sage's arm, coaxing the young king to release Nestor.

"The truth is not the issue, Your Majesty," he warned. "The Topaz Knights have convinced people that you're protecting Prince Briar at the expense of the kingdom. They're demanding actions be taken."

Sage let out a long breath and dropped his hand. His voice remained cold. "I will never abandon my brother. Nor will I hand him over to a fringe order of fanatics."

"No one is suggesting that," Aldwin assured him. "But perhaps, if you could just send him away from the capital—for his own safety."

This was the moment Briar had replayed so many times. As unrest grew in Andar. As the Topaz Knights gained momentum. As Sage canceled the public celebrations and then the days of petition and finally closed the castle altogether. This was the moment that he lived over and over again in his mind as he wandered the white tower for a hundred years, locked in his dreams.

Briar closed his eyes, and he was right back there—crouched on the cold flagstones with the hard cabinet against his back and his circlet in his hands, in the split second between when Aldwin spoke and Sage answered. Wishing that just this once Sage would back down, and wondering if that might have been enough to change everything that happened. But it was just a memory, and Sage always said the same thing, his voice calm and certain.

"Never. Sending him away is tantamount to sending him into the Spindle Witch's arms. Even Nestor can't think that's a good idea." Sage braced a hand against Aldwin's shoulder, dredging up a small, pained smile. "We cannot be ruled by fear. The Topaz Knights won't stop with Briar. He's just the first step in getting what they've always wanted: a war against magic. If we let them, they will topple the orders, and they'll come for the Great Witches, and then who will save us when the Spindle Witch returns?"

The councilors were quiet. Sage let the silence settle before he drew himself up.

"Have faith, my lords. We are not out of time just yet. My sister and the other Great Witches are working tirelessly on a way to defeat the Spindle Witch once and for all . . ."

Briar stopped listening, because he had heard it all before. His eyes fell on the western window, the one choked with roses. Then he looked down and found that without even realizing it his magic had melted and distorted the circlet until it was just a snarl of mangled gold.

A twisted circlet for a twisted prince.

**THE CIRCLET ON** Briar's head felt unbearably heavy as he fisted his hands into his cape, listening to the angry voices of Everlynd's council. He needed to say something—Sage would say something. But if he spoke up now, if he convinced Everlynd to fight for him, would this be one more memory he went back to over and over, wishing for a different outcome? So many people had already been lost trying to save him— Camellia and the Great Witches, and Sage, and everyone else in the castle. Maybe the last thing Everlynd should do was throw in with the ill-luck prince . . .

"Silence! Silence, all of you." The Stone Witch's voice rose above the fray. "This squabbling accomplishes nothing."

"If this is all you have to offer, then my decision stands," Nikor said, pushing up from his chair. "I will not risk the survival of Everlynd on a hopeless cause."

"And what if there was hope?" the Paper Witch asked. Briar looked up and found those glittering blue eyes on his face. "We have discovered a code, left by the Rose Witch herself and tucked away with Briar Rose. We believe it is guiding us to a magic that could defeat the Spindle Witch."

The chamber seethed with whispers. Briar saw the Seer

Witch's hand tighten on Nikor's arm, her long nails digging into his skin.

Nikor frowned. "Why didn't you mention this before?"

Briar had a feeling he knew why. The Paper Witch could be cunning—the type to keep his best card hidden until the final hand.

The Paper Witch only shrugged. "Because it is not complete. We are still assembling the final pieces to decode it. But whatever it is, the Rose Witch pinned all her hopes on it—and on Briar Rose."

Briar felt dread rising in his stomach. He was no closer to finding Camellia's book. And even if he could, they had no proof that what she'd left them could help defeat the Spindle Witch. He wanted to blurt out the truth. But that meant giving up on Everlynd's help—giving up on rescuing Sage. He bit his tongue and kept his mouth shut.

"You are confident you can decipher this code?" Nikor asked. His hard eyes seemed to be asking something else.

The Paper Witch's hand settled like a lead weight on Briar's shoulder. "Yes. He can."

Nikor looked unconvinced, but he exhaled through his teeth, sinking into his chair as he waved them off. "Then I will withhold judgment for now. Keep your promises, Paper Witch—find a weapon against the Spindle Witch and come back when you have more than just vague hopes to offer." Nods passed around the table as the council dispersed.

Briar could barely keep the words down until he and the Paper Witch were alone in the antechamber. He rounded on the man, angry now that the shock had worn off.

"What are you doing? I can't decipher the code. I don't

know what book Camellia used as the key—and even if I did, it's probably in the hands of the Witch Hunters. Or *burned*."

The Paper Witch shook his head. "Patience, Briar Rose. One problem at a time. You are among those who do magic once again, and that means there is a way to uncover the knowledge of the book trapped inside you: a dream walk."

Briar frowned. "I thought only one of the most powerful Witches could create a dream like that."

"And she will." There was a little glimmer in the Paper Witch's eyes. "When I was waiting on your very long bath earlier, Perrin happened to mention that he has some of his great-aunt's dream dust, the same dust she used to put the castle to sleep. There could be no better use for it than to help us now."

Briar felt a shiver on his neck as he thought wistfully of the dreams he'd walked in side by side with his old teacher. She'd been powerful enough to bring all of Andar to one little boy trapped in the walls of the castle. But she was gone. They were all gone.

Briar swallowed hard. "Even if Perrin is the Dream Witch's great-nephew, I don't know him. I don't think he could walk safely inside my dreams. And you know what will happen if I go alone . . ."

Briar trailed off. He was no Dream Witch trained by the Order of the Golden Hourglass. He had spent a hundred years asleep, but even then, he'd been protected by the Dream Witch's magic. Without her, he would fall prey to his nightmares. The sleeping mind was a labyrinth—that's what the Dream Witch had told him.

*Our darkest thoughts are most powerful when we are uncon-scious. In dreams, whatever weakness lies buried in your heart will try to pull you in—and if you succumb to those nightmares, you can become lost in your own mind. Forever.*

*Surely you understand why you of all people must never dream walk alone, Briar Rose.*

The Spindle Witch. It always, always, always came back to her. Haunting his steps. Stalking him from the shadows. The bitter, inevitable end to his story. Briar's hand fisted over his chest. He could almost feel the curl of claws trying to push themselves out of his nail beds.

The Paper Witch squeezed Briar's shoulder. "You will not go alone," he promised. "There is someone who has already been in your dreams. Someone chosen by the bone spindle and your sister to save you. Filore will join you and keep you from losing yourself."

"It'll be dangerous for her," Briar said. There was no telling what she might encounter in his dreams. Briar's darkness, his fears, wouldn't have the same power over her as they did over him. But that didn't mean she'd be able to hold them at bay.

"In desperate times, I'm afraid we all must take our share of the risk." The Paper Witch turned away. "I'll see to the arrangements."

Then Briar was alone. He leaned back against the cold stone wall, wishing it would calm his roiling thoughts. When he turned his head, he was surprised to find a shaft of light cutting through the dark—the giant double doors at the end of the hallway were partway open. Briar was moving toward them before he questioned it.

When he slipped inside, he found himself in Everlynd's

library. The room was beautiful and clearly well loved. Giant mahogany shelves twice as tall as Briar lined every wall, and long wood tables gleamed in the light of small lanterns hanging from stylized bronze hooks. A wide window took up one entire wall, its wooden lattice cradling a hundred tiny panes of winking glass. Braces of unlit candles waited in each corner.

Right in front of the window sat a massive table strewn with open books and what looked like a few letters bound with long blue ribbons. Three different lanterns were lit, two from the library and one that had clearly been brought in from somewhere else. Briar walked closer, noticing the half-full page of notes in Fi's quick scrawl.

It took him a minute to find the girl that belonged with the handwriting, but when he did, he couldn't help but smile. Fi was partway up a high stepladder, a book resting open on her knees. Her hair had dried a little wild, clearly forgotten, and she had a smudge of ink on her cheek. She was totally enthralled by whatever she was reading, eyes wide and bright as she lost herself in the words.

Briar felt a pang imagining Fi in the great Library of Andar, with its two stories of books, the round balcony above lined by sunny picture windows. That was where she was supposed to be now—where they were both supposed to be. Not fighting every single day just to get back what they had lost, barely welcome among the last people of Andar. Not proving themselves worthy of titles they didn't want.

Briar's cape made the loose pages on the table flutter as he passed. Fi raised her head. She blinked a few times, and then her eyes lit up with excitement. "Briar!" she called, closing the book, her finger pinched to keep her place. It felt so good to hear her say his name with no *prince* attached.

"That's a good look for you," Briar said, admiring the stretch in Fi's legs as she perched on the step. And the ink smudge.

"It's a library jacket," she said offhand. Briar didn't really understand, but it was easy enough to smile at her as she balanced precariously on the stepladder, still clutching the book and fumbling down the steps. "You won't believe what I've discovered. Some of these books are centuries old—and I found something." She laid the book aside, tucking a blank piece of parchment between the pages. Then she fanned out the letters with blue ribbons. "One of the antique display boxes was filled with these—letters that the Lord of the Butterflies sent to Queen Aurora."

Briar didn't know the Lord of the Butterflies, but he knew Aurora well. She was the founder of the Order of the Divine Rose, the woman whose giant portrait hung over the stairs in the castle entryway, her golden hair and blue eyes shining and her red lips pressed into a secretive smile. She'd also built the great library, collecting the first books that eventually became the greatest store of magic knowledge ever assembled.

Fi rushed on, barely taking a second to breathe. "That's not the amazing part. I think the Lord of the Butterflies actually knew the Spindle Witch, and they both lived at the same time as Queen Aurora."

"What?" Briar asked, surprised.

Fi smoothed her hand over one of the pages. "In his letters to Aurora, the Lord of the Butterflies talks about a young

Witch of tremendous power, learning to spin it between her fingers into thread."

"Is that even possible?" Briar asked, trying to wrap his mind around it. "Could it really be the same Spindle Witch? This would have been centuries and centuries ago."

"You said it yourself: the Spindle Witch was ancient even before she came to your family's court. If I'm right about this, she's been around since before the founding of Andar. Can you imagine the significance?" Fi marveled, spinning away from the table.

"She could be more powerful than anyone ever imagined," Briar murmured.

"Not just that." Fi turned back to Briar so quickly she had to catch her hands in his cape. "If she's been around that long, and she is that powerful, she could have destroyed your kingdom anytime if she wanted. There's no need for curses or any of it." Fi's eyes flickered to his. "She lived at court, right? She became one the Great Witches and used her magic in service of Andar for, what . . . years? Decades?"

Unease crept up Briar's spine. "What are you saying?"

"I'm saying she must want something from Andar, something she can't get by just taking over the kingdom." Fi was looking beyond him now, seeing something else as her mind worked. "Something that even she, with all her great power, can't find."

Fi's hand slid down his chest, brushing the lapel of his beautiful new vest, but Briar had a feeling he knew what she was imagining. The old coat with its hidden code, the one everyone needed him to solve.

"Briar," she said quietly. "We have to find that book."

Briar felt that same dread roiling in his stomach. Fi seemed to notice his stony expression.

"I'm so sorry—I didn't even ask. How was the council? Are they going to help rescue your brother?"

The hopeful words crushed Briar all over again. They hadn't even talked about going after Sage. He was supposed to be a prince, but he hadn't had any power in that room—and he wouldn't until he had something he could offer.

"There's something I have to do first," he told Fi. "I have to find Camellia's book. The Paper Witch wants me to go on a dream journey. He thinks the answer is inside me, but I . . ."

Briar's mouth went dry. How could he ask Fi to go with him? She'd already risked her life for Briar, over and over, and he hadn't been able to do anything in return.

In the end, he didn't have to ask.

"Well . . ." Fi shrugged, running a hand through her hair. "Whatever it is, we'll do it together. We're partners, right?"

Suddenly, Briar felt like a great weight had been lifted from his shoulders. Maybe, with Fi by his side, nothing was impossible.

The braces of candles by the window sprang to life, hundreds of flames suddenly dancing and reflecting in the glass panes. Fi gasped.

"Did you do that?" she asked.

"No," he said haltingly. At least, he didn't think he had. Fi moved to the window, studying the intricate braces. Then her gaze was caught by something outside.

"Come look!" she urged, laying her forehead against the glass. Briar joined her, only to find that it wasn't just the library—candles were winking on all over Everlynd, hundreds of tiny flames dancing as the city of magic came alive with thousands and thousands of lights. Fi turned to Briar with a bright smile. Her tan skin was glowing, and she'd made the smudge on her face bigger with a careless brush of her hand.

"It's beautiful," Briar said. It felt like he was seeing Everlynd for the first time all over again. Part of him longed to stay here forever, because it reminded him of Andar and everything that had been ripped away from him. But another part wanted to leave this very second, because more and more there was only one thing that seemed to matter to Briar, and she was standing right in front of him.

"The candles are for you, Briar," Fi whispered. "They're welcoming you home."

"Fi," he said hoarsely, searching her eyes. He felt a pull like magic as he bent closer. Fi's head tipped toward him, and he could see the shudder of a breath on her lips. Her eyes closed. Briar felt his heart pounding as he leaned down.

Then, suddenly, Fi's fingers were pressed against his lips, pushing him back. Briar's heart plummeted. Before he could even figure out what went wrong, Fi rushed to explain.

"I'm not pushing you away. But we can't do this—*yet*." Her eyes searched his desperately. "There's something important you need to know first—lots of things, actually. Briar, how much do you know about the Lord of the Butterflies?"

# 16

### Red

**RED STARED OUT** the window, watching the candles flare to life across Everlynd like a field of fallen stars. They probably lit the whole city, but she could only see a tiny corner of it from where she lay propped up against the pillows of a plush bed, her damp curls soft against her neck. She'd been cleaned and bandaged, her ragged traveling clothes traded out for a loose, flowing nightshirt. The gossamer smell of lilac wafted from the vase of flowers on the chintzy dresser. In the warm lantern light, Red's eyes moved from the window to the silver tray set with delicate hand-painted porcelain and what remained of their meal. There was even a soft blanket on the floor where Cinzel slept, his snout twitching with exhausted little snores.

It was the nicest jail cell Red had ever been in. She could almost forget she was a prisoner, except for the guard outside the door and the shackle on her arm.

Red looked down at the metal cuff around her wrist and the chain that snaked across the soft cream blanket, attaching her to Shane. The huntsman dozed in the chair beside her, wearing the other half of the shackles. Red wasn't sure if the sight made her want to laugh or cry—maybe both at once.

She'd been in and out of consciousness since the outpost. All she had were hazy memories of Shane holding her, shaking her. Refusing to let her die.

They bled together with the other memories. Shane yelling at Red to change sides in the Forest of Thorns, Shane yelling her name as they tumbled end over end into the dark of the mines. Shane making her laugh, usually not on purpose. Shane making her heart ache with that steely gray gaze that seemed to pierce right through Red to the withered husk inside.

Shane had been yelling all the way to Everlynd. Demanding to stay with Red. Demanding Cinzel not be left behind. Demanding things *for* Red, demanding things *from* Red . . . Shane was a force of nature, and Red felt like she'd been swept up in a whirlwind.

But somehow, impossibly, Shane had kept her promises. Red was alive, and she was Shane's prisoner. The shackles that connected them had been the condition for bringing Red into the city. Runes in some magic language she couldn't read crawled over the heavy manacle, glimmering as she twisted her hand. It was a relic bound with oath magic that would stop her from using her magic as long as she wore it.

Red swallowed a bitter laugh. As if her magic had ever done her any good.

Red had spent most of her life hating the magic inside her. Her father taught her that magic was a corruption, and in some deep-down way Red had believed him even after he threw her away. The Spindle Witch hadn't needed Red for her magic—she just wanted an extra pair of hands, a little puppet on a string. She'd never had any proper training, no instruction in rituals or spell books or lost magic languages. Just the raw power inside her. Something she had to live with whether she wanted it or not.

That was why she preferred relics. Many of them could only be used by those with innate magic, but ultimately it was still a power that came from outside herself.

The tattoo on the back of her neck itched, like it always did when she thought of her magic. Red gritted her teeth so she wouldn't sink her nails into the skin.

If only something as simple as this shackle *could* get rid of her magic. No—she wouldn't be able to use it right now, but it was still inside her.

Red let the weight of the cuff drag her hand back to the bed. The chain rattled, and Shane's eyes flew open, the huntsman lurching up in her chair.

"Red, are you okay? Do you need anything?"

She sounded worried, and suddenly Red was angry. What right did Shane have to do this to her—to stay beside her, to be so infuriatingly loyal, to push herself into Red's space and her life and her head until thoughts and feelings of Shane forced everything else out?

*Shane. Shane. Shane.* Like a battering ram against Red's heart.

"I'm fine," she said, slumping down into the pillows. She blew a feather of damp hair out of her face. "In fact, the clearer my head gets, the less I can believe you actually brought me here."

"Because you still plan to betray me the first chance you get?" Shane asked warily.

Red's eyes flicked to the porcelain dishes. It would have been so easy to shatter one and make a weapon out of the shards. She hadn't even tried.

"Maybe not," she said, with a half-hearted shrug.

Shane didn't seem satisfied. Shane was *never* satisfied. She leaned forward with her chin braced in her hand, her serious eyes raking over Red's face.

"What would you do if I let you go?" she asked.

Red looked up at the ceiling, feeling suddenly dizzy. What would she do? She hadn't been lying about the Spindle Witch's fury. She also had no place else to go. Red rolled away as far as the shackle would let her so she didn't have to look Shane in the eye.

"Run away as far as I can and hope the Spindle Witch is too busy killing you to come after me."

It would mean never going back to the Forest of Thorns. It would mean never going home. Red tried not to think of what she would have to give up. Her eyes burned, and she squeezed them shut against the tears. Cinzel lifted his shaggy head off his paws, whining low.

Red shivered.

"Are you cold?" Shane asked. She leaned over Red, tugging the covers back up to her shoulder. "The healer said you should be feeling better by now. I'll get you another blanket." Shane started to stand up.

"Oh, you will, will you?" Red gave the chain between them a mocking little shake.

"Oh. Right." Shane sat back down, sheepish. "I'll call for the guard," she offered. "He's not doing anything anyway."

Red almost agreed, just to see if Shane would really order some stone-faced soldier to grab blankets and fluff pillows. But she didn't want some stranger in this space, another reminder of how powerless she was right now.

"Just climb into the bed with me," she said softly.

Shane froze, her expression instantly complicated. "Red . . ."

Red laughed weakly. "Don't worry. I'm too tired to try anything, and frankly, you're not looking your best." It was a lie, though. Even with her lip split and her face bruised, her hair in a tangle down her back, she was utterly captivating, and Red felt out of breath just looking at her.

Shane snorted, using the back of her hand to dab at her swollen lip. "Thanks."

"Besides, that chair doesn't look very comfortable, and you can't possibly go anywhere else." She tugged the cuff and then bit her lip. "Please."

Red hadn't even known how much she wanted Shane close to her until she had said it, but now she couldn't stand the possibility the other girl would say no. She didn't know why she kept asking Shane for things she couldn't have. To run away with her. To make her forget everything, just for the length of a dance. She couldn't remember anymore why she hadn't kissed Shane then, in that one glittering moment on the balcony, the closest she'd ever come to feeling truly free. She wished that was the kiss she had to remember—not their kiss outside the Forest of Thorns, bitter with the word *goodbye*.

She could see the moment the girl caved.

"Scoot over," Shane said, scrubbing her hand through her hair. "And I warn you, I don't want to wake up with that wolf in the bed."

Red smiled as she made a space, trading a quick look with Cinzel. He didn't usually get up on the bed—but she'd like to see Shane try to stop him.

Red felt strangely uncertain as Shane lay down next to her, maybe because there was something more intimate about this moment than any other they'd shared. Shane lay stiffly on her back, and Red suddenly didn't know whether she wanted to curl toward her or turn away. Red wasn't sure what she was asking. She wasn't really sure what Shane was offering.

This moment felt fragile. Breakable. And so unbearably warm. Shane's affection was like a sudden heat, thawing Red's frozen bones. It hurt to have all that feeling return at once, but she still longed for more.

So why couldn't she bring herself to move any closer?

Shane sighed, grumbling under her breath. "Can't sleep like this." Then she rolled over, chain jangling, and suddenly she was right up close, her heavy arm thrown across Red's waist, her eyes stubbornly closed. Like it meant nothing to be this close, even though Red could feel how fast her heart was beating.

Red breathed out, sinking into the heat of Shane's arm around her. Her eyes roved over the huntsman's pale face. She had the sense that she was stealing something, secret little memories she wasn't supposed to have—of the rhythm of

Shane's heartbeat, the twitch of her toes against Red's under the covers, the gurgle of her stomach that made Red giggle in spite of herself. Dreams as delicate as spider silk, just waiting to break.

She could lie to herself for a little while. Feel the supple curves of Shane's body, the tease of her breath against her face. She could play pretend, like she had so many times.

But the reality would always be waiting. There was no safe place in the world for Red now that she had left the Spindle Witch's side. Maybe the Spindle Witch would take her back if Red brought her Briar Rose and personally killed the others, erasing her failure with blood. But she couldn't do it anymore.

Red had lost to Shane in every way imaginable. It was over.

# 17

## Fi

**FI BENT OVER** the table in the library, examining the letters in the low light. All but one candle in the table brace had flickered out. It was long past midnight, and the library was silent around her, the hush so complete she could imagine she was the only person in the whole city. Fi knew she should be exhausted, but she felt wide awake. With Briar's help, she had finally gotten all the letters into chronological order so she could read the story of Queen Aurora and the Lord of the Butterflies from beginning to end. Or at least half of it.

She glanced over at Briar. He was asleep at the other end of the table, slumped in between a stack of books and the unsteady tower of plates on which an attendant had brought their dinner. They'd eaten every crumb. Fi had even used her finger to scoop up the last of the gravy, which was the kind of thing she'd expect Shane to do. Briar had actually picked up his plate and licked it, though, so at least she was in good company.

Fi studied his soft face for a moment, watching his shallow breaths tease a piece of paper trapped under his hand. Then she dragged the sputtering candle closer and turned back to the letters, careful not to drip pearls of wax onto the ancient parchment.

There were twenty-two letters in all. Only a few were dated, so she'd had to use clues in the letters themselves to guess at how they fit together. That was even more challenging because she only had one half of the conversation. All but one of the letters had been written by the Lord of the Butterflies. The only letter in Aurora's hand was the last one, and it seemed unfinished, the crisp ink lines stopping abruptly halfway down the page. Fi wondered if it was a draft or if Aurora had changed her mind and decided not to send it.

She'd read all of the letters through three times already, looking for more clues about the Spindle Witch. There wasn't much to find. Even in his private letters to Aurora, the Lord of the Butterflies only hinted at the Witch's power, and he never called her by a name, only referring to her as *the little spider*. But though she'd gone in looking for something else, Fi found herself fascinated by this glimpse into the relationship between two of the most powerful Witches who had ever lived. She couldn't tell exactly what they'd been to each other, but reading the letters in order, she could watch as their close friendship decayed into something bitter and twisted.

The Lord of the Butterflies's early letters were full of anecdotes from his travels, wondrous places he'd discovered, and ingenious spells he'd devised to solve the problems of lesser Witches. Crammed in between the tight lines of text were intricate diagrams she didn't understand, like the rough sketch of a person over whose body the Lord of the Butterflies had drawn lines of magic instead of veins. Every letter held veiled invitations for Aurora to join him, baited with his disdain for her life at court.

*As my brilliant former student, I trust you'll recognize the significance of this at once. Though if you continue neglecting your magic studies for the drudgery of politics, I wonder if you will in time become someone who needs the answers handed to you.*

Fi traced the line, feeling a rush of excitement. *My former student.* It was a phrase he used several times. She was almost positive that Aurora had studied magic with the Lord of the Butterflies before she became Andar's first queen. He must not have been cursed at that point, and Fi didn't think he was cursed yet when he wrote the letters, either, since he seemed to take great pleasure in skillfully dodging Aurora's invitations to come back to the capital.

Fi glanced down at her fingerless glove. She'd spent the entire last year digging up every scrap of information she could find about the Lord of the Butterflies, but for the first time, she was starting to get a sense of him as a person. He was enigmatic, playful, deliberately mysterious. Fi could tell he enjoyed the game of writing his letters like they were riddles, testing Aurora to see if she could decipher what he'd discovered or where he was headed next. He and Fi even had a few things in common, namely an unquenchable thirst for knowledge. But he was also a Witch of immense power, and he had the arrogance that came with it.

*A Witch came to me the other day. He had grown fearful of*

*his own magic after accidentally starting a fire in his son's nursery. He wanted me to take his power from him. Though I never approve of wasting one's innate talents, in his cowardice the man presented me with a golden opportunity to investigate something I had been thinking on for some time. The veins of magic within Witches can be manipulated, the flow widening or narrowing as a Witch's power grows or withers away unused. But could they be severed entirely?*

And then on the next page:

*As agreed, I extracted all of the magic from the Witch and severed the veins of power inside him. The spell stripped him of his magic, but it produced an intriguing side effect that I had not anticipated, and which will require further consideration before repeating the experiment. Delman Bellicia is not only magicless, but completely immune to magic of any kind. I am eager to find out if this immunity will pass to his descendants.*

Delman Bellicia. The name had practically leapt off the page when she read it. Delman was Armand Bellicia's ancestor, the first Duke of Bellicia, and apparently the source of his family's immunity to magic. The Lord of the Butterflies hadn't just severed one man from his power, but his entire line. And he thought it nothing but a curiosity. The Witch's genius was undeniable, but so was the callousness with which he approached his magical research and spell crafting.

The Spindle Witch didn't show up until the ninth letter— or rather, *the little spider*. Fi could tell the Lord of the Butterflies had been fascinated by her magic, what he called her *limitless potential*. That was when the letters started to change. Where the Lord of the Butterflies had been friendly, Fi began to detect a sour undercurrent of resentment, which built until every word dripped with condescension. By half-way through, it was obvious they were in disagreement about the Spindle Witch. She wished she had Aurora's letters, too, but she tried to piece the argument together from the Lord of the Butterflies's biting replies.

*Each new letter from you brings a new disappointment. You are becoming dangerously ordinary, Aurora, swayed by the petty concerns of very small minds. Do not expect that a Witch of your ability will be able to keep the little spider forever locked in a cage. Her magic is truly unique. Neither of us knows what she might be capable of.*

Fi shivered. The Spindle Witch had been locked away. And the Lord of the Butterflies had wanted to free her. Knowing who *the little spider* would eventually become, the implications were chilling.

The silence felt oppressive now, as if she were waiting for something to break it, listening for any sound in the dark library. Fi knew this time of night could play tricks on the mind, but she couldn't deny that the candle seemed to shudder every time she traced her finger over the line about the girl learning to spin. The rustle of the paper was like a whispering voice, someone speaking urgently to her from very far away.

By the last of his letters, the Lord of the Butterflies was downright hostile. Fi could almost feel him hunched over the parchment, writing so fast the words came out tight and angry.

*I have made my decision, Aurora. Don't flatter yourself that you can force my hand.*

Fi wondered what he'd made a decision about. She lifted

Aurora's half-finished letter, wishing it filled in more of the blanks. In looping handwriting that reminded Fi of the Divine Rose script, the letter opened stiffly and formally: *I regret that we parted on such bad terms.* After that, there were a few lines scratched out, the heavy quill strokes gouged into the paper. When she held the letter up against the light, Fi could just make out a few more phrases: *I miss our closeness*, drowned in black ink, and then much angrier, *It is not your decision to make.* But she kept stopping on the next paragraph—the same place Aurora had stopped, leaving it forever unfinished.

*We have known each other a long time, but don't make the mistake of underestimating me. Your magic may be greater than mine, but I will do whatever I must to protect the people of Andar. I will not allow anyone to stand in my way.*

That was where it ended. Fi didn't know if there had been more letters, lost or destroyed over the centuries, or if the two Witches had stopped writing each other at that point, their friendship severed. Whatever had happened, their story was long over.

*Or was it?* Fi looked at her gloved hand, dark against the paper. The Spindle Witch was still around. Fi carried the Lord of the Butterflies's curse, and Briar was Aurora's descendant, a Rose of Andar with light magic just like hers. Maybe Briar was right, and there was a reason they'd been pulled together after all.

Fi checked one more time to make sure Briar was asleep. He hadn't moved, his head still pillowed in the crook of his arm. The last candle guttered in the pool of wax. Her chair creaked as she eased her glove off one finger at a time, revealing the swallowtail butterfly mark. In the unsteady light, it seemed to flicker, and she could almost feel those paper-thin wings prickling on her skin. She hated looking at it, but she couldn't pretend that was why her insides were squirming into a knot.

She still hadn't told Briar about the curse. She'd meant to, the moment he found her in the library. But she'd gotten caught up in the letters, and so had Briar. Fi knew she should wake him up right now and tell him the truth before she lost her nerve. But even in the soft light, his face looked so tired. He was carrying so much on his shoulders—the hope of an entire kingdom. How could she add to that burden?

Fi folded her arms on the table and leaned forward to rest her chin on her crossed wrists, studying Briar's face from only a breath away. He was beautiful, always, even with circles as dark as bruises under his eyes. The gold circlet had slid out of his hair and lay forgotten on the table. A little smudge of gravy on the side of his mouth made her smile. She squinted, struggling to read the paper hidden under his hand until she realized she wasn't seeing letters, but numbers. Briar had fallen asleep over Camellia's book code. His splayed fingers covered most of the page, but Fi didn't need to see it—she'd looked at it so often she had the numbers memorized by now.

Briar had said the answer was in a dream journey, and she'd promised they'd take it together, as partners. Fi glanced at the butterfly mark one more time. Then she slipped the glove back on. The candle went dark, as suddenly as if she'd snuffed it out.

She hadn't even been in Everlynd one whole day. She still had time. They would take the dream journey together, and then she'd tell him—everything.

# 18

~~~»> «<~~~

## Shane

**PERRIN'S HOUSE REMINDED** Shane of a mix between the Nenroas' artifact-filled estate and a homey kitchen. She liked it. She liked the easygoing boy who'd joined them for breakfast at the prison-slash-guesthouse, too, passing around the melon slices while Fi perched on the end of the bed, too busy waxing on about the library to notice Cinzel stealing her honey bread. Briar nodded along, never taking his eyes off her, but if he'd actually absorbed any of what Fi said, Shane would eat her boots.

Shane thought it said a lot about Perrin that he'd left two total strangers in his kitchen unsupervised while he went to collect Fi. Briar was apparently meeting with Nikor, *again*. Shane didn't envy him. One quick meeting with that stuffed shirt while he looked down his nose at her and told her to be grateful for Everlynd's overwhelming generosity had been more than enough.

Shane leaned back against a high workbench covered with a jumble of tools—knives and hanging brass scales, but also hammers and spools of thread, a corkscrew, and two knitting needles poked through a worn pair of socks. Next to her, Red peered at a shelf clustered with stoppered bottles and small glass vials. The whole room smelled strongly of spices, mint and sweet lavender and loamy herbs growing in globes of colored glass suspended from the ceiling.

It was probably a good thing they'd left Cinzel behind. Shane had a feeling he would have gone through the whole place like a wrecking ball.

Red's presence was being uneasily tolerated by the Witches of Everlynd thanks to the cuff suppressing her magic. The wolf, on the other hand, wasn't allowed to roam the city. They'd left him tucked up under the sunny window with a king's ransom of a feast to keep him busy. Red had whistled twice as they left, and the wolf had obediently dropped to his stomach, looking pathetic but not trying to follow her.

It got Shane wondering what Red's relationship with the wolf really was. She'd never thought about how Red controlled the monster wolves in the Forest of Thorns. Shane had assumed all Witches were either like Briar Rose, showing off his magic left and right, or like the Paper Witch, who Shane suspected would take most of his secrets to his grave.

So much of Red was still a mystery. Shane studied the girl as she ran her fingers down the row of bottles, her nails clinking against the jewel-bright glass. She wore a cream-colored blouse under a black bodice, paired with a red traveling skirt that swished around her ankles. Shane had borrowed some new clothes herself, but she'd held on to her dusk-red coat, now sewn with dark patches and thick cross-stitches like it had its own battle scars.

She was still getting used to the shackles. The chain pulled tight as Red abandoned the shelves and escalated to rummaging through the cabinets.

"Stop snooping around in Perrin's stuff," Shane warned, shuffling closer.

"Aren't you the least bit curious about him?" Red knelt down, her head disappearing into a creaky cupboard. "You're really far too trusting of your allies."

"I don't feel like you're in any position to be telling me that," Shane groused.

"Actually, I'm in the perfect position," Red threw over her shoulder. "Since I took advantage of that trust myself. I'm just watching out for you."

Shane didn't believe that for a second. Red's finger slid greedily along the worn spines of oversize spell books, pausing on the thickest one.

"Now, this is interesting."

"Red!" Shane protested as the girl stood, pulling out a heavy tome. The leather cover was cracked and soft from wear, but by far the most interesting detail was the metal runes that ran like a chain along the top and bottom. "Is that a locked spell book?" Shane asked, drifting closer.

Locked books were extremely rare and often worth a fortune. Of course, the spells inside were supposed to be astoundingly dangerous. The treasure hunter inside Shane itched to pry it open.

"Well, now who's curious?" Red teased. She hefted the spell book, considering. "There's usually a trick to opening these." She ran her finger along the runes. When nothing happened, she braced her hands on either end of the spine and pinched the edges. The cover sprang free with a small click. With a conspiratorial look at Shane, Red flipped the book open.

"What are you doing with that?" Perrin demanded from the doorway.

Shane jerked in surprise, and the book flew out of Red's startled hands. The pages crunched as it splayed facedown on the floor.

Fi appeared behind Perrin, rushing over to pick up the book and dust it off. She was still wearing the librarian's jacket, and she'd crammed a few papers and pens and a lump that looked suspiciously like a whole book into the giant pockets.

Red crossed her arms. "That's at least half your fault for startling me," she said defensively—not an apology even by Shane's standards. But Fi was too enthralled by the book to notice, sliding onto a high stool as she used her thumb to smooth out the bent pages.

"No real harm done," she decided after a moment of inspection.

Shane wasn't so sure. Perrin still stood frozen in the doorway, a strangely wary expression on his face. At first Shane thought he was looking at Red. Then she realized he was staring at the spell book Fi was practically nose to nose with.

"That isn't a book that should be opened lightly." Perrin's hand gripped the doorframe with bruising force, and the note of warning in his voice immediately put Shane on edge.

Of course, it went right over Fi's head. "What? Why?" she asked absently, not even looking up.

Perrin pursed his lips. "We could all get into a lot of

trouble over this book," he admitted. "I'm not even supposed to have it, much less show it to outsiders. No offense."

"None taken," Shane said with a shrug. "But it's a little late for that." She jerked her thumb at Fi, who had leaned in close and was flipping back and forth between two pages, her lips forming silent words.

"Look, it can't be read," Perrin insisted. "Trust me, I've spent many nights trying. The spells inside are all locked, and the words are in an old code. You're just wasting your time." He leaned over the table, holding out his hand for the book.

Fi finally lifted her head. "The spells may be locked, but I can read some of the text."

"What?" Perrin breathed. He sidestepped the table to peer over Fi's shoulder. "Impossible. Which part?"

Fi angled the book to face him, and Shane craned her head to get a look herself. Not that she really knew what she was looking at.

"See these lines here, the ones that look like they were written in a different hand? It's sort of a code, but it's one I recognize."

"And you're sure you can read it?" Perrin asked, his voice strained.

Fi shrugged. "For the most part. I don't know all the words, but I can piece it together. This part says *oathbound by blood*. I think they're talking about early Witches giving up their names and taking Witch titles."

Shane felt Red tense. *At the mention of blood magic?* The thorn rod flashed through Shane's mind, snarled with those bloodstained threads. Shane didn't know exactly what spell had bound Red to that rod, but in her experience, things that had to be sworn *by blood* always took a nasty turn in the end.

Fi was in full lecture mode, tracing the old runes that had been penned in along the spine. "A historian named Notarra found a diary left by Aurora's king consort. He used this code, which she theorized may have been the basis for the Divine Rose language. It's fascinating, really."

"Not as fascinating as you think," Red coughed none too quietly under her breath. Shane couldn't stifle her snort.

Perrin stared intensely at Fi, his face torn with indecision before he let out a long, slow breath. "There's a passage I want to show you," he said. His hands trembled slightly as he pushed up his sleeves and started flipping through the pages, faster and faster. "Something that might be the key to everything if you could translate it . . ."

Shane cleared her throat. "And you're sure you want to show *all* of us this passage?" she asked, tugging meaningfully on the cuff that bound her to Red. She didn't want to be left out, but she wasn't trying to stir up trouble, either.

Perrin froze. His eyes cut between them uncertainly.

"We'll make ourselves scarce," Shane offered, ignoring Red's offended little huff.

"Wait." Fi held up a hand. "I don't think you should go." Her sharp eyes fixed on Perrin. "This is about the Spindle Witch, isn't it?"

Perrin didn't answer, but he didn't have to. His grim expression said it all.

Fi's fingers gripped the edges of the book. "When I was in the library yesterday, I found clues that the Spindle Witch has been searching for something in Andar for a long time. You know what it is, don't you?"

If Perrin clenched his jaw any harder, he was going to break a tooth. "I have a suspicion," he admitted.

"You've trusted us this far," Fi pressed. "And I doubt there's much about the Spindle Witch that Red doesn't already know. Maybe she can even fill in a few blanks."

All eyes turned to Red, whose lips were sealed so tight Shane thought it would take a chisel to pry them open.

"All right." Perrin's body sagged, and he flipped to the middle of the book, smoothing the page down where the corner was fraying. "It's this part right here."

Fi laid the book onto the table, bracing herself above it. "It's the same code, all right. See these hatch marks that look almost like *X*s? That's not a mark that appears in the Divine Rose script." Fi's chin jerked. "Shane, get over here. I need your hands."

"As long as you don't need my brain," Shane grumbled. It all looked like a bunch of Witch gibberish to her. Still, she pressed her fingers to the page where Fi indicated, covering all the sharp little X marks jutting up like thorns. She could feel the faded ink sticking to her fingertips, the parchment crackling with age.

"So if we cover these, we reveal the true message, and what we're left with is . . ." Fi tugged at her earlobe. "It's an account of the first Witch Queen Aurora concealing . . . no, maybe *forbidding* some kind of magic. It's about the method she used. But this can't be right." Fi's eyebrows lifted to her hairline. "Aurora was—*unraveling?*—something called the Siphoning Spells."

Red flinched. Perrin banged his fist into the table. "I knew it!"

"What are the Siphoning Spells?" Shane asked, feeling like she'd missed something.

"They're extremely powerful forbidden spells, locked away since Aurora's time," Perrin explained. "The only surviving references I've found are in the most ancient and obscure texts. From what I've been able to piece together, they allow a Witch to drain life and magic from any living thing and take it for themselves."

Fi looked troubled. "That sounds similar to the Spindle Witch's magic."

"I thought so, too," Perrin agreed. "But these spells are on a whole different level. I can only imagine what someone as powerful as the Spindle Witch would be capable of if she had them."

"She'd kill thousands."

Red spoke up suddenly from Shane's side. Her face was ashen, her whole body tensed as if ready to run.

"She'd drain the life from entire cities, leaving everyone dead. That magic she takes—it's what keeps her alive and restores her power. I saw it sometimes, when I brought her relics to drain the magic from. She never took the veil off, but her hands . . ." Red swallowed, her eyes white and terrified. "Sometimes they're smooth and warm and human, and sometimes they're hard and brittle as bone . . . when she needs to eat. No matter how much she takes, it's never enough."

A nasty taste like bile hit the back of Shane's throat. The Spindle Witch had drained Andar down to the marrow, transformed it into endless wastes and spitting sandstorms. And *that* wasn't enough? "I see why the wicked Witch wants these spells, but what good are they to us?"

Perrin tugged at his chin. "That's what I've been *borrowing* forbidden books to find out. Aurora deemed siphoning magic so dangerous it had to be sealed away forever. But I think the Siphoning Spells could also be used against the Spindle Witch, to drain all the magic she's stolen and end her life once and for all."

That sounded far too good to be true. "So crack open the spell book," Shane suggested. "Let's do that."

"If only it were so simple." Perrin lifted another heavy tome onto the table, this one with gilded roses set into the cover. He flipped through the delicate pages, stopping on a spread inked with the twining script of the Divine Rose. "Try to read this page," he suggested, pushing the book toward Fi.

Fi dutifully bent over the book, reaching out to trace one of the rose vines. The ink came to life under her finger. The curls of the script slithered away from each other until they were nothing but a tangle of pen strokes, the swooping runes vanishing into vines and heavy roses.

"That's the magic you were just reading about. Aurora literally *unraveled* the knowledge." Perrin scrubbed a hand through his short hair. "This page isn't even one of the Siphoning Spells—it's just an entry where they're mentioned. No one knows where the actual spells are or how they're hidden, but it's said only Aurora's descendants can reach them."

Shane gritted her teeth. *That explained why the Spindle Witch was so hell-bent on getting Briar Rose.* The room suddenly felt colder, the shadows pressing close against her back.

"Why didn't Aurora just destroy the spells entirely?" Shane growled, waving her hand and accidentally tugging Red closer. Red still looked pale and shaken. Shane fought the urge to put an arm around her.

"Because Aurora knew no knowledge, once discovered, is ever really gone. The best she could do was leave it in the right hands." Perrin closed the book slowly. "The reason I've been going through these books is because I think that before Andar fell, the Great Witches were working on crafting their own Siphoning Spell. I've been trying to find it."

Fi's eyes lit up. "Maybe that's what Camellia's code is pointing to. The Great Witches' spell. Or even the original Siphoning Spells. She was head of the Order of the Divine Rose, after all. If anyone knew how to access those forbidden spells, it'd be her."

Shane wrinkled her nose. "So ultimately, everything is still riding on whether Briar can dream up the right book."

"Maybe not." Perrin's eyes lit up. "If the Spindle Witch really is after the Siphoning Spells, I might have another lead. The man who was said to have created those original Siphoning Spells was a great scholar of magic."

*A great scholar?* That sounded awfully familiar to Shane. "I think we took a detour through his mines," she said, remembering the cavern where all the crystal had been gouged out. "Real homey place."

"And I'm pretty sure I know who that scholar was." Fi's voice was quiet, her gloved hand curled into a tight fist. "Because I was just reading about a Witch who experimented with draining the magic out of other Witches. The Lord of the Butterflies."

"What?!" Shane reared back. "*That* Lord of the Butterflies?" she demanded, looking pointedly at Fi's hand. Fi shot her a look sharp enough to draw blood. Like Shane would go blabbing her partner's secrets right here in front of everyone!

"But we saw his mark in the mines," Red protested. "It wasn't a butterfly. It was like an X and some eyes." She grabbed one of the blank pieces of parchment on the workbench, scratching the mark with a long goose quill. "See? Doesn't look much like a butterfly to me."

"Are you sure?" Fi asked, reaching for the quill. Red handed it to her, and Fi bent over the paper, adding one swooping line to either side of the X to make wings. Shane gave a low whistle. She could see it now: a butterfly with the eye pattern on either wing, staring back at them.

Perrin waved a hand. "The scholar, the Lord of the Butterflies—whoever he was, one of Everlynd's oldest logs mentioned a workshop of his at the very boundary of the city. It's hidden in the waterfall cliffs. It didn't mean anything to me when I read it, but now . . ." He shrugged. "Maybe there's nothing about the Siphoning Spells there. Still, as long as we have a treasure hunter on hand . . ."

Those words were music to Shane's ears. She grinned, clapping Red on the shoulder. "I guess that means we're up."

Red's mouth fell open in surprise. "You can't be serious."

Fi looked equally incredulous. "You're going to search out the Lord of the Butterflies's secret workshop *handcuffed* . . . to *her*?"

"I'm right here," Red protested.

Shane snorted. "Well, I'm definitely not taking these

cuffs off till we're miles from this city and I know Red can't get up to anything."

"Still right here," Red repeated, annoyed.

Fi's face was pinched into that classic worrywart expression she got so often Shane wouldn't be surprised if it stuck that way. "Shane, you can't. It's too dangerous," she protested.

"Says the person who's about to go face down *someone else's* nightmares." The dream journey hadn't sounded all that safe when Perrin explained it over breakfast.

Fi still looked put out.

"Oh, come on—you know how these treasure hunts go," Shane consoled her. "*If* it's even there, *if* we've got the right Witch, *if* there's anything left after all this time . . . I can handle it."

"I don't suppose I get a say in this?" Red asked, miffed.

"You're my prisoner," Shane reminded her. "Prisoners don't get a say in anything."

Fi gave her a long, hard look. Then she sighed, rubbing her forehead. "I guess I can't stop you," she muttered.

Shane slugged her shoulder. "That's the ringing endorsement I was hoping for."

Perrin eased the spell book back into the cabinet. "Sorry I can't go along. As the only Witch who uses dream magic in Everlynd, I have to stick around here in case anything goes wrong with the dream journey. But there's a map that shows that area of the falls. Maybe in the archives?"

*Maybe in the archives* didn't sound like a fun start to Shane. Nor did it sound very wolf friendly.

Perrin seemed to guess what she was thinking. "Sorry I

can't be more specific. No one's really explored out there, since it's so close to the storm. It doesn't take much to get thrown off the cliffs. You'll have to be careful—not least because that's the area closest to where the Witch Hunters have been encroaching."

"Sounds about right for a secret Witch lair," Shane replied. But she wasn't put off. After all the sitting around she'd been doing, she wouldn't mind a little exercise—or the chance to bust some heads.

Perrin latched the cabinet closed and shot Fi a smile. "Well, unless anyone else has any forbidden secrets they want to share, it's about time to get ready for your dream journey. Why don't we go save Briar from Nikor?"

Briar would probably appreciate it, Shane thought, after having his ear talked off by stuffy councilors for hours on end. Just one more of those little official things Shane had escaped by ditching her crown.

Still, Fi hesitated. "I wish I was going with you," she said, fidgeting with her glove.

Shane knew what a lead on the Lord of the Butterflies meant to her partner. Honestly, Briar was lucky she wasn't ditching him to chase down that ruin right now. "We can always go back. And I promise I'll take a charcoal rubbing of every rune and squiggle and ugly sigil in the place, just for you."

Fi rolled her eyes—fondly, probably. "Just be careful," she said, nudging Shane's shoulder.

"Right back at you."

# 19

## Fi

**THE SILENT LAKE** spread out around Fi and Briar like a pool of gleaming black ink. The night sky was dark, the stars muted by a layer of clouds. They sat face-to-face in a small rowboat on the great lake at the center of Everlynd. Briar pulled the oars into the boat, leaving the little craft to drift, turning gentle circles in the water. Fi lowered her hand over the side, dragging her fingers to make ripples across the surface. The cold water made her shiver. Lanterns glowed along the shore, a glimmering halo of lights that danced in the mirror of the water.

Her eyes fixed on the brightest glow: the lantern in Perrin's hand as he stood at the end of the dock, growing smaller and smaller.

Fi looked down at the glass bauble in her lap. It was the heart of a small hourglass, barely the length of her palm. The golden sand inside shimmered as she tipped it back and forth. Their second day in Everlynd had gone by in a whirl, and though the Paper Witch and Perrin had explained the dream journey several times, Fi still felt like she had no idea what to expect when she broke the stem of the hourglass and plunged them into the dream.

"NO ONE'S ATTEMPTED *anything like this since the Dream Witch herself was alive," Perrin admitted, spinning the little hourglass with an absent finger. "My great-aunt was born in Everlynd. When she gave up her name and took her Witch title, they gave it to the lake in her honor. Use her dream dust at the heart of Evista Lake—that's where it'll have the most power."*

*He unhooked the glass bauble from its frame and handed it to Fi.*

*"To find your answers, Briar is going to have to get into the deepest parts of his subconscious. It can get dicey in there without a guide."*

*"I take it you can't guide us?" Fi guessed, folding her hand around the cool glass.*

*Perrin shrugged. "I'm not nearly that powerful, I'm afraid." His smile faded as he caught Fi's shoulder, looking at her with strangely serious eyes. "Fi . . . when you walk into dreams like this, there's no way to avoid nightmares. If Briar is able to reach the deepest parts of his own mind, he'll be at the mercy of the darkness inside him. It'll be up to you to protect him until he finds what he needs."*

The words rang in Fi's head as she looked across the boat at Briar. She would protect him, no matter the cost. Over his shoulder, she could still see the great whirl of the sandstorm at the edge of the horizon, but here the wind was soft, only strong enough to chase Briar's hair into his eyes. He had left the cape behind and was dressed much as he had been the very first time she saw him: in soft tailored pants under a cream silk shirt, with his old blue coat rippling from his shoulders, the velvet ragged in a few places but cleaned and patched. Perrin had helped Fi find an outfit that suited her, too, pants and a vest under a black coat that reminded her of the old brown one. She felt a little more like herself, though she still missed her traveling hat.

Fi took a steadying breath and glanced back toward the lights of Everlynd. She'd already spent one night and one full day here; almost half her time was gone before the Butterfly Curse would catch up. She shook the thought away. The only thing she could do now was not waste another second.

"Are you ready?" she asked. Briar nodded, their knees brushing as he leaned toward her. Fi leaned in, too, until they were crouched in the center of the boat, only a breath apart. "We only get one chance at this," she reminded him, closing her fist around the tiny hourglass.

Briar gave her a small smile. "Then we'll have to make it count."

Fi squeezed the delicate glass between her hands, snapping the tiny stem between the two globes and letting the sand run out into the boat. The fine dust rose into the air, twisting like a living thing—a sparkle of gold in the darkness that surrounded them.

Fi expected to choke as the dream dust filled her lungs, but the breath she took felt more like the warm air of a sunny afternoon. Fi's eyes were suddenly unbearably heavy, and she felt herself slumping into Briar. Her last impression was of the hazy stars overhead, growing farther and farther away.

Fi blinked at the sudden brightness, shading her eyes against the daylight. She was still on the lake, she thought at first, looking around at the expanse of water and the distant golden cliffs. Except it didn't look quite right. The waterfalls were too close, gushing great oceans of water into the lake, which seemed to be rising.

Fi took a step back. She wasn't on the boat anymore. She was standing at the edge of a small island, the water lapping the sand almost like a seashore. Briar lay in the sand behind her. Worry surged through Fi as she rushed over, kneeling beside him.

He was breathing—she could see the steady rise and fall of his chest. He was just asleep. This must be the dream, then, and Briar was in deeper than she was. Perrin had seemed to think the prince's long years of slumber would allow him to get to the deepest levels of the unconscious. Fi just hadn't expected it to happen so quickly.

She looked around, trying to get her bearings. Perrin had said that everyone saw something different. Briar would be in a different place than she was, a different dream. The body lying before her was Fi's desire to protect him taking form.

*"See, you can take control of a dream,"* she remembered Perrin saying, *turning a tall hourglass filled with crystal-bright pebbles. "But it takes focus, and years and years of practice. That's where your guide would normally come in. You guys are on your own. Just remember that your feelings are the most important thing. Feel as strongly as you can, and the dream will respond. It's thinking that will get you in trouble."*

As she got up, looking around, Fi thought she sort of understood what Perrin meant. Her brain wanted to make sense of the landscape around her, but the scene shifted like running paint, the lake at Everlynd blurring into a seashore. The rich colors of a low sun drenched the whole world in hues of red. The water was still dark, just as it had been when they floated on the silent lake. This was her dreamscape of Evista.

Fi glanced back at Briar. He was still asleep, but somehow roses had begun growing out of the sand around him, trapping him in a cage of vines and thorns. Brilliant red roses flared like fire in the deep rust sunset, their petals falling to the sand like drops of blood.

Fi's hand was suddenly wet, and when she looked down, the finger she had pricked on the bone spindle was bleeding, a red ribbon of blood twining around her hand. The drops turned to rose petals as they fell. Fi watched in fascination, reminding herself this was a dream. She wondered if her mind had put the cage of roses around Briar, or if that had something to do with the dream he was in.

A shiver ran down Fi's spine at the same time as a cloud passed over the low red sun. The waters of the lake had become choppy. Waves rose from the still surface, and ripples cut paths across the top as something slithered underneath.

Fi's pulse jumped. Almost as though it could sense her fear, the thing in the water turned, heading right for her. Fi held her ground at the edge of the sand and let it come.

*Don't be afraid,* she reminded herself. *You are the protector of Briar Rose.*

Suddenly, there was a weight in Fi's hands. A rope had

appeared in her fist, a heavy gold ring tied at the end. This she knew how to use. Confidence rose through her, calming her jumping nerves. She unspooled a length of the rope and let it hang at her elbow, ready to spin out into a quick strike.

The thing moving under the water had almost reached the shore. The formless nightmare creature oozed forward until it touched the trailing grains of gold sand. Then it began to uncurl, rising up like a man. Only it wasn't. It was eerily misshapen, the pearlescent green color of dark seawater and only barely in the shape of a person, with overlong limbs. It heaved forward, stretching its neck out toward Fi as its body lurched after it like a rolling wave. Its mouth was wide open, revealing rows of teeth as tiny and sharp as needles. Fi dodged, and the teeth closed over nothing, snapping loudly together.

Fi couldn't stop her heart from stuttering as more lumps of nightmare formed farther out in the water, all heading for the island. This was what Perrin had warned her about. These were Briar's nightmares trying to devour them.

Fi seized the rope, swinging it at her side, and then used her elbow to whip it forward into the creature that was reaching for her. The golden ring struck the long, inky torso with enough force to break all the way through the sludge, exploding out the creature's back in a spray of thick oily drops. The needle-like teeth shrieked against each other as the creature fell back into the lake, dissolving.

*At least the rope worked.*

The victorious feeling was short-lived. There were already a dozen more nightmare creatures headed for her. A glance backward showed that Briar's cage of roses now surrounded his body like a coffin. Fi took a few steps up the shore to give herself more space to maneuver. She had no intention of letting the creatures get any closer to the sleeping prince. She dug her heels in, surprised to find her feet suddenly bare against the soft sand.

Fi had always thought of her rope as a tool rather than a weapon—something she could use to climb, to mark a path, to reach something high. But she had learned to use it to defend herself, too. She forced out a deep breath and started the heavy ring spinning on the end of the rope. The trick with the rope was to think ahead, to know every move she was going to make and not lose any momentum. Even when the rope came back to her, she would try to catch it against her arm or shoulder and absorb the movement into the next attack.

Fi watched six of the nightmare creatures emerging from the glassy water, heads raising one by one, eyeless faces still somehow fixed toward her. Their teeth rattled, gleaming in their translucent forms as they grinned. Fear sat like a pit in her stomach, making those smiles grow wider, longer, crueler. As though they knew. Maybe they did. Perrin's warning about her feelings being the most important thing flashed through Fi's mind, and she tried to fight down her panic, forcing her mind to run scenarios like a chess game.

The first long leg touched the shore, and like a signal, all the creatures were moving toward her at once. Fi was moving, too.

She whipped the rope over her head and then tossed it low, swinging it in a wide arc to take out two of the creatures still forming at the edge of the lake, unable to dodge. That still left four intact. The closest monster had lunged for Fi, just as she had predicted, and she ducked under the inky curl of arm that snatched at her, pulling the rope back so it burst into the creature's head from behind, splattering it into a shower of seawater.

She caught the rope against her shoulder. The next moves she had to guess at. Two creatures were coming toward her, one so tall it bent all the way over Fi like a rotted weeping willow. The other heaved itself across the sand on its misshapen arms. Fi threw the rope forward, slamming it into the teeth of the willow monster with a snap of her wrist that made seawater rain down like blood. As the ring fell toward her, she lifted one foot, glad to find her boots had reappeared as she kicked the ring into the face of the second creature. It flew apart with a silent scream. One branch-like arm shot out toward her, raking through Fi's hair in the second before it disappeared.

Then she heard the snap of thorns. Fi whirled to find that another of the creatures had slipped around behind her, trying to get to Briar through the cage of roses. This one looked more human than the others. She could almost make out a figure in a heavy cloak, or maybe a veil . . .

Fi didn't want to know. She tried not to think about that form or the monsters rising up from the sea behind her. But fear was already choking her, and she could feel herself losing to it. She ran to Briar's side, throwing the rope wildly to strike down the creature tearing at the beautiful roses. Other emotions Fi could fight down or force away, but the idea that she would fail someone she loved—that had always been her deepest, darkest fear.

The nightmare looming over Briar fell to nothing but a shiny puddle. But it was too late. The entire island was being swarmed now, lumps of nightmare smashing like waves against the shore. Some bared grinning teeth, while others bore deep red lips like flower petals pressed together. What was she supposed to do? How was she supposed to protect Briar from this?

The rope in Fi's hand wavered. She forced herself to look at the peaceful face of the prince, to remember every moment, every kiss, every time Briar Rose had saved her life. This was not where it ended. The rope in Fi's hand took on a golden sparkle as she threw herself into battle again.

The golden ring punched holes through the dark of the nightmare creatures, the sparkling rope turning them back to nothing. Fi was a whirlwind of gold like a fire dancer, twisting her body to make the rope move in tight arcs, sailing out and then wrapping around her as she pushed herself to the breaking point. It wasn't enough. For every creature she destroyed, two more took its place. There was almost no golden island left; it had all run away like sand from an hourglass, sliding into the roiling sea. Fi felt the bite of rose thorns at her back as she was forced against Briar's cage. There was nowhere else to go.

*Hurry, Briar,* Fi prayed, as a nightmare limb curled around her wrist. *Please hurry.*

She didn't have a lot of time.

# 20

※》》 《《

## Shane

SHANE INCHED ALONG a narrow ledge, one hand gripping the torch and the other white-knuckled against the rock.
The cliff face, slick with spray from the waterfalls, glistened
in the light of the sickle moon. One wrong step and she would
plunge into the river far below and wash up on the shores of
Everlynd's lake. Or her corpse would, anyway.

Red tiptoed along behind her, her face pinched with a
healthy combination of concentration and fear. The manacle
chain pulled dangerously tight between them. Shane lifted
the torch to give Red more light, though it brought the hissing flames so close they were practically licking her face. If
she had no eyebrows left after this, she knew who to blame.

"Don't slip," she called.

Red shot her a look. "Well, if I do, I'm taking you
with me."

"That's what I'm afraid of."

Shane was starting to understand why no one had bothered poking around this ruin before. She'd never worked so hard and come up with so little. Finding the map had taken half of one day and most of the next, so long she'd honestly thought Fi would be awake from her dream journey and coming along on this treasure hunt. But her partner, who had drifted off with Briar the night before, was still fast asleep.

She'd asked Perrin if something was wrong. The boy smiled and said there was nothing to worry about, but Shane could just hear the unsaid *yet* hanging in the air between them. She wasn't a Witch, though, so she'd left that to the experts and set off with Red around noon, chasing the Lord of the Butterflies.

Though the spot had looked close on the map, it had taken hours to scale the cliffs, not least because she kept having to wait for Red's mangy wolf to catch up. They'd finally left him behind in a copse of scraggly trees, along with their pack— just some food and a couple of blankets in case they ended up spending the night out here. They definitely would at this rate. They'd spent all day searching every grimy slug-infested hole in the cliff face, but so far, they'd found nothing.

A gust of wind slammed into them, rattling the chain. They were only a few hundred feet from the sandstorm. Shane really wished she had someone else at her back— maybe someone with a rope and the good sense not to keep craning her head around. For all Shane knew, Fi was awake right at this moment, tapping her foot and wondering what was taking her partner so long. But Shane refused to go back empty-handed.

She had spotted one more possible entrance, a narrow

crevice behind a spitting waterfall so high up it would almost have been easier to rappel down from the top of the bluffs. She couldn't pull that off handcuffed to someone, though. So inching thirty feet along a ledge about as wide as a knife blade was their only option.

Red's foot slipped. Shane seized the chain, heaving Red against the wall before she lost her balance and dragged them both down. Adrenaline sizzled in her veins as Red threw her a grateful look.

What had she been thinking, doing this with an amateur? This was it, Shane decided—for real this time. They'd check this last cave, and then they'd make their way to back to Cinzel for a few hours of bad sleep before calling it quits.

With a last heave, she pushed off the ledge and scrambled into the mossy hollow behind the waterfall. She pulled the chain taut to give Red a lifeline. Red ducked under the spray of silver water to join her, looking thoroughly put out.

"I can't believe you do this for fun," she said, pushing wet straggles of hair out of her face and shaking out her crimson tunic.

Shane snorted. "Trust me, it's a lot more fun without you chained to my arm like an anchor."

She looked around. The torch hissed as spray hit the oil-soaked rags, the crooked grin of the moon winking through the waterfall. It wasn't much of a cave, more like an alcove— a wet alcove covered in murderously slippery rocks. Shane reached out to steady herself against the wall and then yanked her hand back when something sharp and metallic bit into her palm. Instinctively, she swung the torch up, accidentally dragging Red forward with it.

"Ow! Maybe you could try *telling* me where you want to go instead of just yanking on the chain all the time," Red suggested hotly.

"Sorry," Shane said, only half listening. "But look at these." She waved a hand at the wall, where dozens of little metal spheres no larger than marbles were embedded in the rock.

"What are they?" Red asked.

Shane honestly had no idea. "Well, they didn't grow like that." She brought the torch even closer. The tips of the flames licked a tarnished sphere, and suddenly the metal began to twist, five angular petals uncurling into the shape of a flower.

Red gasped. Shane moved the torch to another sphere, making it bloom under the flames. Fi would have been spouting the whys and wherefores, but Shane was pretty sure whatever these things were, they reacted to heat.

"Let me try," Red said, her voice an awed whisper. Shane passed her the torch, smiling as Red waved it excitedly back and forth, the silver flowers rippling open like winking stars. The flowers were pretty enough, but she really hoped they'd found something more important than bizarre waterfall art.

She leaned in, studying the little blossoms up close. The center of each flower seemed to be a chip of crystal, glowing faintly in the watery light. It reminded Shane of the ancient forge, and she thought again of the dark cavern with all the empty gouges in the wall.

"Shane, look!" Red said breathlessly. The torch waggled as she jumped up to light the last few metal buds, revealing a larger picture set into the wall. The metal flowers glinted in the shape of a giant butterfly, the small crystals lighting the back of the cave like a constellation.

They were definitely in the right place.

"It must be a clue, right?" Red asked. "Or the entrance to a hidden passage?"

"Or both," Shane agreed. She ran her hands along the wall under the butterfly emblem, searching for switches or gears or any crevices that would indicate a doorway. She banged her knuckles against the rock, pressing her ear to the stone and listening for the clang of hollow compartments. The echo didn't sound quite right, but it was hard to tell over the pounding waterfall.

Now would be a great time for an epiphany. She arched an eyebrow at Red.

"Don't look at me," Red said. "You're the expert treasure hunter."

Shane laughed. "Relic hunting can't be that different from treasure hunting."

"Yes, it can," Red assured, tossing her head, "because I only chased down relics *after* some foolish treasure hunter had done all the work."

Reluctantly, Shane had to admit that probably worked. It was way too easy to picture Red working her charms on some treasure hunter drunk on victory and picking his pocket on the way out of the tavern.

She inspected the wall again, yanking on a few of the metal flowers, but none of them budged. Shane considered unslinging her ax, but that was just wishful thinking. This was supposed to be the workshop of some brilliant Witch; it wouldn't be very practical to have to destroy something every time he went in or out.

Shane put one hand on her hip, glaring at the butterfly. It almost seemed to be staring back, mocking her.

"So this is what it's like to be a treasure hunter," Red marveled sarcastically. "Risking death in order to have long staring contests with a wall. How do you handle the excitement?"

"By figuring it out," Shane said, grinning. Red's jab had given her an idea. The reason it felt like the butterfly was staring back at her was because two of the little flowers were set off from the rest in the middle of the hindwings—exactly where the eyes would have been if Shane drew an X through the middle.

The curse mark on Fi's hand was clearly a swallowtail or something else fancy, but this was a moth. Like the big, ugly brown moths with giant eyespots on their wings that infested Steelwight in the summer, hanging so thick on the bramble and blackthorn that the forest seemed to stare at her with a thousand hungry eyes. Her father called them emperor moths. Shayden had been terrified of them as a child, and Shane had spent many a hot night running around their room barefoot trying to capture the fluttering moths in her cupped hands and throw them back out the window.

She'd asked Shayden once what made them so scary. *Because they're like eyes in the dark,* he had whispered, close to her ear. Then, because he was five, he added: *And they're hairy—gross!* The memory made her smile.

Shane reached up, taking hold of one of the metal flowers

set as an eyespot and twisting it. It turned easily under her fingers. Shane could hear some kind of gear clicking behind the rock, but no mechanism engaged.

"Maybe we have to turn them both at the same time?" Red suggested, reaching for the eye on the opposite side.

"Now, that's thinking like a treasure hunter," Shane said. "On the count of three."

Red curled her fingers around the flower, staring directly into Shane's eyes with a smile. Shane's heart did a little backflip, maybe because for just a moment she caught herself imagining a future for her and Red as treasure hunters together—forever.

Shane cleared her throat. "One, two . . ."

"Three!" Red declared.

They turned the metal flowers at the same time. Shane heard the heavy creak of gears moving, and a second later, the stone on the floor between them was sliding back, revealing a narrow staircase that cut steeply into the dark.

*They'd found it!* Shane felt that familiar rush of excitement as she peered into the unknown. She glanced over at Red. The girl's hand quivered as she held out the torch.

"We can wait for morning, if you want," Shane offered. Nobody was going to steal the spoils out from under them— not all the way up here.

"You want to quit now, when it's finally getting interesting?" Red demanded. Then she leaned close to Shane, smirking up at her through her lashes. "I didn't take you for the type to give up so easily."

Red's hand was quivering with *excitement*, Shane realized. That fuzzy, fluttery feeling was back, taking her heart by storm. Shane knew it was ridiculous to be this blown away—as though she hadn't already danced with Red, kissed her, held her in her arms, whispered secrets into the shell of her ear. This was different, though. Maybe because it felt like they'd left all those secrets and shadows behind. This was just them—Shane and Red, and all they could be together.

And they could be amazing.

Red sent Shane a flirty look as she handed the torch back, the soft brush of her fingers setting Shane's every nerve on fire. It was a tease; it was a challenge. It was absolutely irresistible.

Shane couldn't stop her grin. "All right, but let the *expert treasure hunter* take the lead," she suggested, loving the way Red's eyes went wide and dark as she leaned close. "We have no idea what's going to happen down there, after all." Then she led the way down the narrow staircase, her whole body thrumming.

Shane kept the pace deliberately slow and let her left arm dangle behind her so the manacle wouldn't tug Red forward. They'd gone end over end enough; this time, Shane wanted to make it to the bottom still standing.

The stairway descended to a corridor that cut right into stone and then twisted abruptly, veering out of sight. The walls were smooth as marble, but they shone from within almost like lichen on wet stones, silvery gray from a distance and then suddenly glistening with rainbow colors when lit by the torch. Their footfalls echoed against the glassy floor. Patterns of butterflies were carved into the walls, thick patches of them like arrows pointing the way, but Shane hadn't spotted any runes or magic languages. *Yet.*

She felt a prickle on the back of her neck as she passed a whirl of butterflies etched on the wall, those uncanny eyes staring out from every pair of wings. This wasn't just any Witch, after all—this was the infamous Lord of the Butterflies, one of the most brilliant and mysterious Witches who'd ever lived. Shane wondered what Fi hoped to learn about him, other than his part in crafting the forbidden spells.

She lifted the torch higher, feeling her pulse speed up. In her experience, secret lairs very rarely hid pleasant things, and she'd never known a Witch to build a hideaway like this and leave it unprotected. Shane was getting downright antsy. Was it just the hidden door, or were there other traps waiting to spring?

Something cold hit Shane's neck. She practically jumped out of her skin. "Look out!" she hissed, seizing Red and pressing her back against the wall. She waved the torch in front of her, the butterflies' eyes leaping out of the dark.

Red's breathy laugh was hot against her neck. "Is this some kind of pretense, or are you really trying to protect me from a drippy ceiling?"

"Sorry," Shane said sheepishly, watching a fat drop of water splash down from a tiny crack. She stepped away, letting Red up.

"I didn't say I minded," Red said, dusting herself off. When they started off again, Shane could've sworn Red was walking closer, the backs of their knuckles tantalizingly close to brushing with every step. The mood felt somehow lighter, too.

Shane decided to push her luck a little. "You're a Witch, right?" She didn't get an answer, just a raised eyebrow. Shane went on undeterred. "Did you ever think about taking a Witch title? The Red Witch? The Wolf Witch? Flirty Witch, maybe?"

Red's boot heel clipped Shane's toe. Shane yelped. "Oops," Red said, fluttering her lashes. "You do know that only really powerful Witches give up their names for titles, right? That's not me."

"You seem pretty powerful to me," Shane said. "What about those monster wolves that dragged me all over the Forest of Thorns?"

"Those . . . aren't mine." Red's voice was quiet, and Shane caught her looking at her palm, where the puncture from the thorn rod had become an ugly scab. "They belong to the Spindle Witch."

Well, that had soured the mood. Shane should probably know better than to poke her thumb into a sore spot, but . . .

"You must have some power of your own, though. An affinity—that's what you Witches call it, right?"

Red pinned Shane with an incredulous look, like she couldn't believe Shane had the gall to ask another question. Shane got that look a lot. The Paper Witch had sat her down once and told her that she was too nosy—or in his own words, that her prying was like being chiseled at by a very sharp, unrelenting hammer.

*Your point?* she'd asked him.

He'd stared at her coolly. *Pry less.*

Red had turned away, her stiff shoulders drawn up to her ears. Shane cursed her big mouth. Maybe that busybody Witch was right—or at least nobody ever seemed to be mad at him.

"Forget it," she said, but she was surprised when Red sighed in defeat.

"I guess it couldn't possibly hurt anything now." She rounded on Shane, pointing a finger. "But you better not laugh."

Shane held up her hands.

"I can sing to animals," Red told her, a little color dusting her cheeks.

Shane wrinkled her nose. "So what? Anyone can sing to animals."

"And they understand me," Red ground out. "It's not language, exactly, but . . . they listen, and I can communicate my feelings to them."

Shane thought back to the strange song Red had been humming when she'd calmed the stray dog in the marketplace, what felt like a lifetime ago now. She had caught snatches of the same melody sometimes at night, on the road to Everlynd, when the wolf crawled close enough to lay its head in Red's lap.

"I guess that explains Cinzel," Shane said.

Red laughed, a soft, sweet sound. "He's been with me since he was a pup. He's family. The only real family I ever had."

Shane studied the tiny smile on Red's face, so genuine she seemed to glow with it. A memory from the Forest of Thorns flashed through her mind: Red framed against the dark branches, her expression mocking as she said *I wouldn't even recognize the real me anymore.*

Maybe Red couldn't see it, but Shane could. It was the girl who'd lain awake every night in the firelight shadows, her soft fingers combing the tangles from Cinzel's fur. The girl who loved her wolf more than anything.

The passage ended around the next turn. Shane held the torch aloft as they came to an opening. This one was clearly door-shaped, carved directly into the stone wall. She peered into the space beyond. A narrow hallway stretched out maybe twenty feet before dead-ending into a metal door. The floor was covered in a honeycomb of interlocking white tiles, each about a foot wide. Shane would bet her entire meager fortune there was a trap waiting for them inside.

"Careful," Shane warned as she stepped cautiously onto the first tile. She tapped it twice with her boot and then put all her weight onto it, holding her breath. Nothing happened. She jerked her chin for Red to join her.

Red tried to step onto the same tile, but her toe caught against Shane's boot, and she overshot, stumbling out onto the next row.

Only the shackles attaching them saved her life. Shane felt the rumble and saw the flash of steel at the same second as a thin ax-like blade swung like a pendulum from a slit in the wall, flying toward Red.

Shane dropped the torch and yanked the chain with both hands. Red shrieked as Shane's arms locked around her, hauling her to safety. The ax sliced through the air twice, close enough Shane could feel the breeze of its passing, then it disappeared back into the wall.

Mechanisms had also screeched to life behind them. Shane turned just in time to see an iron door slam down, closing off the passageway they'd come through.

Red struggled out of Shane's arms and snatched up the torch before it rolled away across the tiles. Her hand shook from the near miss. "Now what?"

"We go forward," Shane said, trying to quiet her own galloping heart. "Doors that close behind you are pretty much a given when treasure hunting." Ruins never left you a way out for long. She knelt down, staring out across the floor. "If certain tiles trigger the traps, there's probably only one safe path through. We just have to figure out how it's marked."

Red didn't seem convinced. "They all look the same to me."

Unfortunately, she was right. There were no squiggly Witch runes, no symbols, not so much as a scuff mark. Each tile was completely smooth and blank.

"Stand back," Shane said, unslinging her ax. She hefted it in one hand and then brought the blunt back of the head down on the next tile over.

The blade sliced out from the wall again, swinging at deadly speed. Shane yanked her arm back before she lost it. She flattened herself to see how much space was under it, but the curved blade nearly kissed the floor at its lowest point. There would be no crawling under that. And there was no telling how many tiles were rigged or exactly what they did. There could be more swinging blades, or other weapons waiting to skewer them from the floor or ceiling.

*Only one way to find out . . .*

Shane leaned precariously out over the floor, banging her ax down on the farthest tile she could reach. A row of metal spears rushed out of the walls on either side, nearly ripping the ax out of her hands. This time it was Red who hauled Shane back, both of them panting as they leaned against the sealed door.

"This is useless!" Red snapped. "Are people just supposed to get stuck in here and die?"

"That's pretty much the point of a trap," Shane muttered. "But whoever used this workshop had to get through somehow, which means we can, too." The Lord of the Butterflies clearly came and went just fine, because there wasn't a skeleton impaled on one of these spears.

Shane tipped her head back against the cool metal door, squinting as something glinted out of the dark over her head. Tiny metal spheres, like the ones from the entrance, were embedded in the ceiling. Shane nudged Red's elbow, pointing up.

"Hey. Recognize those?"

"Give me a boost," Red suggested, an answering smile spreading across her lips.

That was easier said than done while shackled together. Shane's arm was cranked halfway around her body while she hoisted Red up on her back, the torch swaying dangerously close to her head.

"Ow! Watch it," Shane yelped as Red's razor-sharp knee dug into her ribs.

Red huffed against her hair. "Maybe if you weren't so short."

*Look who's talking*, Shane thought, but she knew better than to mouth off with Red's elbow so close to her split lip.

When Red finally slid down, Shane could see the girl had managed to open a dozen of the little metal flowers, their crystal centers glimmering.

Red surveyed her work. "I don't get it," she said, hands perched on her hips. "But it looks like some of them didn't open all the way. I'll go back up."

"No need. The path is right there. Look." Shane took

the torch, holding it behind them so its light was blocked by their bodies. The petals Red thought hadn't opened all the way were actually casting shadows onto the corners of some of the tiles—in the shape of butterflies.

Shane tested out the first butterfly-marked tile carefully and then motioned Red to follow, navigating them onto the safe path. Every few feet, they had to stop for Shane to lift Red and the torch up, but now that they knew what they were looking for, it was easy to pick their way through the traps. At least until they were almost across.

Three rows of tiles remained, but there were no more spheres set into the ceiling. Did that mean none of the tiles were safe? Shane judged the distance to the iron door, and then studied the sinister slit in the wall. Would it be spears? Another blade? Something worse?

"Do we turn back?" Red asked, biting her lip.

"Nope," Shane decided. "We're going to dive forward together, roll up, and go through the door."

"And if it's locked?" Red wanted to know.

Shane grinned. "Then we flatten ourselves against it and hope we don't lose any toes."

Fi would have been spluttering in protest, insisting she could figure this out from the air quality or the tension in the tiles. But Red just stared long and deep into Shane's eyes, and then cracked a smile.

"You really are dangerous," Red whispered. She tossed her head back, a daring sparkle in her beautiful brown eyes. "Get me killed, and I'll haunt your corpse."

That seemed fair. "On the count of three," Shane said, locking their fingers tightly together. "One. Two."

"Three!" they said together.

Shane threw the torch ahead of them and dove forward, rolling fast as she hit the tiles. There was a metal screech, and two blades swung from either side of the hallway, crossing in the middle right where their heads would have been. The torch clanged against the door. Red's body was pressed tight to hers, her pulse hammering through their joined hands as they scrambled up. Another trap whirred to life behind them, long sword-like blades knifing up from the floor just behind their feet.

"Go!" Shane shouted, slamming into the door and jerking the handle. It turned almost too easily, opening on silent hinges. Then they were toppling through into the darkness beyond—Shane and Red and the torch—and Shane just hoped there wasn't something worse on the other side.

# 21

## Briar Rose

**BRIAR WAS BACK** in the white tower. Roses fluttered all around him as he sat in the lonely window of his prison, staring out. Except that it wasn't the castle of Andar spread out below him, or the dark Forest of Thorns. It was like Briar's tower had become so high that it was part of the sky instead. A sea of clouds seethed below him, wisps of them catching in the climbing vines that encircled the tower. It was beautiful—more beautiful than any of the dreams he'd had when he was actually asleep in this cage.

It only took Briar a moment to acclimate to the dream. He'd had a hundred years of practice, but still not enough, apparently, to keep from ending up here. This was the last place Briar had ever wanted to return to. He moved into the room, running his hand along the familiar gauze curtains that swayed gently around the empty bed. A shiver of revulsion turned his stomach. He hated this place, but it still felt like home. Briar dreamed of the white tower most nights, and each time, he woke with a small flare of panic as he wondered, just for a second, if Fi and everything else had been a dream.

Briar's hand had curled into a fist without him realizing it, and his fingernails, short only moments ago, had started to stretch like claws. They ripped through the delicate curtain without a thought.

*Briar!* a low voice whispered. *Briar Rose.*

He spun around, his blue coat flaring, but saw no one. The voice seemed to be coming from everywhere at once, whispering his name over and over until the small tower was filled with it. There was a hiss of air almost like a whisper at his neck, and Briar stumbled back, ripping his clothes on the tangled rose thorns. His hands struggled for purchase in the soft curtains, and Briar found himself falling through them, trapped within the layers of gauze as though they were thick spiderwebs.

"Briar Rose!" This time the voice was right in front of him. Briar tore the curtains away until a figure appeared. It was a woman. He could just make out her black curls and loose golden robe as he pulled the last layer of curtain from between them.

"Dream Witch," Briar said, staring at the woman who now stood at the center of the tower.

Her beautiful brown eyes met his, crinkling with her smile. "Briar Rose."

"Are you real?" Briar asked. She looked just like he remembered, warm and welcoming, wearing the same secretive smile as she always had when she'd taken his hand as a child, leading him into a dream.

The woman pressed her lips together with a hum. "Dreams are tricky like that, aren't they?" she agreed. "You created me, if that's what you mean."

"But *what* are you?" Briar persisted. Dreams *were* tricky—it was easy to get lost in them and end up wandering, your own mind creating what you wanted to see and luring you further and further in.

"You walked with the Dream Witch in your sleep many times when you were a child."

The woman smiled fondly, and Briar could suddenly feel the memories tugging at his mind: being a little boy tucked up in the castle window, stuck inside watching a celebration or festival through the glass. Then the Dream Witch would sit on the windowsill beside him and blow a pinch of dream dust out of her palm, plunging him to sleep. When he opened his eyes, he was always somewhere beautiful—a distant sliver of Andar painted from the Dream Witch's memories. He'd walked barefoot through shimmering glades of aspens with ruby leaves and marveled at the eastern city of the artisans, shining with high spires and great silver bells. He'd even raced up the ice towers of the Order of the Rising Rain while the snow sparkled around him like diamond dust. Those dreams still lived inside him, which meant part of the Dream Witch did, too.

"You're beginning to understand," the image of the Dream Witch agreed. "I'm not really her. I'm just a manifestation of your subconscious, a form your mind chose to guide you, created from your most precious memories."

It was her, but it wasn't her. The cage of roses slithered across the wall, and Briar stared into those kind eyes and felt

234

a sudden stab of loss and grief. Being back in this room made him feel those hundred years of emptiness all over again. Outside the window, heavy gray rain had begun to fall.

"Gone is never really gone," the Dream Witch said. She laid a warm hand against his cheek. "You remember me. And you must remember other things, too." She stepped back. Sand had gathered around her bare feet. "That's why your mind wished for a guide. You're looking for something."

"Yes," Briar said. "I need to know about a certain book."

"You need to know a great many things, young prince," the Dream Witch said. "How it all began. How you got tangled up in the middle of it."

This was his own mind trying to lead him astray. Briar swallowed, digging his fingernails into his palms even as his mind raced. "No," he said firmly. "The book—I just need to know about the . . ."

*A baby wailed behind him. The cry wasn't strong, but weak and sickly, and something in Briar's chest clutched as he spun around. He was no longer in the tower, but in an elaborate bedroom. A giant four-poster bed sat against the wall, blankets of the softest velvet and rich sheets of fine silk scattered around the woman lying in the center. She reached her hands out toward the crying baby that lay in the cradle beside the bed.*

*"Please," she was begging. "Please don't let him die. I would pay any price—just save my baby. Save Briar Rose." Her blue eyes glowed with love and desperation as she pushed up on one shoulder, reaching for the cradle. The baby had stopped crying, its body limp and ashen.*

*Briar didn't want to be here. He didn't want to see this, but he couldn't look away. His mother had sweat on her brow. Her* golden hair was tangled and matted, and her white nightgown hung limply from her shoulders, but she was still more beautiful than any painting he had ever seen. Briar hadn't thought he had any real memories of his mother, Queen Amarise.

And yet these images were inside him somehow. Or were they?

Cold snaked through his chest. Perrin had warned him the world of the unconscious blurred the borders between people— especially those who were deeply connected. Was this Briar's memory . . . or the Spindle Witch's?

"Any price, Your Majesty?" Another figure swept into the scene, a woman in a long black dress with a train that dragged against the fine rugs. The lacy edge of her black veil fell just past her nose, leaving her ghostly pale skin and bright lips exposed.

"Any price, Spindle Witch," the queen said. The baby didn't stir even as his mother's hand rubbed his chest. Briar wondered if he had died that day.

A smile spread across the Spindle Witch's lips, and for just a moment, Briar thought he saw the glitter of her eyes. Then she reached beneath her veil, pulling forth a long golden thread and twirling it through her fingers.

Tears splashed from his mother's eyes as she scooted to the edge of the bed, wrapping Briar's tiny hand in her own. The Spindle Witch loomed over them. She looped the end of her golden thread like she was tying a knot. Then Briar watched in horror as she seemed to slip it into the baby's chest, right over his heart. Her deft fingers pulled the loop tight, and Briar's breath hitched, almost as though he could feel the thread tightening around his own heart. The other end had snaked up to wrap around Queen Amarise's hand like a manacle, sliding under her skin.

The Spindle Witch began spinning the thread between them,

*her hand twisting deftly, faster and faster. Even as Briar watched, the baby's skin began to regain its color as the queen grew gray, her own life pulled from her and given to her son.*

*Briar had known that his mother died for him, but he hadn't known it was like this—that he had sucked the life from her, or that the Spindle Witch had tied one of her threads around his heart. He clutched his chest, trying to hold back the agony that threatened to overwhelm him.*

*The Spindle Witch looked up suddenly, as the queen collapsed lifeless into the bed and the baby began to wail. Her head twisted until she was looking over her shoulder, like she was looking right at him—like she could see him. A predatory curve spread across her red lips. Briar lifted his foot to take a step forward . . .*

A hand came down on his shoulder, pulling him back. When he turned again, the Spindle Witch was gone. He was back in the tower, the Dream Witch's fingers clamped around his sleeve.

"You should be careful," his guide warned. "Your connection to her is very strong."

Briar was still reeling from what he had seen. "Why would the Spindle Witch do it?" he demanded, shaking free. "She had to know she'd be exiled or worse for killing the queen."

"You already know the answer to this. The Spindle Witch is looking for something." The room around them was still dotted with bloodred roses, but now the tangled vines looked more like black thorns. "Something worth risking everything to put that thread inside your heart. Something the Rose Witches of Andar have safeguarded for centuries. You're part of that legacy, *Briar Rose.*" The Dream Witch snapped his name at the end, forcing him to look her in the eyes. He felt calmer under that gaze, some of the turmoil fading as he suddenly felt warm sand under his bare feet.

Briar took a deep breath. "That's why I have to remember the book."

The Dream Witch nodded. "There are other things you could know about the Spindle Witch," she offered. "Things that could help you . . ."

It was tempting. Briar could almost see images forming behind his eyelids: the Spindle Witch carving something of white bone, even the hazy vision of someone who looked like Queen Aurora with her rose crown, reaching out to snap a golden thread . . . He could learn so much. He could find out everything there was to know about the Spindle Witch, her greatest weakness—but there was no guarantee he could ever come back. If he wandered off in this dream, there would be no one to find him. Briar had to trust that Camellia had left him what he needed.

"Just the book," Briar whispered, focusing all his feelings on memories of his sister. "That's all that matters."

Even though he knew she wasn't real, the proud smile on the Dream Witch's face still made him feel warm all the way through. He held it close as he slipped into another memory—this one twice as vivid because he could actually recall it now that he was seeing it in front of him.

CAMELLIA SAT AT her writing desk, framed by the spray of pink roses blooming in her window. The soft wind played in her golden hair, the paper rustling as she scribbled away with a long ink pen. Briar watched as a young version of himself, maybe six, clambered up into her lap, making Camellia laugh as his knee bumped the desk and almost overturned her inkwell.

"Careful," Camellia said, and Briar closed his eyes, overwhelmed. Even from across the room, he could almost feel the warmth of her arms around him, the sweet smell of roses tickling his nose.

"What are you reading?" his younger self asked, and Briar took a step closer, peering over Camellia's shoulder. A book was spread open against the dark wood, the thick cream pages broken up here and there with beautiful illustrations. A storybook? He recognized Camellia's careful handwriting scratched into the margins—but before he could read what she'd written, Camellia snapped the book closed.

"Aren't you supposed to be in your dancing lessons?" Though her voice was teasing, she left her hand braced over the book, as if she were afraid it might spring open. Briar couldn't make out the title through her fingers.

The younger Briar grinned. "Are you going to tell on me?" Camellia smiled fondly. She never did. The child studied the book again. "Will you read it to me?"

Camellia ruffled a hand through his hair. "Someday." The child pouted, but Camellia leaned close, dropping her voice like she was sharing a secret. "I have a theory about this book," she told him, holding it up between two fingers. "But I need a little more time to work it out. When you're older, I'll tell you everything."

Distantly, Briar could hear them laughing as Camellia bent to tickle him, digging her fingers into his sensitive ribs. But Briar's eyes were locked on the cover of the book, painted with a dark tower set against a starry sky. A girl stood in the tower's lighted window, her golden hair tumbling over her shoulder. Briar blinked at the title. *The Eye of the Witch, and Other Fables.* It was a collection of children's stories, including a version of one of Andar's oldest folktales, the story of the Witch in the tower whose eye became the moon. It was a book they'd never read, but one he'd seen on Camellia's desk many times, one she'd always carefully tucked away. Somehow, the secret of Andar was hidden in that book.

Briar had what he needed. He knew he should break from the dream, get back to Fi, to Everlynd, but . . .

Camellia slipped an arm under Briar's knees and swung up from her seat, turning around and around in circles, the boy in her arms giggling and kicking his feet. The scent of the roses was so strong Briar could hardly breathe. It felt like if he closed his eyes, he'd be right back in that moment—not just in a dream, but really there, in that bright castle, in his beautiful green kingdom, with his sister alive and laughing. Maybe the last hundred years were the dream, and all of this was still ahead of him . . .

"Briar," Camellia called.

"Briar!" Then the name seemed to twist, growing desperate and strained—and suddenly, he realized it wasn't Camellia's voice at all. It was Fi's.

"Briar . . . hurry!" Fi was calling to him from somewhere far away, her words distorted like she was behind glass. He didn't have any time to waste. He might already have put Fi in danger.

That thought, more than anything, broke him from his reverie. The memory fuzzed around him, becoming his tower of roses for one moment and then a dark rush filled with nothing but falling sand. He was inside an hourglass, the figure of the Dream Witch in her flowing robe disappearing grain by grain.

"I have to go to her!" Briar said as the Dream Witch held him back. "Fi needs me." Now that he was listening for it, it was like she was right next to him. He could hear her screaming and struggling, fighting with nightmares. He felt like a charged lightning bolt, a tempest in a bottle, his magic flowing into him effortlessly the way it always did when he was dreaming.

"Not your magic, Briar Rose! You must find another way," the Dream Witch said, her voice low with warning. "Don't use that power here. You will call the Spindle Witch to you."

The words weren't hers. They came from Briar's own mind—a thousand different warnings from his sister and the Great Witches to be careful, to be sparing with his magic. All those whispers seemed to surround him at once, threatening to suffocate him.

"Then what am I supposed to do?" Briar demanded. His only answer was the whipping wind as golden sand swirled around him, the image of the Dream Witch disappearing.

When Briar could see again, he was inside a very different cage of roses. This one was like a coffin, twined all around him where he lay in the sand. A golden rope sliced through the air above him, and Briar watched as nightmare essence dissipated, a dark tendril falling away from where it had been ripping through the fragile roses over his heart.

Briar surged up, covering his face with his crossed arms as he tore through the cage. "Fi!" he yelled. He had the information they needed—now he just had to get them out of this dream.

Fi's head snapped around. She had her feet dug into the sand, the rope swinging around her as she tried to keep the inky creatures at bay. Her relieved expression vanished as a snake-like arm seized her ankle, yanking her down. Fi gasped as she was dragged backward on her stomach, but she managed to flip over, wrenching the rope over her head and bringing it straight down through the creature's gaping mouth.

"Watch yourself!" Fi warned. Briar blinked, trying to get his bearings. His cage of thorns had been protecting him, but it was gone, nothing but red petals under his feet. He ducked as a bulbous head snapped at him, sharp teeth slicing inches from his shoulder. Sparks snapped almost unbidden to Briar's fingers as he stumbled out of the way, but he held back. He couldn't use his magic. He just had to wake them up, find the escape from this dream. But he couldn't think, couldn't move as the surge of darkness closed him in.

Fi screamed. One inky tendril wrapped around her chest and squeezed. She ripped at it with her fingernails, but it was useless, and her body jerked in panic, her lungs heaving. Her wide hazel eyes found Briar's through the sea of nightmares.

Suddenly, Briar's hands were on fire. His magic poured into him, humming under his skin until he felt he must be glowing. He had never felt so powerful, or so out of control. The magic rushed out of him angry and fierce, light exploding from his hands and engulfing the entire island, burning away every speck of darkness. Nightmare creatures crumbled all around him, sinking into the glittering sea.

"Fi!" Briar shouted. She was on her knees, struggling to breathe.

Briar only made it a few steps before a flock of crows surged out of the ocean, swirling between them in a maelstrom of beating black wings. Razor claws shone, and the air rang with a cacophony of crow laughter. Briar was buffeted back as all of the crows came together, disappearing in a rain of feathers and leaving a figure rising up in their wake.

The Spindle Witch wore a black dress covered in lace. The collar was high and stiff, and the veil swept down her back like a cape, crawling like a shadow over the golden sand. Her hands were tucked in her sleeves as she straightened to her full height.

"We meet at last, Briar Rose." The voice was softer than he had expected, but cold enough to send a shiver down his spine. Briar choked on the lump in his throat.

"Spindle Witch."

This was the Witch who had killed his mother. The Witch who had been alive at the dawn of his kingdom. The Witch who had spun her thread around Briar's heart and brought out the monster he sometimes became. The power he reached for when he was angry, the dark power at the deepest core of him, wasn't his own. It belonged to the Spindle Witch. That's what the Great Witches had been trying to protect him from all his life: reaching for his power and finding hers.

Shadows crept over the sun. Briar looked up to find that the lake was gone and the Forest of Thorns had reared up around them, sharp juts of dark trees closing in like a cage. Vines bristling with razor thorns slithered along the ground. Only two patches of gold sand remained—one beneath his feet, and one around Fi.

This wasn't a manifestation of his unconscious. Briar had called the Spindle Witch to him.

"This is my dream now," the woman said. "And I can do whatever I want here." One of her hands slipped from her sleeve, encased in a silky glove. She flicked her fingers, and crows took off from the ground all around her, a wave of black that rose as one and then dove sharply, streaming toward Briar.

He fumbled to call light to his hand. Sparks fizzled on his fingers, his reserves nearly tapped by the wave of magic he had used against the nightmare creatures. The crows descended on him. A vicious talon sliced into his forearm. The pain gave him a moment of clarity, just enough to make the power sizzle at his fingertips. He waved the light as he beat the birds back with his hands, singeing a few feathers and scattering the crows. They retreated to the thorns, watching him from the highest branches with beady eyes.

"So the little prince is not completely helpless," the Spindle Witch said with an amused smirk that Briar would have given anything to wipe off her face. She wasn't looking at him with fear, not even irritation, but the way a child looks at a particularly interesting plaything. "I've waited so long to have you in my grasp—I'm relieved you're not a complete disappointment like the rest of the Witches of your family."

The memory of his mother was still raw, and so was the loss of Camellia. Briar's hatred burned in him. What remained of his light magic simmered like boiling water under his skin. He struck out before he lost control of it again, hurling a searing ball of light at the Spindle Witch—the same fiery flash that had destroyed all the nightmare creatures. The most magic Briar had ever wielded at once.

The Spindle Witch pulled her other hand from her sleeve, revealing a handful of golden thread on a white spindle—a new bone spindle. With a flick of her wrist, she sliced the sharpened tip of her spindle through Briar's light. It disappeared like it had been swallowed. The Forest of Thorns seemed even darker than before. The Witch laughed, cold and cruel, her teeth gleaming behind her red lips.

"Your paltry tricks will not work on me. You're mine, Briar Rose." Her head tipped forward, her eyes—just a glitter behind the veil—locked on him. She reached out into the space between them like she was grasping something in the air and then tugged.

Briar gasped, doubling over, his hands fisting over his coat. It felt like she had reached directly into his chest and was pulling at his heart. Maybe she was, Briar thought, remembering the golden string tied around the baby's heart. The Spindle Witch made a thoughtful sound, tugging again, and Briar couldn't stop the scream that ripped out of him. It was like a vise around his heart, a suffocating hand that squeezed him from the inside. Briar forced his head up, trying to fight the pain back. He lifted his fingers, calling on his flagging magic to do something, anything.

A golden ring struck the Spindle Witch's raised hand, making her hiss. It was Fi's rope. The golden weapon flashed around Fi like it was braided of pure fire.

Briar sagged in relief as Fi whipped the rope out in a second swing, aimed at the woman's head. The Spindle Witch caught it midway, her gloved fingers tightening around the ring. The rope snapped, disintegrating into gold dust as the Spindle Witch squeezed. Fi jerked back, her retreat blocked by sharp thorns.

"You are an annoyance I meant to have dealt with much sooner," the Spindle Witch crooned. "Well, you know what they say. If you want something done right . . ."

The Witch spun in a whirl of skirts, raising the spindle. Golden threads leapt toward Fi, wrapping around her arms and legs, snaring her like a butterfly in a spider's web. She struggled uselessly, hissing in pain as the golden threads grew tighter.

"All the years you could have lived," the Spindle Witch purred as she began to twist the spindle with one finger. "And now they all belong to me."

Briar watched in horror as Fi tipped back, the color draining from her face. Suddenly, he understood exactly how this magic worked. All people, all living things had a precious drop of magic in them. The Spindle Witch was going to suck that magic out of Fi, and with it, her life. Just like she had his mother. Soon Fi would be nothing but a husk, drained and empty.

Briar lunged out of the sand. The Spindle Witch raised her free hand, twisting that invisible thread between her fingers, and the pain slammed into Briar's chest like a mailed fist. He fell to his knees, feeling his heart splitting from the double agony of the Spindle Witch's thread and the sight of Fi going boneless, hanging limply like a broken doll.

"No!" Briar yelled. He couldn't lose Fi, too.

*He couldn't be this useless!*

Briar reached for power. He didn't care where it came from. He didn't care what it made him. He only cared that he would be strong enough not to lose everything he loved.

Something snapped inside him, and like a dam had broken, a great sweep of magic rushed through him. Suddenly, Briar was on his feet. His fingers had become bone claws, his coat bloodred as it flared out behind him. He could feel the sharp spiral of horns jutting out of his skull like a ram's, and all of it, every bony protrusion, was filled with rich, dark power. Briar's anger roiled in him like a living thing. His eyes fixed on the Spindle Witch.

"Now, that is surprising." Her lips were still smirking. Briar was going to wipe that expression off her face. He darted forward, a red glow like a sunset bleeding through the black trees as he dodged her upraised hand and seized the Spindle Witch by the neck.

She swung the bone spindle, the golden threads abandoning Fi as they raced toward Briar. His bony claws cut through them easily. Bits of the Witch's web rippled in the thorns as he forced her back, feeling her pulse pounding under his grip.

"Oh, Briar Rose. You *are* special," the Spindle Witch said. "And I'm not going to have to find you, because you're going to come to me all on your own." Then she began to laugh. Her head tipped back, even as he lifted a second bony hand and tightened it around her throat. She laughed and laughed until Briar squeezed so hard he heard something snap.

The Spindle Witch fell backward, suddenly nothing but a murder of crows fleeing in all directions from the little island in the black sea. Briar watched them go, feeling the rush of victory. The Spindle Witch wasn't dead, but she had lost—lost to Briar Rose using her own power against her. And when they met for real, she would lose again. Briar would make her pay for everything she had done, everyone she had hurt.

*Fi.* The thought was like an electric shock. She was getting slowly to her feet. Briar rushed to her, reaching out to pull her up, only to have Fi recoil from his long white claws.

"Briar, what is this?" she asked, looking scared.

Briar swallowed hard. He didn't need her concern. He didn't need one more person telling him what he was supposed to do with his own power.

"It's just part of the dream," Briar said, kneeling next to her. "Everything will be back to normal when we wake up."

Fi didn't look convinced, but she nodded. "How do we . . ." she began.

"Just let go," Briar told her, pressing his hand to her cheek and pretending he didn't feel her flinch. "It's already happening." Darkness was narrowing his vision, and Briar let it take him. All they had to do was sink back to sleep until the last of the dream dust lost its hold on them.

They'd gotten everything they'd come for—and more. Briar could feel how addictive the magic of the Spindle Witch was, and how dangerous, and he understood now why the Paper Witch and his sister and the Great Witches had warned him to be careful. But they were wrong. Even if the power itself was evil, Briar could use it for something else—to bring down the very Witch who had destroyed his kingdom.

He wasn't going to be satisfied with small wishes anymore.

# 22

Shane

**SHANE GROANED, FORCING** her eyes open as the world stopped spinning. Her arm was bent awkwardly under her where she'd tried to cushion Red's fall, and her wrist howled from being torqued by the manacle. On the bright side, nothing felt broken. The torch sputtered on the floor just out of reach. In its thin light, she could see that Red had landed hard, her shoulder slumped against the wall, her face a mess of disheveled curls.

"Red, are you okay?"

Red groaned. "*No.* I just crashed into a wall. But I guess that's better than being decapitated or run through, so . . ." She waved her hand dismissively.

"So thank you, Shane, for saving my life for the third time," Shane filled in. The only response she got was Red's elbow digging into her side as she pushed herself up, grabbing a small groove running along the wall for balance.

"Ew!" Red jerked back, scrunching her nose and scrubbing her hand on her tunic. "There's something sticky in there."

Shane shook her head. Sticky wasn't exactly a top priority right now. Then again . . . Shane picked up the torch, examining the groove. It cut across all four walls, branching off in a few places and forming an intricate pattern. It reminded her of something Fi had once mentioned about another hidden study.

Red had gone from complaining about her sticky fingers to groaning over the ugly stain she'd left on her shirt. Shane ignored her, tipping the torch until the flames touched the carved wall. Blue fire sprang to life in the groove, racing from wall to wall along the channel and surrounding them in an eerie glow. It burned out in seconds, except where the flames had caught in sconces high on the wall, each one glittering behind beveled glass. Red hummed admiringly, turning a slow circle, and Shane ground the now-useless torch under her boot heel.

The workshop wasn't very big, maybe the size of a modest bedroom. Nothing shone with the telltale glitter of gold or silver or jewels. The bookshelf was stacked high with sheafs of paper and vellum scrolls, but strangely it all looked blank. The Lord of the Butterflies had also clearly been stockpiling ink. Bottles and bottles of the stuff sat in rows on the next shelf down, all of the wells crusted and dry.

The other side of the room looked a little more promising. There was a chest-high workbench that looked like it had been used for metalworking, tiny links for jewelry and half-finished necklace chains gleaming beside a dull pair of tongs.

Next to them sat a bucket with dry rags dangling over the lip, one still marked with a dusty handprint. On the far wall was a desk with several drawers. A giant gilt mirror hung over it, and Shane was willing to bet the small engravings along the edge would be butterflies if she looked closer. The mirror rippled like water in the flickering firelight.

Red stepped forward. "Let's check the desk—"

"I see something on the workbench."

Shane and Red spoke at the same time, and then looked down at the cuffs. Now would have been a great time to split up.

"Ladies first?" Red suggested, her lips pursed into a teasing smile.

"That's not going to solve anything between us," Shane pointed out. "But sure, why not? Desk it is."

The desk stretched across the entire back wall, and the heavy wood shone with an almost-black luster. The top was empty except for another sheaf of blank paper and a handful of blue ribbons. Shane opened the first drawer cautiously. Nothing popped out at her, and the contents were utterly boring—more quills, a blotting sheet, a handful of rings that caught her eye until she realized they were just worthless pieces of beaten steel. The next drawer held a stack of leather-bound journals, and Shane scooped them out greedily, excited until she unwound the string around the first one to reveal that most of the pages had been torn out. All that remained were little dabs of ink and the edges of letters ripped off near the binding.

Either the Witch who had designed this place really cleaned up before leaving, or another treasure hunter had beaten them here. Shane slammed the drawer shut with more force than was necessary, yanking out the last one. It was filled with bird bones—tiny little skulls and delicate wings, some of them tied together with glinting threads. That was just creepy, especially since Shane was sure no bird had flown down into this cave and died in this drawer on its own.

"Lovely," Red said, making a face.

"That's one word for it," Shane agreed, shutting the drawer more carefully. This hidden workshop was supposed to belong to a great scholar of magic, so where were the books? The notes? The towering stacks of dusty old tomes waiting to crush them? Every other scholarly type she knew, from Perrin to Fi to the Paper Witch, stuffed every square inch with books like they were amassing their own libraries. At this rate, there wasn't going to be anything to report back to Fi at all.

Could they be in the wrong place?

"Fine. You win. Let's try the workbench," Red announced, dragging Shane across the room. Together they rustled through the sparse tools on the tabletop, looking for anything valuable or out of place.

Shane's eyes landed on something shiny. She scratched her nail over it, and the fleck of color popped out—just a tiny bit of ruby embedded in the table's surface, no more than a shaving. Someone had definitely been crafting jewelry down here. Shane wasn't counting a little gold dust and a few jewel filings as a very worthwhile find, though, not with what she and Red had gone through to get here.

Red swept the chains and trinkets aside, moving the bucket of rags. Then her hands darted forward in excitement.

"Look! A jewelry box," she said, pulling a small curved box out of its hiding place dug into the wall. It was made of the same dark wood as the desk, and the top was smooth, with no inscription or design. There also didn't seem to be a latch of any kind. Red tugged at the top and then braced it under her arm, trying to pry the lid up with her fingernails. "It won't open."

"Let me take a look," Shane said, holding her hand out. "There's probably some kind of trick. You're doing it wrong."

"I am not," Red said indignantly. "It's just locked or stuck or something." It flew out of her hands as she tried to pry at it again, landing on the workbench with a thud.

Shane chuckled. "That's no way to force a lock."

"By all means," Red said, annoyed, pushing the box toward her with one finger. "Show me how a pro does it."

Shane picked the box up carefully, admiring the soft feel of the polished wood and running her finger along the top seam. Red was right: there didn't seem to be any kind of trick or mechanism. But there was more than one way to get the contents of a box.

She lifted the wooden box high and brought it down as hard as she could against the corner of the workbench. Red cried out, aghast, but the box didn't even crack. Shane raised it again.

"Stop! You'll break something," Red protested.

"Yeah—hopefully, the jewelry box." Shane smashed the little box down again with all her might. The edge of the wooden workbench splintered, a huge chunk breaking off and crashing down right on Shane's foot.

"Ow!"

"Told you so," Red said smugly.

Shane scowled at the innocent-looking lacquered box, trying to ignore her throbbing toe. "All right. You asked for it."

She dragged Red over to the desk and set the jewelry box down on top of it. If the wooden workbench wasn't hard enough, then this box could try her ax on for size.

"Stand close to me, Red, as close as you can," Shane said, unslinging the ax. It would be hard to get a good swing going one-handed.

Red scooted up behind Shane until she was practically flush against her. Shane enjoyed that feeling, but not nearly as much as she was going to enjoy busting this box into kindling. She swung her arm, loosening up her shoulder as she raised her ax over the box. Then suddenly, a low voice rang out right in front of them.

"As amusing as this is to watch, I feel compelled to tell you it will never work. That jewelry box is sealed by magic."

Shane jumped back, feeling Red's arms squeeze around her in surprise. She nearly dropped her ax. A man had appeared in the gilt mirror. He looked like he was sitting in this very study, in the heavy chair Shane had pushed out of her way, his head leaned into his hand as he watched them with interest. He wore a red robe over a black high-collared shirt, and his long brown hair was pulled back in a loose half ponytail, the rest cascading down his back.

A quick glance determined they were still alone in the room. The man was only in the reflection.

"Who are you?" Shane demanded, leveling her ax at him.

"*Who* is entirely the wrong question," the man said. His deep green eyes were piercing in his tan face. "*What* I am is far more interesting."

"You're a relic, right?" Red said, emerging from behind Shane. "Or at least that mirror is."

"Very good. Think of me as a vessel of knowledge." The man waved a careless hand. "This workshop belonged to a Witch known as the Lord of the Butterflies. He—or rather I—didn't trust anyone but myself. Some Witches hide their notes and spells behind locks or encode them in secret languages. But every lock can eventually be broken. The Lord of the Butterflies cast spells on his own reflections, imbuing us with certain knowledge and thoughts instead of writing anything down. Much more secure, don't you think?" His gaze bored into Shane. "I *am* the knowledge of the Lord of the Butterflies."

Shane's chest clenched with excitement. "You know everything he did?"

"Hardly." The man clicked his tongue. "I'm just one sliver of his knowledge. One chapter of his spell book, if you will. A single moment of his thoughts captured in this mirror."

Shane reluctantly set her ax aside. "Any chance this particular sliver knows anything about forbidden siphoning magic?"

The man's eyes flared, bright with a dangerous gleam. "What a fascinating question. Though less the question than how you ask it." He steepled his fingers under his chin. "So Aurora's going to make it forbidden. She really ought to know better. We never desire anything so much as what we can't have." He slid his finger along the lip of the jewelry box in the reflection. "Siphoning magic was one of the Lord of the Butterflies's obsessions, but it's not my particular area of expertise. My little corner of knowledge has to do with what's inside this box."

Red perked up. "Can you tell us how to open it?"

"Technically, that would be encouraging you to steal, which is one of the things I was left here to prevent," the reflection mused. "On the other hand, I suppose it's unlikely the real me is coming back for it after all this time." He straightened, his eyes searching Shane's. "Maybe it's time I let go."

Shane wasn't about to trust some ancient Witch, especially not the figment of himself he'd left in a mirror. "What's in here, anyway?" she asked, prodding the box suspiciously. Something rattled inside. When Shane pushed the box forward, an identical box slid across the desk in the reflection.

The man reached out, placing a finger over the lid. The rattling stopped. "A powerful magic relic—but only under exactly the right circumstances."

"What does that mean?" Shane demanded. She really hated Witch riddles and doublespeak.

The man leaned forward, his long brown hair sliding over his shoulder as he studied them. "Would you rather know the answer to your question or have the box open?" he asked.

"Both," Shane grumbled.

"The box open," Red insisted, shooting her a look. "We can figure out what it does later."

"Interesting, but not surprising," the Witch said, tapping his fingers against the box thoughtfully. "Most people would rather have relics than knowledge. I suppose it's not an unreasonable position. Granted."

"What?" Shane stuttered. The Witch smiled enigmatically. Then he laid his hand over the lid of the jewelry box in the reflection. He pulled the top gently, and the box sprang open—on the desk in front of them.

Red sucked in a surprised breath. She reached carefully into the jewelry box, lifting out a delicate hairpin. It was about the length from her thumb to her little finger, and the burnished metal shone in the low light. The end was capped with a bloodred ruby, rough-hewn but polished till it glowed. Three chains, as small as necklace chains, hung down the back. Intricate butterfly charms dangled from two of them. Their tiny bodies were made of the same tarnished metal, with long curling tails and fiery rubies set into their open wings. It looked like at one point there might have been a third butterfly nestled between the other two, but now it was just an empty chain.

It was nice enough, Shane supposed, for something that apparently had great magical power under *exactly the right circumstances*. Fi probably would have been gushing, but Shane had been hoping for something more impressive—like some kind of weapon.

"What are we supposed to do with this?" Shane asked. She jerked her head up, but only her own disgruntled face stared back at her from the mirror. The Lord of the Butterflies had disappeared. "Hey," Shane protested, knocking a fist against the glass. "Come back here! I have a lot more questions for you!"

The mirror remained stubbornly blank.

At her side, Red held up the hairpin, turning it in her hand. The pin was a safe distance from her hair, but it still took all Shane's self-control not to snatch it from her fingers.

"You realize that thing is probably seriously dangerous, right?"

Red pulled the hairpin away, looking at it askance before handing it to Shane. Shane shoved it deep in her pocket. A relic was a relic, after all, and one that had belonged to the Lord of the Butterflies. Maybe Fi or Perrin could figure out what to do with it.

*Fi.* Shane wanted to kick herself, thinking of her partner. She had met the Lord of the Butterflies, even talked to him— or at least a piece of him—and she hadn't gotten the chance to ask anything important!

"You know relics pretty well, right?" Shane asked, turning to Red. "Can we make him appear again, or is he gone for good?"

"I don't know," Red said quietly, approaching the mirror. She met Shane's eyes through their reflections. "I guess that would depend on what spell was originally cast on the mirror. But . . ."

"But?" Shane urged.

"Didn't he seem *too* real to you?" Red asked with a shudder. "And he's been in there for centuries, right? Maybe he only appears when he wants to."

That was a cheery thought. "Then I guess we'll just wait and see if he comes back."

At first Shane paced in front of the mirror, until Red yanked the chain hard enough to bruise and warned her she was going to chew her hand off to get free if Shane didn't let her get some rest. Reluctantly, Shane took a seat beside her, leaning back against the cold wall. She kept her eyes trained on the mirror, but there was no sign of the Lord of the Butterflies's reflection, nothing but the fire shadows dancing in the silvery glass.

The silence stretched out. Shane was about to suggest they give up when she felt Red's head slump against her shoulder. She was fast asleep.

Shane studied her quiet face, her lips softly parted and her dark eyelashes fluttering against her cheeks as she dreamed. She looked peaceful for once, all of her troubles far away. It couldn't hurt to let Red get a little shut-eye before they headed back. Shane rested her cheek against Red's hair, listening to the soft in and out of Red's breath like a gentle tide.

Before she knew it, she'd drifted off. She woke who-knew-how-many hours later to Red shaking her arm.

"The torch," Red hissed, dragging Shane up and grabbing the torch from the floor. The fire had died down as they slept, only one sconce still burning near the door. Red thrust the torch into the flames, and it leapt back to life just as the final lick of flame in the sconce went out with a hiss of silver smoke.

"Good save," Shane said. Her legs felt creaky from sleeping on the cold floor. Her eyes cut back to the mirror, but she wasn't surprised to see only their reflections in the dim glass. She'd just have to drag her partner back here. If anybody could figure out how to pry an ancient Witch from a mirror, it would be Fi.

They made their way back through the ruin without

trouble. Somehow, it was always easier to get out of these places than to get in.

When they emerged from behind the waterfall, Shane had to blink against the blinding midday sun. They'd been away a lot longer than she thought. They'd better hurry back to Everlynd before the Paper Witch sent a search party after them—or worse, ratted them out to the stuffy council.

They'd almost reached the grove at the base of the falls when Shane pulled up short. Something was wrong. The cluster of trees was too quiet, and she could see their pack had been ripped apart, their few belongings strewn over the rocks. Worse, she caught a glimpse of something moving in the underbrush, a flash of tarnished chain digging into white-and-tawny fur—

"Cinzel!" Red screamed out.

"Red, no! Wait!" But it was too late. Red darted into the clearing, dragging Shane along with her—right into the teeth of the Witch Hunters waiting for them.

There were six of them in all. Shane couldn't even make a grab for her ax before two of them were on her, wrenching her shoulders and wrestling her down into the dirt. Red shrieked as the manacle cut into her hand. A woman with close-cut hair pressed a dagger to Red's neck.

Shane turned her head and found herself staring at Cinzel, crouched on his belly with a chain wrapped tight around his neck. Shane recognized the man towering over him—Von, the giant with the pike who'd given her such a nice bruise between the shoulder blades.

But how had the Witch Hunters found them? More importantly, how were they even *here?* Everlynd was supposed to be protected.

Shane forgot her questions as a heavy boot stomped down on her back, forcing her face into the gravel. She choked as she recognized the figure leaning over her—or at least his horribly crooked nose.

"Tavian," Shane spat. The bald Witch Hunter looked just as fanatical and unhinged as the last time she'd seen him, howling in rage and pain after she defeated him outside the Black Pines lodge. From the way his boot heel dug into her spine, he'd apparently been nursing a grudge.

"Well, if it isn't the Witch from the woods," Tavian said, his greedy eyes fixed on Red like he was planning to devour her. He tapped his jagged broadsword against Shane's cheek. "And you. You, I'd never forget."

"If this is about the nose, let me up and I'll fix it for you," Shane growled. This time, she'd use her ax to hack it clean off. Tavian's boot twisted, forcing the breath out of her.

"Somebody's chained you up for me already. That'll help. Get them back to the camp!" Tavian roared to the Witch Hunters. Then his expression grew sinister as he leered at Red. "Ivan's been waiting for you."

Red's face went ashen. She threw Shane a wild look—but there was nothing Shane could do, outnumbered and outmatched. Cinzel whined low in his throat, a hollow, desolate sound. The chain rattled as the Witch Hunters hauled her to her feet.

"Who the hell is Ivan?" Shane demanded.

It was the giant with the pike who answered, throwing

her a nasty grin. "Ivan's the one who gets to decide what happens to all the little Witches we catch. You will regret meeting him."

"I already do, pal," Shane muttered.

Wicked swords gleaming, the Witch Hunters marched them out of the grove, turning them away from the city. Shane threw a glance over her shoulder, a sick feeling in her stomach. What was happening in Everlynd? And what was happening to Fi?

# 23

## Fi

FI WOKE WITH a gasp and found herself staring right into Briar's eyes. It took her a minute to get her bearings. She could hear the water lapping as she lay on her side in the rowboat. Briar was curled in the same position, their bodies only inches apart in the cradle of the hull. When the dream dust took hold, they'd fallen toward each other. The sky above them was rosy with early afternoon light and loud with the shrieks of wheeling birds. Fi exhaled in relief. They were back on the lake.

As the last wisps of the dream faded, she peered into Briar's eyes, searching for any hint of an angry red glow. His nightmare image was burned into her mind, the twisted bone horns and the gruesome claws. But the eyes that met hers were beautiful crystal blue, his expression soft, his blond hair spilled around his head like a halo. He was just Briar again.

"The book . . . ?" she asked hopefully.

"I found it." Briar smiled so wide Fi couldn't help smiling back. He seemed light and free, like the weight of the world had slipped from his shoulders. "Fi, we did it." Briar reached out, grabbing hold of her hands, and as his fingers squeezed hers, Fi finally let herself believe it.

"We can save Andar," she whispered.

Briar's eyes sparkled. "We can save everyone."

He lifted a hand and laid it against her cheek. For just a second, Fi had the fleeting sense of his warm skin against hers, the impression that their bodies fit perfectly together—then Briar pulled back, frowning, staring at his hand. Where he'd brushed her cheek, his fingers came away coated in dusky-gray flecks, like snowflakes or . . . ash?

Fi bolted up, the boat rocking under her. The wind shifted, and suddenly the air was thick with it, countless gray specks swirling down out of the glowing sky. Briar sat up, too, his eyes unfocused as he stared in horror at something over her shoulder. It was all Fi could do to make herself turn.

Everlynd was burning.

Fi gripped the bow of the rowboat, her fingernails digging into the wood. The boat had drifted to shore sometime during the night, and from this close, she could feel the wave of heat breaking over her as red flames rioted against the stone walls, a pristine tower collapsing into a pile of smoldering rubble before their eyes. A dark haze of soot hung over the city. The flames had chewed the red pennants on the shining towers into sooty rags, flapping weakly as the wind threw the sparks up in swirls. The world that had seemed so silent a moment ago was suddenly full of the roar of fire and scared voices shouting, the pop of shattered glass, the distant sound of something breaking. Fi thought it might be her heart.

She turned back to Briar, breathless. "Briar . . ."

Briar didn't seem to hear her. For a long, terrible moment, he stared at the wreckage of the golden city, his eyes clouded like he was losing Andar all over again. Then his face contorted, and he vaulted out of the boat, scrambling through the reeds, racing toward the flames. Fi was right behind him.

*How could this happen?* The question was so loud in Fi's head it felt like she was screaming it at the top of her lungs. Could the Spindle Witch have reached Everlynd through them, through the dream? She'd never heard of any magic like that. There was some explanation, but her mind couldn't find it. All she could think, over and over, was that this couldn't be happening—not now, not like this. Not when they were so close to getting everything they needed.

In the narrow streets, the smoke made it hard to breathe. Fi's skin prickled as they sprinted past a crumbling house, orange tongues of flame licking through the windows. A beam crashed to the road behind them. Briar banked around a corner, and suddenly Fi found herself in front of the Main Manor, the wide courtyard a flurry of motion as red-caped soldiers led frightened citizens away from the flames. The air was thick with the sound of children crying. Fi stared into faces streaked with soot as the people of Everlynd limped away from their broken city, following the guards toward the golden cliffs.

Briar headed for a woman in a red cape. She was supporting an old man, his reedy arm flung over her shoulder. "Captain Hane! What happened?" he asked.

"Witch Hunters," Captain Hane answered tersely, barely sparing Briar a glance as she passed the old man along to one of her subordinates. "They attacked at noon—two dozen or so. No one was prepared." She wiped a frustrated sleeve against her chin, smearing the soot. "They were like a pack of feral dogs, running through the city and burning everything they could. We managed to keep casualties down, but they did a lot of damage before the Red Ember rallied and drove them off. They'll be back, though, and in greater numbers. We have to evacuate."

"How is this possible?" Fi could barely get the words out, her tongue thick in her mouth. "Everlynd is protected. The storm—"

Briar grabbed her arm. "Fi. Look."

Fi followed his pointing finger, squinting at the wastes beyond Everlynd, the low hills rising outside the city. Then she realized she could *see* those hills, which until now had been hidden behind a whirl of dust. The sandstorm, the barrier that had protected Everlynd for generations, had vanished without a trace.

*The Spindle Witch*, Fi thought. It had to be. Demolishing the sandstorm would have taken immense power, maybe the most powerful magic the kingdom of Andar had ever known. But something was niggling in her mind, a tiny seed of doubt that she couldn't shake. If the Spindle Witch could take down the sandstorm, why hadn't she done it before? And why now, after Briar had banished her from the dream? Nothing had changed in Everlynd in nearly a hundred years, nothing except . . .

Except that they had come here. Fi had come here.

An awful thought struck her—one that made her entire chest feel like it had caved in.

*No. Please, please, no*, she begged in her heart.

There was a great groan and crack as a window burst from a house at the end of the street—*Perrin's house*, Fi realized, in the second before she took off running. Her lungs burned, the air around her livid with sparks. She dodged just in time as a window lattice came down over her head, churning with flames.

"Perrin!" she shouted, skidding up to the house. Was he still inside? The door had crumpled, wedged in the frame, but she threw herself against it with all her might. The door didn't budge. Fi took a step back, her body shuddering as she glimpsed the main room through the scorched window. Every book had been reduced to a hollowed-out shell, every hourglass an explosion of shards, all the beautiful magic locked up in those glass bulbs just a glitter of sand on the floor. And the painting of Perrin's father was withering, scorched by the flames . . .

"Fi, stop!"

Suddenly, Briar was at her side, his arms locked around her waist as he wrestled her away from the fire. Fi fought him even though she knew it was too late.

"Perrin!" she choked out. "What if he's—"

"Filore!"

Fi whipped around at the sound of her full name. The Paper Witch was hurrying down the road toward them, Perrin outstripping him with long, lanky strides. Briar released her, and Perrin pulled up short next to them, throwing his arms out as if to prove he was still in one piece.

"It's okay," Perrin assured her. "It's only trinkets in there. All the important things made it out."

He was lying. Fi knew what he was losing, what it felt like to have irreplaceable things ripped away. Her eyes fixed on the man behind him—the one person who could either absolve her or condemn her. The Paper Witch's mouth was set in a grim line, his crystal earring shivering as he looked at her with solemn blue eyes.

Fi pushed past Perrin and seized the man's robes. "How long?" she croaked.

"Fi," Briar started, but she only shook her head.

"How long were we asleep?" she demanded, still praying with every fiber of her being that she was wrong.

His silence was deafening.

It was Perrin who answered at last, glancing between them with concern. "Something went wrong," he told her. "It was like you were trapped in the dream. I tried to bring you out of it, but I was afraid if I interfered too much you could wind up lost and unable to return at all."

"How long?" Fi whispered again.

The Paper Witch pressed a hand down on her shoulder, looking pained. "Two days."

Fi felt numb with shock. She sagged against the Paper Witch. Only her fingers fisted in the tall man's robe kept her on her feet. *Two days.* She'd slept right through the third day. The Butterfly Curse had caught up with her, and it had done to Everlynd what it always did to beautiful places: ripped them apart. The Curse of the Wandering Butterfly had been the undoing of the most powerful Witch who ever lived. The enchantment that protected Everlynd had been no match for its malevolence.

"I'm afraid there's more, Filore," the Paper Witch said.

*More? How could there possibly be more?* Fi didn't think she could possibly take one more thing.

"Shane and Red were taken. During the battle, the scouts of the Red Ember saw them being led away by the Witch Hunters. They were too far away to mount a rescue, especially in the chaos."

Fi choked, her breath burning inside her. *Not Shane,* she thought desperately. *Not my partner.* The one person she'd started to think she could never lose. She felt violently ill.

The Paper Witch had warned her so many times what her curse could do, and still she'd tempted fate. She'd heard the prediction of the Seer Witch and thought arrogantly that she could keep it from happening. That she had it all under control. That all the misery and suffering were behind her.

She'd never been so wrong. And she'd never paid so dearly.

Fi stared up at the flames devouring Perrin's house. The Witch Hunters might have carried the torches, but she had set fire to Everlynd. She was the reason the Witches were no longer safe, that people had been hurt, that Shane was gone. She was the reason her mother would never get to see this beautiful city. When the Witch Hunters came again, and they would, they'd destroy everything: the library, the oasis, the dazzling golden tower. She felt like she was back in the snow again in front of a burned-out manor, the storm whipping around her frozen body, watching the agony flicker across her aunt's face.

*You did this.* Those words were in her head as Briar grabbed her arms, forcing her to face him.

"Fi! Look at me. What's going on?" He sounded angry, but more than that, he sounded lost and scared.

"I . . ." Fi swallowed, her stomach heaving like she might throw up. "I did this."

"What are you talking about?" Briar was practically shouting now. Those fingertips that had been so soft against her cheek dug into her shoulders. "The Witch Hunters did this."

"Because of me," Fi tried to say. "Because of my curse. Briar, I'm so sorry—"

"You!"

Fi flinched as the Seer appeared in the street, leaning heavily on the Stone Witch's arm. The woman's robes were stained with soot, and her face twisted in a hateful snarl as she stopped in front of Fi, disheveled gray hair flying about her shoulders.

"You and your curse have delivered us all into the hands of the Spindle Witch!" She spat the words like daggers. Fi felt Briar tense beside her, but she couldn't bring herself to look up into his face.

The Stone Witch surveyed the burning house for a moment before he raised his hand, curling stiff fingers into a fist. The golden stone crumpled like he'd smashed it in his palm, the streaked walls curling in around the flame until it suffocated and went out. The whole structure collapsed into a heap. Even Perrin winced at the crunch of splintering beams.

The Stone Witch's eyes passed over Fi, tired and resigned, but when he spoke, it was to the Seer. "There will be plenty of time to assign blame later—and plenty to go around," he added. "Everlynd is lost. For now, we must see to the people."

Fi watched them go through a fog. She couldn't think, couldn't breathe—her head was pounding from the smoke and the heat, but mostly from the knowledge that all of this was her fault.

Briar stood in front of her, outlined by the curls of smoke spiraling up from his city. Her eyes stung. Fi turned away, crushing the heels of her palms into the tears to keep them from falling. She couldn't do this right now—not in front of Briar Rose. She had to get away from him, put the distance between them she had sworn to keep from the start.

She'd only gone three steps before Briar's voice caught her.

"Fi?" he asked. "Is it true? What she said—did you do this somehow?"

"Yes." Fi squeezed her eyes shut, waiting until she had swallowed the tears and her expression was blank before she faced him. "That mark on my palm . . . it's a curse mark. A curse I've carried a long time." Her throat was closing up, her eyes hazy. "They shouldn't have let me into this city. If I hadn't come here—if I hadn't been chosen by the bone spindle—" When had it all started, anyway? What was the moment she should have turned back?

Briar seized her shoulders. "Don't do that," he said, shaking her. "Don't talk around it. This one time, just give me a straight answer. Did you know your curse could bring this on Everlynd?"

Fi wasn't even sure she knew the answer to that question. She had lived with the curse for so long—it had consumed her every waking moment, her every thought, and then she had become Shane's partner on this quest, and then Briar's partner, and she'd thought about it less and less. Had she forgotten how dangerous it was, gotten swept up in a fantasy of being the hero of Andar?

"I tried to tell you," she said, pressing her hands against his chest. "I was going to. I . . ."

Briar's eyes were hard and cold, and Fi swallowed. He wanted it straight. That was the least she could do. She took a deep breath, forcing her shoulders back.

"It's the mark of the Wandering Butterfly. It means I'm cursed to bring misfortune on any place that takes me in. As long as I keep moving, I can outrun it, but . . ." She shook her head. "Three days. That's all I get anywhere before something happens."

"Something?" Briar's voice was tight enough to snap.

Fi broke from his hold, backing up. "Something bad, Briar. I don't get to know what. I don't get to weigh the pros and cons and then decide. It's a curse! The more I care about something, the more misery the curse brings."

"So Everlynd . . ." Briar began, his mouth open in horror.

"I loved it because it was part of your kingdom, Briar. I loved it so much I destroyed it. I'm sorry—I'm so, so sorry."

"Because it's my kingdom," Briar repeated softly. His hands curled into fists. "How could you not tell me?" he demanded, his voice rising. "Maybe we could have done something differently—stopped this from happening! How could you put all these people's lives in danger?"

Fi's heart was a burning piece of paper crumpling in her chest. "I was trying to help you!" She couldn't stop the tears streaming down her cheeks. "I meant to be gone long before my time was up. I never wanted to let this curse touch you. That's why I . . ." *Why I couldn't tell you I love you, too.* But she couldn't say it. She couldn't put that on Briar after everything she'd cost him. Fi ground her hands into fists. "I thought I had it under control . . ."

"Well, you didn't," Briar hissed. "You made that choice all by yourself, and you made it for everyone, and now we all have to pay for it."

"Briar," Fi begged.

"You should have told me." His voice was low and certain, and the words rang between them with hollow finality.

She should have. She meant to. But it was too late for regrets. It was an impossible curse, one that was hers to bear alone, and this moment right here, when the sky was filled with ash and tears and Briar was looking at her with anguish and disgust—this was the Butterfly Curse working. This was what it was meant to do. This was why the Wandering Witch had disappeared from Andar, never to be heard from again.

Fi turned on her heels, tucked her face into her collar, and headed for the gates of the city.

"Where are you going?" Briar called after her, though he didn't follow.

"Away, where I can't hurt anybody else." Fi looked up at the sky and the flecks of ash falling overhead. Then she ran.

# 24

⟫⟫⟫⟩—⟨⟨⟨⟨

## Shane

THE WITCH HUNTERS' camp didn't look all that hospitable, especially arriving as a prisoner. A huddle of squat tents and torn black pennants flapped inside a jagged fence of sharpened pine logs, where the main attraction seemed to be the massive bonfire pit ringed in scorched granite slabs. All that was missing was a pile of skulls by the gate.

"Hurry it up," Tavian snapped. "Don't want to keep Ivan waiting."

Shane's mouth was bone dry, but she made the effort to spit into the dirt. The blunt edge of a pike cuffed her in the back of the head, not for the first time.

"Ow. I'm going." She shot a glance over at Red, but the girl wouldn't meet her eyes. Her jaw was clenched, her eyes wide and terrified. Cinzel whined, trailing on his chain.

They'd been marching like this for hours, the Witch Hunters flanking them as they moved up the hills and into a dense pine forest hung with threads of yellow moss. Shane had no idea what had happened to the sandstorm, or to Fi, but she wasn't in any position to worry about it right now. Tavian had seized her ax, and it hung from his belt, taunting her. At least they were finally here—even if *here* was the last place Shane had ever wanted to be.

Tavian hustled them into the heart of the camp, past more Witch Hunters than Shane had ever seen in one place. Two men playing dice stopped to watch them pass, their faces twisted with glee at the sight of Red in chains. Cinzel growled, but it wasn't very convincing with his scrappy tail between his legs. The air stank with the sulfur of a blacksmith's forge, and Shane could see a stooped man pouring molten iron into molds for more ugly saw-toothed blades. She should have known that was the Witch Hunters' own design.

"Ivan!" Tavian called. "Something I think you'll want to see."

Shane's stomach dropped as a pale-skinned man stood from beside the fire, wiping grease off his bloodless lips.

Ivan was pretty much exactly like Shane had pictured, except two feet taller. Sharp-featured and ugly as a gargoyle, his ears bristled with topaz studs, and his hair was shorn close enough to his head to show off decades of scars. He looked like the kind of guy who was most comfortable sitting around picking his teeth with a bone. Two saw-toothed swords were strapped over his broad shoulders. He moved forward with a nasty smile.

"Looks like you're bucking for another promotion, Tavian."

Shane took a furtive glance around. Except for the wooden staves holding a chunk of roasting meat over a cookfire, she didn't see anything she might turn into a weapon. The charred smell was enough to make her gag. Or maybe that was the hooked grin on Ivan's face as he seized Red's chin, yanking it up and turning her from side to side.

"So it is you," Ivan said, amused. "I heard rumors of a little girl and her wolves prowling the Forest of Thorns, licking the Spindle Witch's boots. You never did know how to keep yourself out of trouble."

Red tried to spit in his eye. Ivan was faster, forcing her head down and gripping Red by the back of her neck.

"Watch yourself," he hissed. "You know there's nothing the High Lord hates more than problems he's already solved coming back."

Red's words flashed through Shane's head. *A Witch born the daughter of Witch Hunters.*

Cinzel was snarling now, straining at the end of his chain and baring his teeth. The eerie sound set Shane's teeth on edge as Witch Hunters in black robes closed in around them to watch the show. Red was breathing hard, but her eyes were defiant, glaring up at Ivan through her bangs.

"Really? I thought what he despised most were failures like you. Isn't that why you're out here with nothing while he rules over the Eyrie?"

The amusement fell from Ivan's face. He tightened his grip until his bony fingers dug into Red's skin, right over the tattoo, and something sharp and sour shot through Shane's gut as Red bit her lip, refusing to cry out in pain. "My failure wasn't my own. Last time, there were limits on what I was allowed to do. You won't get that lucky again."

That was about all Shane could take. Before anyone

could stop her, she jerked forward on the manacle chain and slammed the heel of her boot into the stake holding the roast out of the fire. The arch of her foot throbbed where it had slammed into the wood, but it was worth it for the look on Ivan's face as the whole spit tumbled into the flames, the Witch Hunters' dinner going up in a burp of black smoke. A shout went through the spectators, and Tavian lunged out of the crowd, wrestling Shane away from the fire. Ivan whipped around to stare at her, his eyes blazing.

"Wow. My bad. I have no idea why that seemed like the right place to put my boot." Shane met Ivan's stare evenly, ignoring Tavian's arms hooked tight under her shoulders. "Your men could have killed us on the spot, but for some reason they dragged us all the way here. You need us alive for something. That sounds like a limitation to me."

Ivan looked like he was tempted to unsheathe one of his swords and carve Shane up in place of dinner. Shane didn't care. Ivan had released Red, and his attention was on Shane now, the girl at his back forgotten. Red was looking at her, too, but Shane couldn't even guess at the expression on her face.

"And what have we here?" Ivan asked, studying their shackles. "Another Witch?"

"Treasure hunter," Shane replied. Tavian's arms jerked uncomfortably tight around her joints, and he shoved a boot into the back of her knee.

"She's the huntsman—the one who discovered the lost ruin of the Rose Witches."

Ivan gave a little chuckle. "Ah. The one who broke your nose."

Shane got a whiff of his foul breath as he leaned down to peer into her face. He took the ax off Tavian's belt and turned it over in his hands. Shane bristled at that nasty vulture pawing all over a legendary weapon from Steelwight. She longed to seize the roughed-up handle and put the blade right through Ivan's skull.

Ivan beat the flat of the ax against his palm. "It's a beautiful piece. Well made. I bet you were someone important once. But now you're just one more thing bound for the fire."

He swung toward the crowd of spectators.

"Get the horses and the wagon ready. I'm taking them to the Eyrie." As Witch Hunters scurried to obey, he turned back to Red, patting her cheek so hard it sounded like a slap. "I have no idea why the High Lord wants you alive, but it won't last. As soon as he's wrung every scrap of knowledge about the Spindle Witch out of you, I'll have the pleasure of killing you with my own hands. And trust me: I won't botch it this time."

*This time.* The words banged around in Shane's head. She wanted to wipe that nasty expression off Ivan's face with her dirt-caked boot heel.

"We found one more thing." Tavian let Shane go so he could dig out the butterfly hairpin he'd taken off her when he searched them for weapons. "It's some kind of magic relic, but they won't tell us what it does."

"We don't know what it does," Shane said, rolling her eyes.

"Then let's find out, shall we?" Ivan twirled the hairpin, the butterflies glinting. "Most relics work especially well on Witches. Luckily, we seem to have one on hand." His hungry eyes settled on Red.

"Don't you dare!" Shane shouted, only to find herself

held back by Von and two other Witch Hunters as Red was forced to her knees in the dirt. The manacle chain rattled, stretched to its limit. Red stuck her chin out defiantly, unwilling to give Ivan the satisfaction.

Cinzel was whining and crying, as though he could sense the danger Red was in. Shane had no idea what that hairpin would do to Red. The Lord of the Butterflies had said the relic would only work under certain circumstances, and there was no telling what those were. Still, Shane found herself frantic, fighting against the hands that forced her down to her knees. Her hands fisted in the dirt and closed around a tiny shard of bone, sharp as a knife. If she could just get up, she'd go for Ivan's throat—

Ivan grabbed a hunk of Red's hair. He twisted it into a knot and then shoved the hairpin in. Red squeezed her eyes shut. The whole camp seemed to freeze as everyone waited for something to happen. Long seconds passed in silence, then a minute.

Ivan scoffed. "Just a useless bauble," he spat, shoving Red away. She fell backward into the mud, her face streaked with dirt and tears. "Oh well. I have plenty of ways of dealing with you. Get them into the wagon."

A battered wood cart rolled up beside them, the horses stamping at the nearness of the fire. Shane bristled watching Ivan strap her ax to the headboard, next to the drivers' feet. She slipped the bone shard into her pocket as Tavian hustled her up, the shackle digging into her wrist.

"What about the wolf?" Von asked, with a wary glance toward the snarling creature on the end of his chain. "Should we kill it?"

"No!" Red screamed, her voice hoarse with fear. "Don't you dare touch him!" She fought to get to Cinzel, but Ivan had her tightly by the arm, his fingers leaving white marks on her skin.

"Foolish girl. Always wearing your weakness on your sleeve." To the man with the pike, he said, "It lives—as long as she cooperates."

All of the blood had drained out of Red's face. She looked like she might crumple. Ivan offered his prisoner a vicious smile.

"There," he said, patting Red's cheek. "Helpless and defeated. That's the girl I remember."

Red turned her head away.

Fury roared through Shane like a riptide. She broke free from the grip on her arms, throwing herself at Ivan with a feral growl. She managed to land one satisfying blow to his jaw before something heavy struck her from behind. The last thing she saw was Red looking at her with wide eyes as the world went dark.

Shane came to in the wagon, her body bouncing as the cart rolled over uneven road. Her head felt like a melon someone had split open. She hissed in pain, pressing a hand to an egg-size lump at the base of her skull.

A wet rag hit her in the face. Shane took it gratefully, pressing it to her head before looking up at the girl that had thrown it.

Red sat beside her in the cart, curled around Cinzel. The butterfly pin stuck out of her hair at a crooked angle, the little charms clinking with the motion of the wheels. Her eyes were red from crying, and her voice, when she spoke, came out hoarse.

"I'm supposed to tell you Ivan hopes you learned your lesson." Her hands never stopped petting Cinzel, stroking little circles into his fur.

Shane ground her teeth. She had learned her lesson all right. She had lost her temper and made a reckless move, but that was the last mistake she'd make. Her gaze flicked to Ivan, just a dark shape riding at the head of the line.

"What did he do to you?" Shane asked.

Red's face crumpled, tears welling in her eyes. But all she said was, "A long time ago, I had two wolf pups. Now I have one." Then she leaned down, burying her face in Cinzel's matted fur.

Shane's heart clenched. Her gaze flickered to her ax on the headboard, gleaming in the red light.

She didn't know Red's whole story, but she didn't need to. She would free Red and take down every last Witch Hunter. She had a lot of pain and heartache to pay back.

# 25

**Briar Rose**

**BRIAR STOOD FROZEN** in the street, the smoke whipping around him as he stared at the place where Fi had disappeared. The crackle of the fire was almost gone now as the Stone Witch and others extinguished the flames one building at a time. But Briar could still taste the bitter ashes in his mouth.

He didn't understand how everything had gone wrong so quickly. One moment he was staring into Fi's eyes, the whole world stretching out before them, everything possible, and the next it was all burning. Part of him wanted to run after Fi, because he knew he was losing her, but another part of him, the part that had watched this city rise like a mirage out of the sand—that part was rooted to the spot.

Maybe a prince didn't get to love someone like her. Maybe Fi, with her curse, wasn't a risk he could afford to take. It made him a coward, though—a coward who had promised her a hundred times nothing would ever change how he felt about her. Were his promises really so empty?

His lungs burned as he sucked in a breath, feeling the losses mounting around him. How could it not matter? The last piece of Andar, the last haven of magic was decimated.

But was it really Fi's fault—*all Fi's fault?*

Fi thought so. He had seen that on her face. But Briar knew, deep down, that some sliver of it was his fault, too. Because he hadn't cared about the people of Everlynd, not really. Not more than he cared about her.

Shame and anger swirled in him, suffocating as the smoke. These were his people. The people who had welcomed him with open arms—who could have helped him save his brother, the castle, and all of Andar. And now that tiny glimmer of hope was snuffed out, too. He was disgusted thinking of what Sage would say if he could see him now.

He didn't know how long he'd been standing there, frozen, before the Paper Witch moved to stand beside him.

"Give her some time," the man suggested, wiping his soot-stained hands against his robes. "A curse is a difficult thing to bear, and there is still much to be done here."

The measured words left Briar cold. "You knew," he whispered. "You knew everything about her curse. You could have gotten her out of here—stopped all of this from happening."

The Paper Witch sighed, suddenly looking very tired. "Not without risking you, Briar Rose. And not without losing the chance for the answers we needed."

Briar rounded on him. "And it was worth losing Shane to the Witch Hunters? It was worth *all* this?" He waved his hand at the crumbling buildings and the streets glittering with broken glass.

It wasn't just Everlynd. It was Sage and Camellia and the Great Witches and everyone else who had sacrificed for him, over and over, to keep him safe. Briar was so sick of watching things burn for him.

"I did not know how dire the consequences would be," the Paper Witch said, shaking his head. "I grew up here, Briar Rose. And Shane is like family to me. Do not pretend to understand how difficult this decision was for me. But the ultimate defeat of the Spindle Witch is more important than any one person or city. The people of Andar would have known that, and the people of Everlynd will soon remember."

Briar suddenly felt sick to his stomach, recalling the Paper Witch's harsh expression as he warned the councilors they could no longer hide. "You wanted something like this to happen."

The Paper Witch looked stricken. "I assure you I did not *want* any of this—"

"But you'd do it again, wouldn't you?" Briar said. "Tell me that if you could go back, you'd change any of it!" He was yelling by the end, and he sidestepped the hand the Paper Witch reached out to him, silently waiting for his answer.

The Paper Witch let out a very slow breath. "I would do it again," he admitted.

Something inside Briar was crumbling piece by piece, just like the city around him. There were words in his mouth, bitter words, and he spit them out.

"We're done."

The Paper Witch's eyes widened. "There are things I can

still do for you, Briar Rose," he said, his crystal earring quivering.

"You can get these people to safety," Briar snapped. "That's what you can do, or I will never trust you again."

The Paper Witch searched Briar's face. Then he bowed his head, tucking his hands in the sleeves of his robe. "I will do as you ask," he said dutifully. "But what will you do—if I may be permitted to inquire, Your Highness?"

"What I should have done from the start." Red sparks crackled at his fingertips as Briar's anger seethed in him like another fire, devouring all other emotions.

The Paper Witch reached out for Briar and was forced back by a hot spark of red light that struck at him like a viper. Briar felt a little flare of satisfaction as the Paper Witch clutched his hand to his chest, fingers singed. "Do what you must, Briar Rose," the man said, "but do not use that power in anger. It is more dangerous than you know."

"Oh, I know *exactly* what it is," Briar promised darkly. "Another little secret you failed to share with me."

The Paper's Witch's eyes grew flinty. "Everything I have done is to protect Andar and you."

"And now I can protect myself," Briar said.

The Paper Witch seemed like he had more to say, but then his gaze cut down to Briar's red fingertips. His mouth thinned into a tight line. "As you wish." He bowed stiffly, sweeping off into the city. Briar watched him go, eyes narrowing as the Witch leaned close to speak to Perrin before he disappeared. Perrin jogged down the street toward Briar.

"Did the Paper Witch send you to talk sense into me?" Briar asked suspiciously.

Perrin blinked. "No. He just said you were going on a journey and could use help finding some supplies." A crooked half smile slid onto his lips. "I did plan to invite myself along, though."

Briar frowned, confused. "Why would you want anything to do with me? We're the reason your home was destroyed. You all could have kept living here, safe and protected, if it wasn't for us."

"For a while, maybe." Perrin's face grew serious. "But that safety, it was always an illusion." He turned away, looking out across the city. "You know my parents were part of the Red Ember. What I didn't tell you is that they were Rangers—the division that left the city and tried to rescue Witches who were caught by the Witch Hunters. It's a division that doesn't exist anymore. After my parents died, Nikor decided Everlynd was stretched too thin to help anyone else."

Briar gritted his teeth. "All the more reason we should never have come here."

"No." Perrin shook his head. "We gave up too much. First it was going out and rescuing others, then accepting outsiders, then we started turning away our own people—people like the Paper Witch—just because they disagreed with the council. We're nothing like we used to be."

Perrin fiddled with something at his neck—a tiny hourglass on a pendant chain. The golden sand winked in the last light of the fires.

"I want the people of Everlynd to remember what we've been waiting for all this time. It wasn't to survive for one more day. It was to take back this kingdom."

Briar swallowed. "I'm not sure I can do that," he admitted, feeling so hollow.

Perrin offered him a strange smile. "Did you know that sometimes dream Witches have flashes of memories in their sleep—the memories of other dream Witches? I know you, Briar Rose. In a way, I've known you all my life. My great-aunt believed in you. So I figure you're worth taking a chance on."

There it was again, that feeling when he looked at Perrin. Perrin wasn't the Dream Witch, but there was still a connection between them, the last precious fragments of something he'd lost.

The wind blew a flurry of ash past them. Briar looked down. "What about Everlynd? Don't they need you here?"

Perrin gave a rueful laugh. "The council can manage just fine without me. I'm not going to be that welcome right now anyway, since I'm the one who defied Nikor and brought Fi into the city."

The reminder stabbed at Briar—all the warnings ignored, all the ways this could have been avoided. Perrin dropped a hand on his shoulder before the dark thoughts got the better of him.

"Everlynd is lost, but Andar isn't. Once they get to safety and regroup, the Witches will rise again, and they'll remember how much they love this kingdom. You are the last prince of Andar, Briar Rose. So earn that loyalty. Give them something worth fighting for."

The words should have buoyed him, made him feel less alone. Instead Briar felt like he was being suffocated, crushed by the weight of a responsibility he didn't know how to carry.

"What if I'm not meant to be a ruler—if I can't do it?"

Perrin raised an eyebrow. "I think saving the kingdom comes before worrying about who's going to rule it." His expression softened. "I know a little something about the burden of great legacies. That's when it pays to have good friends around."

"I could use a few more of those," Briar admitted, feeling a wan smile crack his face. "Thanks."

"Besides, I'd like to see you get anywhere without me. You're a hundred years out of date, remember?" Perrin said with a cheeky smile. "I may not be a very powerful dream Witch yet, but I am pretty handy with a dagger." He took a few backward steps toward the quarter of the city that bordered the lake. Mercifully, it seemed to be mostly untouched by the destruction. "I'll figure out where they've stocked the supplies. Can't fight world-ending evil on an empty stomach."

Briar started after him. "I'll help."

Perrin pinned Briar with a significant look. "Don't you have something more important to do?"

Briar's stomach knotted. He still didn't know what he was going to do about Fi, or what he could possibly say, but Perrin was right. He had to go after her before it was too late.

"We'll wait for you outside of Everlynd," Briar promised. Perrin gave a quick wave before heading off.

Briar started at a walk, but he found himself running faster and faster as he reached the edge of the city. He had been so shocked and numb when Fi walked away, he hadn't done anything but watch her go. Now a small curl of panic seized his chest. What if she was long gone?

His heart was a jumble of warring emotions, but the one

thing he was sure of was that it would be unbearable to lose her. Fi was his savior—the light that had guided him out of the darkness of an everlasting dream. He had loved Everlynd for three days, but he had loved her for so much longer than that.

As he reached the edge of the city, he noticed something that he hadn't on the way in: a dirt track that climbed up into the rocky hills, visible in crisp detail now that the sandstorm was gone. Briar's footsteps pounded in time with his thudding heart. Where would Fi have gone? How far had she made it? The questions chased each other around in Briar's mind as he scanned the copses of pines.

Then he saw her. Fi hadn't gone anywhere. She had stopped just outside of the city, tucked under a tree with her knees pulled to her chest and her head buried in them. She was crying—crying in a way Briar had never seen before. Her shoulders shook as she sobbed. Guilt joined the other emotions swirling in Briar's stomach.

He was beginning to agree with the Stone Witch. There was plenty of blame to go around, between the Paper Witch and the reluctant council of Everlynd—and Briar himself. He should never have put it all on her.

A lump formed in Briar's throat. He had the urge to run to Fi, to brush the tears from her cheeks and promise that he would never push her away again. But he couldn't do it. He hadn't sorted out all his feelings yet, but he did know things were never going to be simple between them again. Now that he knew about her curse, and what it would mean for them to be together, it wasn't so easy to shrug off his own burdens as a prince of Andar. The last thing Fi needed was Briar making a bunch of promises he couldn't keep.

His anger at Fi drained away, and all it left behind was a well of sadness. He still cared for Fi, more than could ever fit inside the painful cracks in his heart, but it was a bitter-sweet ache. This didn't feel like a great destined love, the love he had dreamed about for a hundred years. Maybe they were just supposed to be partners, like Fi had promised, *until Andar was saved.* And then he would let her go.

*We kiss, and we go our separate ways.*

He wasn't sure he could do it. But he wasn't sure what other choice he had.

Briar approached slowly, snapping a few twigs under his boots to let her know he was there. Fi stiffened, rubbing her face against the sleeves of her jacket. Her tears had stopped by the time she looked up at Briar, but nothing masked her defeated expression.

Briar opened his mouth, then closed it again. How did he keep getting to the most important moment without figuring out what he wanted to say?

In the end, he said the only thing he could.

"We can still save Shane."

Fi's eyes widened. "How?" she asked helplessly. "I've ruined her chances along with yours. Without Everlynd's help, we have no hope of taking on the Witch Hunters."

"Yes, we do." Briar held up both hands in front of him. It barely took a thought to make them burn like they were on fire. The power came easier than it ever had. He swirled his hands around, quenching the red flames in tight fists. "That's the other thing I found in my dream, Fi. My magic is stronger than ever."

*Stronger even than the Spindle Witch*, he added silently.

Fi looked desperate and hopeful all at once. "Do you think it could be enough?"

"I do," Briar promised. "But we'll still need a really good plan. Think you're up for it?" Briar reached out a hand.

Fi tipped her head up, her hazel eyes determined. "Whatever it takes." She slid her hand into Briar's and let him pull her up.

It wasn't what Briar really wanted to say, but those words still felt trapped inside him. For now, they could be partners in saving Shane. By the time they did, Briar intended to have found an answer—one that wouldn't force him to split his heart and walk away from something he loved.

Down the dirt track, Briar could see Perrin heading their way, a few heavy packs slung over his shoulders. Perrin waved at him, and Briar waved back, more grateful than he knew how to show. They needed all the help they could get.

He turned to find Fi was staring beyond them, her gaze locked on the low northern hills and the churning clouds of a storm that loomed in the distance. Thunder rumbled from far away. Perrin jogged the last few steps, slinging the packs down into the dirt.

"If we don't want to be right in the middle of that storm, we'd better get moving. As for our destination . . . ?" He let the question hang.

"The Witch Hunters' headquarters," Fi said firmly.

"The Eyrie," Briar echoed.

Perrin whistled low under his breath. "Well, it's close, at least—only about two days' travel. We'll need to make it up to that ridge to start." He pointed at a row of black-barked pines meandering into the northern hills. "There's a road that runs straight to the tower, but since it's a Witch Hunter road, we're better off not getting too close. How do you feel about a shortcut?"

A ghost of a smile touched Fi's lips. "Shortcuts I can do."

Lightning rolled through the black clouds, the thunder crackling in its wake. Briar felt an answering crackle from the magic inside him. He hefted one of the packs over his shoulder. Then he followed Fi and Perrin toward the swirling clouds and tried not to look back at Everlynd, still smoldering behind them.

# 26

***

## Shane

THE STORM WAS coming. Shane could feel the wind's teeth sinking into her as the cart rattled up a narrow dirt track cut into the side of a steep hill. The dark clouds had rolled in fast, snuffing out the weak afternoon light. If Shane knew anything about summer storms, they were all about to get drenched.

She peered out of the cart, every muscle tense. The forest on the upward slope seethed with spindly trees charred to black husks, like a forest fire had roared through not long ago. The horses' hooves sank deep in the soft soil. To her left, the road fell away so fast and so far Shane couldn't see the bottom. A few feet the wrong direction, and the whole cart would plunge over the cliff into the valley below.

She glanced over at Red, curled tightly around her wolf. The butterfly pin was still snarled in her hair. She'd barely said a word to Shane since she'd come to, but she had plenty to say to Cinzel—her forehead was pressed against his fur, and she whispered urgently into his tawny ears.

"Look!"

Shane's guts clenched as one of the drivers shouted. She followed the pointing finger to a dark smudge a short distance up the road. More Witch Hunters—at least three of them, mounted on gray horses that whickered and stamped at the approaching storm. With Ivan's party, that made nine.

Ivan's face soured. "The High Lord's dogs have come to meet us."

As the wagon creaked into motion again, Shane inched across the weathered boards to bump Red's shoulder. Red's eyes flicked up to her face. "Hey," Shane hissed. "It'll be okay. I'm not going to let anything happen."

Red's face was drawn, but she managed a mocking smile. "I think it's your boundless optimism I'll miss the most when we're dead."

Shane scooted back, fingering the sharp little bone shard wedged deep in her pocket. She slipped it into her palm before the wagon jerked to a stop.

The first fat drop of rain hit Shane's face as Tavian lowered the footboard. "Out," he snapped. She and Red struggled out, manacles clanking. Von dragged Cinzel out by his chain.

Ivan was waiting for them at the head of the wagon. Mounted on horseback, he seemed horrifyingly tall, and Shane felt Red flinch as his gaze roved over them, glowering through a black eye so big Shane was downright proud of it. Shane stepped forward so she stood between Red and the Witch Hunters, just specters in flapping robes. She didn't know who the new vultures were, but Ivan didn't seem any happier to see them than she was.

"What is the meaning of this, Keres?" Ivan called to the woman riding at the head of the party, a hard-eyed figure with a ragged ear.

"We're here to take custody of the Witch."

Thunder rippled through the clouds as she spoke. The rain was starting to fall faster now, a silver curtain that washed over them in a whip of the wind. Ivan's boots squelched as he dropped out of the saddle onto the wet earth.

"She's my catch. Which means she's my kill. Those are the rules every sect agreed to under the High Lord's leadership." Ivan was close enough now that Shane could watch the lightning fork in his eyes. He looked more monstrous than ever, cruel and gleaming from the rain as his gaze slid to Red. "I've made promises to her, and I intend to keep them."

Shane could almost feel Red trembling behind her, and Cinzel gave a low whine, a ghostly sound that echoed through the barren trees. *Don't let him get to you*, Shane thought to Red. *Just hang on. I'll get you out of this.*

"The High Lord has other plans." Keres's voice was dispassionate. "I'm to bring her to the Eyrie—alone."

Ivan ground his teeth. "And the other one?"

The woman cast a disinterested eye over Shane. "Do whatever you like with her."

Shane was beginning to feel a little underappreciated by these Witch Hunters.

She could feel Red's hand pressed to her back, a single point of heat under the cold rain. She didn't know what Red was trying to tell her with that touch—to give up, to forget her, to save herself. Shane didn't want to hear it. She would never let Red be dragged off by these monsters. Her eyes flicked to her ax strapped to the wagon's headboard.

Ivan seethed. But at last he turned on his heel, tramping back toward his horse. "Bring the Witch," Ivan said, jerking his head at Tavian.

"Forgetting something?" Shane asked. She waved one hand, showing off the manacle.

Ivan's eyes narrowed. He stared into her face like he was looking for something, but if it was fear, he wasn't going to find any. He hissed a breath out through his teeth. "Unshackle them. Take our treasure hunter back to the camp. It's been a while since we had new fodder for the fighting pit—we could use some entertainment."

Tavian fumbled to get a lockpick off his belt. Shane felt the bite of nails in her back as Red fisted her hand in Shane's shirt, pressing closer.

"Shane," the girl started. "I—"

"Shut up," Shane said. "Anything you want to say to me, you can say after."

Red choked. "There is no *after*."

Shane chuckled. "Don't you ever get tired of being wrong about me, Red?"

She could feel Red's confusion, but Shane didn't turn around. Her attention was fixed on the Witch Hunters, every one of them armed with pikes and sickles and saw-toothed swords. All together, it was nine against one. Those were probably the worst odds of Shane's entire life, but giving up this chance meant giving up on Red. At least most of the Witch Hunters were on horseback—she'd take out the few on the ground first and improve her odds. *Unless the guys on horses run you off the cliff . . .*

She squeezed her hand around the sharpened bone hidden in her palm. Her heartbeat was as loud as the thunder. She'd have one chance. The second the manacles came off—

Tavian shuffled in and picked the lock on Red's cuff. The chain plunged into the mud. Red rubbed her raw skin, looking scared but defiant. Tavian turned to Shane.

"Not her."

Ivan's voice was like a knife in Shane's stomach. Tavian wheeled to face him, and so did Shane, horrified by the knowing smile on his lips.

"I have a feeling we're going to want to keep that one chained up."

Shane stared at the Witch Hunter, one second from total panic. The world closed in around her as Tavian bent to grab the empty manacle. Her eyes found Red's over his shoulder, those scared brown eyes locked on her, and Shane sucked in a breath like it was her last one. Then she jerked back and drove the sharp bone deep into the flesh of Tavian's thigh, ripping a scream from his throat. Tavian went down hard, the lockpick flying from his fingers.

*Nine to one—in chains. Bring it on.*

"Stop her!" Ivan roared.

"Red! Get out of here!" Shane shouted. She prayed the girl could hear her over the howl of the storm, the heavy rain pelting them as lightning tore through the dark clouds. In the flash of the strike, Shane saw Tavian in the mud, Ivan shouting, Cinzel yanking against his chain. Then the Witch Hunters were all around her, and she had no more time to think.

Shane caught the first Witch Hunter with a kick to the ribs, and shoved her fist, manacle and all, into the stomach of the second. They went down in a pile and almost slipped right into the ravine. The rain had made the narrow road even more treacherous, turning the path into a river as chunks of earth broke off and slithered over the cliff. *Watch your feet*, Shane reminded herself as she dove into the fray.

The three new Witch Hunters leapt out of the saddles, the hooves of frightened horses flashing around Shane as she drove her heel into one man's knee. Bones crunched under her heavy boot. She could barely see anymore, the rain spitting right into her eyes. She dodged a sword strike and found herself in the mud. At least her chain was good for one thing—Shane rolled onto her elbows and whipped it out across the ground, mowing Witch Hunters down at the ankles, like she'd seen Fi do outside the barn a lifetime ago. *Thanks, partner*, she thought distantly as she got to her knees.

A handful of Witch Hunters were hobbling away from her, making for the trees on badly sprained ankles. So they weren't all willing to die for the cause.

Through the clamor of voices, she searched for Red. A flash of scarlet drew her eyes toward the wagon. The girl had the butterfly hairpin in her hand, fumbling as she tried to pick the lock on Cinzel's chain—but Von was right behind her, pike raised, his face twisted in a snarl. Shane yanked herself up. She slid between Red and the Witch Hunter just in time to feel the *crack* of that pike staff crashing onto her shoulder blades.

Her brain went fuzzy. It was worth it for the shocked look on Red's face. Shane tried to wink, but it came out more like a wince. Then she looped the chain of her shackle over the pike, bracing the weapon against her shoulder as she spun and drove the blunt end right into Von's temple. The giant man toppled like a dead tree. Shane felt so light she thought she might fly.

"How do you like that! *Entertaining* enough for you?" she crowed.

Something crunched into the side of the wagon inches from her shoulder. Red screamed, and Shane ducked as splintered wood exploded in her face. Her stomach swooped when she turned to find Ivan not a foot behind her. He'd unslung one of the saw-toothed blades from his back, and it gleamed in the storm, every spike flashing. Ivan wrenched the sword back and took a good chunk of the wagon with it.

Shane fumbled to get hold of the pike, but Ivan's sword knocked it out of her hand before she could even get a grip. The blow was so strong that for a second Shane thought he'd snapped her wrist. Then she realized it was just the pike staff.

Red and Cinzel were running. Shane wanted to be mad that they'd abandoned her, but under the circumstances, she wished she were running, too. She darted a glance at her ax, still strapped to the head of the wagon, but it was too far away.

Ivan swung again, wickedly fast for such a heavy weapon. Shane dodged, not quite in time. The sword's teeth caught in her hair. A yell tore out of her throat as those rusty saw-teeth snarled in the knot and ripped through it, throwing chunks of severed brown hair over her shoulders. Her head roiled with the shock of the pain. Before she lost something that didn't grow back, Shane threw herself into the mud and rolled away from him under the wagon. Ivan's sword thunked into the wood, but Shane just kept rolling, slipping through the gap between the wheels and coming up on the other side. The horses startled and shied away from her.

"No one gets away from me," Ivan shouted. Then he had to move or go over the cliff, as the cart creaked, the scared horses driving the wheels closer and closer to the ravine.

Shane shoved her newly short hair out of her eyes. "First time for everything."

"Shane!"

Red's scream took her by surprise. Shane had figured the other girl was long gone. But there she was, clutching a tree with her hair plastered to her face—and there was Tavian, coming at Shane with his sword raised. The cloth at his thigh was slick with blood where she'd stabbed him with the bone, but from the feverish light in his eyes, Shane doubted he was even feeling it.

The chain was all she had. Shane barely had time to yank it into a block before the Witch Hunter was on her, slamming his blade into the chain over and over. Shane's elbows buckled. Tavian pressed in with all his weight, and Shane stared into those narrowed eyes through the twisted chain. The links were bending, the metal shrieking under the force. One more good hit, and the chain would snap.

A streak of white-hot lightning knifed through the storm, striking a spindly tree up the slope. For one moment, the whole sky was white fire, the crack of the splitting tree disappearing into the angry boom of thunder. A giant branch sagged from the trunk, rippling with flames. Shane seized the moment and slammed her foot into the nub of sharp bone embedded in Tavian's thigh, driving it farther in. Tavian howled as he hit his knees.

Shane didn't waste a second. She wrapped the chain tight around his sword. With one good yank, she had the saw-toothed blade.

Tavian clawed at the mud, wriggling away like a worm as Shane lifted the sword high. Then she twisted the hilt and plunged the sword down toward him.

"That's for the black eye," she spat. She stumbled away, shaking from the cold rain—then Red was at her side, picking the lock with the butterfly pin. Shane felt a flood of satisfaction as the manacle clicked open and tumbled off her wrist.

"Thanks," Shane tried to say. But the words got lost in a terrible moan, followed by the Witch Hunters shouting as the crack of splintering wood split the air.

Shane spun around. The tree that had been struck by lightning had come loose in the wet mud, the dangling branch towing it downward until a huge chunk of the mountain broke off, sliding straight toward them. The whole slope was rolling like a wave. Shane had never seen a mudslide before, and she didn't need to see one up close now.

She turned, shoving Red hard. "Go! Go, go!"

Red didn't need to be told twice. Cinzel leapt out of the trees, loping at her heels. Shane was right behind them. The horses dragging the cart barreled past, nearly flattening them. Over her shoulder, Shane could see the Witch Hunters scrambling to get out of the way, shrieking for their horses. Then the mudslide swept across the road, and all Shane could hear was the great roar of the earth, the crackle of black trees splitting as they were pulled under by the wave. The Witch Hunters were gone.

She caught Red's gaze, panting, hardly daring to believe they were still alive. Then something reared out of the fog—Ivan on his gray horse, both saw-toothed blades slicing through the rain. Shane threw herself back from the churning hooves. Ivan must have mounted up after she lost track of him, fast enough on horseback to get out of the way of the mudslide. *Or he's come back from the dead to get revenge*, Shane thought. She wouldn't put it past him.

"Keep going!" she shouted to Red, ducking as Ivan struck at her again.

Red hesitated, unsure. Cinzel was howling, his yellow eyes narrowed to slits. "But—"

"Just go! You're the one he wants!" Shane clenched her teeth before she could say the rest—that if she was distracted worrying about Red, she'd be no match for Ivan.

Red backed away. Then she pressed her fingers to her lips and gave one sharp whistle. Cinzel surged out of the mist around the horse's hooves, sinking his fangs into Ivan's leg and dragging him from the saddle. The Witch Hunter bellowed. One of his swords spun out of his hand as he hit the ground, and Shane leapt on it. Her fist clenched around the muddy hilt. Red took off, a scarlet streak fleeing into the trees, and then it was just Shane and Ivan, watching each other through the blinding rain.

*Well*, Shane thought. *One is better than nine.*

Ivan got slowly to his feet, wiping a hand across his cheek.

His eyes glowed like coals in his scarred face. "You can't stop me," he told Shane. "You can only slow me down."

"Then I'll slow you down," Shane promised through gritted teeth.

It had been a long time since Shane trained with a sword. Every movement felt rusty, and the saw-toothed blade was unbearably heavy. Her muscles ached just lifting it. She could feel herself shivering, her boots sliding in the mud as she lunged at Ivan and missed. Ivan whipped his sword through the air like it was nothing. Shane ducked, but realized too late that she'd jumped into his range—Ivan's elbow cracked against her chin, and Shane stumbled back, blinking dark spots out of her eyes. She swung for his legs. Ivan stepped easily out of the way, blocking her wild strike with a flick of his wrist.

Shane's sword sank into the dirt. The Witch Hunter leaned in, leering out of the gloom.

"Maybe I misjudged you. Maybe you can't slow me down."

For the first time, Shane felt fear crawling in her stomach. It made her reckless, her strikes coming fast but weak—Ivan batted her sword aside each time, barely turning, closing the distance with every block. Shane could hear her grandmother's voice in her head, telling her to calm down, to focus. But she was exhausted and sore, and the long fight was catching up with her, her knees threatening to give out.

Suddenly Ivan was right in front of her, his sword rushing at her shoulder. Shane blocked, and her aching wrist crumpled. The blade slipped through her fingers. Ivan grinned. He raised his boot, and the air rushed out of her as he drove his foot into the soft part of her stomach, kicking her back across the road. Shane groaned as she slammed into something.

"Pathetic."

Shane's vision swam. Ivan was coming toward her, one sure stride at a time. Lightning sparked in her head as she sat up, trying to figure out what she'd hit. A tree? A rock?

No. Ivan had thrown her against the overturned wagon, tipped on its side and sunk half a foot into the mud. The braces must have snapped as the horses fled. One wheel was still turning, and the headboard hung from one hinge, something gleaming in the low light.

Shane stared. *It couldn't be.*

Suddenly, her head was crystal clear. She got her feet under her just as Ivan's sword crunched into the earth, right where her leg had been.

Ivan almost looked amused. "You should have stuck to treasure hunting. You're good, but you're not nearly good enough to face me."

"Swordsmanship isn't really my thing," Shane bit out.

Ivan chuckled low in his throat. He lifted his sword, the wicked teeth rippling with a flash of lightning. "Oh no? What weapon would you choose to die with?"

"An ax," Shane answered.

With a surge of blood, she leapt for her ax, feeling the whoosh of air as Ivan's sword just missed her. The leather straps seemed to spring free at her touch. Shane snatched the handle, her heart singing at the feel of splintery old wood under her fingers—then she turned and slammed the swell of the handle into Ivan's jaw with all the strength she had left. His head snapped back with a satisfying *crack*.

Shane dug her heel into the mud. She spun once, whipping the ax behind her. With an audible crunch, the ax head smashed into Ivan's ribs. He took a staggering step back, sword flailing. The wet earth gave under his feet. Then the edge of the road seemed to crumble, and suddenly Ivan was slithering down toward the ravine. He howled, his long fingernails raking through the dirt as he plunged over the edge and disappeared.

Shane's stomach wrenched as the world tilted underneath her.

It wasn't just Ivan. She was slipping, too.

Shane felt herself sliding. She tried to grab for a handhold, but everything was slick, the chunks of earth sliding through her fingers. At the last moment, she sank her ax head into a dead stump right at the edge of the cliff—then she was over, her legs churning in empty air, the stump groaning as her fall lurched to a stop. Shane clung to the ax, panting hard. She squinted up into the rain. The handle was slick, and her arm was already shaking—she could only hold on like this for a second. Her empty hand waved through the air, searching for something, *anything*, to grab on to—

"Shane!"

Shane's head jerked up. Someone was calling her—and she would recognize that voice anywhere.

*Fi!*

# 27

## Fi

**"SHANE!" FI SCREAMED.** The name tore out of her throat as she watched her partner slide over the edge of the road, the earth falling away beneath her. The storm was so thick Fi couldn't even see the steep drop—just an ocean of swirling fog beyond the cliff, and Shane about to vanish into it. Her body was moving before her brain had even finished processing.

Fi had never thrown her rope so wildly or so fast. She didn't even watch to be certain it had wrapped around the thick branches of the tree she'd aimed for—or that the tree was alive and not already leaning into the treacherous slope. She just raced at breakneck speed for the cliff, the rope spooling out behind her. She cursed as the mud sucked at her boots. Shane had managed to sink her ax into a gnarled stump, and she was clinging to it, her whole face twisted with the effort. Even Fi could see it wouldn't hold long.

It was a shame she had gotten separated from Briar and Perrin, Fi thought as she hurtled toward the edge, because someone was going to have to pull Shane up, and she could really use the extra muscle.

They'd made it to the ridge just as the rain started coming down in sheets. The ashy slope of skeletal trees instantly turned to sludge, so they'd decided to risk taking the Witch Hunter road until they reached the next hill, where the pines that had escaped a recent forest fire might provide a little cover. It hadn't seemed like much of a risk. What Witch Hunters would be out in the downpour?

That had been a mistake. One minute they were hurrying through the gray haze, and the next a trio of Witch Hunters had appeared, racing for the trees.

The rest was a blur. Fi remembered yelling for Briar and Perrin to run, and then she was scrambling for her rope as a Witch Hunter with sopping blond hair came right for her. But the Witch Hunter didn't even seem to see her—he plowed into Fi's shoulder and then just kept going, limping away into the black trunks. By the time Fi looked up, her companions were gone. She could hear a distant roar as the slope up ahead began to waver, a mudslide carrying the burned carcasses of trees over the cliff. Then Fi heard the wolf howl, and she knew. Shane was alive, out here in the rain, fighting for her life. Fi took off running.

And now somehow, impossibly, Shane was right in front of her, about to slip out of her grasp forever.

Shane seized a handful of mud, trying to claw her way up the cliff, but the chunk of road broke off under her hand. Fi's heart barreled into her throat. She threw herself over the edge, one hand looped into the rope, the other reaching out desperately as far as she could.

Her hand closed around Shane's arm just as the ax ripped out of the stump. Shane's body jerked, and Fi jerked with her, her boots scrabbling at the loose earth as she fought to hold on. Shane's surprised eyes flew up to Fi as the excruciatingly painful sag of her weight burned in Fi's arm. She didn't let go.

"Fi!" Shane shouted. She clenched her hand around Fi's wrist. Her gray eyes darted between the thin rope and the muddy cliff. The earth groaned as another chunk came loose, and the rope sagged a few inches lower.

Fi had saved Shane from falling—but she was at a loss for what to do now. She had no handholds, nothing to rest her weight on, and no way to climb the rope as long as she was holding Shane. They'd slipped so far down that Fi couldn't even see over the edge of the cliff anymore. There was no chance of Briar or Perrin spotting them. The rain stung as it whipped into her eyes, and her worthless, crumpy little finger ached like it was breaking all over again. Fi sank her teeth into her bottom lip. She'd finally found her partner, but at this rate, it was going to be a really short reunion.

"Shane," Fi shouted—then the rope went suddenly slack, the line slithering free through the mud. She felt it coming loose in her hands. Her stomach plunged down at the rush of weightlessness.

And then there was a shout, and the rope caught again.

Fi's head shot up. That hadn't been Briar's or Perrin's scream. She peered through the fog, her gaze fixing on the last person she'd ever expected. Red was teetering at the edge of the cliff, straining to keep hold of the rope. She pushed a straggle of hair out of her face with her elbow, her skin slick with the rain as she yanked back with all her might. Fi could see her whole body shaking with effort.

"Red, back off!" Shane yelled. "You're not strong enough. You can't—"

"I am so sick of you telling me what to do!" Red shouted. "Just shut up and let me rescue you!"

Fi's body felt like it was going to split from being yanked in two directions. She closed her eyes, trying to ignore the storm and the pain in her straining joints and just concentrate. There was a way out of this. There had to be. She just needed to *think*—

"Red!"

Fi's eyes sprang open at Shane's cry. Red's boots were right at the edge, her toes licking the open air. The girl pitched forward helplessly as her footholds crumbled. Just in time, a pair of lanky arms shot out and closed around her, two strong hands seizing the rope.

"Gotcha!" Perrin said.

The pair vanished over the edge as Perrin hauled Red backward, pulling her to safety. For a long moment, nothing else happened. Fi held her breath, her heart racing, her eyes fixed on the spot where Perrin had been. Then the whole rope shuddered, and she felt the line begin to inch upward one jerk at a time.

When Fi was finally close enough to dig her heels into solid ground, she could see Perrin had wrapped the rope around a sturdy tree and was using the counterforce to ratchet them up. He shot Fi a relieved smile. Red was waiting at the edge of the cliff, and she wrapped her hands around Shane, yanking her up. Some part of Fi tried to remember that Red could still be an enemy, but it was hard to see an agent of the Spindle Witch in the bedraggled girl with sopping clothes and wide, scared eyes.

With one last heave, they all collapsed in a muddy heap. Fi lay on her back, her lungs quivering. Her hands throbbed with bright red rope burns. But she would take those burns any day over the alternative.

Perrin jogged over to join them, and he held out a hand to help Fi up. She took it gratefully. Her adrenaline rush was abating, and she had a feeling she was about to have a major case of jelly legs.

"Never a dull moment with you people," Perrin said with a smile.

Fi huffed out a laugh. "A dull moment might be nice at this point."

Coughing and panting, Shane got to her knees, wiping a splatter of mud from her face. Her cheek was swollen, and her hair looked like someone had hacked it off with dull garden shears, but none of that stopped her giant grin as her eyes met Fi's.

"Your timing couldn't be better, partner," Shane wheezed gratefully.

It was nothing compared to how grateful Fi felt—deep, abiding relief that left her weak kneed. She'd truly thought her partner was lost forever, but here she was, smiling and teasing and mostly in one piece. It didn't wipe out anything that had happened in Everlynd, but the jagged hole in Fi's heart felt a little less empty.

Red knelt off to one side, looking out of place. She squeaked as Shane leaned in and banged their shoulders together, catching her eye.

"I guess I owe you a thanks, too," she added.

Red shook herself and stood up. "It was Cinzel who followed you," she insisted. The soundless gray shadow of the wolf slipped out of the trees and padded over to Red. He was soaking wet, his fur matted and slicked down against his muddy white legs.

"Well, I'm not thanking that fleabag," Shane warned, rising and slinging her ax into the braces on her back. "Besides, if you want to get technical, it was Perrin who kept us all from tumbling to our deaths."

Perrin laughed, holding out his mud-splattered hands. "You're just lucky my arms are so long."

Fi knew she should agree, laugh along, thank Perrin profusely—anything—but she felt rooted to the spot, suddenly overwhelmed by the enormity of what had just happened. If she had been one minute later, Shane would have fallen to her death. If the rain hadn't led them to take the Witch Hunter road, Shane would have died. If Perrin hadn't agreed to be their guide . . . If Fi had spent one more second crying alone . . . If she'd even slipped in the mud as she ran . . .

Shane would be dead. It was too close a call.

There was a splatter of footsteps as Briar skidded into the clearing, his eyes wild. "Is everyone okay? I'm sorry, I got caught in the trees . . ." His gaze leapt between them and then stopped on Fi, his eyebrows drawn in concern. "Fi? What's wrong?"

Fi's throat felt too tight to get a breath. She shook her head hard. Nothing was wrong—she wasn't even the one who'd been in the worst danger. But everyone was looking at her now, Briar and Red and Perrin and especially Shane, reaching out as if to rest a hand on her shoulder.

"Hey. Are you okay, partner?"

*Partner.* The word made her choke. Fi jerked away, unable to bear it.

"This was all my fault," she whispered.

"I think you're giving yourself a little too much credit—" Shane began.

"It was," Fi cut her off. She lifted her hand slowly, peeling off the fingerless glove and holding up the butterfly mark. Briar's words rang in her head. *How could you not tell me?* She owed Shane the truth most of all.

As the storm faded to an icy drizzle, Fi took a deep breath and told Shane everything—the truth about the Butterfly Curse, the truth about Armand and her family and the Lord of the Butterflies, the truth about what she had brought down on Everlynd, what she had brought down on Shane. It all poured out of Fi at once, the words rushing out like the dam inside her had broken. She couldn't even bring herself to look at Briar, too scared of what she'd see on his face.

"I'm the reason for all of it," Fi finished, wrapping her arms around herself. The rain had let up, but she felt chilled to the bone. "I should have known better—I *did* know better, but I brought the Butterfly Curse down on all of you."

Shane just stared at her for a long moment. Then she dropped her hands on Fi's shoulders, squeezing tight. "That's a lot to be carrying alone," she said quietly.

Something about the softness, the sympathy behind those words, made Fi's eyes prickle. She blinked quickly, looking away. "Now you understand why I never wanted a partner."

"No," Shane said, pulling Fi into a quick, rough hug. "Now I understand why you need a partner more than anyone."

"But . . ." Fi gaped over Shane's shoulder, not quite sure she believed it. Could Shane really not blame her? "You could have been killed!"

Shane snorted. "Yeah. Lucky I have this ridiculously reckless partner who threw herself over a cliff to stop that from happening." She pulled back far enough to offer Fi a cheeky grin. "And you're supposed to be the smart one."

Fi choked on the laugh wedged in her throat. That was just Shane all over. A few grateful tears slipped out of the corners of her eyes, and she turned her head away, scrubbing at them. It wasn't very effective with her wet sleeve.

Shane seemed to sense that it was too much for her. She let go and clapped Fi on the back. "Come on," she said. "I'm soaked all the way through to my skin. I vote we have the rest of this conversation in front of a fire."

"I know a place we can make camp," Perrin offered. "And if we can find the packs again, we'll have dry things."

Fi hadn't even thought of the packs. She'd ditched hers the moment she heard the wolf howl. Only Briar seemed to be wearing his. He was still looking at her with some expression she couldn't read. But he didn't look angry. At least, not that she could tell through the blur of her tears.

The last few minutes were catching up with Fi, including the fact that she'd just poured her heart out in front of no fewer than four people—two of whom she didn't even know that well. Embarrassment sent a wave of heat through her. But she refused to regret it. She was soaked, muddy, and exhausted, but she had told Shane everything. And she still had a partner.

"Lead the way," Shane called to Perrin. Then she hooked an elbow around Fi's neck, dragging her close enough to mutter, "I hope you know you're stuck with me now."

Fi wondered how Shane always knew exactly what she needed to hear.

# 28

### Briar Rose

BRIAR SAT FORWARD on the fallen log, relishing the warmth of the fire on his socked feet. It had taken a while since everything was wet, but between his magic and Fi's handy flint and tinder, they'd finally managed to get a fire going. The rain had passed, and the moon had risen into a clear sky with only a few wisps of clouds.

The tall pine grove wasn't much of a camp, but the ground was flat, and the thick needles had kept out the worst of the rain. Perrin had passed out spare clothes from the packs. Their mess of wet jackets and cloaks lay over the rocks to dry as though having their own private gathering, while the rest of them crowded around the fire.

Briar stirred thick soup bubbling in a big, dented cookpot they'd scavenged from the Witch Hunters' overturned wagon. As the steam hit his face, he felt a flush of warmth in his chest. It wasn't from the fire, though, or the dry tunic, or even the prospect of a hot meal. It was the sound of laughter washing over him as Fi knelt behind Shane, tugging her fingers through her partner's shorn-off hair.

"Just cut it all off," Shane insisted. She was looking a little ragged around the edges and a dark bruise stood out on her cheekbone, but she was in high spirits.

"With what, your ax?" Fi asked, arching an eyebrow. "Because I can guarantee that haircut would strike fear into the hearts of your enemies—and your friends."

Shane chuckled, and Briar saw a smile spread across Red's lips. She kept petting the wolf at her feet, whether to calm the animal or herself, Briar didn't know. Red was no longer cuffed to Shane, but she moved as though she were, staying within arm's length as if the huntsman was the only thing keeping her here. For all Briar knew, she was.

Perrin had removed the butterfly pin from Red's hair and was studying it carefully in the firelight. As the only one with nothing more important to do, Briar had been left in charge of the soup. But he kept forgetting about it, losing himself in watching Fi's little smile as she waved the silver dagger from Shane's boot.

"Without scissors, I take no responsibility for how this turns out," she said, before sawing at the long hair trailing from one side of Shane's head.

Shane chuckled. "You can't possibly do a worse job than the last guy."

Briar caught a flash of black on Fi's palm. Her fingerless glove was among the rest of the wet things. It felt strange to see the butterfly mark out in the open after she'd hidden it so long. Fi seemed more open, too, relaxing into the heat of the fire and rolling her eyes as Shane pantomimed a Witch Hunter fight that had to be at least a little embellished.

Briar finally understood all the guilt and fear Fi had been carrying as long as he'd known her. He'd felt it like a physical blow, listening while she poured her heart out to Shane. Shane had brushed it all away so easily, like the curse changed nothing between them. Briar hated that he hadn't been able to do that in Everlynd—that in the middle of the smoke and the ash, he hadn't wrapped his arms around her and promised she would never be alone.

Perrin suddenly slumped forward, as if he'd nodded off. His leg jerked like it was about to go into the fire.

"Perrin!" Briar banged the spoon against the pot. "Hey, wake up."

Perrin's head shot up in surprise. "What?" he asked, blinking.

"You fell asleep," Red told him.

"Of course I did." Perrin tapped a finger against his forehead. "Dream magic, remember? I was getting a better look at this hairpin."

Red seemed wary but interested. Briar found himself leaning forward, too.

"There's an extremely powerful spell locked inside this relic," Perrin said, turning the metal shaft and making the butterflies clink together. "But I have no idea what *right circumstances* would activate it. There's definitely a piece missing"—he pointed to the empty chain—"but for all I know, that could be intentional. Maybe there's a final butterfly that brings the whole thing to life."

Briar frowned at the bloodred rubies winking in the fire-light. One more piece of a puzzle they couldn't put together.

Fi was staring so hard at the relic she nearly took off the tip of Shane's ear.

"Hey!" Shane protested. "Are you cutting my hair or just yanking it out? I said short, not bald."

"Sorry," Fi said sheepishly.

"So you don't think it did anything to me?" Red asked, looking relieved.

"No," Perrin said with a smile. "The magic is locked tightly inside it. It's perfectly safe. Well, mostly safe." He gave it a mistrustful look. "Probably safe. You know, on second thought, I'm just going to put this away." He wrapped the pin carefully into a handkerchief and tucked it in his pocket.

"There. Done," Fi said, mussing her hands through Shane's newly shortened hair. It was a little intimidating, swept back from her face and standing up in wild spikes.

"How do I look?" Shane asked. She struck a pose, but it was somewhat undercut by the loud growl of her stomach. "How's that soup coming, Briar?"

"It's . . . boiling over!" Briar leapt to his feet, gaping at the broth bubbling down the side of the pot and hissing into the fire. He cast about, totally at a loss. Then Fi was right beside him, wielding his wet cream-colored shirt. She wrapped it around the pot handle, and Briar grabbed on next to her, both of them heaving the pot off the flames.

Briar coughed out a lungful of smoke. "I guess that got away from me."

Fi gave him a flat look, poking him in the chest with the ladle. "Next time, I do the cooking, and you do the hair-styling."

*Next time.* Those words made Briar's chest so tight he couldn't breathe. He wasn't sure she'd want a *next time,* at least not with him.

"I didn't even know you could burn soup," he admitted.

"Typical prince. You can burn anything—I would know," Shane assured him. "But most of it's edible anyway."

Briar was relieved to find Shane was right. The soup was hot enough to scorch the inside of his mouth, and Shane spit out one lump of char after scraping the bottom of the pot for seconds, but after so long in the rain, it was warm and satisfying and delicious. Fi perched next to him on the log, and the feeling of her elbow bumping against his was as wonderful as it was distracting.

"Last bite," Shane said, leaning over the stew pot and digging at the bottom. She trailed off when the wolf got suddenly to its feet. The animal hadn't moved from Red's side all evening, lying with his head on his paws, just watching them with its bright eyes. Now Cinzel padded up to Shane, who was still awkwardly stretched out over the cookpot, holding up the ladle. The wolf dodged forward and pushed his nose right into Shane's face.

Shane squawked, rocking back on her heels. "Hey! Keep your drool to yourself, pal."

"He's expressing his affection," Red explained. "It's how wolves say hello. They look each other right in the eyes, push their noses together, and lick each other's teeth."

"They what?" Shane demanded, then sealed her mouth shut as Cinzel squished his nose against hers and licked a long, wet stripe over her lips. Perrin burst out laughing.

"It means he accepts you as a pack mate," Red said. "You'll hurt his feelings if you pull away. You're lucky— Cinzel doesn't like many people."

The wolf licked all the way from Shane's chin to her forehead twice more before looking back at Red proudly, tongue lolling. He seemed like a different animal all of a sudden, playful and assured. His eyes closed to dark crescents, and for a second, he almost seemed to be smiling.

"Oh yeah, real lucky," Shane muttered, wiping at her sticky face. Then she yelped as Cinzel stole the last scraps out of the pot. "Hey! You rascal."

Fi was laughing so hard she almost slipped off the log. Her fingers fumbled for something to hold on to—and then her hand found Briar's, squeezing it tight, and something swept through him, such a big warm feeling it had to be magic.

This—being right here with Fi—was the happiest he'd ever been. It was a happiness he hadn't even dreamed of, locked away in the castle, and now that he had it, he never wanted to let it go. Titles and kingdoms and curses, everything he'd been wrestling with since Everlynd—it all seemed so small compared to the feeling inside him, a vast ocean of light that crashed over his heart as Fi met his eyes, her face glowing. Briar smiled right back.

How could he ever think of letting her go? He couldn't imagine a future without her anymore. Whatever he had to give up to be with Fi would be worth it if it meant a lifetime of her smiling at him like this.

Suddenly, it was all so simple. Briar knew exactly what he wanted to say to Fi. He just didn't want it to be in front of a crowd.

Cinzel lay down at Red's feet once more. Briar watched the rest of his companions settling down around the fire, trying to think of a compelling reason he and Fi had to go into the woods alone, so he could get everything off his chest. He hadn't come up with one yet when a pine cone smacked his arm.

Briar jerked around to see Shane with her hand out-stretched. "That wasn't aimed at you," the huntsman said, not looking particularly sorry. "Do me a favor and peg Fi with it instead."

Fi had been staring intently into the fire, her forehead creased in thought. She blinked as Shane hefted another pine cone. "Why? What did I do?"

"I recognize that expression," Shane said, throwing again. Fi ducked. "That's you getting ready to leave me out of some harebrained scheme. Like maybe taking on the Witch Hunters' headquarters all by yourself? How am I doing—getting warm?"

Red hot, judging by the guilty look on Fi's face.

*Take on the Witch Hunters? Just them—alone?* Briar hadn't even thought about what their next move would be now that they'd gotten Shane back.

Fi raked a hand through her hair. "Shane, you and Red just escaped from the Witch Hunters—"

The third pine cone finally hit Fi straight on, bouncing off her shin. "All the more reason I deserve to kick the tar out of them. Don't make me give you the partner speech again," Shane warned.

"Why would you want to go to the Eyrie?" Red asked, her eyes troubled.

"Two reasons." Fi held up a hand, raising one finger. "My curse took down Everlynd's protections, leaving them vulnerable to the Witch Hunters. They'll never be able to join Briar against the Spindle Witch with the Witch Hunters at their backs." She looked down, fisting her hand around the butterfly mark. "I'm the reason they're in danger. I have to make it right."

"I'm all for cracking Witch Hunter skulls," Shane said. "But I don't think we're exactly equipped to take on an army."

"We wouldn't have to," Briar said, realizing what Fi must be thinking. "According to Captain Hane, the Witch Hunters' alliance is fragile. The only thing holding them together is their new leader. Without him, the Witch Hunter sects would fracture again. They'd still be around, but they wouldn't be nearly as dangerous if they were busy fighting each other."

Red's face had gone ashen. "Kill the High Lord of the Witch Hunters? In his own tower?" she whispered, looking a little sick. "Impossible."

Shane frowned. "Wouldn't it be safer to draw him out?"

"Which brings me to the second reason." Fi held up another finger. "The book we need to solve Camellia's code."

"It's an old book of collected stories from my sister's private library," Briar said, tossing a pine cone into the flames. "The Witch Hunters took the only copy I know of. We think they're keeping it at the tower, among all the other relics they've been collecting."

"If we could succeed at either one of those objectives," Fi murmured, "we could make a difference."

Silence hung in the air for a moment before Shane broke it by cracking her knuckles. "Well, I'm feeling pretty good about my odds right now."

"It won't be possible without a plan," Perrin said, fiddling with his hourglass necklace. "But if we can come up with something that has even the slightest chance of working, I'm in."

"What do we know about the watchtower?" Fi asked.

Perrin sighed, leaning back on his hands. "It's all but impregnable. It was constructed during the great wars, in the time before Queen Aurora conquered the warring duchies and unified Andar. It's built right on a rocky outcropping between two ravines, with no way in or out but a few rope bridges."

Perrin scooped up a twig of firewood and drew a rough sketch in the dirt: the circular tower with a chasm on each side. The four rope bridges, all in a row, looked precarious even in sketch form.

"That'll pretty much leave a frontal assault," Shane said.

Briar shook his head slowly. "I don't know. The way Captain Hane was talking about it, I got the sense it would be a hard fight even with the full might of the Red Ember."

No one had anything to say to that except the crickets. Maybe Briar was reading into it, but their chirping didn't sound very encouraging.

It was Red who broke the silence. "If it would be useful to know the layout of the watchtower, I can give it to you. I've been there—lived there, actually, when I was little. Anything you want to know, I can probably tell you."

Briar wasn't sure what surprised him more: that Red had

a connection to the Witch Hunters *and* the Spindle Witch, or that she was actually willing to help them. Or maybe that wasn't surprising at all, given Shane's talent for getting through to people.

They spent an hour talking around an attack on the Eyrie. Red quickly proved an invaluable source of information, describing its ins and outs, including a side passage that led into the tower at the ground floor, near the soldiers' barracks. They might even have a fighting chance if they could get inside the building.

The problem they kept coming back to was the four rope bridges that were the only means of reaching the tower. There was no way they could all sneak across unseen, and even if they managed to lure the Witch Hunters out, five against an army was no one's idea of good odds. No matter how they tweaked the plan, they seemed to come back to a doomed frontal assault. Shane and Fi were winding up to go through it again when Perrin got to his feet.

"Let's call it a night," he suggested. "We're going around in circles. We can look at it again in the morning with fresh eyes . . . and fresh brains." He stretched, rolling his shoulders. "I'm going to get some more firewood."

Red had withdrawn into herself as they talked, her eyes fixed on the tower drawn in the dirt. She sat up when Cinzel raised his head, his ears perking up as he watched Perrin leaving.

"Do you want to go hunting?" she asked the wolf. Cinzel got immediately to his feet. "Come on, boy. Let's go." The wolf bunted his head against her hip, twining around her legs as she vanished into the dark space under the trees.

Shane sighed, stuffing her feet into the boots that had been warming by the fire. "I'll keep an eye on her."

"Do you trust her, Shane?" Fi asked, catching her partner's gaze.

"Against the Spindle Witch?" Shane frowned. "I'm not sure. But against the Witch Hunters—absolutely."

Fi nodded, satisfied, and Shane took off, sweeping rain-speckled pine branches out of her way. Briar's gaze flickered to Fi.

It was just the two of them now. They still sat side by side, barely a foot apart, but it felt like an impossible distance. Fi's eyes were fixed on the fire, and Briar knew she was still thinking about the Eyrie, turning the problem over and over in her mind.

He wished he could chase her worries away. Fi had rejected his plan of drawing the Witch Hunters out and taking them on himself with his magic, but right now, Briar felt like there was nothing he couldn't do. He'd heard that Queen Aurora could use her magic to summon lightning out of a clear sky, that she could heat magic in her hands until it screamed into a battle like a giant fireball. That was how his magic felt now—limitless. If only there was some way to prove it to Fi.

Briar's eyes settled on the fire. Then he smiled. He cupped one hand and twisted his fingers, just like he had long ago, at another campfire. Fi sucked in a breath as a crimson rose unfurled in the seething coals, the yellow tongues of the flames softening into petals. But Briar could do more than that now—so much more. He kept twisting, and the petals curled into buds, spinning tighter and tighter until they burst open into dozens of new blossoms, a cascade of roses in every color of the flames from blazing scarlet to blinding white.

"Briar . . ." Fi breathed. It took him a moment to understand why. Without even meaning to, he'd built something else into the illusion: a white tower ringed in roses. The tower Fi had rescued him from.

Her crooked smile said she recognized it, too. Briar held her gaze as he closed his fist, feeling the hum of magic in his fingers—then he released it, and the roses erupted in a shower of petals, swirling upward until they faded away to sparks.

Fi was looking at him now. He liked what the low light did to her eyes, making the flecks of gold and green in the hazel shine. His tongue felt thick in his mouth, and his pulse was racing, but he knew this might be his only chance.

Briar inched forward until he was right in front of Fi, close enough to rest a hand on her knee. She jumped, but she didn't pull away.

"Fi, listen." The forest was quiet, the whole world leaning in to hear him. Briar leaned in, too, his voice barely a whisper. "You were right about us. You were right about everything."

Fi's eyes widened a fraction in surprise. Briar took a deep breath, ready to blurt out everything he needed to say. Then suddenly he was choking, and so was Fi, both of them scrambling to get out of a cloud of billowing smoke. The wind had turned, sending the heavy smoke from the fire right toward them. Briar's eyes burned as he coughed into his sleeve.

"That really shouldn't have surprised you," Perrin quipped, stepping out of the trees with a pile of wood clutched in his arms. "They say smoke follows beauty, after all." Fi arched an eyebrow, and Perrin added with a wink, "I'm referring, of course, to the lovely prince."

"Of course," Fi said, the tips of her ears a little red. She was already on her feet, dusting bark chips from her legs and refusing to meet Briar's eyes.

"I'm not interrupting anything, am I?" Perrin asked, glancing between them.

"As a matter of fact," Briar began, at the same time as Fi said, "Absolutely not." Then she practically dove into the packs, strewing blankets and supplies all over the camp as she engineered five bedrolls.

Briar slumped back against the pine trunk, frustration bubbling up in him. He'd missed his moment, and once again, he hadn't managed to say anything important—he'd barely said anything at all! He could tell Fi was already over-analyzing those few words, twisting them around in her head. But there was nothing he could do about it now. He'd just have to watch for another chance, and this time, he wouldn't let it slip away.

Briar knew what he wanted. Now he just had to convince that hopeless skeptic she wanted it, too.

# 29

## Red

**RED STOOD ALONE** at the edge of the cliff, staring into the dark chasm far below. The night was filled with the smell of wet earth and the shimmer of raindrops hanging heavy on the pines, and the air seemed to hum with a thousand tiny sounds.

It was *alive*—that was the word for it. The whole world was alive with insects and trickling water and animals calling in the brush—and Red was alive, too. She didn't know what to think about that.

Cinzel had walked with her as far as the forest, then bumped her legs affectionately before disappearing after some prey. She could sense his happiness in his tail twitching, the ease of his body as he loped off into the trees. She wished she felt the same rush of relief being off her chains. But all she felt was a new kind of dread.

She had a feeling Shane would be coming after her, but

she wasn't ready to be found. So she just sort of drifted, until at last she found herself at the edge of the steep drop with nowhere else to go.

A tiny stream trickled over the edge and splashed on the rocks down below. Red's hands clenched into her skirt. Her skin was rough and raw, the red line of the rope burned into her scarred palm. She closed her eyes and felt it all again—the icy rain on her face, the pounding of her heart, the ache in her arms from holding on so tight as Shane and Fi hung defenseless over the drop.

She should have let them fall. That's what *the right hand of the Spindle Witch* would have done. In one swoop, without lifting a finger, she could have gotten rid of her most dangerous enemies, crushed Briar Rose's spirit and crawled back into the Spindle Witch's good graces. All she had to do was *not* save them. But that wasn't the choice she'd made.

Worse, it hadn't even been a conscious decision. Her body had moved on its own the moment she realized Shane was in trouble. Her treacherous hands had been taking orders only from her heart as she clung desperately to the frayed rope. She'd been ready to die to save Shane—or to die with her.

Whether she meant to or not, in that moment, she had chosen a side. But what else was she supposed to do, when Shane had just saved her from the Witch Hunters—from Ivan, her oldest and darkest fear?

Heavy footfalls through the brush alerted her to a presence at her back. Red didn't even need to turn around to know who it was. She was beginning to think the huntsman was part bloodhound; she always seemed to be able to sniff Red out.

"Shane," she said, not taking her eyes off the rocks far below.

"Red." Shane sounded strangely wary. "Do you want to come away from there?"

She didn't. She didn't want to face the huntsman, to see that complicated look in her eyes. She just wanted to linger right here, on the precipice of something she wasn't ready to give in to yet. She'd lived her whole life here, between the darkness and the long fall.

Red wrapped her arms around her stomach. "I hate being so close to the tower. It makes my skin crawl." She couldn't see the Eyrie over the ridge, but she could imagine it, the watchfires burning into her like furious eyes. Her past was waiting for her there—every horrible, rotten memory she'd tried to bury.

Shane stepped closer. "Hopefully, after tomorrow night, we can put it all behind us."

Red choked on a laugh. Wasn't that the most ridiculous part of all? After everything that had happened, after barely getting out with their lives, Shane and her companions were still determined to go after the Witch Hunters again. They were asking her to lead them to their deaths. If she really cared about Shane, about any of them, Red should disappear right now before she told them anything else about the Eyrie and they all got themselves killed.

The drop licked at her toes. Red stretched her arms out, sucking in a deep breath of cold night air. "Do you think a person can ever outrun their past?"

"No." Shane didn't even hesitate before answering. Red

flinched. "But I think they can face it, and accept it, and eventually learn to live with it."

"And maybe change?" At last Red looked over her shoulder. Shane's gray eyes were a storm of emotions. Worry. Anger. Fear. Longing.

"Of course," Shane said softly. "That's how you live with it. By making it right." Her hand rose and then fell, as though she were desperate to reach out to Red but not sure how to do it without risking pushing her too far. Red was one step from the edge, after all.

Red closed her eyes. "You make that sound so easy."

The back of Shane's hand whispered against hers—just the bump of their knuckles brushing, the sudden flush of heat as Shane hooked their middle fingers together. "Easier than looking at yourself in the mirror and hating what you see."

Red's eyes prickled with tears. She kept them tightly shut. She wanted to believe Shane—that she could twist something deep inside her, and everything would be different. But what if she faced the truth of herself and found she wasn't worth saving?

Red had always done whatever it took to survive, and she'd never felt bad about it. People were cruel. People used each other. People only helped when they had something to gain. She'd truly believed that . . . until she met Shane. The huntsman did the right thing, always, even when there was nothing in it for her—especially then. People like Shane weren't supposed to exist. But if she did, then Red really was a monster. Just like her father had always told her.

She shook her head too hard. "You should have let me die."

"Never," Shane hissed, fisting their hands together. "Don't ever wish that, Red."

The tears were getting away from her. She felt one racing down her cheek. "I've done so many awful things."

Shane surged forward all at once, seizing Red's arms and spinning her around. "So do something good this time," she said, her eyes flashing. "Help us bring down the bad guys. You survived the Witch Hunters as a little girl, and you survived the Spindle Witch, too. But now it's time to do more than survive. Come with us—come with me, Red, and *start living*."

Shane's words broke over her like a wave. Red ached just looking at her—windswept and wild-eyed, holding on so tight that even though Red was still teetering on the edge, her heel gaping over empty air, suddenly she felt like she could never fall.

Red hadn't felt anything in so long. She lived in comfortable numbness, everything low and muted as if through water. She'd been safe in the deep, drifting away, until Shane yanked her up and breathed life into her. Shane made her feel like an exposed nerve, raw and vulnerable, unable to hide the most fragile parts of herself.

She wasn't sure she could handle it. That rawness. That ache.

"Where were you all those years ago?" Red whispered. "Why didn't you save me back then, when it still mattered?"

"Red . . ."

She couldn't read Shane's expression through the blur of tears. She felt those warm hands fall away from her shoulders, and she stiffened, wondering if Shane was about to step back and leave her. But all she felt were gentle fingers sliding into her hair as Shane pulled her close, pressing their foreheads together.

"Hey. Look at me," Shane said softly.

Red tried. But Shane's eyes were blinding, so calm and steady, staring right into the heart of her. She found herself trying to pull back, certain somehow that Shane would see all the worst things she'd ever done.

Shane held her tighter. "Don't look away. Don't close your eyes."

Red swallowed hard. She knew she must look blotchy and horrible, but Shane didn't make any move to push her away. She just breathed in, and Red breathed in with her, taking refuge in the tiny secret things that only belonged to them. The heat of Shane's exhale. The shining silver starlight in her gray eyes. The soft scratch of her thumb tracing tiny whorls on the nape of Red's neck, right over the tattoo.

"I'm here now," Shane said, a little catch in her voice. "I'll save you anytime you need it."

Red choked on her tears. "You and your promises," she whispered. But in spite of everything, she believed it. Shane had saved her, over and over. She was the only person in Red's life who'd ever made her a promise and kept it.

Shane huffed out a laugh. "I told you, you can't scare me away." She entwined their fingers, lifting Red's hand and pressing a kiss against the ugly scar the rod had left on her palm.

And then Red's body was moving on its own again. She felt so lost—but her heart knew what it wanted. She rocked forward on her toes and pressed her lips to Shane's. The kiss was desperate and breathless, and Shane's arm clenched around her, holding her tight to keep them from falling. But Red didn't care if they did fall. She just wanted to live inside this fragile dream as long as she could.

Shane had burrowed all the way inside her, strong as a heartbeat. Red didn't think she could go on without her anymore.

She might have kissed Shane forever, if not for Cinzel. The wolf was suddenly right beside them, banging his big furry head into the back of Shane's leg and almost sending them both over the cliff.

"Hey!" Shane protested, her arms windmilling. "Watch it, you mangy mutt."

Red couldn't help laughing at her grumpy expression. It felt like the laugh broke something inside her—some jagged, sharp thing she'd been carrying for so long. Red closed her eyes and let it break.

As they stepped apart, Shane scrubbed her hand through her hair, her eyes lingering on Red's lips. "So, uh . . . what did that mean?"

Red couldn't help but smile. The huntsman was so determined, so forceful, breaking anything that got in her way, but she was always so careful with Red. Probably the only person in the world Red could trust with her oh-so-cracked-and-breakable heart.

"Ask me again if we live through this," she said.

Shane just grinned. "Sounds like a damn good reason to live."

# 30

## Fi

FI LAY IN her bedroll stiff as a board, staring up at one narrow strip of stars through the pine branches. Sleep seemed miles away, but she resisted the urge to toss and turn. If she rolled over, no matter how hard she tried to avoid it, she knew her eyes would settle on Briar. After all the nights they'd spent traveling together, she could tell he was still awake—his breath was too light. If she looked at him, he'd open his eyes and look back at her, and then . . . she had no idea what would happen then.

Fi pressed the heels of her hands into her eyes. *Think about the Eyrie*, she told herself. *Think about the Witch Hunters. Everyone is counting on you to come up with a plan.* Every tiny stick on the ground under her felt like a log, every pebble a boulder. She brushed her fingers over Camellia's code tucked inside the deepest layers of her shirt. Fi didn't have to pull it out to picture every set of numbers lined up in neat rows . . . but no matter what she tried to fix her mind on, all she could think about was Briar's hand warm on her knee as he leaned toward her, his words chasing each other around in her head: *You were right about everything.*

What did that mean, *she was right*? Had Briar realized they didn't belong together? Had everything he felt for her withered and burned away now that he'd seen what the Butterfly Curse could do? Or was he talking about something else entirely? He'd been leaning in, his expression soft, his eyes steady on hers. Surely he wouldn't have kissed her right before he rejected her . . . though Fi supposed she had done exactly that to him.

Fi made a face. She needed some air.

She sat up quickly, working her boots on and slipping out of the camp. Perrin had offered to take first watch, and she gave him a quick nod as she tiptoed past, pushing blindly through the pines until she came out on a grassy hill. Clouds feathered over the crescent moon, and when they cleared, the whole hill seemed to glow, the wet grass glittering with silver light.

She heard footsteps behind her and turned to find that Briar had followed her, a cloak tucked under his arm. She supposed she should have expected that. Maybe unconsciously she'd come out here to end this. They stared at each other across the starry hillside.

"I need to finish what I was going to say before," Briar began, looking serious.

Fi nodded, steeling herself for whatever came next.

"You were right. It would be impossible for a prince of Andar to ever be with someone under a curse like yours."

Fi's stomach plummeted. She had expected that—deserved it even, after what she had brought on Everlynd—but it hurt. It hurt like the curse searing into her flesh all over again.

"I'm still not finished," Briar said gently, but she couldn't even look at him. They couldn't be together. Wasn't that enough?

"Fi . . ." Briar moved forward until she could feel his gaze burning into her bowed head. "A *prince* could never take that kind of risk—so I'm going to give it up. I'm going to abdicate my title and leave Andar."

Fi's head shot up, her mouth falling open in shock. "What?"

"Don't give me that look. I'm not going to abandon anyone." Briar's blue eyes twinkled with amusement. "We're partners until we've saved Andar, remember? But when it's over, I'm going to leave with you no matter what."

In the moonlight, he was otherworldly, radiant and beautiful with star-bright eyes. His expression was soft, a confident smile on his lips. He was serious. He was dead serious. Fi felt like he had picked her up and shaken her. She wasn't sure whether her heart was trying to soar or sinking like an anchor, because what Briar was suggesting, it was impossible.

Fi shook her head. "I can't let you do that for me. You have so much to lose—"

"*Let me?*" Briar's eyebrows shot up. "It's not your decision, it's mine. It's my life, and I get to decide what's important to me. And it's you, Fi—it's us."

She couldn't tear her eyes away from his. "But you've waited your whole life to get Andar back," she whispered.

"No. I haven't," Briar said. "Of course I want to save

Sage and everyone else, but I've never wanted to go back to that castle. My whole life, what I wanted more than anything was to get away and see the world. Being out here with you is the happiest I've ever been."

*Of course.* She should have realized that. All the signs were there—the way Briar was delighted by everything from old ruins to fuzzy caterpillars, his endless curiosity to see more, know more, do more. And that dazzling smile he had shot her as they stood side by side in the Stone Manor, and in the sandstorm, and in Everlynd, as they uncovered the secrets of Andar together. They were more alike than she sometimes imagined.

Briar was moving toward her, erasing the distance between them one step at a time. "You didn't put me in a cage. You saved me from one." Briar's words were barely a breath. "I love you for that—and for so much more."

He was right there, an arm's length away, the tips of his boots bumping hers. Fi stared down at their feet, almost dizzy, trying to figure out how they'd gotten so close so fast. She shook her head, but she wasn't sure who she was trying to convince. "Briar, the odds against us working are—"

"Stop." He held up a finger, pressing it to her lips. "You can reject me, but not because of what-ifs and worst-case scenarios. I'm going to say it one more time, and I want you to answer me, not with your head, but with your heart."

Fi's chest squeezed. She felt hot and cold all at once. It wasn't that she didn't know the answer. She wanted to throw her arms around Briar, tell him that she loved him, too—more than she'd ever thought was possible. But she was afraid. Fi had lost so many things to this curse, and she didn't think she could take any more. Everlynd was another scar that she would carry for a long time.

Briar took a breath, holding Fi by the shoulders and squeezing her softly. "I love you, Fi. Let me travel by your side forever. Please."

It was the *please* that undid her—because he was asking to stay, just like he had the very first night they met, after they'd been entangled by the bone spindle. Just like he had looked at her so many times along the way, earnest and warm and full of hope. And suddenly Fi was feeling instead of thinking.

She had built walls around her heart to keep out all the things she shouldn't wish for, shouldn't believe in, but Briar's words brought them tumbling down. All at once she was imagining her and Briar traveling side by side through Andar and Darfell, all the way to the coast, camping out and staying in shoddy inns and hiding out in rocky hollows to escape the rain. And when they reached the seashore, they would sit in the golden sand and jump through the crashing waves, and Briar would waste his time collecting far too many shells because he was fascinated by every one. There were other dreams, too— Briar the bad dancer embarrassing himself at parties, Briar her faithful light holding a handful of sparks as they delved into old, secret places. Briar with his silly billowing sleeves caught in the brambles of a blackberry bush, smiling at her with a thoroughly purple mouth. She could almost feel his hand entwined with hers as they lay in the grass of some other hill on some new, strange night, trying to count the stars. Fi wanted that life with him—and more than that, and more, and more.

Fi breathed out. She pressed her hand to the soft fabric over his heart.

"You're sure I'm what you want?" she asked.

Briar laughed. "I've been sure since the beginning. It's you I've been trying to convince all this time." He leaned closer, his smile joyful. "And it looks like I finally have."

Every time Briar had kissed her, there had been some wall between them—some secret. This time Fi put all of herself into it, leaning up to meet him, memorizing every feeling: his soft fingers and the cradle of his hands and the blush of heat from his breath on her face in the seconds before his lips finally touched hers. Her heart was beating so fast she thought it might stop. When Briar drew back, Fi locked her elbows around his neck and dragged him down again, fisting her hands into his coat to deepen the kiss. It was faint, but Fi swore she could taste the salt of ocean spray on his lips, and the soft tang of lemon tea—the sweetness of all the things they hadn't done together yet, but they would. They would save Briar's kingdom, and then they had the whole world ahead of them, just waiting.

When she finally let him go, Briar choked on a laugh, his eyes bright. "That was worth the wait," he told her. Fi elbowed him in his stomach, which just made him laugh harder. She shivered as a breeze swirled through the trees, and Briar started, glancing around before reaching down to pick something up. "Oh—sorry. I brought this for you, but . . . let's just say I got caught up in the moment." He wiped dewdrops from the bundled cloak and swung it around Fi's shoulders.

"Thanks." Fi pulled the cloak on gratefully. Then she blinked, looking more closely at the bright fabric. "Briar . . . this is an Everlynd cloak," she said, pointing out the white tower stitched into the red cloth.

"I guess," Briar said with a shrug. "Perrin brought them along."

"Did he bring any more?" Fi asked, excited. "More cloaks just like this?" She waved the cloth in his face.

"I think so—they're doubling as blankets," Briar said, confused. "Why?"

"I figured out how we can even the odds with the Witch Hunters," Fi said. "Or at least make them think we have."

"I knew you'd come up with something brilliant," Briar whispered. Then he leaned down and touched his lips to hers, and something ignited in Fi's chest like a flame.

It was hope, she realized. Against all odds, they might actually have a chance.

# 31

## Fi

**FI CLUNG DESPERATELY** to the wooden plank, hanging precariously from the underside of the rope bridge. The entire structure moved and swayed as a Witch Hunter passed overhead, his heavy boots creaking on the weathered boards. Fi squeezed her eyes shut, staying as still as possible and trying not to imagine the sheer cliffs and the dizzying drop into the ravine below. It wasn't easy, since she'd spent the entire crawl toward the bridge staring up at the Eyrie until the landscape was seared into her mind.

The tower reared up against the sky like a vicious clawed hand erupting from the earth. It was built of gray stone and crowned with sharp battlements that gleamed in the last of the dusk. The glow of fires through the slit windows made it seem like the whole structure was burning from within. The tower sat on a single spit of rock between the ravines. On every side, the ground fell away into sheer cliffs. The only path across was one of the four rope bridges stretched over the gaping chasm, each of them about fifteen feet apart and creaking in the soft wind.

A drip of sweat ran down Fi's spine. *Someday I will be the kind of strategist who makes plans in front of a map, from a safe distance*, she thought to herself, continuing the climb.

Her first task was to cross the underside of the rope bridge without being spotted or falling to her death, and it would have been hard enough without the heavy boots stomping around above her. At least she should be hard to spot. She had borrowed a dark shirt of Perrin's to wear under her new black coat, and unlike Briar, she didn't have a halo of golden hair or glowing porcelain skin to give her away. Besides, the Witch Hunters had no reason to look down. This was easily the most dangerous thing Fi had ever done, and she doubted anyone else would be desperate enough to try it.

Her muscles ached with the effort of holding up her own weight. She tipped her head, trying to gauge the distance to the other side. Somehow the bridge that had looked so short before had grown immensely long, and she was only a little over halfway. Her arm shuddered. Before she could lose her grip, Fi swung her boot up over the edge and tangled it in the crisscross of ropes that served as the bridge's railing. She hooked her elbow over the top, too, hanging for a moment to ease the strain on her muscles. Her boot and elbow would definitely be visible if another Witch Hunter passed, but clearly Fi had overestimated herself a little bit.

She wished she could have let Shane take this job. The huntsman had volunteered as soon as Fi told them someone had to make the dangerous crossing in the dark. Unfortunately,

Shane was also their main fighting force, and they were going to need her right where she was for the rest of the plan to work. Assuming they got that far.

Fi let herself rest for one moment more, breathing deeply. Then she unhooked her elbow, forcing her stiff fingers to grab the next plank. She was about to unhook her boot when the bridge began to shake and rattle as a heavy Witch Hunter jogged across. The splintered tip of the plank broke off in her hand, and Fi swallowed a scream as she lost her grip and sagged toward the chasm, her boot tangled in the ropes suddenly the only thing holding her up.

The darkness spun dizzily beneath her. Her stomach muscles shuddered as she struggled to lift herself with sheer will. She got her fingertips around the jagged plank just as the Witch Hunter passed overhead.

*Don't look down,* she begged silently. Luckily, the Witch Hunter seemed to be in a hurry. He rushed across without stopping. Fi didn't move until only the gentle sway of the bridge marked his passage.

All she wanted to do was wrap her whole body around the planks and hold on for dear life, but that wasn't an option. She was already behind. Her companions would be getting antsy, and she didn't imagine it would take too much antsiness for Shane to abandon all reason and start the doomed frontal assault she'd advocated for repeatedly. Fi sucked in a breath and pressed on.

She was sweating hard by the time she finally reached the other side. The torch rising from the bridge post seemed almost too bright after navigating in the semidarkness. Two sets of boots gleamed above her—a pair of sentries stationed at the end of the bridge. Slowly, muscles shaking, she shifted her weight to the rock wall, staying below their sight line and inching along the cliff face until she was far outside the ring of torchlight.

Fi peered up at the tower. From this close, she could see that the dark walls were pockmarked with crags and hollows, the snarling faces of the stone gargoyles worn away after hundreds of years enduring the storms of the wild north. The main door into the tower was held open by a barrel of saw-toothed blades.

She could cross *falling to her death* off the list of ways this plan could get her killed. The next item down was *impaled by Witch Hunters*.

Fi pulled herself over the rocky ledge as quietly as possible. She darted forward and pressed her back against the tower, then reached down the front of her shirt, pulling out the cloak she'd stowed out of the way while she made her crossing. It wasn't one of the beautiful red Everlynd cloaks; this one was made of stiff canvas dyed pitch black, with a silver buckle at the neck. She unrolled it quickly, catching the topaz pendant tucked into its folds before it hit the ground.

These were Witch Hunter clothes. Shane had retrieved them from the site of the battle, returning with a grim expression, and Fi had chosen not to ask about the dark stain along the hem. She slipped into the cloak and lifted the hood. With any luck, she should blend right in. Fi wasn't infamous among Witch Hunters, after all, so she wasn't likely to be recognized, even face-to-face. Another reason she was the right choice for this job.

The topaz pendant swung from her neck as Fi made her

way around the base of the tower, heading for the hidden side entrance Red had told her about. There was supposed to be a small door tucked behind one of the gargoyles, an old servants' entrance into the barracks kitchen.

It took Fi a minute to spot it in the gloom. The door was so weathered it looked more like a plank of wood someone had left leaning against the wall. She tugged the handle, wincing as the warped wood groaned, but the dark hallway beyond was empty.

So far, so good.

Fi dug out her flint and tinder, and smiled down at the scratched-up fire starters. She had a feeling her father couldn't have imagined just how often they were going to come in handy when he'd given them to her. From her other pocket, she pulled a sprig of black thistle, wound with a little curl of paper for easy kindling. Fi set the nettles at the foot of the gargoyle's pillar and then lit them with a spark. They went up in a quick flash of green.

That was the signal for her companions to start moving. The next part was up to Briar and Shane—Fi just had to sell it.

With no time for misgivings, Fi ducked inside the weathered door. She passed through a damp hallway and a dark kitchen, stopping when she reached the barracks. A few torches burned in sconces, throwing long shadows over the lumps in the rows and rows of beds stretched out through the base of the tower. Everlynd's council had been right about one thing: the Witch Hunters were definitely gathering at the Eyrie. Other doors led deeper into the tower. Only a few Witch Hunters were awake. Three men and one woman played cards at a battered table near one of the slit windows. A pile of gold and other loot changed hands as the cards fell.

Fi gulped, moving until she stood beside the window. She tilted her head up as though she were looking at the sky. Instead, her eyes were fixed on the darkness across the ravine. No one had even looked at her twice, dressed as she was, but Fi still felt like she stuck out like a sore thumb. She tried to loosen her shoulders, make her pose look less stiff.

"Hey, boy! Outta my way!"

Fi jumped, only realizing when a meaty hand came down on her shoulder that the barrel-chested Witch Hunter was talking to her.

"You're between me and my card game!" he slurred, clearly drunk.

Fi twisted her face into her best approximation of a Witch Hunter glare. "Go around," she suggested coldly, shrugging the man's hand off.

He chuckled, his giant shoulders rippling. "You're no more than a slip of a thing anyway," he decided, crashing through a few empty chairs to the card table and pushing the man with the smallest pile out.

Fi's heart was racing madly on the inside, and she decided then and there that she didn't have the right nerves to be a spy.

Her eyes darted back to the dark landscape outside the window. What was taking her companions so long? Had they run into some kind of trouble? A hooting laugh from the card table made her start, and she glared at the back of the Witch Hunter's head.

Long minutes passed as the moon rose high in the sky. Fi was about jumping out of her skin when it finally happened.

A tremendous crash of steel split the silence, ringing through the night. If Fi hadn't known it was a big pile of cookware they'd raided from the Witch Hunters, rigged to crash down on the rocks, she would have sworn it was the sounds of battle. At the same instant, a hundred fires sprang to life, glowing between the hills like lit torches carried by a force of soldiers. Fi's heart leapt. Those were Briar's flames, burning like a field of stars.

Then the flags began to go up. One by one, poles with the red sigil of Everlynd rose on the other side of the ravine, rippling in the night wind. Fi knew the whole plan—had in fact come up with it—and she still would have believed an army was marching on the Eyrie instead of just a ragtag band with a bunch of torn-up Everlynd cloaks on sticks, helped along by a little of Briar's magic.

Now for the finishing touch.

Fi sucked in a huge breath. "We're under attack!" she shouted as loud as she could. "It's a sneak attack by the Witches of Everlynd!"

Witch Hunters woken by the crashing cookware surged from their beds, grabbing for their weapons. The card players threw their game aside, rushing to the windows to spot the fires and the flags and taking up the call to arms. Fi ducked away, slipping into the chaos before she could be pinpointed as the one who'd shouted. The darkness was working in their favor, making the Witch Hunters easy to manipulate with just a little suggestion from Fi.

In moments, all the Witch Hunters were up, shoving each

other out of the way to get to the windows, and word that Everlynd was attacking in retaliation for the burning of their city was flying through the ranks. Fi joined a line of men and women arming up. She hid her disgust as a stringy-haired Witch Hunter shoved a saw-toothed blade into her hands.

"There's a whole battalion and more coming!" she hollered, inching toward the open front doors. "We have to get across the bridges before they can pin us down!"

Her gaze locked with that of a harsh fox-faced man, and for one awful moment Fi thought she had pushed this too far. But then the man howled, raising his saw-toothed blade in the air. Bloodthirsty battle cries filled the tower. Fi found herself swept outside, carried along in the mob of Witch Hunters charging for the bridges. She barely managed to get out before she was crushed to the center of the pack and forced to join the attack. Breathing hard, Fi slipped away, pressing her back to the stone of the tower and watching as the Witch Hunters rushed across the bridges, disappearing into the darkness.

Fi could hear Shane's battle cry in the distance, followed by a clash of steel. She sent up a silent prayer. Each of her companions was trying to take the place of at least ten soldiers, engaging the Witch Hunters just long enough to keep up the ruse and then falling back, luring them farther from the tower.

The last of the Witch Hunters trailed across the bridge. Fi watched them go, swallowing around a lump in her throat. She counted their entire force at well over fifty—too many to keep occupied for long.

She'd better hurry.

Fi threw the saw-toothed blade aside, trading it for the dagger she'd tucked into her belt. While her friends kept the Witch Hunters busy, Fi would cut down all but one of the rope bridges, leaving just a single path to the Eyrie. Then Briar and the others would race across to join her, and she'd sever the last of the ropes, cutting off the watchtower completely and trapping the Witch Hunters' main force on the far side of the ravine. If it worked, they'd be able to look for the High Lord and Camellia's book without facing an entire army—just whoever was left.

It was a lot more *if* than Fi was comfortable with in a plan, but it was all they had. She left her disguise on as she headed for the first bridge, hoping that if anyone caught a glimpse of her, she'd just look like a scrawny Witch Hunter late to the battle.

The two sentries hadn't joined the fight like Fi had hoped. Both had stopped at the edge of the ravine, staring out over the chasm. Fi made for the bridge farthest from them, her ears wide open for any shouts or footsteps.

She got to work, taking the first of four heavy ropes in her hand and sawing through it with the sharp silver dagger. The rope was thick, almost as big as its anchoring post, and the bristling strands frayed and snapped as Fi carved madly. The last strand fell away, leaving the planks of the bridge tilted, held up only on one side.

Fi looked up only long enough to determine the sentries weren't bearing down on her before slicing through the thinner ropes that served as rails. They snapped easily. The whole bridge shuddered, hanging from a single rope. She'd only cut halfway through it when the rest of the strands broke under the weight, her end of the bridge dropping away into the dark ravine below.

*One down, two to go,* Fi thought, racing for the next bridge. She wasn't far from the sentries, so she ducked low, falling to her knees and cutting at the ropes anchoring the base of the bridge first. Fi kept her head down, working so fast she barely remembered to breathe. She had just sawed through the first rope when a voice stopped her cold.

"You there! What are you doing?"

The Witch Hunter was right behind her. Fi had to think fast. She dropped the dagger, lifting the sawed-off end of the rope as she turned. "Look, sir," she said, really hoping that sometimes Witch Hunters called their superiors *sir.* "Someone's cut the ropes. Do you think it could be sabotage?"

"Let me see that!" the man demanded.

Fi held the rope low, forcing the tall man to bend over to get a good look. Then she whipped the rope up, twisting it around his neck and pulling hard. The man let out a strangled gurgle, clawing at his neck as she cut off his air.

Adrenaline gave Fi the strength she'd lacked under the bridge. She pulled the rope tighter, dodging as the man swung at her with a wild fist. That was why Fi had waited until he was bent over—she could never overpower a Witch Hunter unless she already had him down.

Fi held the rope tight until the man passed out, his body slumping down so hard it almost wrenched her shoulder out of its socket. Fi let go of the rope and sagged backward into the dirt. She stared at the craggy face for a moment before scrambling to her knees, sawing through the last ropes and sending the second bridge plummeting into the dark.

There was only one more to cut, but it would be the hardest one. She'd left the bridge near the sentries for last. One man stood by the brace of torches, while the other had moved partway across the bridge, a pike with a long blade resting against his shoulder. The metal gleamed along the sharpened edge. Fi bit her cheek. She had to get rid of them—this had already taken too long.

She unwound her rope from her belt, holding the ring in her right hand and the dagger in her left. Her stomach lurched at the thought of what she was about to do. It was the kind of thing Shane would come up with—the kind just as likely to get her killed. Fi's partner was really rubbing off on her in a bad way.

With one last breath, she chambered the rope and took off running, headed straight for the bridge.

Just outside the circle of torchlight, she released the rope. The metal ring slid down onto the bridge post with a tinny clang, and as the sentry whipped around, searching for its source, Fi hit the dirt and slid right into his knees, kicking the Witch Hunter toward the abyss. She caught a glimpse of his wide eyes before his boots slipped over the rocky edge and he plunged into the dark.

The rope and her momentum carried Fi the rest of the way to the post. She let go of the rope and threw herself at the bridge, digging the dagger's teeth into the frayed knots. The cord of the bridge railing bit into her hand. She could do this. She could make it.

"Stop! Intruder!"

Fi didn't know what had tipped the other sentry off—his companion's grunt or her skid in the dirt or just the bridge under his feet shuddering as Fi cut the railings away. It didn't matter. She was too close to stop. The Witch Hunter staggered toward her, stumbling on the unsteady bridge, and Fi forced the knife faster, sawing at the thick rope that held all the wooden planks in place. It felt like she was moving in sand.

The Witch Hunter pounded toward her, swinging his weapon over his head—then the rope snapped, and the bridge groaned. Fi ducked as the blade whizzed over her head, so close that she wouldn't be surprised to come out of this with a haircut that matched Shane's.

The Witch Hunter scrambled to hold on to the swinging planks, the bridge sagging over the chasm as all its weight strained at one ragged rope. Fi plunged her dagger into the knot. The rope tore free, and the Witch Hunter and the bridge disappeared with a sickening crack. Fi fell to her knees in the dirt, struggling to catch her breath.

Her fingers shook as she freed her ring from the bridge post and stuffed her rope into a belt loop. Still, she couldn't fight a smile as she made her way around the tower. She had actually cleared their path—and she was still alive to celebrate it!

Fi stopped at the end of the last bridge, her heart hammering away as she lit the second flare and held it high. She used her sleeve to wipe sweat from her brow, only now feeling the chill of the wind. The silence prickled in her ears. The rope rails were still; there was no pounding of feet on the planks.

Where were her companions? There was no way they could take on fifty Witch Hunters, and any minute their ruse would be discovered. All it would take was a single straggler exiting the tower and finding her—one voice raising the cry, and then Fi would be completely cut off from her friends as Witch Hunters poured back across the bridge, overwhelming her.

"Briar," she called uncertainly into the dark. "Perrin? Shane?"

There was no answer.

# 32

### Shane

SHANE WHOOPED AS she slammed the blunt back of
her ax into a Witch Hunter's shoulder and he went down in a
pile of scrawny limbs. Something whizzed over her head, but
she'd already lost as much hair as she could afford. She spun
on her heel and clocked another Witch Hunter in the mouth
with the butt of the handle.

The man fell back with a groan, spitting a mouthful of
blood and more than a few teeth. Shane showed hers off in
a wild grin as she hefted her ax and took off, scrambling up
a high jut of iron-streaked rocks to get another look at the
battlefield.

A sea of small fires surrounded her like fireflies, the torn
Everlynd cloaks flapping in the icy breeze. The night air
was thick with the sounds of a fight, steel against steel and a
counterpoint of angry shouts as the Witch Hunters searched
for their enemies in the dark.

This side of the ravine was riddled with rocky gullies cut by winter runoff, which was why they'd chosen this spot for an assault. The Witch Hunters had to split up to search the maze-like channels, which made it easier to keep a force of dozens busy with a force of, well, four. Startled faces bloomed out of the darkness as small pockets of Witch Hunters reached each circle of firelight, and then Shane was on them, her muscles singing with the sweet elation of a good old-fashioned brawl.

As their only real fighter, Shane had taken the farthest position from the bridge. They were just supposed to engage the Witch Hunters long enough for Fi to cut the first three bridges. Shane was probably *engaging* a little more than necessary. Her left wrist was still sore from the fight with Ivan, but she hardly felt it. In fact, she felt downright invincible.

Shane caught a flicker of movement—a shadow in a dark robe creeping toward the torch below her. A saw-toothed blade smashed the bundle of sticks and torn cloth to the ground.

"There's no one here!" the Witch Hunter growled in frustration.

Shane could fix that. She slid down the rock face with a rush of gravel—and before the man could even figure out where she was coming from, Shane had introduced his face to the sole of her boot, crushing her thick heel right into his nose. The Witch Hunter reeled away, clutching his face. Crooked, badly healed noses were going to be the new Witch Hunter look.

A figure reared up out of the dark, her sword almost taking a chunk out of Shane's shoulder. Apparently, the Witch

Hunter hadn't come alone. There were two other black-robed figures in the narrow gully with her, so close they were practically breathing down her neck. Shane dropped onto her back as the sword came down again, blocking high and planting one foot in the snarling woman's gut, then using the angle to throw the Witch Hunter over her head. The woman slammed into the rock face and crumpled next to the broken torch.

Something whistled past her ear. The remaining Witch Hunter bellowed as a quicksilver dagger struck his hand, knocking his blade into the dust. Perrin leapt down from the rock ledge and drove the hilt of his second dagger into the man's kneecap, taking him out of the fight for good. He retrieved his first dagger with a graceful flourish.

"You're better than I expected," Shane admitted. She had been glad to see that Perrin knew how to use the pair of daggers he carried, even if those weapons had abysmally short range. "Where'd you learn to fight? I thought you Everlynd Witches were all shut-ins."

Perrin laughed. "I have Captain Hane to thank for that. She's no slouch."

"Well, good for her." Shane had a feeling she might get along with Captain "No-Slouch" Hane if they ever crossed paths.

Perrin jerked his head toward the bridge. "Red's waving her flag. She saw the signal."

That had been Red's only job, the one cushy position in the whole plan: hiding near the last bridge and waiting for Fi's flare so she could wave them in. Shane squinted back toward the bridge. Red had improved on the original plan and lit her flag on fire just to make sure she had their attention.

"Briar is already ahead of us," Perrin filled in.

Even as he spoke, Shane saw a brief flare of light in the next channel over, Briar blinding a few Witch Hunters with a blistering flash of magic. She still couldn't shake the image of him at the beginning of the battle—Briar with his arms outstretched, lighting all the torches at once without so much as snapping his fingers.

Perrin scrambled up the rock, and Shane followed, jumping between the outcroppings until they could slide down near the bridge. Just in time. A sallow-faced Witch Hunter had crowded Red back toward the bridge's anchor posts, his sword gleaming in the light of the burning flag.

Red whipped the fiery cloth at him, but she clearly had no experience with a staff. Cinzel lurked behind her on the bridge, snapping and growling low in his throat.

Red screamed as she swung her flag too far and the Witch Hunter seized the pole, yanking her toward him. Shane sped up and slammed into the man with her shoulder. The Witch Hunter grabbed helplessly for the bridge ropes as he slipped over the edge of the chasm, the burning flag spiraling down after him.

Shane watched him fall, breathing hard. When she turned back, Red was watching her. The girl's hair was a mess, and one sleeve of her tunic was burned where she'd gotten too close to the fire, but she offered Shane a tiny smile.

"Let's go!" Briar shouted, skidding up beside them.

Shane could see Fi waving from the other side, jumping up and down with both arms wheeling over her head, pointing at something on their side of the ravine. Then she realized what Fi was trying to tell them. A whole knot of Witch Hunters, maybe fifteen strong, had spotted them and was streaming back toward the bridge. Shane gave Red a shove, and the girl started across at a run, Cinzel and Briar hot on her heels.

"Stop them! Don't let them reach the tower!"

That voice was close, closer than the army of Witch Hunters. Shane spun around. A broad-shouldered man had burst out of the nearest channel of rocks. His bloodshot eyes shone in the glow of the torch. She jerked her head at Perrin.

"Go already!" Then she choked up on her ax and chopped through the torch.

The bundle of twigs and oil-soaked rags hit the first planks of the bridge, and there was a sound like someone taking a quick breath as the fire rushed outward, licking hungrily at the frayed old ropes.

Shane threw the Witch Hunter one last look before she fled to the bridge, pounding across the shaky planks. She should have long enough to reach the far side, but by the time the rest of the Witch Hunters showed up, the bridge would be done for.

The bridge shuddered. Shane stumbled and then almost somersaulted right into the chasm as something crashed down behind her, making the whole bridge sway. Her stomach flipped. The broad-shouldered Witch Hunter had leapt over the flames, chasing her onto the bridge. He bared his teeth in a furious snarl as he swung his great saw-toothed sword.

Shane leapt back. He missed her by a foot, but it almost didn't matter as the bridge rocked from side to side. Shane was thrown against one railing and then the other. A second wild swing cut right through one of the thin rope rails. Shane's knees locked, her ears filled with the crackle of the approaching fire.

"Cursed Witches!" the man shouted.

"Shane!"

She could hear Fi calling her, but all she could see were the flames growing stronger, devouring the ropes that anchored the bridge to the cliff. Any second, the last strands were going to split, and then this Witch Hunter would be the least of her problems . . .

There was a horrible crack. Shane felt the bridge twist under her as the second rope railing snapped, its charred end whipping through the air in a shower of sparks. She tucked her ax under her arm and ran, stumbling on the swaying planks, praying she wouldn't feel the rake of rusty steel teeth in her back.

She was almost to the far side when she heard the whine and snap of the ropes going. The bridge lurched. Her stomach dropped straight into the ravine. The Witch Hunter bellowed in rage and fear, and Shane threw herself forward, clinging to the crevices between the boards. As the bridge dropped out from under her, she swung with it and hit the cliff. The air went out of her like she'd been kicked in the gut, but at least she was still alive to feel it.

Shane gasped in relief as her companions hauled her over the edge. For a long minute, all she could do was breathe and resist the urge to kiss the thin blades of crabgrass under her cheek. Finally, she rolled over and pushed up on her hands. The ax fell at her feet.

"Everyone in one piece?" she asked.

"You were the one in the most danger!" Red pointed out, tugging at a loose piece of Shane's hair. Shane tucked it behind her ear, trying to pretend that little motion hadn't warmed her down to her toes. She didn't feel half so fond about Cinzel bracing a paw on her knee so he could smear his slimy tongue down her cheek.

"Are you still good to go on?" Fi asked, with a worried frown.

"Never better," Shane said, accepting the hand Perrin offered to pull her up and ignoring all her accumulated aches and pains.

Red took the lead as they headed into the empty Witch Hunter tower—or, mostly empty. As soon as they stepped inside, Red darted to the left, shutting and barricading a door that seemed to lead down to an armory. Shane could hear footsteps in the depths of the tower in the second before the door slammed shut. The arms master was probably still down there, and she really didn't want to stick around to find out who was with him.

"This way," Red said, pointing to a narrow iron staircase coiling up into the dark. She'd promised that the Witch Hunters would keep anything of value in the tower's highest room, the inner sanctum, which only the High Lord himself was allowed to enter. It had once been the watch chamber where the signal beacons were lit, before the Witch Hunters took over.

Together they raced up the stairs. Shane watched in amazement as Red expertly jumped a missing step without even looking down. The girl really did know her way around.

As they wound higher, Shane glanced out a tall arched

window. They were facing away from the rope bridges now, toward the high cliffs that rose beyond the second ravine. A plank bridge hung down against the rock face, its chains barely glinting in the moonlight. When pulled taut, it looked like it would just reach the top floor of the Eyrie.

It wasn't part of the original design—Red claimed the High Lord had added it so that he could scurry away and save himself if the tower was under attack. Shane wasn't surprised. Power-hungry tyrants always had a back way out. Any other time, she'd be disgusted. Right now, she just hoped the winches and pulleys were in good condition, since that bridge was their way out, too.

At last they stood before the heavy door at the top of the stairs. The wood was warped from the elements, with white salt stains pressed into the cracks of the boards. A gargoyle glared down at them from the ledge over the door.

"It's locked," Fi confirmed, tugging on the tarnished brass handle.

"No problem," Shane said, pushing her way to the front. This wasn't some giant hulking double door guarding a fortress or an iron door designed by a powerful Witch—this was a good old-fashioned wooden door, and Shane knew what to do with one of those. "Back up," she suggested, hefting her ax.

In three swings, the ancient door was nothing but splinters.

The room beyond was eerily silent. Shane peered around as they stepped inside. Giant bookcases spanned from one wall to the other, curved to fit the round shape of the tower. A cold breeze through the high arched windows set her teeth on edge. Lanterns hung from cast-iron hooks above a collection of worn tables and chairs, and the furniture was piled with mounds of old books and ancient relics the Witch Hunters had seized. Every inch of the shelves was covered in more of the same, along with a few things Shane didn't want to think about, like the tarnished blades of saws and a skull with hollow black eyes.

Someone had set a fire in the low brazier at the center of the room. Shane wondered with disgust how many priceless artifacts the Witch Hunter had already burned.

The hairs on the back of her neck rose. Shane's head shot up. She wasn't sure why, but suddenly she had a very bad feeling about this. Her eyes zeroed in on movement in the dark corner of the room as a man in a white tunic stepped out of the shadows, a topaz amulet glinting at his neck.

Red tensed. "The High Lord," she hissed. Cinzel whined, pressing low at her heels.

Shane hefted her ax, studying the man. He had sallow skin and gray hair trimmed around his mouth into a sharp beard. His brown eyes were sunk deep into a harsh, bony face, and his thin lips were turned down in what Shane suspected was a perpetual frown. A saw-toothed blade hung from his thick belt.

The Witch Hunter paused next to the iron brazier, his impassive gaze moving across them.

"I'm surprised you made it this far." His voice was rough and gravelly, and there was something strange about the smirk twisting his lips, as if it didn't fit the contours of his face. "I suppose they have you to thank for that." His eyes locked on Red.

Red shivered but held her ground. "Well, when it comes

to betraying family," she said bitterly, "I learned from the best, Father."

*Father?* Shane jerked around, feeling like she'd been punched. Behind her, Fi sucked in a sharp breath. But Red wasn't looking at any of them. Her eyes were fixed on the man in front of them, her expression warring between fear and hatred.

"You're the daughter of the High Lord?" Perrin asked, horrified.

"I was." Red's fists dug into her cloak. "Until my father cast me out and tried to have me killed. At that point, I assumed we were done."

Shane clenched her ax in white-knuckled hands, the rush of blood in her ears drowning out everything. Red wasn't just the daughter of *a* Witch Hunter—she was the daughter of *their supreme leader.* Suddenly, all the puzzle pieces of Red fell into place. Her anger and her despair; her distrust and her bitterness. And the way she looked at Shane sometimes, like she'd been living in the dark so long she could barely stand the light.

Red's shoulders were trembling, but she stepped forward, facing down the Witch Hunter. "You're alone now, and there's nowhere to run. You're not getting out of here alive."

The man barked out a laugh. "Why would I run? I've finally got everything I need right here."

"What do you mean?" Red demanded.

"You."

Shane's stomach roiled as the Witch Hunter uncurled his hand, holding it out to Red.

"I've missed you, my daughter. More than you can imagine.

Not a day has gone by that I haven't regretted how I lost you. Come back and reclaim your rightful place by my side."

Something was very wrong—with the Witch Hunter, and with the tower. The shadows seemed to be growing darker around them, the air close and suffocating. Something brushed Shane's leg, but she couldn't tear her eyes away from Red.

"*How I lost you?*" Shane bit out. "You mean how you threw her out like garbage and tried to have her killed?"

But Red didn't even seem to hear her. She looked stricken, her face gray, her arms locked around her stomach like she was holding herself together. Or holding herself back.

Shane's heart crunched.

No way. There was *no way* Red could seriously be considering crawling back to him. Shane only knew a fraction of what her father had put her through, but even that was too much for anyone to forgive. Her eyes locked on the faded tattoo on the back of Red's neck.

"Red—you can't—"

"*Shane!*" Fi hissed, her hand fisting in Shane's coat.

Shane whipped around. Her partner's eyes were wide and desperate, and in a second, Shane understood why, along with what was so wrong with the High Lord of the Witch Hunters.

*Red!* She tried to shout, but it was already too late. Golden threads had crawled up her legs, and now they surged around her throat, choking the words down. Fi's hand was yanked away from her, and Shane's stomach lurched as she was heaved up, suspended over the floor in the web of gleaming golden threads.

They'd walked right into a trap. And not one set by the Witch Hunters, but by a far, far more dangerous enemy.

Below her, Red inched forward. One trembling hand unclenched from her cloak.

"Yes," the man crooned, beckoning her. "I love you. I've always loved you. Come back."

*No, Red!* Shane yelled in her heart, as she watched the girl take one unsteady step and then another. Thrashing only made the threads tighter, each one biting into Shane's skin. The same threads that had trapped the people of Andar's castle—the unbreakable threads of the unbeatable Witch.

# 33

## Red

RED'S HEARTBEAT THROBBED with every step she took toward her father. The air stuck in her throat, each breath acrid with the rot and the smoke and all the memories she'd left festering here. The tower was a blur. All she could see was her father and his outstretched hand.

*I love you.*

Red hadn't even realized how much power those words still had over her. Everything she felt for her father—everything he'd done to her—was a wound Red hadn't examined in so long. But now that wound had ripped open, and all of the pain and longing and anguish poured into her until she was dizzy and bruised with it. Red didn't even know everything she felt. All she knew was what she wanted—to take the hand reaching out for hers.

"It's not too late for us." Her father's eyes were sunken,

lit by a feverish gleam. "We can still be a family. All you have to do is come home."

Revulsion and yearning rose up in Red. *Never* was on the tip of her tongue. But she just couldn't seem to get the word past her quivering lips.

She thought she'd come here resolved to face him, hardened by her hatred. But then he'd called to her, and suddenly she was eight years old again, desperate for him to look at her just once without his lips curled in disgust.

There was none of that on his face now. His usual harsh expression was blunted by a strange smile, almost soft. The voice she still heard in her nightmares calling her a monster was welcoming her instead, asking her to come home. As if *home* were a real place Red could go, and not just a sour memory.

Red stared at her father's hand. The hand that had combed the knots out of her hair, that had lifted her into the highest branches of a hawthorn tree bursting with honey-sweet blossoms. The hand that had held her down while she screamed and the hot pain of the needle seared the tattoo onto her neck. The saw-toothed blade glittered on his belt, jagged teeth grinning at her.

The High Lord of the Witch Hunters couldn't love Red, because she was a monster. And Red shouldn't love him, because he was a monster, too.

But maybe that just meant they deserved each other after all.

Red stretched out her hand.

Something jerked her back. Cinzel had seized a mouthful of her cloak, his teeth sunk deep into the fabric. The wolf crouched against the floor, whimpering low in his throat. Red had never seen him so terrified—not even when the Witch Hunters snapped the chain around his neck.

Red shook herself. She hadn't come here for her father. She'd come here for Shane. Shane who should be right beside her, shouting at her, shaking her by the shoulders. Why was she silent now, when Red needed her the most?

Red turned to look back. Her heart leapt into her throat. Behind her hung a tangle of gleaming golden threads—and her companions, snared like insects in a spider's web.

"Shane!" Red cried out.

Shane's face twisted in a grimace, her mouth gasping for air. "Red . . . run . . ." she wheezed, all she could get out through the suffocating threads.

Red backed away. This didn't make sense. She knew this magic intimately. But it couldn't be here, in the heart of the Witch Hunters' tower. Only one person could wield those golden threads . . .

"Don't look at them. Look at me," her father snapped, dragging Red's gaze back to him. "I'm offering you everything you ever wanted. Just take my hand, Red."

*Red.* That one word finally broke through her daze. Red staggered back, ripping her hand away before those gnarled fingers could close over hers.

"You're not my father," she spat. "My father would never call me *Red*. He would have called me by my real name—the name my mother gave me before she died. Assora."

Now she could see all the ways he was wrong. His eyes were dark and greedy, his mouth stretched into an unnatural smile. This was nothing more than a puppet wearing her father's skin.

She should have known he could never look at her that way. With compassion. With love.

"Who are you?" Red demanded.

The High Lord straightened. His soft look melted away as he lowered his hand. The shadows seemed to writhe around him, thrashing like black thorns.

"I'm hurt you don't recognize me. I thought we'd gotten so close."

Red shrank back. Her heel collided with something—a short bronze dagger that spun carelessly across the floor. She froze as she recognized the Divine Rose blossoms engraved on the handle. Now that she was looking, she could see other familiar relics strewn among the spoils. A gnarled oak branch strung with tinkling copper beads, an old spell book with half the cover torn away. A set of five rings linked by delicate chains. All of them relics that Red had hunted down herself and personally delivered to the milky-eyed crow.

"No," Red whispered. "You can't be." She couldn't say it, couldn't even think it.

"So it's Assora. Pity." The man clicked his tongue, his smile winnowing down to a thin-lipped smirk. "It's always the little details that give you away," he lamented, curling his fingers and watching the sinews move under the skin.

The figure reached down, grabbing his topaz amulet and yanking the chain from his neck. Instantly, he began to change. The sallow features of the Witch Hunter dripped off like running paint. The white tunic rushed into long black skirts pooling on the floor, his gray hair disappearing into a lace veil that revealed only the faintest impression of the smooth face underneath. A familiar smirk curled her painted lips.

"Spindle Witch." Red's heart slammed against her ribs like a caged creature. Terror urged her to drop to her knees and beg for mercy. "But how . . . ?"

"It's just a bit of illusion magic. Thanks to this." The Spindle Witch lifted the amulet she had yanked off—not an amulet anymore, but a little glass vial covered in runes. A sinister crimson stain dripped down the inside. "All it required was a little blood—and getting rid of the original, of course."

The Spindle Witch swept aside to reveal a slumped form, half-hidden behind a mountain of gold and jewelry set with precious gemstones. Some had fallen across the body, leaving the corpse slung with winking silver coins and glistening pearls. The Spindle Witch tossed the relic she had been wearing carelessly onto the pile.

"Father . . ."

Red darted forward, falling to her knees by the body and turning the figure in her arms. The skeleton crumbled the second she touched it. The High Lord had been dead a long time.

Red stared down at her hands streaked with dust. That was all that was left of him: dust and scraps of fabric and old bones, and his topaz amulet, the glittering yellow crystal cracked through the middle. The man who haunted her nightmares withered down to a desiccated corpse. Red felt locked inside her body, utterly numb.

Footsteps clicked at her back. Red felt the Spindle Witch leaning down over her, the ragged hem of her long black veil shivering against Red's neck.

"It's a shame. If you'd just taken my hand, you could have had your reunion and never known the truth."

There was a strangled shout behind them. The Spindle Witch straightened, turning her attention to the prey caught in her web.

"If you keep trying to speak without permission, you'll cut your throat," she warned. Carelessly, she crooked one finger, loosening just the threads around their necks. The figures sagged, all of them gasping for breath.

"Get away from her!" Shane wheezed out, wrenching against the snare. The threads held her fast. Shane still clutched her ax, eyes blazing, but Red had no idea what she hoped to do with it. Only the Spindle Witch could break those threads.

Fi wiped her face against her shoulder, leaving a streak of blood from the cut on her cheek. "How could a Witch like you have gotten to the High Lord of the Witch Hunters?"

The Spindle Witch smirked. "I didn't have to. Three years ago, he came to me seeking a solution to a problem that caused him perpetual grief: a beloved daughter, cast out for being a Witch."

Red didn't want to hear this. She wanted to slap her hands over her ears, to sink into the floor and disappear. She'd wished her father was dead so many times. But not like this. He was supposed to have been a monster to his last breath, and Red was supposed to feel nothing but relief.

"The Witch Hunter was looking for a way to suck every last drop of magic out of his daughter. And quite by coincidence, I was looking for a spell that could do the same thing."

"The Siphoning Spells," Briar said hoarsely.

The Spindle Witch flicked her hand dismissively. "He

didn't know to call them by that name. The foolish man thought he could use me until he got what he wanted. But I decided he could serve me best as a corpse. He was in such a perfect position, after all: paranoid, isolated, and with all the power of the Witch Hunters at his fingertips."

Fi's eyes widened as she put the pieces together. "So everything the Witch Hunters have been doing—gathering relics and spell books, searching for the Rose Manor. That was all you pulling the strings from the shadows."

"The rank and file never knew the difference." The Spindle Witch tossed her head in amusement. "The little parasites are very useful for digging up old relics and keeping the Witches out of my way. But no one could seem to bring me what I wanted most. Fortunately, he's come here himself—as I knew he would." Her glittering eyes fixed on Briar Rose.

Briar's fist crackled with light magic. "I'm not going to let you have your way," he promised.

Red fought down a hysterical laugh, looking up at her companions. She hadn't really believed they were a match for the High Lord of the Witch Hunters. They were woefully— *woefully*—unprepared for the Spindle Witch.

She swallowed down the bitter air, sharp as bile. Hadn't she told Shane, over and over, that going up against the Spindle Witch was certain death? That from the moment she'd betrayed her, she was on borrowed time? So why did it hurt so much to be there on her knees, watching everything play out exactly as she'd expected?

Somehow, in some tiny corner of her heart, she must have actually started to believe—that they would make it out of this, that she could be redeemed. She hated Shane for giving that to her, if it was just going to be taken away.

Cinzel was crying, cowering on his belly as the Spindle Witch loomed over Red.

"I suppose, in a way, I owe all of this to you." Her smile made Red's skin crawl. "Your father never would have dirtied himself seeking the counsel of a Witch if he weren't so desperate to save you. So I'll give you one last chance."

The Spindle Witch reached into her sleeve, drawing out a sinister black rod studded with thorns. The relic Red had lost—the symbol of her pact with the Spindle Witch. The Witch Hunters had taken it straight to their *master*. Red's hand burned with the memory of those thorns sinking into her skin, of the hungry pull of its magic and the Spindle Witch's power seething like poison in her veins.

But there was also the memory of Shane's lips brushing the old scar, promising to save her.

The Spindle Witch held out the relic.

"Take the rod, return to my side, and I'll overlook your little transgressions. Otherwise . . ." She slid one curved thumbnail along her throat. "Side with my enemies—for whatever few precious minutes they have left to live."

Suddenly, everything felt so clear. Red's father had hated her. Despised her. Driven her out. And then regretted it. And whatever tiny sliver of love he'd still held in his heart for Red, that was what had driven him to the Spindle Witch. Red was the poison.

His love for her had killed him. Her love for Shane was going to kill them all.

Red stood up slowly, her legs shaking. Fear was a wild

animal gnawing at her insides. She stared at the rod, her hand stretching out to hover in the air.

"Red, don't do it!" Shane was thrashing wildly. Beads of blood slid down her arms and throat where the threads cut into her. Her fierce gaze locked on Red, her gray eyes storming like a sea.

Red's vision was blurry with tears. "I have to, Shane," she said. Trembling, Red wrapped her fingers around the rod. The thorns bit into the tender flesh of her palm, that achingly familiar pain sending warm tears down her cheeks. Because Red knew she would never be free of this rod again.

Somewhere Shane was screaming her name.

"You made the right choice," the Spindle Witch said, her nails raking Red's scalp as she stroked her hair.

"I know I did," Red whispered. Then she ripped free of the Spindle Witch and threw herself toward her companions, slashing the rod through the golden threads.

The Spindle Witch shrieked in fury. Her hand snatched at Red's cloak, tearing it from her neck—but then Red was free, hacking wildly at the threads, just hoping she'd get enough of them.

Only the Spindle Witch's magic could break the threads. Red would use it one last time to free Shane and the others— the only good thing she'd ever done with it.

Shane's words from the cliff rang in her head. *That's how you live with it. By making it right.*

That was all Red wanted. To be able to live with herself— for the last precious minutes she had.

The black rod writhed in her hand, the angry thorns burrowing deep into her skin. Red could feel the magic of the

Spindle Witch's relic turning against her, her legs buckling as the spell sucked her magic away. She clenched her teeth and held on.

The final threads broke with a snap. Her companions' bodies slammed into the floor, each of them kicking the golden strands away—then Red was wrenched backward, the Spindle Witch's bony fingers fisted in her hair.

"Foolish girl," the Witch spat. "After everything you've done to survive, in the end you throw it all away."

Red lashed out with the rod, slicing at the Spindle Witch's face. All she managed to do was rip a jagged hole in the black veil. The Witch caught her easily by the wrist, squeezing hard enough to force Red to her knees. In one smooth motion, she tore the rod out of Red's hand, taking a chunk of flesh with it.

Red screamed. The thorns had carved bloody ribbons into her skin—but the pain inside her was so much worse, the sensation of all the power the Spindle Witch's rod had granted her being ripped away. Her whole body felt scraped out and raw. Blood slithered down her arm, dripping onto the old tower floor.

Blackness swam in Red's vision. She'd broken her pact with the Spindle Witch. Her protection was gone, and the things she'd left in the Forest of Thorns were lost to her forever. But somehow her only thought was that she hoped Shane was proud.

"I'll show you one last mercy," the Spindle Witch promised, raising the rod. "I'll kill you first."

"No!" Shane shouted.

Red's eyes flew open just in time to see Shane throwing herself between them, swinging her ax up as the Spindle

Witch slashed for Red's throat. The wicked thorns screeched across the metal, leaving deep grooves in the silver knots. The force of the blow ripped the ax right out of Shane's hands. Shane let it go, throwing her arms around Red and rolling with her across the floor.

Red gasped as they skidded across the flagstones. In half a breath, Shane had scrambled up, kicking the legs out from under the brazier. Hot coals spilled onto the floor at the Spindle Witch's feet. The decorative rugs caught fire instantly, tongues of flame licking the old furniture and the ragged pages of books. Cinzel surged out of the gloom, sinking his teeth into Red's tunic and wrestling her back from the fire.

"Get the bridge down!" Shane yelled through the smoke, where Red could just make out Perrin's form racing toward the window. Then Shane stripped off her coat and threw it over Red, hunched on the floor cradling her bloody hand. "No one's dying on my watch—especially you."

Red had no strength to reply. She couldn't even stand. All she could do was lean into Cinzel and press Shane's ragged coat to her wound, arm throbbing and head spinning, and hope she had done enough.

# 34

## Briar Rose

**EVERYTHING WAS CHAOS.** One minute Briar had been scrambling to his feet, watching the Spindle Witch about to strike down Red, and the next the whole room surged around him, everyone taking off in different directions.

Fire raced along the floor, crawling like a living thing. The Spindle Witch's boot slammed down against the spinning brazier. Icy air poured in the window behind her, smothering the flames gnawing at the hem of her skirt.

"Very well. I suppose this tower could use a few more corpses."

The Spindle Witch tossed the thorn rod aside, drawing from her sleeve a bone spindle on a shining gold thread. The spindle began to twirl. As it spun, she pulled the golden thread taut between her fingers, so tight it cut white lines into her flesh.

Briar's pulse pounded as he stared at Andar's oldest foe. Here she was—the Witch who had killed his mother, destroyed his kingdom, and taken everything from him. He could feel the rage swirling in him, so hot and thick he could barely breathe. But could he use it? And would it be enough?

Shane had seized the rusty saw-toothed blade from the Witch Hunter's corpse and hurled herself at the Spindle Witch. Perrin had run for the far wall, kicking coals and burning sticks of furniture away from the winches that lowered the chain bridge. The wolf stood bristling in front of Red, his long yellow teeth bared. And Fi . . .

He had lost track of Fi! Briar whipped his head around, frantic until he spotted her. She had Camellia's code in one hand, her finger dragging along the spines of books as she desperately searched the shelves. Fi was determined to get the book. She was still thinking ahead, already imagining a battle after this one. Which meant it was up to Briar to make sure there was an *after.*

Perrin would get the bridge down, Fi would get the book. The High Lord of the Witch Hunters was already dead. It wasn't too late to come out of this with everything they wanted. All Briar had to do was buy them some time.

Shane tumbled backward, crashing into an overturned table. Briar gathered light magic in his fingers, imagining it growing hotter and brighter, fierce enough to scorch. He needed his magic to be stronger than ever before—not Camellia's *small wishes,* but Queen Aurora's great battle magic.

He threw it before he lost control. Lightning streaked out of his hands, darting toward the Spindle Witch. She didn't even bother to dodge. The sharpened shaft of the bone spindle slashed through the air, slicing Briar's magic into a harmless shower of sparks. The Witch's eyes locked on him.

"You are trying my patience, Briar Rose."

*Briar Rose.* He hated the way his name sounded on her tongue—like she owned him, like he was nothing. And wasn't he? Even at its strongest, his magic was so weak compared to hers.

The Spindle Witch twisted her hand. Golden threads slithered through her fingers, forming a vicious snare. Then a steel-bright dagger cut through the smoke, flying at the Spindle Witch's exposed neck. The Witch jerked her head back, the spell in her hands unraveling. The dagger clanged off the wall and clattered to her feet.

Perrin stood with his hand outstretched. Briar shot him a grateful look, and Perrin grinned back.

"Pesky vermin," the Spindle Witch spat. "None of you can stop me from taking what I'm owed."

A shimmer of golden thread whipped across the room and wrapped around Perrin's arm, pinning him to the wall like a fly in a web. Perrin sawed at it desperately with his remaining dagger, but the golden thread was unbreakable, tightening until the boy cried out in pain.

"Perrin!" Briar shouted. He flooded his hands with magic, hotter and hotter, until they glowed like a searing brand. Heart in his throat, he leapt the overturned table and seized the Spindle Witch's arm, pressing that blazing hot magic into her skin. Where the magic burned her, her skin charred and withered, aging right before his eyes.

The Spindle Witch hissed in pain, her furious eyes boring into him. Briar held on tight. But a second later, it was like all his power was draining out of him, vanishing so suddenly he almost crumpled to his knees.

Briar looked down. The Spindle Witch had looped her golden thread around his wrist, the gleaming tendril sucking the magic out of him. She twisted two strands over each other, and Briar suddenly felt lightheaded and ill. It was like the moment Red had slashed him with the thorn rod, only worse, because instead of just draining away, Briar could feel the power being drawn out of him, devoured by the Spindle Witch. The charred skin on her wrist turned smooth and pale again, as if he'd never burned her.

Shane's battle cry rang through the tower. The huntsman leapt off a low table, swinging the rusty saw-toothed blade. The Spindle Witch yanked Briar close for one second—close enough to see the malice in those glittering eyes. Then she flung him aside. As his back slammed into a heavy shelf, Briar felt something inside him snap—a rib or worse. He slumped to the ground.

Briar could barely breathe. His gasps were short and tight, crawling down his throat. Through dancing black dots, he watched as Perrin tore at the golden threads, as Shane scrambled to pick up her ax and Fi raced to the next shelf of books. Briar pressed one hand over his broken rib.

He'd fought so hard to control his magic, to throw off the shackles of his old life, but in the end, he was just as powerless to save himself as the day he'd fallen under the curse.


BRIAR KNELT IN the soft spring grass of the secret rose garden, feeling the sun warm on the shoulders of his blue velvet coat. Birds called in the poplars along the garden wall, and when Briar looked up, the white marble of the Grave of the Rose Witches spread out above him, each branch shrouded in red blossoms and supple green vines. Briar thought of it as his grave, as well, though his name wouldn't be bound into the marble among all the other Roses of Andar. He would leave nothing behind.

Briar's world had been getting smaller. His whole life was marked by the things he hadn't done, the places Sage had never taken him and the magic Camellia refused to teach him despite all her promises of someday. Someday he would leave these walls. Someday the Spindle Witch and her curse would be gone. Someday he would be free.

Only someday never came. An assassin had snuck in during a feast and nearly taken Briar's life, and now Sage had closed the castle to outsiders. His magic lessons had been canceled out of fear that the darkness of the Spindle Witch had crept inside him. The council had splintered, and the Topaz Knights were growing stronger every day. Andar was crumbling. Sage rode through the territories, trying to hold the fracturing kingdom together, while Camellia and the Great Witches hid themselves away in their tower, working on some secret spell. And Briar sat in the castle, just waiting.

In the shadows near the tree trunk, Briar noticed a tiny rosebud drooping on its stalk. He lifted it with one finger. Light gathered in his hand, and the struggling rosebud opened just a little, the soft petals peeking through. Briar smiled bitterly, wondering if that was the last magic he'd ever perform.

It was his sixteenth birthday, after all.

Camellia had woken him at dawn to give him a single birthday present: a soft blue velvet coat, the collar and cuffs embroidered with tiny scarlet roses. The fabric felt like water under his hand. She held her smile as he slid his arms into the rich sleeves and examined himself in the mirror. "Happy birthday, Briar," she whispered, pulling him close so he wouldn't see the tears streaming down her face.

He was out of time. The Spindle Witch was coming for him, and Briar knew what would happen next. His world would get smaller again. He would be confined to the white tower, the highest tower in the castle, to keep him safe. He would lose one more piece of himself, staring out the window and waiting for the curse to fall.

Briar sat back on his heels, engraving the image of the rose garden onto his heart. Everything seemed so bright—the radiant blue sky and the flush of green from the white-barked poplars, and the rings of rosebushes all around him. Red petals drifted down from the marble tree. The garden was his sanctuary, tended by Camellia and protected by Sage and all of his ancestors, all the way back to Queen Aurora. Now he was losing it, too.

His gaze caught on something white gleaming among the roses. Briar got to his feet, curious. It was buried in a cluster of deep red blossoms, so dark the petals were almost black at the tips. Whatever it was, it glistened beautifully in the sunlight. Mesmerized, Briar lifted a hand to push aside the thorny vines. Was it a white branch? A white ribbon, inscribed with a blessing or a wish? Some old stone relic hidden here long ago?

The world narrowed to the bloodred roses. Briar barely felt the thorns digging into his hand as he reached for the white shaft. It was a spindle, carved of polished bone. It seemed to leap under his touch, the sharp tip biting deep into his flesh.

Briar jerked back. A drop of blood slid down his finger and curled around it like a wisp of thread. There was a rushing in his ears, like a great wind had begun to thrash in the poplars, except the wind was inside him, pounding in his head. His body felt far away, like he was watching everything unfold from the bottom of a dark well.

Briar sagged to his knees, staring at the finger bound with crimson blood. Then he realized the roses were falling around him, the red petals splashing the ground and leaving the twisted branches bare. Every one bristled with wicked thorns. Birds cried in the trees, but not the songbirds and jays that usually chattered in the gardens. These were great crows. Their black wings stretched like a rising storm over the garden as they filled the sky.

With the roses gone, Briar could see that the earth beneath the rosebush had been disturbed, marked by blood-spattered feathers and the gnarled foot of a crow bound in a knot of golden thread. The bird's mangled body must be just beneath the surface. Dark magic had been eating away at Camellia's protective roses, right here in the castle. Brittle branches snapped, and the delicate bone spindle fell through the black thorns, shattering into pieces.

And then Briar was falling, too. The darkness rushed up to meet him, snuffing out his last glimpse of the sky.

He should have felt himself hit the ground, but he felt nothing—just the lurch of his body plummeting eternally down, into the blackness. It felt like he was breathing it in, like it was suffocating that pool of light inside him. Briar's hands clawed at the darkness, desperate to catch hold of something, anything.

And then something caught him—two hands that grasped his arms and pulled him to a stop. Briar opened eyes he hadn't even realized he'd closed to see the Dream Witch standing before him, shining in a golden robe. Her curly hair whipped around her in a maelstrom of sand as she held on to Briar, determined and fearless.

Briar recognized the golden robe and the small islet of sand beneath her, spreading out until he could feel the shifting grains beneath his feet. It was the way she always looked in dreams, dressed in the robes of the Order of the Golden Hourglass. Whatever darkness was trying to tear Briar away, the Dream Witch had come into his mind to save him.

"Briar Rose."

He sucked in a breath at the sound of his name in that familiar voice, forever laughing. She wasn't laughing now.

"This is it, isn't it?" Briar said softly. "This is the curse." He had spent his whole life knowing this would happen, and somehow he still wasn't ready. The darkness was roiling beyond the edge of the sand—Briar could feel it creeping toward him, thick and oily as tendrils of ink, something wicked whispering in the shadows just behind him. "It's going to consume me," he choked out, fighting the overwhelming urge to look back.

"No." The Dream Witch caught him just as he was about to turn his head, holding him steady with her warm hands on his cheeks. "Look at me. Only at me, Briar Rose. The curse is very powerful. If I lose you, I'm not certain I can find you again."

Briar swallowed. "Is Camellia . . . ?"

The Dream Witch shook her head. "I cannot bring her here. I'm sorry."

Briar blinked hard, trying to force the tears away. After so many years of memories—Camellia laughing with him, reading to him, chasing him through the gardens as the flowers unfurled beneath her feet—his last memory of his sister was going to be Camellia in tears. When he knelt beneath the Tree of Roses, he hadn't known he was saying goodbye to her.

Briar could feel the blackness pressing in around him again, like a crush of dark wings. He forced himself to stare into the Dream Witch's eyes. She looked older than he remembered, her lips pressed together and lines of silver in her black curls. But there was still a spark of magic in her eyes, her brown skin glowing as she smiled at him, the wisps of sand glittering around her like a halo of stars.

"You will not fall to this, Briar Rose."

There was a soft, sweet scent in the air, one that made Briar's chest ache as he recognized it. The scent of roses. He could see something now beyond the sand: twisting green vines that clambered up and up until he was surrounded by pillars of climbing roses holding the darkness at bay, the tangled vines erupting with a thousand fiery blooms. Briar gasped. He'd know this magic anywhere.

The Dream Witch nodded. "The Rose Witch has found a way to keep you from losing yourself to the darkness. You will sleep here until your sister can find her—the girl who can break the curse."

The roses were growing faster, binding together vine upon vine. The blossoms glowed brighter, blinding like a stained-glass window lit by the setting sun. And then, suddenly, Briar knew where he was, as white stone reared up out of the darkness and became rough walls, a ceiling, a small arched window seething with red blooms. The white tower, thronged in roses.

The Dream Witch had started to disintegrate. Her expression was wistful as the sand whipped around her, raining down like it was running through an hourglass. "Don't let yourself forget, Briar Rose. This is not forever. A girl will come, and she will save you with a kiss." The last grains of her fingers slipped away from his face. "So just keep believing. Wish hard, because that's what magic really is. Wishing."

Then the sand rushed at his eyes, and when Briar blinked it away, the darkness had vanished and he was alone in the white tower, with nothing but a few golden grains trapped in his outstretched hand.


AND SO HE'D waited, and wished, and believed for a hundred years. And Fi had found him. He wasn't a prince locked in a tower any longer. He was her partner, and he was not going to fail.

Briar pushed himself up from the floor. There was a great

power inside him, beating like a second heart, begging to be unleashed. The pain in his ribs drained away as he reached for it. That dark power lurking under his light magic might have been the Spindle Witch's once, but it belonged to Briar now. He didn't have to hold back anymore.

Briar lifted one hand, feeling the rush of magic as his fingertips erupted with wild red flames.

The Spindle Witch's threads had snared his companions again. Shane struggled furiously, trapped with her ax in mid-swing, while Perrin sagged against the wall with his arms wrenched unnaturally over his head. Red lay in a heap beside her torn cloak. Only Fi was still free, not paying attention to anything as she clung to the top rung of a stepladder, desperately thumbing through the books. The Spindle Witch loomed behind her, the sharpened point of the bone spindle gleaming as she raised it over Fi's unprotected back.

"Fi!" Shane shouted in warning. Fi turned too late, her eyes wide. The bone spindle plunged toward her.

Time seemed to slow down. Briar felt the magic crawling over him, enclosing him like a tight, painful skin. His bones ground together inside his body. The ends of his fingers erupted into long juts of bone with sharp claws, and he caught a flash of red eyes in the dark glass of the window. Briar gritted his teeth, willing it to stop there. He was in control. This power was his.

Before he even felt himself move, Briar was in front of the Spindle Witch. His claws sliced effortlessly through her golden threads as he ripped the bone spindle out of her hand and flung her across the room. The Spindle Witch crashed through a burning table, splinters of ash flying as her body cracked against the wall. She barely caught herself on the windowsill, her long nails digging into the stones.

Fi was staring at him. Briar could just imagine what he looked like in her eyes. He reached one bony hand out to her, trying to explain—then all the hairs on the back of his neck prickled as laughter erupted through the room.

The Spindle Witch unfolded, slowly rising to her full height. "If only Camellia could see you now. So desperate to beat me that you welcomed the darkness in." An amused smile crawled onto her lips. "Just who do you think that power belongs to, boy?"

"Me," Briar said. "It's mine." He could feel it surging through his veins, answering his every call. The Spindle Witch had underestimated him, and he would make sure she *didn't* live to regret it.

"Then let's see you use it." The Spindle Witch lifted her hand, the spindle whirring.

Golden threads shot out so fast Briar could barely see them. He raked his clawed hands through the air. The threads snapped before they could reach him, fluttering down around him in charred shreds.

He was free—but he wasn't the one the Witch had been aiming for. Golden threads wrapped around Fi's wrist and her neck, trapping her with one hand raised. She was staring right at Briar, but her expression wasn't one of fear. As soon as their gazes met, Fi's eyes cut sharply down, and Briar realized she had a book clutched to her chest—a familiar book with curling silver words etched into the spine. Camellia's storybook.

It wasn't over.

Briar called the bloodred magic to his bony hands. He whirled toward Fi, slicing her free. Then he launched himself at the Spindle Witch. He slashed through the last curtain of threads and found himself right in front of her, this nightmare specter that had ripped everything away from him. He was close enough to watch her throat bob as his claws shot toward her neck.

The Spindle Witch's head snapped back. She raised her empty hand, holding it right over Briar's heart—then she twisted and pulled, like she was yanking something.

Briar gasped. Suddenly, his lungs were on fire. It felt like she had torn something out of his chest, and now the dark power he had unleashed was filling the space, flooding every part of him.

He stumbled back, his arms thrashing as he clawed at his own chest. Someone was screaming, and it took Briar a moment to realize it was him, his howl of agony drowning out everything except the Spindle Witch's laughter. The sound rang in his ears like a crow cackling.

"Finally," she breathed. "I waited a hundred years to get my hands on you—the prince the Great Witches sacrificed everything to protect."

Briar thought he heard his companions yelling for him, but the sound was impossibly far away. He was drowning in a vast ocean, waves of darkness crashing over him one after another as the greedy pull of that magic dragged him down. He had felt this before, a century ago, when he'd pricked his finger on the bone spindle. Camellia's magic had saved him then. But what would save him now?

He could feel the bone horns bursting through the skin

above his ears. The flow of dark power was an unimaginable tide, washing away everything that was Briar. The Spindle Witch towered over him, her eyes glowing as she grabbed his chin.

"To think," she said with a click of her tongue. "I almost killed *her*"—she forced Briar's head around to look at Fi—"because I thought she might keep you from using that power. If I'd known she was going to drive you right into my arms, I wouldn't have bothered."

Fi's hazel eyes were wide and terrified. Her arms clenched around the book as the Spindle Witch let go of Briar's chin, tossing him aside.

*Fi. Fi could save him.* That was the only thought that made it through the haze. Briar dug his claws into the stone, leaving deep furrows in the floor as he dragged his bony limbs up, stumbling toward Fi. His vision was getting narrow, but he could still make her out, one pinprick of light in a dark, rippling world.

"Oh, Briar Rose." The Spindle Witch's voice thundered in his ears. "It's far too late for that. You belong to me now, and with you, all that Camellia and Aurora and the rest of the Witches of Andar have kept from me for far too long."

Briar lurched forward, his clawed hand writhing with red fire as he reached for Fi.

That was the last thing he saw: the horrified look on her face as she flinched back from the monster Briar had become. Then there was no Briar, the last spark of his light snuffed out by the darkness.

# 35

## Fi

**FI COULDN'T BELIEVE** this was happening. She had listened almost numbly to the fight as she frantically searched the shelves with only one thought in her head: *If she could just find the book, they might stand a chance.* And then she had, her hands shaking as she dug the thin volume out from behind a huge leather tome, but somehow it was already too late, and everything had gone so wrong. Her fingers tightened around the scrap of code tucked in her pocket, the precious book shoved into her vest.

Briar was still reaching for her, only he wasn't Briar anymore. He was . . . transforming. That was the only word for it. His fingers had lengthened into claws. His eyes had begun to shine with a red gleam, and as Fi watched, ivory spirals of bone horns erupted from his head, curling above his ears. Fi recognized that form. He was becoming the monster from the dream space, the nightmare creature Fi had thought was just a figment of those dark dreams.

His breath rattled in his throat, his eyes desperate as his hand stretched out toward her. Fi wanted to grab it—to hold on to Briar before he slipped further away—but she was frozen. Everything in her heart screamed for her to step forward, and still she hesitated, whirring through possibilities, trying to understand what was happening and why.

Red overtook the blue in Briar's eyes. He threw his head back in a wrenching scream.

"Fi—do something!" Shane's yell broke through her daze. Her partner was still trapped in the threads, but her eyes blazed into Fi's. "Briar needs your help!"

The words jolted Fi out of her head. She lunged forward, grabbing for the monstrous hand, but Briar had already ripped it away. His claws raked through his golden hair as he clutched his head. Long juts of eerie white bone thrust up from his back, tearing through his flesh and ripping his ragged blue coat. Fi stopped thinking and just ran for him.

"Briar!" She ducked under his thrashing limbs, grabbing the shreds of his coat and pulling him against her. She wrapped her arms tight around his chest. His red eyes were unfocused and filled with pain, and Fi searched for some glimmer of her Briar in them.

She shivered as the bone fingers slid down her back, feeling the prickle of those claws even through the layers of fabric. But she wasn't going to pull away from Briar, never again. She tugged him closer until their foreheads were pressed together, praying her touch could pull him back from the brink of whatever the Spindle Witch had done.

Briar's head fell onto Fi's shoulder.

"Fi . . ."

She heard her name, barely a whisper. Her heart leapt. Then his head jerked back, and he howled, writhing in pain. Over his shoulder, Fi watched the great ivory protrusion at his back unfurling into black wings ribbed like the skeleton of a bat.

"Briar, no!" Fi grabbed both sides of his face, forcing him to look at her. "Stay with me!"

She held on tight as the wings snapped open and closed. His red eyes began to clear, the dullness fading.

"Yes," Fi begged. "Please, Briar. You've got to come back to me."

His hand curled around her arm. Fi watched a small smile stretch across his lips. She smiled back, a tear slipping down her cheek in relief. Then his claws clenched like a vise, and Fi gasped as Briar wrenched back and threw her aside like a ragdoll.

She barely felt the pain as her body slammed into a wall, the book flying out of her vest and spinning across the floor. It stopped just short of the smoldering coals. Fi heaved herself up, staring in disbelief at the cruel smile playing across Briar's lips. Singed golden threads slithered over the stones as he flapped his dark wings and lifted off the ground, dropping into a crouch at the side of his new master.

The Spindle Witch stepped forward, the toe of her black boot coming down on top of Camellia's book. "So this is where the Rose Witch hid her secrets." She flicked her fingers toward the book, and Briar obeyed, snatching it up. Fi choked at the sight of the book they'd risked everything for, the key to Camellia's precious last message, dangling carelessly from a bony claw.

Briar's transformation had been completed by those giant wings. Now, at the Spindle Witch's side, he looked every inch one of her twisted creations. The jointed claws were at least twice the length of normal fingers. His golden hair swept around the white horns, curled like a ram's, and the giant bat wings glowed with a sinister luster in the fiery light. Worst of all were the red eyes that held only malice, none of the kindness or curiosity or love that always sparkled in Briar's blue eyes.

The Spindle Witch gestured again, and Briar tucked the book into his ragged coat. Fi watched it disappear, her last hope that this had been a ruse, some trick on Briar's part, vanishing with it.

"Finally, I will have what Aurora stole from me," the Spindle Witch seethed. Fi could only see the hint of the Witch's glittering eyes through her veil, but it was enough to know she was outmatched. She would never be strong enough to take Briar back from that dark power by force. She had lost him.

That was an answer Fi couldn't live with. Her hand curled around the paper with the code.

The Spindle Witch's head tipped, as though she had heard that little crinkle of paper. She waved one careless hand. "Briar, my pet, kill them all."

Briar didn't hesitate. His red eyes fixed on Fi, the giant leathery wings stretching out from his back as he jerked up from the ground.

"Wait!" Fi yelled. She snatched the book code from her

pocket, holding it up high. "Do you know what this is? It's a code left by the Great Witches, meant to guide Briar Rose to the Siphoning Spells."

Fi could feel every eye in the tower fixed on her. Perrin's face was horrified, like he couldn't believe what she was saying. The Spindle Witch toyed with her golden threads, disinterested. "And now I have Briar Rose," she pointed out.

"But not his mind. Not his knowledge. Just his . . . meat." Fi couldn't stand to look at Briar as she said it. She focused on the Spindle Witch. "Briar Rose may be the key, but do you know where the lock is—where the spells are hidden? Are you willing to wait another hundred years to find out?" Fi waved the code. "This could lead you right to them. Everything you want—right at your fingertips."

"Fi, what are you doing?" Shane hissed.

Fi's fought down a shudder as the Spindle Witch's eyes fixed hungrily on the scrap of parchment. Then she threw the code into the spilled coals.

"No!" the Spindle Witch shrieked.

The paper caught fire in an instant, all the numbers vanishing into a curl of blackened ash. Briar launched himself at her. His bony hand seized Fi's throat, forcing her back against the wall. She could feel the cold claws choking off her breath. All he had to do was squeeze, and he would snap her neck.

"I still have the code!" Fi gasped out. "It's right here." She tapped her temple. "I memorized the whole thing— every number."

"I'll just drag it out of you, then," the Spindle Witch hissed. Her spindle whirled as she fingered a long golden thread.

Fi dredged up her courage. "I don't think so," she said. "I don't think you can reach into people's minds. Otherwise, you could have taken the information you want from the Rose Witch a hundred years ago and ended all of this." She forced herself to sound confident, but it was just a hunch—her last desperate play. "If you want the code, you'll have to bargain with me."

Briar's grip tightened around her neck. Then he let her go, the Spindle Witch recalling him with an invisible tug of thread.

"What is it you want?" she asked, almost curious.

"Briar," Fi choked out. "I want Briar back."

Without him, she could never get the Siphoning Spells. But the Spindle Witch knew that, too.

The Witch laughed long and deep, her veil fluttering in the icy breeze. "A page of numbers for the prince of Andar? I think not." The Spindle Witch lifted a hand, petting it down Briar's cheek. "Allow me to make a counteroffer. Find the Siphoning Spells and bring them to me, and I will return this boy to you. If you can memorize that little code, then surely you can solve it."

Fi swallowed. "But you have the book."

"So I do," the Spindle Witch agreed. "And it's coming with me. I suppose you have a choice to make." She stepped forward, crushing splintered coals under her black boots, until she and Fi were face-to-face. "Work for me and win Briar Rose's freedom, or fight him now and die."

"Don't listen to her, Fi!" Shane shouted. The huntsman had worked one hand free, and her ax clattered against the floor as she yanked at the golden threads. "Don't even think about it," she warned. "We'll find another way!"

But there was no other way. The Spindle Witch was too powerful. If they lost that book, they lost any chance of ever finding the Siphoning Spells, the only glimmer of hope of defeating her.

And Briar. Fi would lose Briar, too. Forever.

Fi's heart was a tangle darker than the Forest of Thorns. Was she really going to help the Spindle Witch—lead her to the forbidden spells the Witches of the Divine Rose had spent centuries protecting? But what other choice did she have?

Going meant gambling that she could outsmart the Spindle Witch and solve the code out from under her before the Witch got everything she wanted. It was a terrible risk, with an entire kingdom on the line.

"Well?" The Spindle Witch held out her hand. The golden threads looped around her fingers glittered like a dozen rings. The fire was spreading, slowly crawling up the bookcases and devouring the dry old parchment spines. Soon the whole tower would be ablaze.

Fi looked at Briar one last time, imagining his sparkling blue eyes, his playful smile, their kiss under the endless stars. They were supposed to have forever.

"It's a deal." Fi took the outstretched hand, feeling the prickle of the Spindle Witch's long nails as they sealed the agreement.

"Come along, then," the Witch said. She swept toward the window, her dress rippling behind her as if she was wading through a deep black pool. The window was suddenly a wall of beating wings, and the Spindle Witch stepped out into the air, rising with the storm of crows. Briar leapt after her, swooping through the sky and then turning back to hover just outside the window.

Fi climbed up on the windowsill, reaching for Briar's monstrous hand.

"Fi, no!" Shane screamed, but Fi's mind was already made up.

"I'm sorry, Shane," she said.

With the Spindle Witch gone, the golden threads were unspooling fast. Shane hit the ground in a roll, scrambling to her feet. Their eyes met, and Fi tried to convey so many things—how grateful she was, how much she loved Shane, how sorry she was to end it like this.

Fi dredged up a tiny smile. "I guess this time it really is goodbye . . . partner."

Then Briar's cold hand closed around Fi's, and he drew her out of the window, sweeping her up into his arms before gravity could drag her down. His great black wings stretched out against the darkness, bearing them up into the sheer mountain air. The last thing she saw was Shane framed in the red window, her face quickly becoming a distant speck, her voice disappearing in the rushing wind.

Briar's grip never faltered as he carried her into the night, following the Spindle Witch's crows. Fi wrapped her arms around Briar's neck. She didn't know where they were going. She had no idea what she was going to do. For the first time in her life, she didn't have a plan. She wouldn't let the Spindle Witch have her way—but she wouldn't let her have Briar, either. Fi had promised his story wouldn't end in darkness and pain, and that was a promise she didn't intend to break.

The arms around her were stiff, without a trace of Briar's warmth or love. His red eyes never flickered to hers, but he was in there somewhere.

"I'll get you back," she whispered into his ear, her lips brushing the spiral horn. "No matter what it takes."

# EPILOGUE

⟶⟫⟩⟩ ⟨⟨⟨⟵

## Red

**RED STOOD AT** the edge of the rocky cliff, staring out at the burning tower. Her singed hair blew across her face, thick with the smell of sulfur and char. She'd bound the ragged strips of her red-lined cloak around her hand to staunch the bleeding. The smoke that had nearly choked her still burned in her throat—but somehow, in spite of everything, she was alive.

They'd barely escaped in time. In a mad dash, Perrin had managed to crank the bridge into place, and then Shane, sweaty and glowing with the light of the flames, had hauled Red to her feet and half dragged, half carried her across the dark chasm, herding Cinzel over the creaking plank bridge with her knees.

The flames that had raced through the tower's highest chamber were already guttering, snuffed out by the ancient stone walls. Something was burning in that fire, some part of Red, but not the part she had expected. Cinzel stood beside her, pressing his comforting weight against her leg. She didn't take her eyes off the tower.

Her father was dead. Red's fingers squeezed around the topaz amulet in her fist. She hadn't meant to pull it from the body, but somehow, the moment her fingers clenched around the gem, she hadn't been able to let go. Sharp silver letters were carved into the back. *Assora*. The name she had left behind so long ago.

Red shivered. She'd spent so much of her life running away from her past, always afraid the Witch Hunters were about to catch up with her. She was relieved it was over. She was relieved her father was dead. And yet . . .

She wrapped her arms around her stomach, listening to Shane and Perrin arguing farther up the slope. Shane was determined to go after Fi and Briar. If she had wings, she would have taken off already. Perrin was trying to convince her that their best chance was to meet up with the Witches of Everlynd. It didn't really matter what they chose. One way or the other, Shane was going after her partner, and Red wouldn't try to stop her. Even if it was a lost cause.

The sky was still thick with smoke, the crescent moon scratched out to the east, where Briar Rose had flown away with the storm of crows. Red had stood right where Fi had, a long time ago, with the Spindle Witch reaching out her hand, holding something too precious to lose. She'd taken that hand, lived that life. Maybe she, more than anyone, understood why Fi had made her choice.

The Eyrie had gone dark, the last ashes burned out to nothing. Red pressed her lips into a thin line. She'd never expected to make it out alive. Even when the Spindle Witch disappeared out the black window, Red couldn't bring herself to move—just slumped to the floor beside her father's skeleton, wondering if she had come back here to die with him. Two monsters lost to the flames.

Then Shane had burst through the smoke, coughing and dirty and fierce, and she'd swept Red up and carried her away from the tomb of the tower. And now she had to go on living.

A hand settled on Red's shoulder. She turned to meet Shane's stormy gray eyes. "Come on. We've got to drop in on some Witches. Perrin knows where the people of Everlynd were headed."

Behind her, Red saw Perrin shaking the ash from his coat, gingerly testing the arm the Spindle Witch had wrenched over his head. At least it didn't seem to be broken. Perrin shot her a tight smile, his face smeared with soot and grime. Red felt too sick to return it.

"Hey." Shane gave her a little shake. "This isn't over. We're not giving up on them. Now, come on. You, too, you singed furball." She reached down, dragging her fingers through Cinzel's matted ruff. The wolf leaned into the touch, moving to follow Shane even before Red did.

Red shook her head as she trailed Shane and Perrin into the trees, tucking the amulet into her pocket. Shane's partner was gone. They had faced the Spindle Witch and been utterly defeated. But Red would follow her anyway, because in spite of impossible odds, she just couldn't bring herself to bet against Shane.

Maybe the huntsman was just leading her to another dark, ashen place where they'd all burn out. Maybe she'd prove Red wrong one more time. Whatever happened, Red had one thing to hold on to. She was no longer alone.

# ACKNOWLEDGMENTS

Everything they say about book two is true—more fun, more anxiety, more incredible moments, and especially more people to thank for bringing this dream to life. I could not have done this without a literal village!

Thank you to my agents, Carrie Hannigan and Ellen Goff—from the magical release of book one through every stage of this series, you have been absolutely amazing! Also thank you to Rhea Lyons, Soumeya B. Roberts, and all of the wonderful folks at HG Literary.

Thank you to my fantastic editor, Ruta Rimas. I'm so grateful to you for adopting me and for everything you've done for Fi & Shane and this book!

Also a huge thanks to everyone at Penguin who made this book possible. Tessa Meischeid, you are the most amazing publicist and your enthusiasm and love for these characters has meant the world to me! Thanks to my talented copy editor, Rachel Skelton, and designer, Suki Boynton. I'm so grateful to Marinda Valenti, Felicity Vallence, Simone Roberts-Payne, and the entire Penguin Team.

This cover blew me away from the first moment I saw it. Thank you to the wonderful designer, Jessica Jenkins, and the incredible artist, Fernanda Suarez!

One of the joys I could not have imagined when this all began was how much I would fall in love with the audiobook. Lindsey Dorcus, you brought these characters to life in the most amazing way! Big thanks to Nick Martorelli, Emily Parliman, and the entire Penguin Audio team.

I absolutely would not have made it through my debut year without the amazing authors of the #22Debuts and the Class of 2K22 Books! Meg Long and Jen Peterson, you are amazing writers and human beings who made this journey so fun! Akshaya Raman, you were there for me when I really needed it, and I can't thank you enough. Also to Sue Lynn Tan, Lillie Lainoff, and Vanessa Len—debuting alongside you was truly a privilege.

Rosaria Munda, you have written one of the most incredible series I've ever read, and I'm so grateful for your friendship and guidance!

Big thanks to Kyle, Christie, Sarah, Jennica, Natalie, Claire, and all the early readers who not only did this the first time, but came back for round two! You are epic!!

Thanks to my family—especially my grandmother, whose belief in me has meant so much. And to my wife's family, the Dotters, who have helped make this entire journey so fun. To my father-in-law, Jim, for so many years of reading and enthusiasm for these stories!

A special thanks (with an asterisk) to my two spoiled house cats. Sometimes because of you, sometimes in spite of you, I got my writing done.

Most especially, thanks to my partner, Michelle. This book—and honestly every book I ever write—will be dedicated to you. You come through for me in ways I never even knew were possible. You're there in the good times and the bad, and you somehow always make me smile. You're the most amazing partner a person could have and none of this would be possible without you!

Finally, thank you to all the readers who showed up in such a big way for this series. I couldn't even have imagined the wonderful outpouring of love for Fi and Shane. You've made my heart burst with happiness, and this book is for you!